The Persuasion of Miss Jane Austen

-A Novel -
wherein she tells her own story of Lost Love,
Second Chances, and Finding her Happy Ending

Shannon Winslow

A Heather Ridge Arts Publication

Copyright 2014 by Shannon Winslow
www.shannonwinslow.com

All Rights Reserved
Except for brief quotations, no part of this book may be reproduced or distributed in any manner whatsoever without the written permission of the author.

Except as otherwise noted, the characters and events in this book are fictitious or used fictitiously. Any other similarity to real people, living or dead, is coincidental.

Cover design by Micah D. Hansen
Original cover art by Sharon M. Johnson

This book is dedicated to every fan who has wished Jane Austen herself might have enjoyed the romance and happy ending she so carefully crafted for all her heroines.

I have endeavoured to grant your wish.

Respectfully,
Shannon Winslow

Soli Deo Glori

Prologue

December 1817

La Comtesse de la Fontaine basked in the sun's afternoon rays with eyes closed, listening to the varied music of daily life and commerce afloat on the Grand Canal twenty feet below. Venice, for all its antiquity, remained as novel to her as the day she arrived months before, following her marriage to the count.

"There you are, my darling," said her husband, pushing aside the heavy drapery to join her on the iron-railed balcony.

She reached out to invite him closer, but he was already at her side. A now-familiar thrill raced through her as he bent to brush her lips with his kiss. Then, their faces only inches apart, they exchanged a knowing look, a flicker of a smile passing from one to the other.

"What have you got there?" she finally asked, hearing the crackle of paper in his hand.

"Ah, yes. I was momentarily distracted, but I came to show you this item in the news. When I saw it, I recognised at once that it would be of singular interest to you. Just there," he said pointing to a small paragraph near the bottom of the page.

Madame la Comtesse addressed her attention to the article he indicated in the English language paper:

<u>Author of Popular Novels Identified Posthumously</u>
It is now known that the well-received novels **Sense and Sensibility**, **Pride and Prejudice**, **Mansfield Park**, and **Emma** (as well as two more titles only now coming to light) were written by the daughter of an obscure English clergyman. Unfortunately, she will write no more, having suc-

cumbed to an undetermined illness at the age of one-and-forty. She reportedly died five months ago on the 18th of July, and was subsequently buried at Winchester Cathedral. Thanks to the efforts of her brother, Mr. Henry Austen, **Northanger Abbey** and **Persuasion** have recently been published in a four-volume set prefaced by his biographical notice identifying the authoress as his deceased sister, Miss Jane Austen.

"Your favourite authoress, dead," said the count. "Sad news indeed, my darling."

Madame frowned and slowly shook her head. "If it were true, but I cannot believe it. I *will* not! Surely there has been some error."

"What? Do you think the newspapers invent these things?"

"I daresay they do not. More likely, they are simply mistaken in this case... or misinformed. No, this report does not upset me, I assure you. Although I am glad to be told that there are now two more of her books out in the world, I am quite certain that this business about Miss Austen herself is a gross falsehood. I feel it in my bones. In fact, I would wager anything you like that she is every bit as much alive as I am. Will you take my bet?"

"O-oh, no!" he laughed. "Be so foolish as to make a wager against *you*? Not likely – not when I see that particular gleam in your eye. I perceive, my darling, that you know much more about this business than you are telling."

"You think me clairvoyant, then? What if I told you that I have already dismissed this report about Miss Austen as of next to no importance, and that the gleam you see in my eye is entirely for you, husband."

"If that be the happy case, madame, then I will call you a mind-reader instead, for you seem to know my thoughts as well as I do myself." He took up her hand and brought it to his lips. "So then, come with me, my darling exile," he said, helping her rise and leading her inside through the cinnamon-coloured velvet curtains.

Part One

What people may hereafter say about my life, I cannot control. My biographers, if any, must do the best they can with the sources available to them. It is necessary that this, my own account, shall remain for some time to come concealed from their eyes. For now, the story belongs to me alone – to me and to that one other. – J.A.

- 1 -

August 1815

It is time.

I could not have done it even a few years ago. But now the pain – though never far from my mind – has eased to a familiar, settled presence that I can bear without distraction, and the memories are objects I can view with more tenderness than despair.

Sitting at my writing desk at our beloved Chawton cottage, I gaze out the window toward the path that leads to the door. No one is there; no one ever is, at least not the one most fondly looked for. And yet looking has developed into a habit of longstanding duration, an unconscious exercise in futility over the twelve years since he went away.

Now the wars against the French are finally at an end, and still he does not come. So, it is time to lay aside any lingering hopes I have secretly cherished in that regard. My fires are at last tolerably quenched, and I have reconciled myself to the prudence of never fanning the remaining embers ablaze again. Instead, I have determined to steep the warm essence of my recollections into a novel about youthful errors, mature love, and second chances – to write the story I would have preferred for myself, one which embodies all the early promise of the genuine article but a more felicitous conclusion than providence has seen fit to authorise.

I shall call my captain Frederick Wentworth, and his lady will be Anne Elliot.

My breath catches in my throat as I hold my pen, suspended over the sheet of pristine paper. This is the moment that both thrills and terrifies me, the moment before commencing a new novel when all things are possible but nothing has yet been achieved. To begin is to risk everything – crushing defeat, utter failure or, worse still, mediocrity. However, not taking the risk is unthinkable. I have come through successfully before, but that hardly signifies. With each new work the familiar doubts and niggling questions resurface, chiefly these. Do I really possess whatever genius it takes to do it again? And if so, what is the best way to go about it?

With the hero of my story, the heroine, and their early meetings, I am already well acquainted. Having their basis in life has given these things an early birth in my mind. I know all about how the two met, every detail of their falling in love, and in what cruel manner their happiness was cut short. And yet the tale will not end there – not with the regrets of the past, but rather by redeeming the promise of what might still lay ahead. First, however, it is my job to set the stage, to construct a world of persons and conditions that will give their story substance – a worthy backdrop against which Anne and her captain will act out their poignant play.

The lady's family should bear scant resemblance to my own, I have already decided. At its head, I will situate a vain and rather foolish baronet instead of a sensible country parson. There is no need – nor any advantage – to mirroring the real circumstances, long gone by, too closely. Not that I fear discovery. Few indeed are those who know the particulars of my... my disappointment. That is what Mama persists in calling it, although "disappointment" seems such a singularly inadequate word for describing what transpired. When I consider the pain and the peace of mind it cost me –

No. I must put such feelings to one side for the sake of the task I have now set for myself – the *twin* tasks of recording in this book my recollections and, at the same time, writing alongside it the novel they inspire.

Moreover, despite what knowing the man took from me, it gave me far more. It gave me a true knowledge of what it means to be in love and, therefore, the ability to translate that consummate wonder into my stories. Without it, where would I be? Experience is vital to a writer, and painful experience even more valuable. Or so I have heard it said. I pray it is true, that not one moment of anxiety or one shed tear has been wasted; that would be the greatest tragedy of all.

I shake off these contemplations, and my suspended pen at last touches paper. I begin the work with these words:

Sir Walter Elliot, of Kellynch-hall, in Somerset-shire, was a man who, for his own amusement, never took up any book but the Baronetage; there he found occupation for an idle hour, and consolation in a distressed one; there his faculties were roused into admiration and respect, by contemplating the limited remnant of the earliest parents; there any unwelcome sensation, arising from domestic affairs, changed naturally into pity and contempt, as he turned over the almost endless creations of the last century – and there, if every other leaf were powerless, he could read his own history with an interest which...

A familiar creak of the door interrupts my progress, alerting me to someone's approach.

"What? Are you writing again, Jane?" asks my mother, bustling into the room. "I thought you finished that tiresome book weeks ago."

"This is a new one, Mama," I answer evenly.

"A new one! Good gracious, girl, will you never be satisfied? A little poetry now and again, such as I myself have written, would do you no harm, but I cannot understand this obsession with the novel. How many will it take to get this fever out of your brain once and for all?"

"Writing novels is not an illness that need be recovered from. It is my work; it is what I do."

"Yes, so you have told me. But all the same, I thank heaven no one much beyond the family knows of it. Though your father may not have objected, *I* cannot think it a perfectly fit occupation for a young lady. I never have. It is far too taxing on the mind and it will one day ruin your health completely; mark my words. You see how my own health has declined, and you are so thin that I sometimes worry you cannot be quite well either."

"My constitution is perfectly sound, Mama, as is yours. Besides, my earnings help to put food on our table," I remind her.

"Nevertheless, I should have put an end to the business years ago had I known the mischief to which it would lead. Sensible girls stop believing in fairy stories when they grow up, else how are they to marry ordinary men and be happy? That was always your problem, Jane: expectations set too high. You had your chances – suitable men, any one of whom would have made you a very satisfactory husband – but nobody could measure up to Mr. Darcy or Mr. Knightley, I suppose."

Experience has taught me that arguing this recurring charge would be pointless. So I bite my tongue and wait for Mama to continue on her way and out of the room.

She is entirely wrong, of course, as to where the problem lies. Mr. Knightley and Mr. Darcy are not to blame, for it is against *quite a different gentleman* that every other whom I meet with is measured and found wanting. Although through subsequent revisions I have imbued each of my literary heroes with portions of *his* character, not one of them embodies the original completely. Perhaps Mr. Bingley best portrays my captain's amiability, Darcy his essential integrity and aristocratic air, and Mr. Knightley his spirit of true nobility. Poor Colonel Brandon has the misfortune to share the same haunted expression of having witnessed first hand too much of the cruelty of which men are capable.

Each one of these sketches is an incomplete portrait, however; it is only in Captain Wentworth that all the true qualities will at last be united. In him I will duplicate what I remember from our early meetings and add the traits I have ascribed to the gentleman since. Whatever else, I must believe him on some level constant to me even now, in life or in death. At this juncture, only God knows if he has survived the war. At least I have every reason to believe he long since forgave me my weakness at the critical moment. I could not bear it if he were alive in this world and still thinking ill of me. Or is it possible he no longer thinks of me in *any* way? Is that why I have never heard one word from him?

These are home questions – ones I will have to take courage and address eventually as the chapters of my book progress. For the moment, however, I intend to entertain myself with other, less perplexing personalities.

Anne Elliot's family begins taking shape on the page before me. I write of a foolish father whose extravagance has sunk the family's finances, a prudent mother who died far too young, an imperious older sister, and no brothers at all – everything my own family is not. Only Lady Russell bears a tolerable likeness to a person of my own circle. In her, I revive something of my former friend and mentor Madam Lefroy, now ten years gone and more.

So many of our family and friends have left us: my father, Madam Lefroy, Eliza, Anne, Elizabeth, and Fanny, as well as Cassandra's Mr. Fowle. Although gone from sight, they remain in my mind and a few live again and forever on the page, thanks to my pen. It is one type of immortality, or is that presuming too much? Books come and go much like people do. And, even with the degree of success I have been so fortunate as to achieve, it is not to be supposed that the humble literary efforts of a clergyman's daughter will make much of a lasting impression on the world. Doubtless a hundred years from now, no one will remember a sea captain called Wentworth or have read his story.

And yet, I must try.

Continuing at my labour, I introduce William Walter Elliot, Esq., and name him heir presumptive to the Elliot estate of Kellynch. Surely, had the young man any manners at all, he ought to thank me for the gift of his one day being made a baronet, as he has clearly done nothing to earn the honour and much to disparage it. Still, it is for the current baronet that I reserve my greatest scorn and severest censure – for his absurd airs, for his monetary irresponsibility, and for his failure to value the one of his three daughters truly worth esteeming. To make clear the father's faulty views on his offspring, I now write…

> *Elizabeth had succeeded, at sixteen, to all that was possible, of her mother's rights and consequence; and being very handsome and very like himself, her influence had always been great, and they had gone on together most happily. His two other children were of very inferior value. Mary had acquired a little artificial importance, by becoming Mrs. Charles Musgrove, but Anne, with an elegance of mind and sweetness of character, which must have placed her high with any people of real understanding, was nobody with either father or sister: her word had no weight; her convenience was always to give way; – she was only Anne.*

Poor Anne is consigned to the shadows – by loss of bloom and by neglect of her own family. She must bear her sorrows and their disregard a little while longer, but not forever. Her true radiance will eclipse them all in the end; I will see to that.

The hours pass without my noticing, and soon my first chapter rests before me – complete if not yet perfected. It is a good day's work, an excellent beginning, and I know I will enjoy pleasant dreams tonight. But will they be dreams of Captain Wentworth or of Captain Devereaux? In truth, it makes no difference, for to my mind they are one and the same.

-2-

I first set eyes on Captain Philippe Devereaux on the last day of 1797, at my brother Henry's wedding to our cousin Eliza de Feuillide.

I was just barely two-and-twenty years of age then, and arguably at the pinnacle of my modest looks and charm. For a season at least, I did possess a very particular attraction for members of the opposite sex. Having discovered this capability a few years earlier, I had since given it free reign, taking every opportunity for dancing and flirting that our limited society could afford.

I had had a consummate teacher, after all, in my older and much more sophisticated cousin Eliza, whose wider experience of the world made her a creature of endless fascination for an impressionable young girl such as myself. But I was not the only one who had proved susceptible to her inherent appeal; two of my own brothers and nearly every other gentleman in our circle had succumbed as well. To one extent or another, they were all bewitched by the vivacious Comtesse de Feuillide. Here at last, I thought, was an example of how a woman might gain a measure of power over men. And although I did not aspire to Eliza's metropolitan way of life in general, this seemed a lesson worth attending to.

I daresay flirtation came as naturally to my cousin as breathing. Not so for me. But after years of narrow observation, I did begin putting what I had gleaned from her into practice myself. I soon discovered it to be a most delightful sport, especially when lucky enough to be matched with a partner likewise devoted to the game. I never enjoyed it more than when, in the December I turned twenty years of age, I practiced the art with a handsome young Irishman by the name of Mr. Tom Lefroy.

"How do you like my morning coat?" he inquired of me two days after our first meeting at a ball at Manydown. He was come into the neighbourhood for a Christmas visit to his Aunt and Uncle Lefroy at Ashe, where this conversation unfolded. "Do you find it fashionable?" he continued, preening for me like a peacock.

We had liked each other at once upon being introduced at the ball, but now a new uncertainty at this second meeting needed to be overcome. Our footing with each other had to be tested once again to establish that the camaraderie we felt the other night was solid and genuine.

After a moment to ponder his question, I shrugged and replied, "It appears a serviceable enough garment. That colour, though…" I made a face and shook my head.

He tugged the white coat into sharper order and checked his reflection in the window glass. "I am surprised at you, Miss Austen. I would have you know that this is the same shade as the one worn by my favourite literary hero Tom Jones."

"Is that so?" My countenance and manner of speaking betrayed nothing more than mild interest in the subject, when in actuality his reference to Mr. Fielding's work intrigued me very much indeed. "Now it is you who have surprised me, Mr. Lefroy, for I did not have you marked out for a great reader. Although again, I am compelled to question your taste. Perhaps you are unaware that novel-reading is not considered quite respectable in certain circles."

"What about in *your* circle, Miss Austen?" he asked, leaning a bit closer. "Yours is the opinion I most wish to hear at the moment. Do you admit to reading novels?"

I drew back in mock horror. "Really, Mr. Lefroy, this is terribly forward! I am afraid you presume too much upon our rather brief acquaintance. Is not this a very personal question to be asking a lady whom you have known for so short an interval?"

"Quite possibly so," he said, examining the well-manicured nails of his left hand. "I truly cannot say, for I admit that I am somewhat mystified when it comes to these complex social niceties. They seem, in general, to accomplish very little of value while at the same time requiring a great deal of effort."

"What nonsense you talk, Mr. Lefroy."

"Do you think so? Then I must be in error, but not irretrievably so, I trust. I am not a hardened case; I am perfectly willing to be guided by the wisdom of one more expert in these matters."

I nodded my approval, and he went on.

"Perhaps *you* would consider undertaking the challenge of reforming me, Miss Austen. And you might start by settling the original problem for me. What would be the appropriate time to ask my impudent questions of you, such as the one concerning your reading habits? If not at our second meeting, then when?"

Instead of being so obliging as to answer at once, I deliberately left the gentleman in doubt of any satisfaction by adopting a pensive expression and taking one full tour about the room before returning to him. Then presently I said, "As to undertaking your thorough reformation, Mr. Lefroy, I can promise you nothing. That monumental task may require more time and industry than I can spare at present. However, it is my judgment that you may safely ask your more personal questions upon our third meeting."

His aspect brightened. "This is most encouraging news, Miss Austen. So you believe we *shall* meet again, then, do you?"

"I think it highly probable we shall, Mr. Lefroy, especially if you are determined to persist in the neighbourhood for some little while. In fact, such an occurrence could hardly be avoided. So I suppose I must prepare myself to answer your impertinent curiosity by and by. For tonight, however, we had much better confine our discourse to the usual polite topics."

"The weather and the state of the roads, I suppose you mean. How dull," he said, finishing with a sigh.

I smiled. "It needn't be, Mr. Lefroy, with a little imagination. For example, I was just about to remark that, although you may know how to wear this light coat to best effect, I fear it may not hold up well in the rain."

He bowed, acknowledging the compliment. "Ah, I see what you mean. And if imagination is what discussing the weather requires, then I am only too pleased to employ it. I can imagine the effects of a downpour easily enough, and that this…" He teasingly brushed one finger across the thin muslin fabric of my sleeve. "…this insubstantial gown you wear would fare no better in the rain. Yes, I can picture the results of that calamity very well indeed," he said with an especial gleam in his eye. "There, is that what you had in mind, Miss Austen?"

Our eyes held for a long moment before I answered. "That remark, while somewhat predictable, will do at present, Mr. Lefroy. Now, you really must excuse me. Here are other gentlemen waiting to discuss the weather with me. Would you not allow that it is only fair they should have their share of my conversation as well?"

"I would by no means allow any such thing. As I have often heard it said, all is fair in love and war."

"I have heard your saying as well, and yet, even if that were true, I hardly see where it applies here. Which do you presume this to be, Mr. Lefroy? An occasion of love or war?"

"Oh, war, Miss Austen. By all means, war."

"I see. You fancy me your enemy, then."

"Not an enemy. A better word would be opponent, for one requires an opponent – a worthy opponent – to engage in any kind of enjoyable sport."

What followed this exchange was an additional fortnight of highly enjoyable sport indeed, with behaviour deemed by some standards profligate and shocking. To my mind, however, it encompassed everything most pleasant by way of dancing, talking, and sitting down together. It was a remarkable time. We played at being in love, Tom and I, and we could not be bothered to hide our infatuation from anybody.

Although I believe Mr. Lefroy to have experienced some embarrassment for the teasing he endured on my account, to this day I can not argue myself into feeling one bit sorry for anything that occurred between us. We may have bent the rules of decorum nearly to the point of breaking, but there was no real harm in it. If there could be any cause for regret, it would be for worrying my dear friend Madam Lefroy, who, seeing how the two of us had been carrying on, did kindly caution me against the danger.

"You are too rational a girl," she told me one day, "to fall in love merely because I warn you against it; and, therefore, I am not afraid of speaking my mind. I would wish you to be on your guard. Do not involve yourself, or attempt to involve him in an affection which the want of fortune would make so very imprudent. You have sense, dear Jane, and we all expect you to use it."

Her words – similar to those which I later put into the mouth of Elizabeth Bennet's Aunt Gardiner in a like situation – were kindly meant but entirely unnecessary, for I am sure the gentleman and I did not fancy ourselves much more than half in love. When he went away, it only confirmed what I already suspected – that my happiness was very little dependent on Mr. Lefroy's continuing in my presence. Although my vanity could not help being gratified by his conspicuous attentions, I found I was in no danger of wasting away under a perpetual gloom of temper when they were withdrawn. I can not suppose Mr. Lefroy suffered so very much for the loss of my company either, not unless I flatter myself that his subsequent engagement to another woman, his marriage, and his begetting of many children were all by way of consoling himself for the overwhelming loneliness which my absence occasioned.

I have no scruple in admitting that I took great enjoyment in that brief interlude with my Irish friend, and I would not be persuaded to part with a single minute of it for any price. Looking back on our short acquaintance, it is clear to me now what a fortunate meeting it was, one that taught me lessons which have served me well. With Tom I gained confidence and I refined my facility for flirtation. With him I practiced a type of imitation love that prepared me for the genuine article when I later encountered it. And I have long since lost count as to how many of Mr. Lefroy's words and mannerisms found their way into the stories I have written.

Yes, Tom Lefroy did me a good turn, and I shall always wish him happy. There were others as well, potential suitors who contributed to the catalogue of memories and experiences upon which I daily draw for the characters in my books. But despite my mother's opinion in the case, not one of them would have made me a tolerably good husband. Or perhaps it would be more correct to say that I would not have made a tolerably good wife, for the problem, in truth, was more with me than with any of them. I could not give my heart; I had no heart to give, for, from age twenty-two, it already belonged irrevocably to Captain Devereaux.

-3-

All through the second chapter of the new book, I delay. I write of Sir Walter's debts, of retrenchment, of quitting Kellynch-hall for London or Bath, and of the danger posed by the insinuating presence of Mrs. Clay – everything but him. In chapter three, I dare to venture a little nearer by expounding at length upon the navy and the merits of its officers. I admire the profession as a whole and, with two brothers also belonging to it, the fate of all sailors has long occupied a prominent place in my mind. But there is still another reason, for, like Anne Elliot, I cannot think of the navy without remembering a certain captain. In Anne's case, it is Captain Frederick Wentworth, whom I finally summon up courage to introduce this way in chapter four:

> ...*who being made commander in consequence of the action off St. Domingo, and not immediately employed, had come into Somersetshire, in the summer of 1806. He was, at the time, a remarkably fine young man, with a great deal of intelligence, spirit and brilliancy; and Anne an extremely pretty girl, with gentleness, modesty, taste, and feeling. Half the sum of attraction, on either side, might have been enough, for he had nothing to do, and she had hardly any body to love; but the encounter of such lavish recommendations could not fail. They were gradually acquainted, and when acquainted, rapidly and deeply in love.*

This is all I write of the young couple's first meeting and brief courtship. Why? Well, I suppose I feel very protective of their privacy at this tender time. And also, no further explanation seems necessary. When two such promising young persons are brought together by fate, there can be nothing *less* extraordinary than their falling in love. Their mutual attraction assures the outcome. It is for them a force of nature as impossible to oppose as the change of seasons. Just as flowers invariably turn their faces toward the sun, so Anne and Captain Wentworth instinctively turn toward the warmth of admiration aglow in the eyes of the other.

It was much the same for us – for me and my captain – only a different time and place.

"Jane, do allow me to introduce to you a very good friend of mine," said my cousin Eliza (newly made my sister-in-law) at the breakfast following her wedding to my brother Henry. "This is Captain Philippe Devereaux."

I looked up and there he was. The second before, I had been laughing and rattling on with someone else – who, I really cannot remember – in a most frivolous fashion. But my chatter died instantly away when I saw the dashing gentleman in naval uniform before me. He was tall, and, as I have now written of Captain Wentworth, *a remarkably fine young man*. My breath caught in my throat as he reached out his confident hand for mine, and I stood frozen for a moment, unable to do anything more than stare at him.

I had beheld plenty of handsome men before, of course, none of whom had demonstrated any ability to deprive me of my considerable powers of speech. This was different, however; I knew it at once, even before Captain Devereaux opened his mouth. Perhaps it was the soulful way he returned my gaze with those searching, dark eyes of his. Or perhaps I had a certain sense, even then, that my life would be forever changed because of the stranger before me.

The gentleman bowed deeply over my hand. "Enchanted," he said in a low rumble. I believe I murmured something unintelligible in response, and then Eliza, looking at me archly, got on with the business of making us acquainted.

"Captain Devereaux has been a friend to me – as he was to my first husband – for many years. He did me a great service at the beginning of the Revolution, seeing to it that my son, my mother, and I came safely away from France." Then, addressing the gentleman, she added, "Dear Jane is by far my most favourite cousin, sir, and it is my considered opinion that two such charming people ought to know one another." With no more than that, she left us together.

We continued to stare at one another until finally the captain said, "I am very happy to make your acquaintance at last, Miss

Austen. In truth, it was all my own idea. So highly has your cousin spoken of you that I insisted on receiving an introduction."

His English was flawless. His elegant accent, however, although faint, was decidedly French like his name. A French expatriate in the British navy? My quick curiosity demanded satisfaction. But first, I nodded, acknowledging his compliment, and I managed to say, "I am pleased that you did, sir."

This is when I should by rights have smiled coyly. Here was my opening for trying my powers of flirtation on a new and very appealing subject. Yet I was too much overcome by the strength of the man's mere presence to attempt it. His nearness made my every nerve come alive. It excited an almost painful mingling of attraction and agitation. Ordinary flirting was out of the question. How could I hope to be clever when I could neither think clearly nor still the violent flutterings inside my breast? Besides, some inner voice told me that this was not a person to be taken lightly.

So instead, I did my best to swallow my discomposure as I said in earnest, "Eliza has the most remarkable friends. I am already intrigued by what she says about you, Captain, that you helped her to escape from France. I can only suppose that there must have been considerable danger involved."

He dropped his eyes for a moment. "Some, yes, but I would not wish to excite ideas of heroism. It was my own life I was saving as well as hers when we sailed for England."

This surprising humility impressed me. "I am sure you are too modest," I said. "May I know more about how it happened?"

A shadow crossed his face. "Oh, no. Reciting my sad history can be of no use on a day meant for celebration. Let us find a more suitable topic. Your cousin has told me that you possess a very keen interest in literature, Miss Austen. Pray tell me, what is the kind of thing you most like to read?"

As disappointed as I was to have been turned aside from the first subject, the second was equally compelling. "*All* kinds, Captain, or very nearly all. How could I chuse only one food when there is a banquet spread before me?"

One side of his mouth pulled up into a half smile. "That is well expressed, mademoiselle. I myself take my reading pretty equally from biographies, plays, poetry, and the papers. For moral extracts, I like Dr. Johnson. Have you read Dr. Johnson, Miss Austen?"

"I have indeed! He is a great favourite with me as well."

"Excellent. We have already found one thing we have in common. I very much look forward to discovering many more."

By this time, my initial unease was fading, nearly done away with by growing exhilaration. Abandoning my last scruple, I plunged ahead. "Then, at the risk of offending you, sir, I will be so bold as to ask you this. Do you admit to reading novels?"

"I do! And furthermore, I am not ashamed of saying so. Although novels may not yet enjoy the respect they deserve, I believe nowhere else is the excellence of the human mind and imagination so well displayed. I have novels to thank for taking me on some very fine adventures – to the far corners of the world as well as to the hidden reaches of the soul."

I could not trust myself to speak at this, so deeply were my already-excited feelings gratified by the captain's warm commendation of that art form which meant the world to me. It seemed there could be no better proof of our compatibility.

"You smile, Miss Austen, and yet I cannot judge what you are thinking. Do not leave me in suspense. What do you say to my confession that I esteem the novel?"

I gathered my wits together again. "I could not agree with you more, Captain, I assure you."

We pursued this happy line for several minutes longer, comparing lists of our preferred novels and discussing in further detail those we had read in common. Nothing could have been more satisfying or more thrilling. It was not that our opinions, Captain Devereaux's and mine, always coincided; they did not, in truth. But here at last was an attractive gentleman – a *very* attractive gentleman – with excellent manners, a well-informed mind, and a wealth of intelligent conversation. I had nearly despaired of finding one such; now he stood before me. And, of equal importance, he appeared to be as taken with me as I was with him.

I saw and heard nothing beyond ourselves. For the moment, my world had contracted to that one conversation, and yet it had at the same time immeasurably expanded to encompass all the pleasurable possibilities as to where it might lead.

After a time, I endeavoured to turn the discussion back to the earlier subject, which I had been obliged to abandon too soon. "It seems we have both been for fine adventures by means of the novel, Captain. Unlike in my own case, however, my guess is that you have indeed experienced things quite equal to those found within the pages of books. Now that we are a little better acquainted, perhaps you will indulge my curiosity and tell me more of your escape from France."

"Are you truly interested, Miss Austen?"

"Why should you doubt it? I am interested, or I would not have said so."

He gave me a long, appraising look. "Yes, I see I can take you at your word. Very well, then. Your wish is my command, but you must promise to stop me if I begin to bore you."

I already knew that was impossible; I knew I could listen to Captain Devereaux speak at length on any subject and never grow weary of it. The deep resonance of his voice was enough to captivate me, and I could have happily lost myself in those drowning eyes. I agreed eagerly so that he would go on, which earned me another of his quick, lopsided smiles. Then he began his remarkable tale.

"As I was saying before, my own life was in danger in France. The Jacobins had already taken my father and brother, you see. And they would have arrested me as well, if I had gone home after I arrived in port. Thankfully, I received the warning in time to set sail again, and some of my friends with me. I have never since set eyes on my home or any of the family I left behind that day."

"How awful for you, Captain! Do you know what became of them?"

"My home? – confiscated. My father was executed."

I gasped; I could not help it.

"Forgive me, Miss Austen. That was careless of me. I have lived with this knowledge for long enough to become accustomed to it, but I had no right to blurt out such a shocking thing to you."

"Do not apologise, Captain. My existence has been less sheltered than you might suppose. I have heard of such atrocities before, and I believe it is fitting that we *should* be shocked by them. God help us if we ever cease to be."

"Quite right. Nevertheless, let us change to a new subject, one better befitting a lady's tastes."

"Sir, I may be a lady, but I am also a rational creature who wishes to hear more of this history you have been relating. Now, if I may ask, what was it that made your father an enemy to the revolutionaries? Was it the same crime that condemned my cousin's first husband and so many others to death – the unpardonable sin of having royalist leanings and aristocratic blood in his veins?"

I saw a new spark of approbation light in his countenance at this question. No doubt he was more accustomed to finding females either uncomfortable with, or out of their depth, in a discussion of world events.

"You have deduced rightly, Miss Austen. Supporting one's king has traditionally been seen as a virtue. But the world seems to have turned upside down, and now such a natural allegiance is enough to send a good man to the guillotine."

"I am truly sorry about your father, Captain. I hope the rest of your family fared better."

"I was told that my elder brother, as my father's heir, met with the same fate. Although I have never been able to confirm that fact, I have no doubt it is true. My mother died when I was young, and my older sister was already in *this* country, so now it is only my younger sister whose outcome is still unknown. She was swallowed up along with so many others in the reign of terror, and I shudder to think what might have become of her since. One day I will return and search her out. This is my solemn vow."

"I trust you will find her safe and well, Captain. In the meantime, however, you are at least not a man without a country," I said, directing my attention to his attire. "I have two brothers in His Majesty's navy, so I am quite familiar with the uniform you wear."

"Yes, as you see, I am an English sailor now. When I fled my homeland in '93, I surrendered my ship – a merchant vessel, as she was then – to the British fleet. She has since been refitted for war. And now, by four years of loyal service to the crown, I have lately earned the right to captain her again – against my former countrymen if necessary."

"Oh, dear! I must pray that, for the sake of all, peace will prevail. If you are forced into action against the French, would not that place you in an untenable position? Divided loyalties, and so forth?"

"No danger of any such thing, I assure you, Miss Austen. What loyalty should I feel for a renegade regime with the innocent blood of thousands on its hands, including that of my family and very good friends? No, I shall suffer no qualms going to war against that unlawful order. The Republic, in its degenerate state, is not the country I knew and loved; it is the monster that has killed everything I once held dear."

I could see he was battling a tide of rising emotion, and my heart swelled with sympathy. Before I could think of what to say, however, Eliza came hurrying over to us with a frown threatening to disfigure her comely face.

"What's this? What's this?" she demanded. "Why do you two look so serious? This is an occasion for gaiety. Now, Captain, tell me you have not been worrying my young cousin with the trouble across the channel; not today!"

"Guilty as charged, my dear Eliza. No, I suppose I must call you Mrs. Austen now!"

"Yes, please do, Captain. I very much like the sound of it. And now promise me there will be no more talk of France."

"Really, Eliza," I interrupted, "you mustn't blame Captain Devereaux. I found his story so compelling that I encouraged him."

"Very well then, but let us banish all sad subjects henceforth. I am a bride, and I command that everybody must be as happy as I am!" Then off Eliza flitted again. I watched her back across the room to my brother's side. Henry attended to a whispered word from his new wife, smiled, and then lifted a glass to me.

"It was generous of you to come to my defense, Miss Austen," said the captain. "But your cousin is right to scold me. A bright young lady, such as yourself, should be free to make merry at her own brother's wedding instead of being expected to lend her ear to the misfortunes of a world-weary exile. Do not allow me to keep you from your friends any longer."

His tone told me clearly enough that I had been dismissed. But for what reason? Had I displeased the captain in some way, I wondered, or was he over scrupulous – truly afraid of monopolizing my time? I could read nothing useful in his countenance. All I knew was that I was profoundly unready to tear myself from his side. My brief encounter with Captain Devereaux had already sunk the fortunes of every other person in the room. For not one of them could I any longer feel the slightest interest.

This excursion to London had promised to be a rare and delightful treat for me. We could not afford that the whole family should make the journey, and I alone had been singled out for the privilege. So there I was, in an unfamiliar city with a company of fashionable strangers, all of whom an hour before had seemed so intriguing. Now, my happy anticipation for making their acquaintance had vanished completely. They were suddenly only a collection of people in whom there was to be found little beauty, less importance, and no pleasure at all.

Nevertheless, since I had been correctly raised, I did what was expected of me. I curtseyed to the man and said, "Yes, of course. How thoughtful you are, Captain. Please excuse me now."

I moved off to join Henry and Eliza's party, but I could not properly attend to the lively conversation going forward there. All my senses were engaged elsewhere, acutely attuned to following the movements of the gentleman I had just left and to deciphering any syllable he might happen to drop within my hearing. My heart raced at my every glimpse of him, and it leapt alarmingly when I happened to be so fortunate as to once catch and hold his eye for a moment. In that look, I thought I confirmed the regard I had seen there before. Yet he never approached me again that day, and he later slipped away without taking any leave of me.

Had I misread his feelings completely? Had the instant attraction I thought we both felt been all on my own side and none on his? In that case, I would see Captain Devereaux no more, for it seemed most unlikely we should meet a second time by chance. He belonged to the navy, and I was for Steventon on the morrow.

But to never again encounter him? A bolt of near panic ran through me at the thought, and my chest constricted to where I could scarcely draw breath. What sort of madness was this, I wondered? How could such a fleeting encounter – our entire conversation had spanned little more than half of one hour – have so thoroughly changed everything? And yet I knew without a single doubt that it had.

-4-

I dearly loved my home and family, but I had never been more unwilling to return to them than I was that next day after the wedding. I lingered on the street as long as possible in hopes of a last-minute reprieve. Then I looked both up and down one final time before entering the carriage. I saw no one – least of all a handsome naval officer – hurrying to stop my departure, or even to bid me a fond farewell. It seemed only Henry and Eliza, already in the carriage, cared if I were to stay or go, so I reluctantly joined them.

We rode in silence for some time – I with my eyes constantly at the window, continuing the watch even as all hope faded away. Once beyond the environs of London, I ceased to be interested in the scenery altogether. I could not even take pleasure from the knowledge that I would soon be back in my beloved sister's company. All that impressed me was the fact that every mile we travelled toward Steventon carried me farther away from the chance of ever seeing Captain Devereaux again.

I repented, over and over, of being so addlebrained as to believe myself in love with a man I had met only once. I had heard of such cases, of course, but I had always deemed them pure nonsense. Only a weak-minded sort of individual would allow herself to be run away with by such fanciful feelings... or so I had supposed. Now *I* was that weak-minded person, for I could not stop thinking of the captain.

Even had I been strong enough to put the gentleman from my head, it would have made no difference, for my companions seemed determined that I should not forget him. Eliza embarked on that line of conversation no more than an hour down the road.

"Jane, dear, you have not yet told me what you think of my friend Captain Devereaux," she said teasingly.

I travelled homeward in the same manner as I had gone to London – courtesy of the bride and groom. Prior to the wedding, which naturally took place in Eliza's home parish, I served as an attendant and chaperone of sorts. Now we all returned for a celebration of that event to be held in the parish of the groom.

"Yes, Jane," added Henry. "Do tell us. Did you find his manners engaging?"

"I hardly know," said I, hoping nothing in my look or my voice betrayed me. "I only spent a few minutes with him, after all."

"It was not too short a time to form a first impression, though, was it?" Henry continued. "And I know you are a champion of the importance of *First Impressions*," he added with a wink.

I pretended to be amused by his small joke, but then I had to correct him. "On the contrary, my dear brother. If you recall, Elizabeth Bennet learns to repent of her reliance on judgments formed in haste."

"Very true, very true," conceded Henry.

"Nevertheless, Jane, I will not allow you to evade my question so easily," said Eliza. "You must have formed *some* opinion of my friend. It only takes a trice to assess a person's looks, for example. Do not you agree that Captain Devereaux is uncommonly handsome?"

"I really did not notice," I lied.

"Did you not?" Eliza asked with a devilish grin. "Strange. I felt quite certain that you had, that you had very particularly noticed that much if nothing else about the man. Allow me to remind you of some of his other assorted attractions. He is well born, well read, and he knows how to speak his mind and heart. And what of his air of continental sophistication? These things must have garnered your attention, for I daresay you do not meet with this sort of quality gentleman every day, especially not in your usual society."

Silently, I agreed with Eliza on every point, but I offered her only a shrug in response.

"Upon my honour, I am surprised at you, Jane," she continued. "I thought writers were required to be careful observers of the human condition. I am afraid this lapse on your part does not bode well for your career… or for the captain's chances with you either."

"You mustn't tease my poor sister so, my love," said Henry mildly.

"Yes, I must indeed!" insisted Eliza. "My introducing her to the captain was by way of a little experiment, and the scientist must know the outcome of his work."

This was too much. "An experiment?" I cried. "But the captain said it was at *his* insistence that you introduced us."

"Yes, that is true enough. But, my dear Jane, who do you suppose made him so curious about you that he insisted, hmm? All lovers need a little help."

"Your imagination has run wild if you see lovers wherever you look," I rejoined, although I could feel the colour rising into my cheeks.

"Aha! See how she blushes, Mr. Austen. I think it is not only my imagination that has run wild. There was something to my idea of putting the two of them together after all."

I took a moment to compose myself before answering this new attack. "Regardless of how it began, Eliza, you will have to give up the notion of reaching any significant conclusions from your so-called experiment. The contrasting elements you put together are now rent asunder again and forever, without issue."

"Perhaps so, and perhaps not. *I* can do nothing further, it is true. But there is always the possibility that fate will take a hand. More surprising things have occurred than that two people's paths, seemingly travelling in opposite directions, should cross again. We shall just have to wait to see if anything develops." Eliza smiled serenely and then returned her attentions to her husband.

I cannot recall ever being held captive to a more uncomfortable carriage ride in my life. The road was not to blame. No, I had the continual billing and cooing of the newlyweds – so obviously in love – to witness, whilst all the while knowing myself to be permanently divided from the only man with whom I could picture being similarly occupied. The torture was acute, and my only escape came in disguise – feigning sleep or a singular interest in the verdant countryside – that I might withdraw my eyes from what soon became too painfully irksome to observe.

~~*~~

Momentary weakness might be forgivable, but a lengthy wallow in self-pity I refused to tolerate. I therefore determined to talk myself into being sensible again by the time we reached Steventon. Nothing truly tragic had occurred, I reasoned. I had simply made an error –

not the first nor the last time that would happen, surely. I had mistakenly wished for a romantic attachment that could never be. The object of that supposed attachment was now gone, and there was an end to it.

Exertion was necessary, and so resolutely did I struggle against the oppression of my feelings that my better self eventually won out. It was with a tolerable semblance of my customary cheerfulness that I greeted my family upon our arrival home. Although nobody paid much attention to me; they were all full of the bride and groom, which was just as it should be.

It was only that night, when Cassandra and I finally retired to the bedchamber we shared, that my self-control faltered. Too weary to maintain the pretense any longer, I let down my guard. And Cassandra, who I sometimes believe understands me better than I do myself, immediately queried me.

"What is it, Jane?"

I knew I had been found out. That did not stop me from feigning ignorance, however. "I have not the pleasure of understanding you."

"Yes, you have. Something is amiss. I suspected as much earlier, but now I am certain. Tell me."

"It is nothing, only a touch of melancholy."

"Not because of Henry and Eliza, I trust. Anybody can see how happy they are."

"No, of course not. I am delighted for them both."

"What, then? You know all my sorrows, Jane. It is only right that you should allow me to share yours as well."

A violent pang of conscience struck me. Poor Cassandra. Less than eight months before she had learnt that Tom Fowle – the love of her life – was gone forever, taken a victim of a tropical fever at San Domingo. She had known him far longer than I had my captain, and between them there had existed something far more substantial: a positive engagement. And yet she bravely carried on. What were my sorrows next to hers?

"My distress is owing to a similar cause, but it does not bear comparing to your affliction, dear Cass. It is just that I met someone at the wedding that I believe I could have cared for, and now I shall never see him again."

"Ahhh," she said with a knowing look. "So it is love."

"Certainly not! How could it be? I only saw him once, and I shall soon be over it."

"The same as you were soon over your infatuation with Tom Lefroy?"

"Yes!" I declared boldly. "No," I corrected. I could lie to myself, if I chose, but I would not lie to my sister any longer. She deserved better. "No, this is different," I added with a sigh.

"I see. Not calf-love this time. No mere flirtation."

"I wish it were, since it stands no chance of continuing, but I am afraid it is not."

With gentle coaxing, Cassandra drew the story from me, bit by bit, until I had related to her the whole of it – how I met the captain, a full description of his person and manners, and every detail of our one conversation.

"He is just the sort of man I could admire," I concluded, "and what I had almost given up hope of finding."

"Now you sound like Marianne Dashwood," teased my sister. "What is it she says near the beginning of the book? Something about never finding a man whom she could truly love."

I had recently revisited the manuscript in question, so the passage to which Cassandra referred was still fairly fresh in my mind. "It goes something like this," I said. I closed my eyes, rested the back of my hand against my forehead, and threw myself into the role, as if acting in our old family theatricals. "The more I know of the world, the more I am convinced that I shall never meet with a man whom I can really love, for I require so much. He must have Edward's virtues, and his person and manners must ornament his goodness with every possible charm."

Cassandra laughed at my melodramatic performance. "Ah, yes, an opinion drawn from the vast wisdom and experience of one who was but seventeen. Can anybody measure up to Marianne's impossible standard, Jane? Does your captain?"

I gazed at the ceiling and considered the question wistfully. "Difficult to say. A longer acquaintance would surely be required to verify his goodness with certainty." Then I grinned. "And, unfortunately, I had no proper opportunity to test the limits of his virtue. But I can vouchsafe the rest. I found Captain Devereaux *highly* ornamental and *everything* charming."

We laughed again and I embraced Cassandra, silently blessing her for lightening both my burden and my mood. Then, before dropping off to sleep that night, I told myself once more that this affair was utterly at an end. There was no use continuing to think of the captain, because I was never to see him again.

I believed it at the time, and I have wondered nearly every day since how things might have turned out differently had it been true.

- 5 -

The fact is that, instead of never seeing Captain Devereaux again, I saw him the very next day.

The party at Steventon, given in celebration of Henry and Eliza's marriage, was well underway, and all our friends were gathered to make merry with us. Papa acted the consummate host. Mama fussed and fretted for fear of running out of the fricandeau, or that the table arrangements might be judged insufficiently grand for the occasion. The bride and groom, arrayed in their finest dress, displayed their happiness and good fortune for all the world to see.

It was a splendid affair, by Steventon standards, and I should have been in my element – taking every opportunity of enjoying myself. Yet, despite my resolution to the contrary, I had once more been daydreaming about Captain Devereaux.

"Do not they look well together, Jane?" remarked dear Madam Lefroy, coming up beside me and resting a hand on my shoulder.

Thus forced into cutting short my reverie, I followed her gaze to where the newlyweds stood talking with my brother James and his little daughter Anna. "Yes," I agreed, "very well indeed."

"One would never think that there was any awkwardness in their ages. Such trifles hardly signify when more important factors mark two people out for a good match. Their temperaments seem entirely suited, and the comfortable bit of wealth Eliza brings to the union will surely make up for everything else. Your brother is a lucky man."

"He *is* lucky, yes, but because he has been able to marry the woman he loves."

"Jane, do not look at me so reproachfully. Only think what it was that enabled Henry to marry where his heart chose. Why, was it not a sufficient supply of funds?"

I had to admit she was right. "I suppose that is true enough, my friend. I still maintain that a good income is not the only ingredient necessary to happiness. However, I am willing to concede that it is one thing which is very difficult to do without."

"Exactly so," she said calmly, giving my hand an affectionate squeeze. "I knew we must come to an understanding, my dear. You and I can never remain at odds for long."

I returned her warm smile, thinking how our own enduring relationship reflected the sentiment this gracious lady had expressed a moment before; a disparity in age did not signify when compared with more important factors, such as mutual respect and common interests. With Anna Lefroy I shared a passion for literature of all kinds. She encouraged me in my writing, and she was always ready to join me in an informed discussion of plays or poetry. The fact that she was closer to my mother's age than to mine merely made her a more reliable counselor. A decade of acquaintance had taught me to trust her opinions, which were always founded on sound judgment and the wisdom of experience.

As usual, my conversation with Madam Lefroy had done me good, talking me back into a more rational frame of mind. Still, it little prepared me for what followed. One moment sense and order reigned; the next, they were completely overthrown again with Captain Devereaux's sudden appearance at Steventon.

Henry, who had spotted him first, was in the midst of greeting his friend. Yet his friend could not attend. Indeed, whilst Henry was still speaking, the captain began to walk away. As if drawn by the strength of my own wishes, he slowly and inexorably moved in my direction, cutting through the crowd with no more notice of them than if he were passing through a field of tall barley.

At first, I did not believe my eyes, and then came the fleeting impression that the glorious image before me must have somehow been conjured from my own mind. Yet this was no apparition, I soon perceived, but rather a man of flesh and blood, alive, breathing, and now no more than two feet from me.

"Miss Austen," he murmured.

Blinking back my disbelief, I said, "Captain Devereaux, what do you do here? I… I had not expected to see you again."

"Perfectly understandable, since I left you with no assurance that you should. Still, I found that in the end… In the end, I could not stay away."

He paused and I held my breath until I should hear what he would say next.

"I could not stay away because… That is to say, I came because I knew *you* would be here."

It was no doubt very forward of him to say such a thing to me on so short an acquaintance, but I swiftly decided to make allowances. He was French, after all – a very passionate race, by all accounts – and it was not to be expected that four years abroad would have transformed his native temperament and manners entirely. In any case, his words, added to the earnest way he looked at me, confirmed everything in a moment. That was all that signified. I had *not* imagined the regard I had seen before in his eyes. I was *not* alone in thinking something special had passed between us in our brief time together two days earlier. He had felt it too, and on the strength of that conviction alone, he had followed me all the way from London. My spirit trilled for joy; my heart was given wings.

"Do you mind," he asked, "that I have come, I mean?"

Before answering, I told myself that I had not the same excuse as he did for speaking so openly. "Not at all," I said with proper English restraint. "I enjoyed our conversation before, and I wondered if we might meet again one day. I had not imagined it could be so soon, however."

"We live in uncertain days, Miss Austen, and I could at any moment receive orders to sail. This is no time for hesitation, no time to hope circumstances alone might happen to forward our acquaintance. I had to take matters in hand myself or risk losing this one chance. You must see that."

"Sir, I hardly know what to say to such a statement," I equivocated, "except that I am extremely flattered that you prize our new friendship so much as this."

"I do, and I believed – that is, I hoped – it might develop into something more, given the opportunity. Forgive me if I presume too much, but I thought perhaps you did return some portion my regard. Was I wrong, Miss Austen?"

What could I say to him that would be both proper and true? My heart longed to shout for joy, but my head again called for restraint. We were not alone, for one thing, and I was worried that our conversation might already be attracting undue attention. "I do like you, Captain," I said in low tones, "very much, in fact. But more than that I cannot say. Decorum prevents me."

He looked pleased. "If your feelings for me are stronger than you are at liberty to openly declare, then I am well satisfied. This is a good beginning. Yes, a very good beginning!"

∼∼*∼∼

We spent every possible moment together after that. Henry and Eliza's presence gave excuse for all manner of parties and gatherings at both Steventon and Ashe, and for Captain Devereaux's inclusion in them. Since we had been enjoying especially fine weather for January, we all took to walking out together as well – the young people of the neighborhood. These outings on foot were our favourite above any other form of entertainment, for they offered the captain and myself opportunity to become more intimately acquainted away from any officious scrutiny.

What can I say about those days of exceptional happiness? Just as with Anne and Captain Wentworth's initial courtship, I am compelled, even now, to keep to myself many details of what actually transpired between the two of us. Such private moments and tender feelings defy words and explanations in any case. This much may be known, however; overwhelming forces had already been set into motion, sealing our fates. What ensued was as irresistible as gravity. Establishing the pattern for the hero and heroine of my novel, Captain Philippe Devereaux and I fell *rapidly and deeply in love.*

We both understood what was happening and rejoiced. Suddenly, all the world was right and beautiful in Philippe's estimation, with his highest praise reserved for me. I felt the same boundless bliss, rightly sighting my captain – in whom all the manifold virtues of male perfection were happy to reside – as the source of my sublime contentment. Past injuries and disappointments were soon forgot, and nothing but the most glorious future lay before us.

Since no positive engagement yet existed between us, we talked about these things only in theoretical terms. He would ask me general but leading questions. What sort of house did I imagine myself living in one day? Did I suppose that the sea air would agree with me, should I, for some unnamed reason, find myself residing in a port town for example? It became a delicious game to us, a delectable way of heightening anticipation – seeing how much we could say to one another without committing ourselves, without crossing the tempting line too soon.

In these roundabout discussions, Captain Devereaux admitted to only one minor reservation for our outlook, and that was his current lack of fortune. He had been forthright about this from the beginning. Although once he had been rich, he had been obliged to start again almost from nothing when he arrived in England. He had his officer's pay, of course, but little beyond at the moment. A minor inconvenience, it seemed in those first heady days of infatuation, for in our exuberance, we believed ourselves more than equal to overcoming every obstacle. Nothing must stand in our way.

Had anybody else perceived the seriousness of the attachment so swiftly forming in front of their eyes, we might have encountered early opposition to spoil our joy. But I had been more circumspect this time – it was part of the game – and only Cassandra could have supposed this was anything to rival my flagrant flirtation with Tom Lefroy two years before. The others seemed to accept the given explanation for the captain's frequent presence in our house – that he was a close friend to Henry and Eliza, come to celebrate their marriage along with the rest of us.

The celebrations could not continue indefinitely, however, and neither could our delightful courtship games. After two weeks all together, Henry and Eliza were due to leave us. And Philippe himself was obliged to go into London on business in a matter of days. He expected it would be a brief absence. All the same, there was always a chance he would find orders awaiting him there and not return. In that case, would I ever see him again?

Then Philippe rode over that fateful morning from his temporary lodgings to propose one more walk to Ashe before the breakup of the party.

"An excellent notion," said Henry, in response to the Captain's suggestion. "Do not you agree, my dear Eliza? It will serve as our take-leave visit."

"Yes, to be sure, although it pains me to think that we must go away tomorrow. Jane, you *will* walk with us."

Looking up from the book I pretended to read, I saw her wink at me. "Certainly, if you wish it," said I, as if it were all one to me.

"I would not lose your company for one hour," continued Eliza, "even to gain that of the Lefroys."

With no one else available to join in, we four set off for Ashe parsonage, walking at a brisk rate to match the bracing chill in the air. Once out of sight of the house, the Captain and I slackened our pace, steadily dropping behind the others, as we had so often done before. Words were not necessary to orchestrate this alteration, or the fact that our parallel paths soon drifted a little closer, to the point where the sleeve of his coat might happen to brush mine occasionally. I could then at least imagine I felt his warmth bridging the gap between us, though we never touched.

"I believe I owe you an apology, Miss Austen," he began at length as we went along.

I looked sideways up at him. "Truly? Whatever for? And please, do call me by my Christian name whenever we are alone." I longed to hear myself addressed so. And, coming from his lips, I expected that one syllable would sound as sweet as the most elegant sonnet.

He paused and looked at me. "Very well, *Jane*."

A wave of pleasure washed over me at his caressing tone, and time seemed suspended for a moment while the exquisite sound hung in the air.

Then he remembered himself, resumed our walk, and continued with his thought. "I owe you an apology, or at least an explanation, for my behaviour to you in London. You must have wondered why I ended our conversation so abruptly, especially when we had been doing so well together."

"You did give me an explanation," said I, determined now to make light of the circumstance that had hitherto given me so much anxiety. "You said you feared detaining me from my friends overly long. Still, I thought I must have said or done something to displease you."

"Not at all. Quite the opposite, I assure you. Perhaps you did not suspect it, but I knew within minutes of our first meeting that I could care for you, that an attachment was indeed already beginning, on my side at least. The longer we were together, the more difficult it would be to break away. And, not being in a strong position to make any commitments, I believed I owed it to us both to part before any real harm was done."

"Yet you followed me to Hampshire anyway."

I stopped and turned to my companion, and he did likewise.

"Yes," he said almost breathlessly. "I suppose I changed my mind."

Perhaps it would have been more correct to demure, but I simply said, "I am so glad you did, Philippe."

This seemed to decide him. Rewarding me with a gratified smile, he took both my gloved hands in his and hurried on. "The world would tell us that it is imprudent to contemplate marrying on so little.

I have some money saved, otherwise there will be barely anything above my pay to live on. But I love you too passionately for delay, Jane, and I am asking you to believe in me. I am resourceful, hard working, determined, and, despite my history, I count myself a lucky sort of person. With you by my side, I cannot fail of achieving great things, both in my career and as regards to fortune. There is plenty of prize money to be made in the war, and I still hope to recover at least a portion of my family's property as well. Dearest Jane..." Here he dropped to one knee. "...will you trust me? I may have no right to ask, but will you marry me now, while I am undeserving? If you agree, you will never regret it, I promise."

Dear God! How long ago that scene played out! And still, I have yet to forget one detail of it – the stray lock of dark hair forming a flawless curl on the captain's forehead; the small puffs of fog created when his warm breath merged with the frigid air as he spoke; the call of a distant rook punctuating the brief silence after he finished. These and other precious remembrances compose a sharply drawn picture in my mind, undiminished and unmarred by the passage of time. The words spoken on that wooded pathway remain so perfectly preserved that I have no difficulty recalling them even now, more than seventeen years later, recalling them and ascribing the substance of my captain's sentiments over to his fictional counterpart. I take my pen and write:

> *Captain Wentworth had no fortune... But he was confident that he should soon be rich; full of life and ardour, he knew that he should soon have a ship, and soon be on a station that would lead to every thing he wanted. He had always been lucky; he knew he should be so still. Such confidence, powerful in its own warmth, and bewitching in the wit which often expressed it, must have been enough for Anne.*

Likewise, it had been enough for me as well. I agreed to marry Captain Devereaux that day, and it would be impossible to say which of us was the happiest – I, in receiving his declaration of love, or he in having his proposal accepted. We laughed and kissed by turns, forgetting to make much progress towards our destination. I smiled so much that by the time we finally did reach Ashe, my cheeks ached for it. If only that initial happiness, that boundless, unlimited joy, had been stout enough to withstand the storm to come.

-6-

We told Henry and Eliza at once about our plans to wed. Since Eliza had played the matchmaker and Henry always supported anything that made me happy, we were sure of their approbation. Their own connubial bliss made them particularly eager to see those they cared for similarly well disposed of, and to believe all would end cheerfully, both for us and for themselves.

Cassandra was more guarded in her reception of my good news, which I told her that night in private. Coming over to sit alongside me on my bed, she asked me gently, "Are you certain it is wise, Jane, to marry on so little, especially with him likely going to sea again. Anything could happen."

From her worried aspect, I knew what she must be feeling on my account. Captain Devereaux and I faced similar circumstances to what had confronted her and her intended – the twin perils of a purse too small and an ocean too uncertain. Cassandra and Mr. Fowle had responded with caution and restraint, choosing to wait for his return to dry land on a more favourable financial footing. It was in keeping with Cassandra's character; indeed, I would have been amazed if she had done otherwise. And yet her caution had not saved her; it ended in tragedy nonetheless.

Vowing she will never marry another, Cassandra remains entirely constant to Mr. Fowle to this day, as devoted to the man after his death as any wife could well be. She has had all the sorrow of widowhood without ever enjoying any of the consequence conveyed by having actually been married.

"I know you mean well, Cass," said I in return. "You would protect me if you could, and I thank you. As to being wise, however, I can only hope that time will prove it so."

"You must do more than *hope* for the future, Jane. You must *think*, and not let your feelings run wild."

I jumped to my feet and spun about with my arms outstretched. "Too late!" I said, throwing my head back and laughing. "No doubt your advice is very sensible, but it comes much too late, my dear. My feelings are already run wild, and I find that I like it. I am sure no one ever 'thought' or 'planned' their way into such happiness. One must simply rush headlong at it when it comes within sight! Now, tell me I have your blessing."

Cassandra, who loved me too dearly to withhold anything that would give me a moment's pleasure, kissed me at once and wished me joy.

I am grateful that Captain Devereaux and I told no one else of our private bliss immediately. As I now write of Anne and Captain Wentworth, we had those few days – a very short period of *exquisite felicity* – before the first signs of trouble appeared, during which we made the most of every moment in each other's company.

> *A short period of exquisite felicity followed, and but a short one. Troubles soon arose. Sir Walter, on being applied to, without actually withholding his consent, or saying it should never be, gave it all the negative of great astonishment, great coldness, great silence, and a professed resolution of doing nothing for his daughter. He thought it a very degrading alliance; and Lady Russell, though with more tempered and pardonable pride, received it as a most unfortunate one.*

Philippe and I were decided on having things formally settled between us before he left for London. Thus, my parents needed to be told. I hardly know what I expected their reaction to be but, in my euphoric state, I could not have imaged anything like what actually occurred.

Alarm shot right through me at seeing Philippe's dark expression upon emerging from his brief conference with my father. He said nothing, just looked at me while working his mouth as if to rid it of an unpleasant taste. Then he snatched his hat from the table where he had left it and made straight for the front door. I stopped him before he could get away, demanding in a hushed tone, "For God's sake, tell me what has happened, Philippe!"

He muttered a mild invective in French, and then continued in English with an accent of bitterness. "I may be from a very distinguished line by most people's reckoning, but it seems I am not good enough to marry your father's daughter."

"Impossible! Is that really what Papa said?"

"I am too French. I am too poor. Call it what you will; the result is the same. He refuses to give his blessing, and he claims he can do nothing to help us if we go ahead without it."

I was so stunned that for a moment I could not speak. Presently, however, I said, "I never had any hope of much in the way of financial assistance, but to be so harsh? That I did not anticipate. Perhaps it is only the shock of the thing. We have been so secretive that Papa was unprepared. This must be the explanation. Surely, he will come round in time."

"Perhaps, but time is in short supply if we are to be married before I am sent to sea. And we *must* be married, Jane. I know you feel it too. Are you prepared for my sake, for the sake of our future together, to defy your father's wishes in this if necessary?"

That was the question at the heart of the matter. I had the week while Captain Devereaux was gone to London to turn the tide in our favour, or be forced to choose.

Philippe went away angry and hurt. I could not blame him. His pride – a natural product of his privileged upbringing – had been insulted by my father's rejecting his suit. And, more importantly, I had been unable to give him the immediate assurance he asked for, that I would side with him against my family and the entire world if he asked it.

~~*~~

I was miserable when he was gone – for missing him, for the manner of our parting, and for what I endured in his absence.

I went to my father as soon as Philippe had ridden away, anxious that the mistake might be corrected at once. It must be a misunderstanding, I thought, not a definite negative as the captain had supposed. I knocked on the door to the study and heard my father's voice.

"Come in, Jane."

Opening the door, I stepped into the familiar room, crowded with beloved books and too much furniture. My father was seated behind his desk, as he so often was, and he wore a sober expression. I opened my mouth to question him, to accuse him. "Papa, how could you…?" That was all I could manage before the threat of tears choked off my words.

My father came round to me at once and silently bundled me into an embrace. He allowed me to cry until I was calm again before holding me at arm's length and attempting an answer. "You ask how I could refuse my permission for this Frenchman to marry you. How could I do otherwise, Jane? Should I allow a stranger to walk into my home and carry off one of my most precious possessions without trying to stop him? Of course not."

"He is not a stranger, Papa. And I thought you liked him."

"He is a casual acquaintance and no more. We have only Eliza's information to establish his character beyond. That may be enough to invite the man into my house, but it is not sufficient recommendation to take him to the bosom of my family!"

"I know him better than you do, and he is a good man, an honourable man."

His tone softened. "He may well be all that you say, but we cannot know it with any confidence on such short association. More time is needed, much more time. Inquiries must be made to determine the facts. Then perhaps… But still, he has no money, Jane – this he freely admits himself – and he is a foreigner besides. Have you forgotten that we are at war with the French?"

"He is an Englishman, by choice if not by birth, and a sailor like two of your own sons!" I broke free of my father's grasp and stalked across the small room. "Captain Devereaux has served the English crown for four years now, and he feels no allegiance at all to the revolutionaries who killed his own father. As to fortune, Papa, Philippe once had more money at his ready disposal than you or I will see in a lifetime, and he will rise again. I believe in him. Even now, he might have had sufficient resources to satisfy your ideas had he not generously given his ship and his occupation over to the navy. Blame him for being too foreign or too poor, but you cannot have it both ways; one argument cancels out the other. He may lack a proper fortune now, through no fault of his own, but he has certainly demonstrated his loyalty to this king and country."

My father did not dispute these facts, but neither would he allow them to sway him from his original opinion. Regardless of how deserving Captain Devereaux might prove to be in the end, he had yet to adequately establish his value and trustworthiness. And we must wait to marry until such time as he did. That was Papa's final word on the subject.

My mother was no more my friend in this matter than was my father. "What do you expect to live on?" was her first question when I approached her for help.

"Money, money, money!" I responded in disgust. "Is that all that signifies in this family? What about love, Mama? Try to understand my position, I beg you. Let me appeal my case to the poet deep in your soul."

"Now Jane," she said sternly, "I may appreciate a good sonnet and even write a pretty verse myself now and again. But I have also, every day of my married life, suffered the challenge of making a small income go a long way. Love is all very well in books, Jane, but I have yet to see it put food on the table or a roof overhead."

Although I battled on for the cause, my arguments failed to sway her either. In the end, my mother's answer was the same as my father's had been; we must wait. If we were prudent and patient, it was possible they would lend their blessing to our union in time. But they could, neither one of them, support us rushing into something that so much portended disaster. I was to give the captain up and speak no more of marrying him at present.

"I am sure they only mean to act in your best interest, Jane," said Cassandra when I complained to her of the injustice. "They would spare you the pain they fear will result from your entering into this alliance too precipitously. You may disagree with their judgment, but you cannot fault their motives. And remember, their answer isn't 'never,' only 'wait,' just as it was for me and Mr. Fowle."

I was quiet for a minute, debating with myself whether or not to ask my sister something I had long wondered. It seemed exactly the right moment for it, however, if there ever was one. Others were free enough with their counsel; I should hear everything my dear sister had to contribute.

"Cass, do you ever regret having listened to their advice," I asked cautiously, "regret having waited, I mean. Do you sometimes wish you had thrown caution to the wind and married your young man before he went away? You would then have had at least a brief season of happiness together."

"And when he did not return, I would have been left a widow. Widows have the most dreadful propensity for being poor, Jane."

"You should have been no worse off than what you are now, surely. And you would have been left with the greater consequence of having been married; with a more complete experience of the man you loved; and, who knows, perhaps with his child too."

A faint blush coloured Cassandra's cheeks and she looked away, first down at her hands and then out the window to where a steady rain beat against the leaves of the trees, making the whole host of them dance erratically.

"Forgive me, dearest," I said presently. "I did not mean to upset you, and you are certainly under no obligation to answer my question. I just wondered about it – on your own account and for the bearing it may have on my situation as well."

Cassandra gave me a sad smile. "I do sometimes think of it. I ask myself if being married first would have made the losing of Mr. Fowle less difficult… or more."

"One cannot know the answer, I suppose."

"That is just what I think, so I take comfort in the conviction that I acted with prudence and honour in the matter, and that nothing I did could be supposed to have added to my own distress or to the distress of others."

Except perhaps adding to the distress of your intended, I thought. As far as I knew, however, Tom Fowle had never pressed my sister for an early consummation of their wedding plans. Captain Devereaux would not be as patient, I suspected.

-7-

With Henry, Eliza, and Captain Devereaux all gone away, I had few allies at my disposal. Cassandra, I knew, would support me in whatever I decided to do. But she could not be expected to take the fight to my parents herself, especially when her own cautious nature tended to side *with* them.

After two days of making no headway against their united front, I had but one significant avenue of recourse left to me: Madam Lefroy. She was a woman of good sense and judgment, respected as such not only by myself but by my mother and father as well. If she backed my position, she could prove a formidable weapon in my arsenal. Perhaps these terms are too strong, and yet I did feel as if I were in a fight for my very life. At all events, it was time to find out what my dear friend and mentor had to say on the subject.

As with everybody else, the captain and I had endeavoured to keep her in the dark about the strength of the interest between us. She was thereby quite unsuspecting when I called very early the next morning to open my heart to her at last.

"Why, Jane, what do you do here at this time of day?" she asked.

I glanced about at the hall and open doorways of Ashe parsonage. "Come with me," I said, leading the way into the small parlour where we often sat to talk. She settled in her favourite wing chair. I shut the door before coming to my customary seat, close by and facing hers. I was too restless to sit down, however.

Madam Lefroy studied me most intently as I paced and fidgeted before her. Did she see only my excitement at the monumental secret I was about to disclose? Or did she also discern the fierce trepidation, which I strove to hide? I felt as if the issue of the next hour would tip the scale one way or the other, my future hanging in the balance. With this one beloved friend's encouragement, I was prepared to stand against all the others. Without it… well, how could I meet the opposition completely alone?

"What is it, my dear?" she asked, lines of worry furrowing her brow. "You clearly have something of great import on your mind."

"It is quite true, Madam Lefroy. I am far too transparent for disguise, it seems."

"So, then, sit down and tell me. What is your news? Let us have no secrets between us."

"It is simply the best news in the world!" I gushed all at once, dropping into my chair to face her squarely. "Captain Devereaux and I are to be married."

This was met with stone-cold silence rather than effusions of joy. When Madam Lefroy did speak, it was to ask, "Am I to understand that you have engaged yourself to Captain Devereaux? No, you cannot be serious, Jane!"

It was a wretched beginning. If Madam Lefroy did not believe such a thing probable, how was I to convince her that it was not only possible but a fully viable plan? "Oh, my dear friend," said I, "you do not know how you wound me! My sole dependence was on you; and I am sure nobody else will support me if you do not. Yet, I am in earnest; I speak nothing but the truth. He loves me, and we are engaged."

I saw her struggling to compose her features and emotions for my sake. "Well then," she shortly continued. "If you say it is so, I suppose I must believe you, although I was never more surprised by anything in my life."

"You must forgive me, then. Had I taken equal care in revealing this as I have heretofore in concealing it, you might have been spared some portion of the shock. I did not wish that anybody should know until we were sure ourselves. Please tell me, though, that you really do not find the idea so disagreeable. Now that you think of it, can you not see the excellence of the match?"

Sidestepping my question, she posed one of her own. "You said your sole dependence was on me. Does this mean that your mother and father have already heard of your plans and oppose them?"

"Yes, but what does that signify? You have always made free to form your own opinions. My mother and father can only see the obstacles; I trust *you* to see beyond them, as I do, to what can and must be."

"I should hope that you might also trust me to tell you the truth about what I am thinking. My darling girl…" She cupped her hand against my cheek. "…you know that I could not love you more were you my own daughter, born of my own flesh. I will indeed tell you my true opinion, once I am in command of all the facts. I have spoken with Captain Devereaux, of course, and have formed a general impression of his character. But I was so far from thinking of him as a prospect for you at the time that I did not endeavour to know him properly. And I could not have had your unique perspective of his merits in any case. Therefore, you must tell me more about his situation before I am asked to render any judgment. Not only that, however, but also why you love him and your shared vision for the future."

I was a little heartened at this, that Madam Lefroy saw the value in these other aspects of Captain Devereaux's suit, not only the baser claims of birth and fortune. And nothing could have been more welcome to me than an invitation to speak to my friend about the man I loved. I did so at length and with more warmth than I would have dared to reveal to any other person alive, save my sister.

I started with the circumstances of Captain Devereaux's high birth, his devotion to his family, his harrowing escape from the revolutionaries, and his loyalty to England. These were things that could not fail to impress. Through misfortune, he currently had little money, I admitted, but he was confident that he should soon be rich again by his profession. He had his own ship to command and, with his unflagging spirit and bravery, it would soon bring him everything he wanted. His determination and brilliance of mind would assure his success. He was handsome, which anybody could see, but he also possessed wit and uncommon understanding. Proud he might well be, and rightfully so, but he was not arrogant. He had already shown himself respectful of my abilities and value as well.

"He loves me even as I love him, Madam Lefroy, and we are both quite determined to be married before he goes to sea again, which he likely will soon. Then he expects to return with prize money. His limited resources will be enough for my simple needs in the meantime. Neither one of us aspires to a grand style of living. So all we want to be completely happy is the approbation of our closest friends, and no one's approval means more to me than yours, dear lady. Tell me, then, shall I have it?"

Madam Lefroy, who had listened patiently and attentively to it all, now sighed. "Oh, Jane," said she. "This is a hard thing you ask of me."

She rose and went to the window. I remained where I was, in silent agony, impatient for her answer and dreading it at the same time. Yet surely she could not resist the earnestness of my appeal, I thought. She, who was always so likeminded to myself, must see the circumstances through sympathetic eyes.

After a few minutes of deliberation, which seemed like an eternity to me, she calmly returned to her seat, leant forward, and took both my hands in hers. "How shall I advise you, my dear?" she began. "How shall I tell you what I am feeling on your account? It is a difficult thing, for I can clearly see that your heart is engaged. I do not wish to injure you, but I fear it must be so. If by a little pain now I can save you from throwing away your whole future, I shall think I have done you a good service in the end."

"No!" I cried, pulling away from her and getting to my feet. "I shall not believe it of you, that you would take my parents' part against me."

"Jane," she chided with great tenderness. "You must calm yourself and be reasonable. You know I would never take sides against you, but I must prove myself your most faithful friend by giving you wise counsel, whether you like it or not. Will you similarly show yourself to be mine by listening to it?"

I could say nothing to this. I sat, crossed my arms, and made ready to defend my position against whatever arguments of logic or sensibility Madam Lefroy should bring to bear.

She smiled encouragingly. "Now then, we shall discuss this rationally between ourselves with candour and charity. Agreed?"

I nodded, and she went on.

"We must begin with the pecuniary problem, although I am quite certain you will say you have heard enough on that aspect from others. No doubt you are sincere in being ready to – and quite capable of – living on very little for a time. In fact, I believe learning to overcome these minor hardships can be beneficial to a young couple. It is the length of time the problem may persist that frightens me. Nothing is more wearing on youth and courage than unrelenting poverty. This must *not* be your fate."

"It will not be; Captain Devereaux is sure to rise, and I with him."

Madam Lefroy shook her head and bit her lower lip. "How can you know this? The navy, upon which all his hopes are based, is an uncertain profession at best. The truth is that your captain has almost nothing but himself to recommend him. Is that not so?"

"Perhaps, and yet in *his* case that is more than enough."

"Such confidence is admirable. You have learnt it from him, I collect, and it was no doubt potently bewitching in the way he expressed it. I can well imagine how it has been enough to convince you, Jane, but I see his sanguine temper and fearlessness of mind very differently. I believe it is rather an aggravation of the evil. He may be brilliant, as you say, but his headstrong temperament only adds to the danger into which he will place you... and himself as well." She lifted my chin, forcing me to look her in the eye. "Jane, dear, I care only for your safety. If you cannot be persuaded to do the same, however, then think of what will be best and most prudent for others, for Captain Devereaux in particular."

"I *am* thinking of him," I said defensively.

"Are you, Jane? Are you really?"

"Yes, this is what he wants; *I* am what he wants."

"I daresay it is so. Sadly, though, what one wants and what is best are not always the same thing. In fact, they are very often quite different indeed."

Inside myself, I had to admit it was true. A willful child wants all manner of things that must do him harm; a parent's duty is to prevent the child from getting them.

"Think now," said Madam Lefroy, returning my attention to the case at hand. "How will it benefit Captain Devereaux's career to be saddled so soon with a penniless wife and the possibility of children? How freely will he then decide his actions in the heat of battle? What additional risk might he invite by his desperation to capture the prize money he has promised you, and what disaster will result? Suppose the worst were to happen. You could find yourself widowed, perhaps with a child or two whom you have no means of supporting, and unable to return to your family home. What then?"

She allowed these sobering questions to sink in for a moment. I had no answers for her, at least none that I cared to acknowledge. My first doubt of my own inerrancy in the question crept into consciousness. Was it possible that my sound judgment, in which I took particular pride, had gone so far astray? No, surely not.

She reached for my hand again, patting it as she continued in the gentlest of tones. "A man must be at liberty to establish himself in this world without the weight of domestic cares dragging him down like a millstone round his neck. Similarly, my darling, you must be allowed the exercise of your extraordinary literary gifts without undue encumbrances. You *will* be a published author one day if you persevere. I know it."

"He would not wish to stop me doing so," was my feeble rejoinder.

"Nevertheless, continuing will be impossible for you when children come along and you have no servant to help. How long will your love last when the harsh realities of life have destroyed all your dreams? How long will it be until he begins to resent you and you him?"

It was a crushing blow. Such persuasive arguments, given by one upon whose kindness and steadiness of opinion I had come to rely absolutely, were more than I could withstand. No adequate rebuttal came to my mind in defence of our plans to marry at once; no re-statement of my beloved's bravado or my own confidence in him sprang to my lips. For the moment, all I could see was the overwhelmingly bleak picture Madam Lefroy had painted of my future. It loomed as large and ominous as a sky full of thunderclouds, obscuring everything else from view, even Captain Devereaux's especial radiance.

-8-

I did not give up the dream willingly or without a fight. The three remaining days before Captain Devereaux's return to Steventon I spent closeted with my own thoughts, doggedly debating every aspect of the case with myself until I was wearied beyond all understanding.

At one moment I stood firm in my initial decision, resisting every argument of the naysayers in my head. I told myself we would be lucky; the gloomy predictions would not come true. I also told myself that my beloved and I were entitled to take our happiness when and where we found it, and that if we missed this chance we might never get another. I placed my every dependence on Captain Devereaux – my sole anchorage within the storm – and drew reassurance from the memory of his strong face, his confident words, and the knowledge that he loved me.

The next moment, however, I found myself listening to the persistent advice of our detractors, repeating itself in my mind. It was wrong to insist on my own way at the expense of others, they said. I had a duty to my family – and to Captain Devereaux – to act responsibly and not give grief where it could be avoided. Would it not be a worthwhile sacrifice to wait a year or two if it meant a better outcome in the long run? When the war was over perhaps (and surely that could not be many months distant), then we could expect to proceed under more favourable circumstances.

The longer the captain stayed away, the more I felt myself beginning to slide towards a giving in, a yielding to those other influences. After all, the dissenting voices were not those of true enemies, despite the way I had characterised them. These were my most trusted friends, the very people who knew me best and wished me safe and happy. How could I ignore them and their wisdom of greater experience? Would it not be the height of foolishness to refuse to heed their kind warnings?

Madam Lefroy's counsel carried particular weight with me. Her wisdom and objectivity had long since earned my every respect. Her friendship and goodwill could not be questioned. But more than that, she stood in place of a second mother, in tenderness of affection and in authority. Such a one could not be continually advising me in vain.

I now write of Anne Elliot the conclusion I ultimately came to for myself.

> *She was persuaded to believe the engagement a wrong thing – indiscreet, improper, hardly capable of success, and not deserving it. But it was not merely selfish caution, under which she acted, in putting an end to it. Had she not imagined herself consulting his good, even more than her own, she could hardly have given him up. The belief of being prudent and self-denying, principally for his advantage, was her chief consolation...*

I hoped Captain Devereaux would understand.

He did not. The caution I suggested, he interpreted as lack of resolve. When I advocated restraint, he railed against allowing ourselves to be bound by the arbitrary conventions of others. I claimed to champion our common good, but he saw only betrayal in it.

The scene, painful to recall even now, unfolded in this way.

I had procured the use of my father's study in advance, in order that I might make the unpleasant disclosure in private. So, when Captain Devereaux came to call as expected at the end of his week away, I led him to that room. Other than a tempered greeting, no words had been exchanged between us, but I had felt his ardent gaze continually on me.

Once the door was closed behind us, rather than taking a seat as I expected, he moved to take me into his arms instead, saying, "Oh, Jane, Jane. My darling, how I have missed you! Pray, do not keep me in suspense any longer. Tell me at once that all is arranged for our speedy marriage. We have not a moment to lose."

I had in some measure forgotten the powerful impression his physical presence conveyed, magnified at that moment by the fact that he was actually touching me for nearly the first time. I wanted to stay there forever, enveloped in the heat of his embrace. It was the most difficult thing I ever had to do, to push myself away from the man I loved and speak the words that would change everything between us. I did it, however, believing at the time it was for the best.

Instantly, his hopeful expression transmuted into one of hurt and incredulity. "You have decided to give up our engagement?" he repeated. "No, Jane, this cannot be so."

"It will not be forever, Philippe. Only for a little while, until circumstances make our marrying more supportable. We must be sensible, after all."

"Sensible! This is not what you said before. A week ago, you said you would marry me. There was no talk then of being sensible, only talk of love. These are someone else's words you now avow. Who has whispered in your ear and made you lose your nerve?"

"It was not one person only, my love; everybody advises against it. Can they *all* be wrong?"

"Yes, by God, they can be, if they say we must be parted."

"You cannot be surprised that they should. You knew of my father's disapproval even before you went away. Since then, others have added their similar opinions. Madam Lefroy says…"

"Madam Lefroy?" he broke in. "What has that lady to do with this?"

"Nothing, only that she is my dear friend and confidante. But you must not blame her for cautioning me. My mother agrees with my father as well, and even my sister is in favour of exercising a prudent restraint. How could I stand against them all, Philippe, especially without you here beside me to give me strength?"

"It is my fault then, I suppose," he said miserably, dragging a hand through his hair. "I should never have gone away and left you alone. I certainly would not have done so, had I any idea that your resolve could be so weak, that your word to me meant so little. Jane, just answer me this one question. Do you love me?"

"Yes, of course I do! More than anything in the world."

"Nothing else matters, then."

"If only that were true! But how can a man of understanding and education, who has lived in the world, speak such utter nonsense? You know it is nonsense, too, and yet you would use it against me?"

"I will use anything at my disposal, fair or foul, to change your mind, to persuade you in favour of love again."

"No one could be more a champion of the idea that love is the only right basis for marriage, but even I acknowledge that love alone is not enough. We all must have something to live on as well. Can you deny it?"

"This argument simply means that you do not trust me to provide for you. You do not believe I will do as I have promised."

"I do believe in you, Philippe."

"But not enough, it seems. Not nearly enough."

My tears, kept at bay with difficulty until that time, began to flow, and I could not reply. My worst fears had overtaken me. Not only was I required to relinquish this man of superior worth – for, despite the current disagreement between us, I still believed with every portion of my being that Captain Devereaux was one such – but I was to have the additional pain of his bad opinion against me too.

He had walked away to the window, rubbing his face with both hands as if assaulted by a sudden headache. Now he returned to me. "Jane, Jane," he pleaded softly. "My love, I ask you to reconsider. Do not do this terrible thing, I beg of you. Do not throw away what we have, what we could have – a future together."

More composed again, I answered, "It is only a delay, not a throwing away. Please understand me! What I do is not for my own convenience or even according to my own wishes. But I believe it is the best thing, the right thing – for you, for me, for everybody involved. If we were to go ahead now, without money and without family consent, we would be risking the happiness of others as well as ourselves, possibly even that of our own children."

A mixture of emotions rapidly played across his face at my mention of the last. I can only imagine that they mirrored my own: embarrassment and pleasure at the thought of our having children together, but also trepidation for the heavy responsibility the idea entailed.

He shook his head, as if to rid himself of that valid concern. "It seems to me that you care more for the opinions of others than for mine."

"No, not more than. But the feelings of one's family, a beloved mother and father, must be taken into some account."

"You believe me ignorant of this fact, then?" he said with some indignation. "I assure you that I loved my own honoured parents well enough. Do you think I have not asked myself, time and again, whether they would have approved my choice of wife? The question, my dear, has been asked and answered. With all my family connections amongst the nobility of France and Belgium, do you suppose they would have congratulated me on my betrothal to an English clergyman's daughter? And yet, I willingly set this and every other objection aside for your sake. All I asked is that you be prepared to do the same for me."

We were both silent for a minute while he seemed to be awaiting some concession from me. I had none to give him. His argument, although perhaps having some validity under other circumstances, could not change the facts in this case.

"Very well," he finally continued. "I have laid bare my heart to you, but I will not grovel. The decision is entirely in your hands. Now once and for all, will you marry me, Jane? There can be no 'later.' There is only 'yes' or 'no.' A man must have *some* pride."

I paused before answering, trembling under a great weight of despair – despair, but also anger that, rather than choosing to understand me, the captain had given me an impossible ultimatum. I would not be dictated to, especially to act against my own conscience. He might have his pride, but I had my convictions.

"I have already given my answer to your question, sir, and my rational explanation for it. Perhaps in time, you will learn to credit them. If, however, your pride is truly so overpowering as to prevent you from seeing reason, then it is well that I have discovered it now, before it had been too late. I will not marry a man without sense, sir. Until you acquire some, I will not marry *you*. Have I made myself clear?"

He seemed undecided at first, and then he straightened himself and replied, "Perfectly, madam. You do not want what I have to offer, clearly. You must forgive me for having taken up so much of your valuable time with my foolishness. I will leave you now." He gave a curt bow, turned to go, and then stopped. In a milder tone, conveying more sadness than ill will, he added, "I have received orders and must report for duty soon. Since it is doubtful we shall ever meet again, Miss Austen, please accept my best wishes for your health and happiness. I truly hope you find the kind of life you seek. Pity it cannot be with me."

With these words, he hastily left the room. His firm footfalls retreated from my presence, and the next moment I heard the front door as he quit the house. The hot tide of my anger receded with him, and I was left with only bitter desolation. Thoroughly spent and unable to support myself any longer, I collapsed into a chair, where I remained for half an hour, weeping inconsolably and hardly knowing what had happened… except that it was over between us. Harsh words had been spoken on both sides, accusations made and countered. It was not to be supposed that such things could ever be recovered from.

~~*~~

Looking back on these events, I can scarcely believe how swiftly they occurred. Captain Devereaux appeared in my life one day, and, in little more than a blink of an eye, he disappeared again. Yet the ramifications live on, even to the present time.

Fate showed me no mercy then; I, likewise, must show none to Anne Elliot now. By the stroke of my pen, I sentence her to undergo the same trial:

The belief of being prudent and self-denying, principally for his advantage, was her chief consolation under the misery of a parting – a final parting; and every consolation was required, for she had to encounter all the additional pain of opinions, on his side, totally unconvinced and unbending, and of his feeling himself ill-used by so forced a relinquishment. He had left the country in consequence.

A few months had seen the beginning and the end of their acquaintance; but, not with a few months ended Anne's share of suffering from it. Her attachment and regrets had, for a long time, clouded every enjoyment of youth; and an early loss of bloom and spirits had been their lasting effect.

I cannot say if my own youthful bloom expired the very day Captain Devereaux went away or not. I am no judge. I only know that, like Anne, for a time this misfortune clouded every pleasure of life – clouded them but did not obliterate them altogether.

It is true that I could not thereafter view any man in naval uniform, even one of my brothers, without a considerable pang. But that I was forever inconsolable, that I fled from society, or contracted an habitual gloom of temper, nearly dying of a broken heart, must not be supposed. In truth, I lived to exert and frequently to enjoy myself. I had my writing to occupy me, my friends – literary and otherwise – to console me, and (thanks to my brothers Edward and James), a growing roster of nieces and nephews to keep me entertained.

It was a full life. Yet I continued to lament the loss of Captain Devereaux and, from time to time, to wonder if I had done the right thing after all in giving him up, especially when I heard how quickly his predictions of success came true. Navy news was not difficult to come by in our household, not with two of my brothers belonging to the profession. Between the papers and the newest navy lists, I discretely kept myself apprised of the captain's rapid progress.

Thanks to him, Captain Wentworth shall now receive the benefit of early prosperity as well. I write…

> *All his sanguine expectations, all his confidence, had been justified. His genius and ardour had seemed to foresee and to command his prosperous path. He had, very soon after their engagement ceased, got employ; and all that he had told her would follow, had taken place. He had distinguished himself, and early gained the other step in rank – and must now, by successive captures, have made a handsome fortune.*

Had both Anne and I given up our engagements for nothing, then? Although it is impossible to know the answer, I have now furnished Anne with a definite opinion. While kindly placing no blame on those who had advised her, after years of separation from her captain and no second attachment to heal the wound, she came to believe that *she should yet have been a happier woman in maintaining the engagement than she had been in sacrificing it.*

A sad outcome indeed. But it shall not be the end for Miss Anne Elliot. As I have said before, my novel is to be about youthful error, mature love, and second chances. Anne's story must not conclude with these regrets over the past, but rather live on to fulfill the promise of a bright future. Would that *I* might be so fortunate.

- 9 -

Both the captain and the young lady made errors their first time out. She had been too much persuadable; he had been too little. No, truth be told, most of the fault fell on the lady's side, I am now convinced. I (and my literary surrogate likewise) had been weak in giving in to pressure, weak and cowardly. That is what it really came down to. However much I might wish to assign an equal share of the blame to both my captains, I found I could not.

Was Captain Devereaux culpable for deserting me when I myself made it impossible for him to stay? He had gone away when I refused to cast my lot in with his, when I declined to trust his judgment rather than the wisdom of other voices. The only thing of which the captain was guilty was the trumped-up charge of his not coming back to try me again when circumstances improved. Even that mayn't have been his fault. After all, a military man often cannot control his own destiny, and I had wounded his pride besides.

With these thoughts in mind, I continue with Anne and Captain Wentworth's story.

> *More than seven years were gone since this little history of sorrowful interest had reached its close; and time had softened down much, perhaps nearly all of peculiar attachment to him. But she had been too dependent on time alone; no aid had been given in change of place, or in any novelty or enlargement of society. No one had ever come within the Kellynch circle who could bear a comparison with Frederick Wentworth, as he stood in her memory. No second attachment, the only thoroughly natural, happy, and sufficient cure, at her time of life, had been possible to the nice tone of*

> her mind, the fastidiousness of her taste, in the small limits of the society around them.
>
> She had been solicited, when about two-and-twenty, to change her name, by the young man, who not long afterwards found a more willing mind in her younger sister. And Lady Russell had lamented her refusal; for Charles Musgrove was the eldest son of a man, whose landed property and general importance were second in that country only to Sir Walter's, and of good character and appearance. And however Lady Russell might have asked yet for something more while Anne was nineteen, she would have rejoiced to see her at twenty-two so respectably removed from the partialities and injustice of her father's house, and settled so permanently near herself. But in this case, Anne had left nothing for advice to do.

This is the little narrative I have now composed to account for the passage of time between Anne's first meeting with Captain Wentworth and her second. For they *will* be given a second chance for happiness, and this time they will not be so foolish as to squander it, I trust. Even so, the waste of seven precious years seems almost criminal, for the locusts have eaten them and nothing can bring them back.

My own history parallels Anne's in essentials, but departs from it in certain particulars. As with her, though time had softened the blow, no second attachment had arisen from my limited society to obscure the memory of the first. I did have other suitors, a fact of which my mother enjoys reminding me even to this day. Some of them deserved my consideration and some did not. Yet as much as I might occasionally have wished it otherwise, not one of them was able to threaten Captain Devereaux's prior claim. Without any effort at all on his part, he continued holding fast to his primary place in my heart. There was no dislodging him.

Unlike Anne, I *did* have a change of place – a removal to Bath when my father retired – yet this served more to aggravate than ameliorate the unpleasantness of my circumstances.

On another point, and as I have now documented, Anne had already received and refused her only subsequent proposal of marriage whereas, at that time, my second opportunity was still to come. It would be a proposal so diametrically opposed to what Captain Devereaux had offered me as to mark out a clear comparison between the two. In January of 1798, I had heeded advice and declined to marry the captain, whom I loved, because he lacked the money to live on. In December of 1802, I would ignore common wisdom and refuse to marry Harris Bigg-Wither, who had wealth beyond my dreams, because I did not love him.

It was an awkward business, really best forgot, except that it proved one thing to me beyond any doubt I might still have harboured on the subject. No matter how unprepared I had been to enter into marriage without money, I was even less inclined to wed without affection.

At first I thought I might overlook my young suitor's many personal shortcomings to do what would please all those concerned and forever secure my own comfort. But, on further rumination, I knew it was impossible. All the Bigg-Wither fortune could not entice me. Money would never compensate for the fact that I could not love, or even respect, the graceless youth who offered to make me mistress of the palatial home he would inherit.

Perhaps if I had known no better man for comparison…

But by then, of course, I did know one infinitely superior, and not only from our first brief courtship, but from our second encounter as well. For, like Anne Elliot, I was also to see my captain again. In my case, it was some four years later rather than seven. This made me and Anne of an age – six-and-twenty, well beyond a young lady's first bloom and approaching uncomfortably close to the years of danger. No one had yet called either of us a spinster, at least not to my knowledge, but it could be only a matter of time.

~~*~~

In 1801, when I was five-and-twenty, my father retired from his work in Steventon parish, where he had been rector for nearly thirty years. The living, as well as the comfortable parsonage that went with it, were to be given over to my eldest brother James, and we (my father, mother, sister, and I) were to sell up and move to Bath.

With my father celebrating his seventieth birthday that year, I should have foreseen that something of the kind would eventually occur. However, I confess that I did not. In truth, I was never so shocked in all my life as I was when I heard of the plan. I fainted dead away, and I am told it took many minutes to revive me.

I had no say in the matter, of course; I was totally dependent on my father for support, and therefore subject to all his decisions. But the parting with my life-long home, friends, and so many of our possessions – our furniture, the treasured contents of my father's library, and my own piano-forte – was to me a great source of sorrow, second only to the loss of Captain Devereaux in its gravity and duration. Still, there was nothing for it other than to make the best of a bad situation.

Most people allowed the town of Bath to be quite fashionable and pleasantly diverting. And for a time it did distract me from dwelling on what I had given up in coming there. One could not contest the fact that there was much more to do in the thriving metropolis than in a sleepy country village like Steventon. The theatre, assemblies, and pump-room had to be attended. And there were new environs to explore, by foot or on a drive, and new people to meet with.

We were not completely friendless in Bath. There was a girl by the name of Bernadette Cumphries, whose acquaintance I had made when we had visited the town before. And my aunt and uncle (my mother's brother and his wife, the James Leigh Perrots) resided there as well. This gave us a start at collecting new society about us. Nothing, however, could make up for the people and place we had left behind, or for the fact that we would too seldom see them again.

My greatest consolation was that I still had Cassandra with me. My greatest loss was the companionship of Madam Lefroy. Despite the pain that had resulted from taking her advice, I did not hold any ill will against her for giving it. Her motives were then and continued to be my utmost good; this I did not doubt for a moment. To cherish a resentment against her over what had happened with Captain Devereaux would have been to willfully inflict a larger injury upon myself, to lose them both instead of the one. But then I effectively lost Madam Lefroy anyway, due to our change of towns.

My writing also suffered during my time in Bath. The confined quarters, the noise, the busier pace of life, and my own lassitude: all these conspired to prevent my making any appreciable progress – on the stories already begun or on anything new of consequence. The one contribution Bath made to my literary efforts was to give me a new location that I could write about with authority.

I have planned that in time Anne Elliot will also find her way to this locale. Not yet, though. First she must reacquaint herself with Captain Wentworth at Uppercross and Lyme.

~~*~~

When Anne parted with Captain Wentworth upon breaking their engagement, she never had any idea of seeing him again. He had been so angry when he went away, so wounded in his soul and in his pride, that his intentionally soliciting a second encounter with her could not be expected.

It is, therefore, incumbent upon me to design a situation wherein they might meet again by happenstance. But what would ever entice Captain Wentworth to reenter the neighbourhood where he had been treated with so much disrespect? Sir Walter and the aloof Elizabeth Elliot had quite looked down their noses at him. And Lady Russell had judged him utterly unfit to marry her friend. Yes, it will require a very altered set of circumstances indeed to tempt him back to Kellynch.

But this is easy enough to arrange; Sir Walter has done it for me.

On account of running up debts in the extreme, Sir Walter has no choice now but to take the likewise extreme measures of vacating his manor home and letting it out to strangers. Ironically, this self-important man, who holds an arbitrary prejudice against the navy, is obliged to give up his house to an officer of that very order, to one Admiral Croft. Furthermore, Mrs. Croft is none other than the sister to Captain Wentworth.

Although the irony of how the tables have turned may be lost on Sir Walter, whose penetration reaches no further than the convenience of his own nearest concerns, it cannot escape the notice of one with a far keener perception. What different sentiments must Captain Wentworth feel upon his reentering Kellynch now! Once despised and rejected, he returns to the place of his previous mortification a decorated war hero and a man rich in his own right. His enemies have fled, forced to give way to his own brother and sister.

But where is Anne to go? She must not stray so far away as Bath, the place of her father's exile, else how are she and the captain to meet again? No, I will instead send her to Uppercross, only three miles off, to visit her own sister:

Something occurred, however, to give her a different duty. Mary, often a little unwell, and always thinking a great deal of her own complaints, and always in the habit of claiming Anne when any thing was the matter, was indisposed; and foreseeing that she should not have a day's health all the autumn, entreated, or rather required her, for it was hardly entreaty, to come to Uppercross Cottage, and bear her company as long as she should want her, instead of going to Bath.

"I cannot possibly do without Anne," was Mary's reasoning; and Elizabeth's reply was, "Then I am sure Anne had better stay, for nobody will want her in Bath."

To be claimed as a good, though in an improper style, is at least better than being rejected as no good at all; and Anne, glad to be thought of some use, glad to have any thing marked out as a duty, and certainly not sorry to have the scene of it in the country, readily agreed to stay.

Thus I have now laid the groundwork for an uncomfortable reunion between the former lovers.

The author of a novel takes license to direct such movements with godlike supremacy. Of her own life, however, she has neither control nor the ability to see the future. Events break in upon her with the most alarming unpredictability, as was the case with me once again in the summer of 1802. Unbeknownst to me, fate had been at work to arrange another meeting between myself and Captain Devereaux, one every bit as improbable as that which I have since devised for my literary friends.

-10-

With the temporary cessation of hostilities against the French, achieved by the treaty signed at Amiens in March 1802, hundreds of English sailors were turned ashore, two of my brothers among them. Frank had his own plans, but young Charles joined us for the summer.

His coming to us was like a tonic. We had been at Bath for a full year by then; we had seen all the sights in every season, attended the assembly rooms a dozen times or more, and begun to tire of our confined and unvarying society. At least I had. Father promised we would go to the seaside again, as we did the summer before, but until then we were consigned to suffer the white glare and dreadful sameness of Bath.

All this changed with Charles's arrival. He blew into town on a breath of freshening air direct from the coast, full of youthful enthusiasm and novel schemes for enjoyment. These benefits of his presence hardly surprise me. What I did not expect, however, was that he would have it in his power to add so valuably to our acquaintance.

"Jane, will you show me the way to Camden Place?" he asked one morning when he had been in Bath only a few days.

"Certainly," said I. "Why do you especially wish to see it? I would not think the place of such renown that you would even have heard it mentioned before."

"It so happens that staying there is a former commander of mine, an admiral, now retired, whom I had the great good fortune to meet and to have take very kind notice of me, though by my rank there was no reason that he should have."

I was at once intrigued. "You are very fond of this admiral, I collect."

"Oh, yes! I believe Admiral Crowe is the very best of men. But for an injury he received, I should have hoped to be lucky enough to serve under him still. Now that I am come to Bath, paying my respects to him and to his wife is the least I can do."

"I should like to see this paragon of virtue for myself." Turning to my sister, I added, "Cass, will you venture out with us?"

"Do you mean to walk or take a chair?" she asked me.

"Why, walk, of course! What need have we to be carried about as invalids?"

"Then you must excuse me, Jane. What you propose is quite an ambitious trek from Sydney Place."

"Nothing that should deter us. We shall have the cool of the morning in our favour. Come along. Here is your chance to meet two splendid individuals and sit half an hour in their well-appointed parlour. We do not taste such luxuries here as they are known to enjoy in Camden Place."

Cassandra would not be cajoled into agreeing. "Climbing up that hill will surely do me more harm than sitting in Mrs. Crowe's fine parlour will do me good."

"Very well. Perhaps, if we find them worthwhile, we shall be able to entice these Crowes to fly down from the heights and return the visit. Then you may meet them with more comfort," I said good-humouredly. "Charles, it appears that you and I must make this perilous expedition alone. I hope you are up to the challenge."

Charles assured me that he was, and we set off down Pultney Street and across the bridge before turning toward the upper part of town. Though I had made light of it, Cassandra was right about the climbing of the hill. It was not an undertaking for the faint of heart. The exertion may have left us in a state of some inelegance at our arrival in Camden Place, yet with our wits and our limbs still under admirable control.

Charles quickly located the house number he was looking for and gave a knock to signal our presence. We were announced and admitted at once, being shown into a generously proportioned drawing-room with large windows, which provided a cheerful quantity of daylight and an excellent prospect of the surrounding countryside. All this I was still taking in a few minutes later when our host and hostess entered to greet us.

The admiral was a man somewhere above forty, still a fine figure despite evidence of some lameness in his right leg. The limp and his reddened, weather-beaten complexion tended only to lend him the authoritative air of a man who has lived widely in the world. Mrs. Crowe, apparently several years his junior, was neither tall nor especially elegant, and yet she had an uprightness and vigour of form that gave her person importance. Her face was agreeably composed as well, possessing a ready smile and intelligent eyes. I liked her at once, and I felt a degree of familiarity with her that was difficult to account for. In her, I was sure I had found a kindred spirit, and I had the sense that she might be someone who could in part fill Madam Lefroy's place in my life. All these impressions I gathered within the first few minutes and confirmed over the remainder of our visit.

With the initial flush of civilities accomplished, Mrs. Crowe invited us to sit down. She immediately fell to my share, as Charles and the admiral gravitated to one another and to talking of the sea.

I glanced about myself once more. "You have a lovely home, Mrs. Crowe," I began. "So well situated and comfortably furnished. How long have you lived here?"

"Thank you, Miss Austen. We have been here six months now and are quite content, although it makes the admiral a little uneasy that he cannot see the sea. A short drive to Bristol now and then relieves his mind."

"Of course. Allow me to say again how delighted I am to meet you and your husband, Mrs. Crowe. One can never have enough interesting acquaintance. I find that, despite the abundance of people in Bath, good company is something often in short supply."

"I am flattered, Miss Austen, naturally, but you give us too much credit. What makes you so certain that we shall prove to be acquaintances worth having? We hardly belong to the first circle of Bath society. And having no children about us to make noise, you will find that the admiral and I live in very quiet retirement."

"None of what you say deters me. The first circle of society interests me not at all, I assure you; your life with the navy does. You may live quietly now, but you must have had adventures, ma'am, and travelled."

"The last part is certainly true, although many women have done more."

"Tell me, then," I encouraged.

"Well, I have crossed the Atlantic four times, and have been once to the East Indies, to Cork, and to Lisbon, and Gibraltar. But I never went beyond the Streights, and I was never in the West Indies – Bermuda and Bahama, yes, but not the West Indies."

"Did life at sea suit you, then?"

"Indeed, it did," she said wistfully. "I can safely say that the happiest part of my life has been spent on board a ship. While we could be together..." Here she looked at her husband with obvious affection. "...there was nothing to be feared. I have always been blessed with excellent health as well, and a tolerance for every climate – things much to be desired in a good sailor. And nothing can exceed the accommodations of a man of war!"

"See, now, you have confirmed my theory. What stories you must have to tell, Mrs. Crowe! I have travelled so little that all these fresh places you mention are of interest to me. I am also a great lover of good stories and, one day, when we know each other better perhaps, I hope you will be so kind as to tell me some of yours."

She nodded, and I could see that she was pleased.

"Why must we wait, Miss Austen?" she asked. "I will tell one to you now, if you wish it. What would you most like to hear?"

"You must not feel obligated to indulge my little whims, Mrs. Crowe."

"Nonsense. It would sincerely give me pleasure to relive some of those happy times through the telling of them. Now, what do you desire to hear about? A shipwreck? Battles? Or an exotic marketplace, perhaps?"

"Thank you, but in truth, it is none of these things. What I am most curious about is how you happened to meet and marry the admiral."

"Ah, so it is a story of the heart that most intrigues you."

"Yes, I suppose it usually is. And especially in this case, because it strikes me that you could scarcely have met in an ordinary way – at church or at the local assembly rooms. If I am not mistaken, Madam, you were not born in this country. You are French, I think."

"You have a good ear, Miss Austen. Much as I may try to hide it – for it is not popular these days to be from that country, you know – what you say is perfectly true. I have lived half my life as an Englishman's wife, but I was born French."

"I will harbour no prejudice against you for it, believe me. You could not choose the place of your birth or control events in that country, not any more than I could dictate policy to the king in this!"

"Exactly. Well then, let us talk about something more agreeable than kings and wars; let us talk of love, as you suggested. Would that please you, my young friend?"

I nodded vigourously.

"It happened like this. Years ago, before the wars, Admiral Crowe – Captain Crowe he was then – received a commission to sail from London with a cargo for Portsmouth. His voyage was barely begun when a sudden storm blew in from the north, driving his ship far off course and nearly dashing it to pieces."

"Dear me!"

"Yes, it was a dire situation, and there was no question of making his original destination or even returning to London, not with the condition the ship was in. So he gave the order to put in to Boulogne, the closest harbour, for repairs. That is where my brother, who is a sailor as well, ran across him. Thrown together by circumstances, they quickly struck up a friendship. And, soon enough, my brother invited the captain home to enjoy our hospitality until his ship could be made habitable again."

"And so there he met the beautiful daughter of the house and quite naturally fell in love," I continued for her. "Yes, I have heard that brothers can be very useful in the business of inviting their friends home to meet their sisters, although I cannot say that I have very much benefited by it."

"I suppose this brother," she said with a nod to Charles, "he is perhaps a little too young to have been of any assistance. Have you no older brothers, Miss Austen?"

"On the contrary, Mrs. Crowe. I have five, but I can only think of one occasion when that served to introduce me to a gentleman of particular interest."

When I said no more, she asked, "What became of this gentleman, if you do not mind saying?"

"Nothing. My family objected and he went away again." I shook off this melancholy reflection and observed, "It seems you have been much luckier."

"I have indeed. Captain Crowe stopped in our home until the worst of the repairs had been completed and his ship was fit to occupy again. Then he stayed in port another fortnight, visiting us nearly every day."

"But he could not remain forever."

"No, he could not, and, oh, how I dreaded the day he would have to go away again! Finally, when he could no longer postpone his departure, he plucked up his courage and came to the point, asking to marry me."

"I daresay you accepted him, or you should not be sitting here talking to me now."

"Of course I did! I was as smitten with my captain as he was with me, and there was no denying it."

My captain, I thought with a pang. How often had I used that phrase – in word or in my mind – to describe Captain Devereaux, erroneously, as it had proved to be. Mrs. Crowe was justified in using the term; I had not been. Captain Devereaux never truly belonged to me. Or if he had, it was only for a brief moment in time.

"He had no reason to fear my answer," she continued. "There was more doubt of my father's. Although Captain Crowe was of a fine family with a creditable fortune of his own, marrying him by no means equalled the lofty alliance my father might have hoped for me."

"Did he indeed stand in your way, then?"

"No, he was a kind-hearted man and sought my happiness above his own. He was so very good to us. He made no objection to our marrying or even to the idea that my husband would sail away with me, perhaps forever. I think, even then, that he had some idea of the trouble to come, and wished me removed far from it."

Though her countenance remained under admirable control when she said these things, I noticed a slight quavering of her voice, which warned me to proceed with care. "You said he *was* a kind man, Mrs. Crowe. Is you father no longer living?'

"No, he fell victim, like so many others, to the reign of terror. I never saw him again."

We were both silent for a minute.

"I am very sorry for your loss, Mrs. Crowe – a tragic and yet all too common outcome. I have heard of these atrocities before."

She nodded. "War is cruel indeed, and it seems those who wage it sometimes become so inured to the horrors of death that they lose all respect for life itself – the lives of others and perhaps even their own."

"God help us when we cease to be shocked by such things."

"Indeed. But you must forgive me, my dear. How did we stray onto this topic? We should return to a subject more befitting ladies."

I could not reply. A niggling itch had begun in my brain, telling me there was something oddly familiar about this conversation. Yet I could not quite put my finger on it.

"Miss Austen?" said Mrs. Crowe. "Are you quite well? You have the most peculiar expression on your face. Said I something amiss?"

"No. No, not at all," I returned presently. "Please excuse my bad manners. It is nothing, I assure you."

Although the impression lingered, I fought it off so far as to be able to finish our stay with no more awkwardness. And, despite that one moment of unease, I was a good deal more than satisfied – not only with the visit itself, but with my new friends.

"They promised to call in Sydney Place soon," I told my sister later. "So you shall meet them for yourself, and you are sure to like them every bit as much as I do. It was the strangest thing, though, Cass. I know it sounds irrational, but at one point I was absolutely convinced I had been there before."

"What do you mean? At Camden Place?"

"It was more than that. It seemed I had been in that same room, or one very like, speaking to Mrs. Crowe, and identical words too."

"Are you certain you have never made Mrs. Crowe's acquaintance elsewhere?"

"Never. How could I have? She was born in France and, since leaving there, she has lived all her life on board a ship or in port towns. And yet, there is something so very familiar about her. She does remind me of Madam Lefroy in a way, although…"

"There," said Cassandra decisively. "You have answered your own question. It is that similarity to your old friend that has made it all seem so familiar. Nothing more than that."

It was a reasonable explanation and the best one I had available at the time. I let the matter drop and did not think much more about it. Only later would the truth become clear… painfully so.

- 11 -

The Crowes proved as good as their word, two days later returning the call Charles and I had paid them. The meeting was an unqualified success. Everybody was delighted with the admiral and his wife, and they with my people as well. Two families so connected with the navy could not fail to have mutual interests and common concerns. Add to this the straightforward, unpretentious natures of the parties, and there was the making of a most congenial group. We were instantly adopted into the Crowes' society, and just as quickly made part of all their plans.

At one of these subsequent meetings, my father chanced to mention that we intended to take a sojourn to the seaside the following month. "We shall be sorry to lose your society for a time," he said to the admiral. "But I have promised the ladies, and I must not disappoint them."

"No," agreed the admiral. "Do anything to keep the ladies happy. That is my advice, Mr. Austen. And of course my sympathies are entirely on the side of anybody desiring to spend time near the sea. Truth be told, I still long for it daily, and I have been trying to enlist Mrs. Crowe's support in a seaside scheme of my own. What is your intended destination, sir?"

"We have made no definite plans, Admiral, beyond the fact that we are definitely going," my father said, chuckling. "The particulars are still matters of spirited debate in this house, especially the location. One is a champion for Lyme Regis and another for Sidmouth. Even Brighton has a staunch advocate. With such divisions, how am I to decide? Making a daughter happy will place me in disfavour with a wife. Pleasing a son comes at the expense of his sister, and so forth. You can appreciate my dilemma, I daresay."

"I can indeed, and I sympathise. I have only one to please, not four, and that is challenge enough. I know not what weight my opinion may carry, but allow me to throw my support on the side of Sidmouth, if you will."

"Certainly. I am happy for any assistance in breaking the current standoff, but I must also hear your reason for this recommendation."

"It is simply this, that the Austens being to go there is sure to settle the matter for the Crowes as well."

"How so, sir?"

"It goes back to my seaside scheme, which I mentioned before. You see, a brother of my wife has written, inviting us to join him in Sidmouth three weeks hence. Mrs. Crowe had thought it better to hold out for him coming to us later here at Bath instead. But now, with the additional enticement of your family's presence there (and absence from here), Sidmouth is bound to win her over."

"Yes, Papa!" I cried, no longer able to keep my opinion to myself. "What could be better? We shall have the seaside to enjoy, and we shall take the very best portion of our Bath society with us." I referred not only to the Crowes in this case, for I had already secured the companionship of my friend Bernadette Cumphries for the excursion as well.

By this time, the others in the room had abandoned their own conversations to attend to what was going forward between my father and Admiral Crowe. All eyes and ears turned expectantly to Papa, awaiting his decision.

He paused before speaking, apparently revelling in the fact that he held the floor. "Very well, then," he began slowly, keeping us in suspense as long as possible. "After considering what you have said, Admiral," and, turning toward the rest, "what you *all* have contributed on the subject, I have very nearly made up my mind. Yes, it comes clear to me now. I am…" One final pause elapsed. "I am for Sidmouth," he pronounced. "We liked what we saw of the place before. And, as I said then, if it was good enough for the king to visit, I suppose it is good enough for the Austen family as well!"

My mother, who had heavily campaigned for Brighton, sighed audibly, but no more severe protestations were forthcoming either from my relations or the admiral's. He had been correct in supposing that the leading of one family would serve to secure the following of the other. Now that Sidmouth was our mutual destination, the place took on an irresistible appeal, even for those who had been less than enthusiastic in the beginning.

I had been in favour of Sidmouth all along. Although we had stopped there briefly the year before, dividing our summer holiday between it and Colyton, I had found the place so refreshing that I was delighted to be returning.

A surprising circumstance arose thereafter, however. All my expectation of finding pleasure in the expedition was soon overthrown, my cheerful outlook replaced by one of deep anxiety and mortification, when I learnt who else I was bound to encounter in Sidmouth.

~~*~~

Mrs. Crowe and I had engaged for doing some shopping together one day, when we stepped into Molland's to escape a sudden shower. Whilst taking some refreshment there and waiting for the rain to subside, I asked her to tell me more about her brother – the one who had invited the Crowes to Sidmouth in the first place.

"You shall see him for yourself soon enough, Jane, and I fancy that you will be very well pleased with him. The ladies always are. He cuts quite a dashing figure in his uniform, if I do say so myself."

"He is in regimentals, then," said I. "There are ladies who have been known to swoon at the very sight of a red coat, but I am not among them, I assure you, Mrs. Crowe. It may not surprise you to learn that I am partial to the navy myself. I do not think there is a finer set of men in all of England."

"You will receive no argument from me on that score, as you may well imagine. And hearing this bodes even better for Philippe, for it is a navy captain's uniform he wears, not army regimentals. I believe I mentioned to you that my brother was a sailor."

"Philippe?" I repeated in a whisper, instantly staggered. The unexpected hearing of that one word, that name of highest consequence in my memory, after so long a silence on the subject, hit me with the force of a physical blow to the chest. For a moment I could neither breathe nor think clearly either.

"Yes, his name is Philippe," Mrs. Crowe continued, unaware. "Philippe Devereaux. Did I not happen to say so before? He is turned ashore by this peace, just like your own brothers."

I only heard half of what she said after that; I could not properly attend in my agitated state. The pieces were falling into place all at once. The details matched; everything was explained in a second.

Of course Mrs. Crowe had seemed familiar to me! She was *his* sister. Though I did not know it at the time, it was *his* father that we had been talking about upon my first visit to Camden Place. No wonder that I had the sensation of having participated in that conversation before. I had carried out one of a very similar description with the man himself four years earlier! I remembered it well. On that same occasion, Philippe had told me that he had an older sister in the country. But of *all* the sisters in *all* the country, what perverse decree of fate had determined that I should be introduced to this particular one who now sat beside me?

What I felt at that moment may be imagined. Anne Elliot now feels the same upon hearing she will likely also be brought face to face with *her* long-lost captain. I write…

> *With all these circumstances, recollections and feelings, she could not hear that Captain Wentworth's sister was likely to live at Kellynch, without a revival of former pain; and many a stroll and many a sigh were necessary to dispel the agitation of the idea. She often told herself it was folly, before she could harden her nerves sufficiently to feel the continual discussion of the Crofts and their business no evil. She was assisted, however, by that perfect indifference and apparent unconsciousness, among the only three of her own friends in the secret of the past, which seemed almost to deny any recollection of it.*

So was the perfect ignorance of the Crowes to the past connection between our families, as well as the equally perfect discretion of my own people. During the intervening years, I had occasionally spoken of Captain Devereaux to my sister, but otherwise his name was never again mentioned by those few of my family and friends who knew of my short-lived engagement to him.

This was generally as I would have wished it. Although I did secretly hope that my father had read (as had I) of the captain's heroism and success, I could not have borne to often hear him spoken of, disparagingly as before or even in admiration. To be continually reminded of what I had lost, or to fear that rumours of the affair had been spread abroad, would have been unendurable.

Had my youngest brother been privy to the information, however, I might have been saved the discomfort of ever setting eyes on Captain Devereaux again. Charles surely would not have introduced us to the Crowes had he known of the business and how much it still haunted me. But now it was clearly too late to avoid this new tie.

I wondered what Philippe's reaction would be to hearing my name spoken again, which he surely would by the same means I had heard his. Would the occurrence affect him as profoundly as it had me? Would he be curious to meet me again or at great pains to avoid it? I could not help but think he would disapprove to know that his sister and I were friends. Or perhaps for him the past was so faded into insignificance as to make it a matter of purest indifference whether he ever saw me again or not. I had to consider that he might even be married to someone else by now. Would I be forced into making his wife's acquaintance to compound my every other misery? Such an event should surely be prevented if it were at all possible.

Perhaps some excuse could be made for cancelling our trip to Sidmouth. My parents might support me in the idea if I asked them. Or they might not. Considering Captain Devereaux's improved circumstances and my advancing age, they would, likely as not, promote rather than deprecate a renewed alliance between us, were the captain still conveniently single. And even if I could stay away from Sidmouth, he was coming to Bath afterward.

The larger question, of course, was this: Did I really wish to avoid seeing Captain Devereaux again? As mortifying as my imagination made the prospect appear, a part of me longed to risk it, longed to take a chance in hopes that there might still be enough affection remaining between us to be rekindled. It would take very little encouragement to fan my feelings ablaze again. I was sure of that much. But would the flames catch him afire as well… or simply burn me alive?

All these contemplations raced rapidly through my mind as I sat with Mrs. Crowe at Molland's. Since it seemed unlikely that I could escape the connection entirely, I had no choice but to own it straightaway. Failing to do so, only to have the truth come to light later, would raise speculation of a most unpleasant kind. I therefore plunged in, saying, "I believe I may already know your brother, in fact."

Mrs. Crowe was taken aback at this. "Do you, indeed?" she said presently.

"Yes, I remember meeting a Captain Philippe Devereaux about four years ago, at the wedding of my brother Henry in London – a

French expatriate like yourself, Ma'am. The name was familiar at once, but it took me a minute or two to recall why it should be."

"Well, this is quite remarkable, Jane! Still, I suppose it must be true. I would wager that there cannot be more than one Philippe Devereaux in the English navy. Only imagine how pleased my brother will be to renew your acquaintance."

I could indeed imagine the uncomfortable scene, but I simply said, "As shall I be in renewing his."

I did not pursue the subject further, and I gave Mrs. Crowe no reason to suppose there was anything more substantial to it than a brief encounter made by chance. I hoped no one else – especially the captain – would let on that it had been otherwise.

-12-

Cassandra had to be the first person to whom I told this startling information, for I knew she could fully enter into all my strong and varied feelings. With her, I had complete freedom. With her, there existed no need to exert myself in holding anything back. I could wonder at the sheer coincidence the situation represented, wail over the perverseness of my fate, and relieve myself of every cause for uneasiness that the possibility of seeing Captain Devereaux comprised. After she had listened to all my hopes and all my fears, and after she had sympathised mightily with me in every respect, I became a little calmer – enough so that I could discuss what to do about the problem rationally.

"I suppose our parents must be told something in advance," said I. "What is your own opinion?"

"By all means," agreed Cassandra. "It would not do for circumstances to overtake them without warning. Who knows but what one or the other of them, owing to the surprise of confronting the captain unexpectedly, might say or do something to expose some portion of the past that you would rather remain hidden from view."

I shook my head. "No, I cannot have that. It would be far better that they were prepared. I have left Mrs. Crowe to think her brother and I were only slightly acquainted. I will drop something similar to Bernadette and to Charles. And I will insist that my parents behave likewise. Oh, Cassandra, I cannot help but shudder when I think that *I* might have been the one taken fully by surprise! How grateful I am to have had this forewarning. Perhaps now, by the time I see Captain Devereaux, I will be master enough of myself to keep from revealing too much. I would not give him the satisfaction of knowing he still possessed any such power over me as I expect he really does… at least not without first being certain he feels the same."

"Now, Jane," Cassandra said in a tender yet cautioning tone. "You must not allow any hopes for such an outcome to take root in your imagination. Four years is a long time, and many things may have changed."

"In my head, I know you are perfectly correct, dearest. Oh, but my heart would say otherwise! My heart would tell me it was but a day or two ago and nothing has changed. It seems true for me, so is it not at least possible the same is true for him?"

"Possible, but I fear unlikely. If that were the case, why has he never attempted to contact you? If he still loved you, why did he not come back to address you again when his circumstances had improved?" She let these questions have their effect before continuing. "Fairy story endings are difficult to come by in real life, Jane, at least according to my experience."

I gave my sister a sympathetic look and a squeeze of the hand to let her know I understood.

Cassandra was right, of course. I had to rely on her good sense and take a more realistic view of things. I needed to banish all thoughts of a reconciliation and turn my attention to merely surviving the ordeal to come. My only goal must be to get through the awkward reunion with my dignity and self-control intact.

After consulting with my sister at length, I spoke to my mother and father in private, telling them what I had learnt. They were surprised, quite naturally, but otherwise undemonstrative. My sense was that they were waiting to take their cue for how to behave from me, a cue which I was more than happy to give them.

"This news does not affect me, I assure you," I told them. "Now that I have recovered from my initial astonishment at hearing it, I am grown quite inured to it. I expect we shall be able to meet as common and indifferent acquaintances, all of us, with no need to talk of what has gone before."

When I had finished this little speech, by which I proved to myself that I might have had a successful career upon the stage, my father nodded firmly and rose to his feet. "It shall be exactly as you say, Jane," he agreed. "Captain Devereaux will be acknowledged by us as a slight acquaintance, but one of no particular significance. There is no need to make too much of something that never came to pass, after all, and certainly no need to allow it to spoil our happy relations with the Crowes."

So, that was that. We were all determined to go ahead with our plans for Sidmouth, and no more thought to the past. As I had intended, I found an appropriate moment to casually drop to Charles that I had met Mrs. Crowe's brother before. And then I looked for the right time to inform my friend Bernadette of the same.

I saw Bernadette Cumphries much as the younger sister I never had (for she was my junior by four years and, therefore, Cassandra's by six). She was a sweet girl whose pleasant company I thoroughly enjoyed. Still, our friendship was based more on our closeness of habitation than similarity of character. If I wanted wise counsel and like-minded fellowship, I went to my true sister. If I needed rescuing from the overly serious contemplations to which I had recently become susceptible, this was Bernadette's office, one to which she was eminently suited by her very nature.

"You simply *must* come with me, Jane!" she proclaimed when she called in at Sydney Place one morning shortly thereafter, dropping round as she often did from her house on Daniel Street, where she lived with her widowed father. "I cannot possibly do without you."

I smiled at her enthusiasm. "Oh, yes? And pray, what is the destination that requires my accompanying you to venture? Do tell me."

"Why, to High Street, of course! I have finally convinced Papa that I must be bought new clothes for my holiday with you at the seashore. Quickly now, let us be off before he can change his mind."

"Very well, then," I said, laughing. "I suppose I shall have to resign myself to it. Shops must be visited; purchases must be made."

"Yes, they must indeed! And there is no time to lose."

I made my explanations to my mother, and then Bernadette and I set off down Great Pultney Street. It was a fine day in the last week of June, when the air is still fresh with the promise of the emerging summer season and not yet too hot to enjoy a walk. Bernadette, having secured the comfort of her father's generous purse, was as gay as could be, cheerfully chattering on about the long list of things she hoped to purchase once we reached town. Having no such friendly financial resources to draw upon myself, I planned no major expenditures, but that did nothing to quash my enjoyment of the outing. I intended to be satisfied with the purchase of a few millinery supplies for reworking an old straw bonnet, that and with vicariously sharing in Bernadette's happiness.

"I wonder if there will be any smart beaux in Sidmouth," she said when we were passing Laura Place.

"They may be in very short supply," I told her. "The settled population is mostly made up of fishermen and shop keepers, I believe. But then perhaps you should like being a fisherman's wife," I teased.

"Lord, no! Can you imagine what such a man would come home smelling of? One would never get the stench out of one's nostrils, I should think. No, it is a gentleman I am after, and the sooner the better. Or perhaps a handsome officer. Do you suppose there will be any handsome officers about?"

The face of one such immediately sprang up before my mind's eye, and for a minute I lost myself in recalling its every appealing virtue in detail.

"Jane? Did you hear me?"

"Sorry." This was the opening I had been watching for, I perceived. "Yes, I know for a fact that there will be at least one – a captain of the Navy, Mrs. Crowe's brother."

"Aha! And being Mrs. Crowe's brother, we are sure to meet him! I hope that he is rich. And he ought to be mightily good looking too. I suppose you would have no way of knowing such things, but you might have heard if he is at least single. Failing that quality, the rest counts for nothing."

"I should suppose the rest counts for a great deal to his wife, if he has one!"

"Oh, I cannot be troubled to look out for her! My interest is for myself alone."

"Then I shall quit my teasing and tell you what you wish to know, dear Bernadette. But I must warn you that my information is very much out of date. It so happens that I met the man – four years ago, at my brother Henry's wedding. At the time, Captain Devereaux was entirely single and very handsome indeed. As to fortune, he had little enough then, but I shouldn't be surprised he has acquired a tidy sum in the war since." I had tried to keep my voice even and my countenance free of telltale expression when I said these things, but even so Bernadette gave me a penetrating look.

"For a gentleman you met only briefly, Jane," said she, "you seem to remember this captain very well. He made quite an impression upon you, I think."

"Yes, perhaps he did," I said lightly. "One does not often come across a sailor with such a sophisticated air. And a Frenchman in the English Navy is something of a rarity, you must admit."

"Very true. Because of what you tell me, I am now even more intrigued to meet this gentleman."

"And so you shall; there can be no avoiding it. Married or single, we are sure to be much thrown together with him in Sidmouth."

So the necessary communication was satisfactorily made, accomplishing two things. It had assured that Bernadette would see nothing particularly significant in finding some degree of familiarity between the captain and myself when we all met. And it had given me one more opportunity to practice thinking and speaking of the man in everyday terms. I only hoped that this careful preparation would mean I could also see him with some degree of equanimity, to be in the same room with him and hear his voice with a measure of composure. It still seemed impossible, and the day I would be put to the test grew ever nearer.

~~*~~

There was nothing remarkable about our journey south from Bath into Devonshire, except for the added benefits of travelling in tandem with the Crowes. Not only did the arrangement provide the promise of ready help in case of mishap, but also the very real advantage of variety in companionship. With every change of horses, there was a simultaneous change of situation for the human beings as well.

Charles had his own horse and sometimes rode, but the other seven of us were confined inside and shifting round at regular intervals. My mother and father travelled with the Crowes for a stretch, leaving the other carriage to me, Cassandra, and Bernadette. Then Cassandra was invited to join the Crowes when my parents returned to their own carriage, and so forth until every possible combination had been tried.

When we arrived at the village of Sidmouth, we were at last forced to part company with the Crowes. They had taken rooms at the York Hotel, facing the sea, whereas we had less expensive accommodations reserved at a lodging house on the east road – the same house we had briefly patronized the year before.

For me, it was a relief to put a little distance between our party and theirs, lest we should by accident run across Captain Devereaux before I was fully prepared. I knew I must see him, of course, but I felt as if I could endure that first meeting much better if it occurred at the time and place I expected, that being the following day at a dinner at their hotel, as the Crowes had proposed. Until then, I hoped to stay well clear of him.

It was too late in the day, and we were all too tired, to venture out of our lodging house once we had arrived. But Bernadette, who had never before been to the seashore, was very keen to have a look at it first thing the next morning. So off we went – Charles, Cassandra, Bernadette, and myself – continuing down the east road to where it ended at the esplanade.

A heavy morning mist still hung in the air, lending cool dampness to every breath I took and casting a ghostly veil over all that we surveyed. The sea itself nearly merged with the white sky at the horizon. And the exposed cliff faces of Salcombe Hill to our near left, which I remembered being bright rust red, were now muted to a soft rosy hue. When I looked to the right, down toward the opposite end of the beach, I could not even make out Peak Hill for the hazy atmosphere.

What I did see, however, was the figure of a man afar off and nearly enveloped in fog. Perhaps it was fanciful of me to think I knew him from that distance, but somehow I was certain it was Philippe Devereaux.

"Let us go back," I said to the others at once. "It is too damp to enjoy the seashore now. We can come again when the sun has broken through the clouds."

"Oh, no!" cried Bernadette. "We cannot go; not yet! I am determined to touch the water and taste for myself if it is indeed as salty as they say." Not waiting to hear any protests, she stepped from the paved walk and dashed off across the roughly pebbled beach.

"Be careful," I called after her. Then I looked sternly at my brother. "Charles!"

Charles took my meaning and hurried to Bernadette's side, arriving just in time to catch her as she fell.

- 13 -

"It is only a twisted ankle, I think," said Cassandra after a cursory examination. Bernadette sat on a bench, where Charles had deposited her, writhing in some pain.

My thoughts were divided between concern for my friend and worry that all the commotion might have attracted the attention of the gentleman down the beach. "We should get her home straight away," I recommended.

"I cannot possibly walk!" wailed Bernadette.

"You won't need to," said Charles, sitting down next to her and directing me to Bernadette's other side. "Now, Miss Cumphries, put your arms about our shoulders. Jane and I shall lift you and support all your weight between us. You only need hold your bad foot off the ground and swing your good one along. It is but a short way. Are you ready, Jane?"

I nodded; Bernadette squealed; and we three rose together as one unit. We reached our lodging house within five minutes, where much fuss was made over the patient by the landlady, Mrs. Tinker. The most comfortable chair in the front parlour was given over for Bernadette's use. Then her feet were swiftly elevated and a cold compress applied to the site of injury.

Having detected the uproar, Mama came in to hear all that had happened. "Goodness gracious," she then said, directing her exclamations to the patient. "I hope it is nothing serious. Your father entrusted your safety to us, my dear, and I should hate for him to charge me with negligence."

Bernadette, a great deal calmer by this time, was able to reassure her. "He would do nothing of the sort, Mrs. Austen. Why, it is only a sprained ankle, and all my own fault besides for attempting the beach with entirely the wrong kind of shoes."

"Still, I suppose our dinner with the Crowes must be quite given up," lamented Mama. "And I had so been looking forward to it."

"Oh, no! I would not hear of it, Mrs. Austen. You must all go ahead as planned, all except Jane perhaps."

"Yes, of course," I agreed instantly. "There is no reason the rest of you may not go. Leave Bernadette to my care. No one can think it wrong while I remain with her."

Mama's eyes brightened. "Dear me, that is a very good thought," she said. "A very good thought indeed. To be sure, Jane, you are by far the properest person to stay with your friend. I may just as well go as not, for I am of no use in the sick room. And I am sure it would only oppress dear Bernadette to have us all sitting about staring at her."

Bernadette nodded, and Mama hastened on.

"You can send for us, you know, at a moment's notice, if anything is the matter; but I daresay there will be nothing to alarm you. I should not go, you may be sure, if I did not feel quite at ease about that."

My initial feelings were all relief at having the inevitably uncomfortable reunion with Captain Devereaux thus forestalled for at least another day. After the others had gone off to their dinner with the Crowes, however, it came home to me that this change had only made my situation worse by extending the period of dreadful suspense. With Bernadette less animated than usual, the minutes ground by slowly. Her lack of chatter allowed my mind to wander to what might be going forward at the York.

How had my parents' reintroduction to Captain Devereaux come off? Had he seamlessly taken his cue from them so that they all behaved as slight and indifferent acquaintances, arousing no suspicion in the eyes of the rest? What had he felt at learning I was not to be of the party after all? Disappointment? No, it must be either indifference or relief, for, had he wished ever to see me again, he need not have waited until now. He might have done what I could not – come to me when events had given him the independence which alone had been lacking before.

I had continually to call my mind back from such useless speculations as these. They were too painful to bear and could profit me nothing. Upon Cassandra I then pinned all my anxious hopes of information as to how the dinner had passed off. But first I had to listen to the effusions of the others.

My brother came back quite delighted in his new acquaintance with Captain Devereaux, and my mother and father were scarcely less pleased with the visit in general. The hotel was very elegant, the food first rate, and there had even been music provided by a string quartet to add to their enjoyment. The company was, of course, exceptional. The Crowes were in their element, acting the gracious hosts and providing every possible comfort to their guests. For Mrs. Crowe's brother, my parents' praise was carefully reserved in nature. But they did finally own that his manners were altogether charming.

What I later found out from Cassandra was to this effect (I write the words now on Anne Elliot's behalf):

He had enquired after her, she found, slightly, as might suit a former slight acquaintance, seeming to acknowledge such as she had acknowledged, actuated, perhaps, by the same view of escaping introduction when they were to meet.

Bittersweet it must be for Anne to learn this of Captain Wentworth at his first coming into Uppercross, just as it was for me to hear it of Captain Devereaux in Sidmouth. I should have been relieved to know that he had not, and would not, give away my secret past – our secret – but in truth, one part of me would have been gratified had he done so, presuming it meant that his passion for me still burned too warmly to be concealed. What vanity!

There had been no uncontrollable passion, it seemed.

"He was calm and gentlemanly in every respect," reported Cassandra. "In fact, he made himself so agreeable that I found myself liking him again, as I had done before, despite what has happened in between. It was most disloyal of me, Jane, I admit it. Oh, and you should be prepared, for he wished me to say that he will briefly call here in the morning, as a courtesy to you and to Bernadette. He and Charles got on famously, and they have formed some scheme together for tomorrow."

So, one more restless night and the moment would at last be at hand, and no escaping it this time.

Charles rose early and breakfasted at the York, with the stated intention of bringing Captain Devereaux by immediately afterward. "The two of us will then be off on a grand explore in the hills," he had explained.

Accordingly, Cassandra waited with me and Bernadette in the front parlour the next morning in anticipation of the promised call.

Bernadette was all aflutter at the idea of meeting the handsome captain. There was no reason for her to behave otherwise, perfectly ignorant as she was of the occasion's significance to me. My dear sister, of course, knew better, and she shared my quiet nervousness as the minutes ticked by until Captain Devereaux should at last be in my presence again. With a thousand feelings assailing me at once, my only consolation was this: that the weeks of suspense would soon be over. Regardless of what happened, it could be no worse than the torture under which I had been suffering since I had known of this eventuality. Let him come, then, and have done.

The front door opened, I heard his tread in the passageway, and the next instant he was before me, looking just as I remembered him. Bernadette kept to her seat, but Cassandra and I rose as my brother began the necessary introductions.

"Captain Devereaux, my elder sister you met last night. May I now present our good friend from Bath, Miss Bernadette Cumphries? And here is Jane, whose acquaintance you will have made four years ago, I understand."

My eye only half met his. A bow and a curtsey passed between us.

"A great pleasure to see you again, Miss Austen," he said to my sister in that familiar voice from the past. "Miss Cumphries, you have my sincere wishes for a speedy convalescence." Then he turned his casual notice to me. "Yes, I wasn't certain I remembered. But now that I see you again, madam, there is something *slightly* familiar in your countenance…"

I understood him immediately. His veiled look and his disingenuous words were meant to coldly convey to me how low I had fallen in his estimation, of what little consequence to him was a person who had dared to give up his affection.

"…and of course your surname recalls an association from the past as well. I once knew a lady who married a man by the name of Austen – Henry Austen. Another one of your brothers, apparently, and it was at his wedding where we were introduced, as my sister reminded me. I suppose it is possible we saw each other again afterward, in his home parish. Steventon, isn't it? That is where I met your parents."

I had intended to make no reply, with the belief that the less I said, the shorter would be my period of heightened discomfort. Then, as he had continued to speak, my irritation rose and my courage with it. I could not allow such an insult to stand uncontested, and what had I to lose at that point?

"Your not remembering me, Captain, I can well understand," I began, forcing a calmness into my words and tone that I did not feel. "You must meet so very many people in your travels, and our brief acquaintance was but a trifling thing, to be sure. Yet I must confess to being more than a little surprised at your scant recollection of my brother and sister-in-law, both of whom you claimed to hold in the highest regard at the time. Did you find such good friends not worth retaining?"

I meant this as a challenge, and I had the satisfaction of seeing it stumble him momentarily. He soon recovered, however. "Well, you pose an interesting question, madam. I can only say that, just as circumstances may bring people together for a time, they are equally apt to separate them again in the end."

"Ah, so you believe that we are all completely at the mercy of chance or fate, then, that we are helpless to resist whatever currents would carry us away from our friends against our wills?"

"It has been known to happen," he said cautiously. "The will of one man, no matter how valiant, cannot stand when a large contingent combines forces against him."

Our eyes locked together while our wits continued the verbal joust, which no longer had anything to do with Henry and Eliza. I fired the next salvo. "Such a man might be thwarted for a time, yes, but he would be foolish indeed to relinquish his object at once, not when a little patience and exertion might have turned the tide in his favour again."

He regarded me coolly as he formulated his response. "It is interesting that you should put the question in terms of the sea, for I have often observed that, where there is no solid foundation of feeling, no firmness of purpose, no committed anchorage, a person is likely to be tossed from side to side, just as the wind blows the waves first one direction and then another."

This arrow hit its mark. I turned away as I felt it pierce my patched-together armour. My voice faltered. "And yet… And yet, even the sea has a constancy of its own."

"How so?" he asked, in a tone softened to match my own. I dared to look at him, and for a moment I thought I observed a tender pleading in his eyes, as if he also felt the pain of exchanged blows, or at least some compassion for mine. Then it was gone again, replaced by steely indifference once more. "What can you know of its constancy?" he asked, all his former bitterness revived. "Have you ever spent time at sea yourself?"

"No, Captain, it is a simple observation. You must admit that, whatever direction the winds may blow, the waves always return to the shore in due course. Quite unlike people, they cannot decide to go away and never come back again, can they?"

Captain Devereaux produced no immediate rejoinder, and our companions, I observed, likewise stood openmouthed. Cassandra was the first to recover, exclaiming, "Well, my goodness! What a philosophical journey you have taken us on, Jane! Since you have met the gentleman before, I daresay the opening civilities could be dispensed with quickly enough, but I am afraid you have rapidly carried the rest of us beyond our depth. At least, it is true for me. Charles, do help us find our way back to the comfortable shallows again."

"Yes. Yes, of course," said Charles, thus prompted into action. At once, he cleared his throat and the look of confusion from his face. "You shall have to tell us, Captain, about the primary sights of Sidmouth, which are not to be missed. I am a newcomer, you see, and so is Miss Cumphries. We will need some expert guidance to make the most of our stay here."

"I would be more than happy to oblige," said Captain Devereaux, his air of assurance reestablished. He flashed Bernadette a winning smile. "In fact, when the fair invalid is returned to good health, I shall make it my mission to devise a personally guided tour of the town for her… and for anybody else who would care to join in. Between the two of us, Charles, I believe we can guarantee that Miss Cumphries will come to no further harm."

The men then began taking leave, and without even a backward glance at me, Philippe was gone.

As soon as I heard the door close, I sank back into my chair. It was over, I told myself. The worst was over. I had once more been in the same room with him, and I had survived it. For the moment, that was all that mattered. I withdrew into myself, to tend my wounds, and only became aware that Bernadette was talking when I heard her mention the captain's name.

"…you told me nothing but the truth about him, Jane. Handsome he most certainly is. And was not that kind, what he said to me at the last about a personally guided tour? I take that as a very particular attention. Do not you think so?"

"Yes, very particular," I mumbled.

"Although he was not so gallant to *you*," she continued, "claiming barely to know you, as if these four years had left you sadly altered. But I daresay it can be accounted for just as you supposed – that he has occasion to meet so very many people in his travels, and that your acquaintance with him was no more than a trifling thing to begin with."

Bernadette was perfectly innocent in saying this, unconscious of how deeply the captain's words had cut me. Altered beyond his knowledge! A devastating charge, although I did not for one minute believe it was true. The intervening four years might not have been as kind to me as they had to him – stealing away some portion of my youthful bloom while only adding a manly confidence to his. Still, the passage of time had hardly left me unrecognisable.

No, the true import of Captain Devereaux's disregard was something far more damaging than what appeared on the surface. It was just as I had feared. He was saying that he had not forgiven me, that he had no intention of forgiving me... ever. I had used him ill – deserted and disappointed him. And worse still, I had shown an inexcusable feebleness of character in giving him up to oblige others. In his eyes, it was weakness and timidity, things his confident temper could neither understand nor endure. I knew then that it was truly over. My foolish dream of reconciliation had been only that: a wish manufactured by irrational thinking. My power with him had vanished, lost and gone for all time.

- 14 -

In the swiftness and certainty of this conviction I soon learnt to take some small comfort, for the knowledge was of a properly sobering tendency. It showed me exactly where I stood with Captain Devereaux, allowing no room for false hope. It therefore allayed my earlier agitation over what his feelings for me would prove to be and what might be the result. The plain truth, no matter how brutal, must ultimately leave one more composed than constant conjecture; it must make one happier in the end, I reasoned.

And yet, taken minute by minute, the decision of reason will not always win out over the claims of excited sensibility, especially when the object of those feelings remains as an ever-present reminder of their source and replenisher of their strength.

The object of my every painful sentiment did indeed remain for some time firmly lodged before my notice, continually looming up like the hind end of the donkey ahead of the person driving the cart: inescapable. In our snug Sidmouth society, I was continually thrust into company with Captain Devereaux. Yet, although we were very often occupying the same room (at the York or at our lodging house) or walking but a few feet apart (along the beach, through the town, or into the countryside), after that first day we had almost no conversation together beyond what the commonest civility required.

Anne must, therefore, now endure a similar ordeal. It grieves me to write of it, but so I must.

I tell how, from the time of her first meeting Captain Wentworth again at Uppercross, Anne is repeatedly thrown together with him as they both become absorbed into the Musgroves' social commonwealth. They all dine together, sit together of an evening, and will not conceive of an excursion where any one of the group should be excluded. At every turn, the contrast between past tenderness and the current cold pains her excessively:

> *Once so much to each other! Now nothing! There had been a time when they would have found it most difficult to cease to speak to one another. There could have been no two hearts so open, no tastes so similar, no feelings so in unison, no countenances so beloved. Now they were as strangers; nay, worse than strangers, for they could never become acquainted. It was a perpetual estrangement.*

Whereas I was seldom called upon to speak to Captain Devereaux, I was very often obliged to listen to him. With three sailors encompassed in our group, there was a great deal of talk of the sea, much of it by the man himself at the urging of the others. His profession had supplied him with tales to tell, and his disposition made him willing to tell them. The listening was, for me, however, a kind of torment – a penance to pay – for at these times, when he fully lost himself in the storytelling, I heard the same voice and discerned the same mind as the man I knew four years earlier. That was the man who had won my respect and my heart, not the seemingly detached version now frequently before my eyes. I could not help but think that, had things turned out differently, it should have been to *me* that he habitually directed these animated reports, to me that he returned after each adventure at sea.

Was it possible that no similar reflections visited him? I could not believe it. Though no tremor of voice or glance in my direction ever betrayed him, once or twice – when the year of our brief engagement was necessarily named by him in his narrative – I glimpsed a look of consciousness in his countenance. He *did* recall, then, though I could draw no consolation from it. For him, it was nothing more than an unpleasant association, a disagreeable remembrance called forth against his will.

For Anne Elliot, I now transcribe whole conversations of the character I myself endured in those first days. She must hear Captain Wentworth speak of his harrowing beginnings commanding a sloop barely fit to be employed, his prosperous days aboard the Laconia, his self-effacing accounts of escapades with friends and victories over enemies, and his views about a ship being no fit place for a woman.

Anne hears him eloquent on every topic; she acknowledges him commanding in presence; she sees him admired, especially by the Miss Musgroves, who hang upon his every look and word. And when the evening turns to dancing, she observes him happy as well:

It was a merry, joyous party, and no one seemed in higher spirits than Captain Wentworth. He had everything to elevate him which general attention and deference, and especially the attention of all the young women, could do. The Miss Hayters were apparently admitted to the honour of being in love with him; and as for Henrietta and Louisa, they both seemed so entirely occupied by him that nothing but the continued appearance of the most perfect good-will between themselves could have made it credible that they were not decided rivals. If he were a little spoilt by such universal, such eager admiration, who could wonder?

Captain Devereaux was not quite so spoilt as I have now described Captain Wentworth being, for he had only one eager, admiring young lady to fall in love with him. She was, of course, my friend Bernadette; and she would be his for the asking.

~~*~~

Captain Devereaux was *not* already married, as I had originally feared he would be – intelligence I had acquired *en route* to Sidmouth when riding with the Crowes – but it seemed he was very much of a mind to be so, if his relations were any authority.

I had been resting with eyes closed, lulled nearly to sleep by the rocking motion of the carriage, when I overheard a conversation going forward between the admiral and his wife. They were speaking in low tones, so as not to disturb me, and I never let on that they had.

"Now that your brother has been put ashore, he will be looking about for a wife," the admiral was saying when I became aware. "And he will make quick work of the business too, unless I miss my guess. Sailors cannot afford to go in for long courtships during times of war, and who knows how long this current peace will hold?"

"I should very much like to see Philippe well married, my dear," returned Mrs. Crowe. "I hope he will not be in *too* much of a rush to the altar, though. It must take more than a little beauty and a few smiles to win his heart. He deserves a wife with a strong mind and a sweetness of temper as well. This is how he has described to me the woman he wants."

"So you see, he has been thinking on the subject seriously."

"Yes, and I trust it will serve as some protection against an overly impulsive choice."

"Ah, that is where you are mistaken, Marguerite. Like all men, he thinks he will judge soundly, but it is more probable he will lose his head and end by make a very stupid match."

"For shame, Caspian! How can you say such a thing? This is no very fine compliment to me, I fear… or to yourself either."

"I deserve no credit, it is true. I lost my head like every other young fool in love, but I had the great good fortune to lose both head and heart to a woman of superior worth. We must hope your brother has the same good luck."

Affectionate murmurings between husband and wife followed, to which I tried not to attend. Instead, I indulged myself with the pleasant speculation that, when Captain Devereaux had described his ideal woman to his sister, he might unconsciously have been talking of me. But this was before we met again and his subsequent coldness banished any such possibility from my head.

What the admiral had said of Philippe being ready to fall in love did seem perfectly true, not that these things were immediately apparent. The state of affairs would quickly unfold before my eyes in the days that followed, however.

At the time, Captain Devereaux had every advantage a young man could possess – looks, health, fortune, and a season of leisure from a prosperous career. What was there to wait for? All he had lacked was the proper temptation. Then, in Sidmouth, fate smiled on him once more by throwing a suitable young lady, Miss Cumphries, in his way just when he would be most receptive to her charms. And if he could manage to court and fall in love with her right in front of the woman who had dared to reject his suit years before, so much the better.

Perhaps I was wrong to suspect Captain Devereaux of so base a motive, but it required no very great stretch of mind to imagine there would be considerable consolation in it for a long-wounded pride.

~~*~~

The "young people," as the two married couples soon took to calling the other five of us, went adventuring about Sidmouth nearly every day that the weather permitted, which it most usually did. Bernadette's ankle had mended swiftly, and then there was no longer any excuse to absent myself from going abroad either. In truth, I did not even wish to absent myself from these scenic wanderings. The exercise and sea air would prove beneficial, I believed, and the sooner I became inured to Philippe Devereaux's company, the better.

The captain made good on his promise of serving as our guide, although the town itself was so small that there really was little more to see than what I had already come upon during our brief stay the year before. A morning's walking tour took us down the east road to the beach, across the esplanade to the west road, north all the way to Mill Cross and back again. Along our route, there were the obvious natural wonders to witness – the crashing waves tinged with pink in reflection of the red sandstone cliffs, which plunged sharply into the sea on both sides of town – and a few noteworthy man-made edifices to admire as well. Otherwise, Sidmouth was nothing more than a sleepy fishing village with a couple of hundred houses huddled close together between and partway up the surrounding hillsides. The place could not even boast a completed sea wall or a proper harbour.

It was exactly these things (the lack of size and industry) that appealed to me most – these and the sea itself, of course. They made Sidmouth a refreshing contrast, an enticing escape from the cosmopolitan bustle of Bath. I felt an almost immediate revival of spirits upon entering its environs, despite the presence of that single irksome element: Captain Devereaux. I was determined to be cheerful – as a matter of personal pride and to show that gentleman how very little his presence mattered. And I suspected the same motive informed some part of his behaviour as well.

When Philippe made a show of inviting Bernadette to fall in beside him on that first walking tour, I pretended not to notice. Later, when we had completed our initial exploration of the beach and he showed concern that she might be fatigued, I was not jealous; I exhibited as much or more care for her comfort as he.

"If you are the least bit tired, dear Bernadette," I said earnestly, "I shall gladly turn back with you now. Let the others go on and we can finish another day. Your recovery is paramount. You must not overtax yourself on our account."

"That is very generous of you, Miss Austen," the captain countered, "but if anybody turns back with your friend, I will be the one who does it." Then addressing her, he continued, "I am entirely at your service, Miss Cumphries."

I believe my pretty friend was mildly astounded at finding herself the object of so much solicitude, for she had also my brother's efforts to contend with.

"Nonsense, Devereaux," said Charles. "The party cannot possibly continue without its guide. *I* will go back with Miss Cumphries. It would be my honour."

"You are all so very kind," said Bernadette, "but I am perfectly capable of continuing – really I am – especially if one of you gentlemen would lend me your arm."

Charles and Philippe nearly tripped over each other in their rush to do so. Bernadette, apparently unwilling to slight either one of them, accepted the assistance of both.

I glanced at Cassandra in time to see her roll her eyes heavenward. She then offered me her arm, that I might not feel completely neglected. And it was much the same the next day and the next. Bernadette continued to bask in the gallant attentions of the two naval officers, while my sister and I consoled each other as well as we might. In fact, it became something of an ongoing joke between us, the vigourous contest for Bernadette's affection and the speculation as to who would win out in the end.

Dear Cassandra. She was my champion and stronghold. I truly do not know what I would have done without her during those days. In that respect, I fared so much better than poor Anne does, for I have given her only Mary – no strength or comfort there. Cassandra kept my soul from sinking. She rescued me from awkwardness time and time again. She taught me to rise above the temptation to self-pity, to feel my own strength, and to laugh at myself. In these disciplines, as in so many other ways, she had gone before me.

I will not pretend it was easy. On the contrary, watching Captain Devereaux pay his addresses to another woman, to my own friend, was one of the most difficult things I ever had to face. Still, following along after every biting pang of loss, I experienced an undeniable thrill of satisfaction in coming through it alive – more than alive, almost triumphant. I began looking forward to each new test as an opportunity to prove myself more than its equal, to feel the exhilaration of overcoming the crippling weight of gravity in order to soar aloft.

I did not always succeed; far from it. Indeed, I often came crashing down in dark defeat. But I fancy that, in my very finest moments, I tasted a little of what the angels must feel. They look down on the strivings and follies of men from a loftier perspective, seeing these things for what they are – mere specks in the vast expanse of time, only light and momentary troubles compared with the glories of heaven.

Or perhaps I only flatter myself by thinking it was so.

-15-

Daily, the sea drew us like a powerful magnet, with not one amongst us able to resist its hypnotic attractions. Bernadette, however, was perhaps the most susceptible. Whereas for the rest of us the devotion was of longstanding duration, she was still in the throes of first passion. After captivating her when she initially laid eyes on it the day after our arrival, the sea continued to hold her fast, drawing her back time and again like an unrelenting lover who will not be denied. Whatever else was planned, Bernadette was sure to insist that at least half an hour be reserved every afternoon for paying homage at the shore.

We were thus occupied again late on the fourth day of our stay. Cassandra and I happened to be walking with Bernadette along the esplanade at the time when she burst out with, "I must live always by the seashore, for surely, there can be no felicity equal to this!"

Her rapture was understandable. Indeed my own heart had been straining to shout out something of the kind as I felt the sun's warmth on my shoulders and watched its rays dance across the water. Waves rushed boldly in at us and then retreated from the beach once more, creating a tinkling music as they tumbled the stones forward and back each time. The perpetual breeze was only freshening that day, not at all cold. And bright gulls hung suspended in the friendly currents aloft. In short, every natural advantage combined to frame a picture of perfect harmony and delight.

The crowning touch to all this grandeur was the fine prospect of Charles and Captain Devereaux, arrayed in uniformed splendour and walking on a way ahead of us women. Bernadette's maritime appreciation soon expanded to include them. "And I so admire the navy. There cannot be a better collection of men than these anywhere in the world. Do not you agree, Miss Austen?"

Cassandra politely did so, and Bernadette was sufficiently encouraged to continue.

"All uprightness and honour as they seem to possess, and such a warm brotherhood exists between them. These are men who know how to live. How I envy them that they should have found a way to remain always close to the sea. A woman cannot hope for such a thing... unless, of course, she is the wife of the man who commands a ship. What a life that must be, to live aboard a man-of-war as the captain's lady! Mrs. Crowe speaks of its comforts in the most glowing terms."

"She has exactly the right temperament for it," I contributed, speaking my thoughts aloud. "Not every lady does, surely. One would need to be able to cope with the confined quarters, the lack of female companionship, the constant motion of the water, and the nomadic lifestyle. And consider the danger, should the ship and crew unexpectedly be called upon to engage in battle! No, I am convinced that it would not suit most women at all."

"I collect that you have given the idea extensive thought," Bernadette observed, with a curious sidelong glance at me. "Do you think *yourself* cut out for a captain's wife, then, Jane?" she teased.

I felt the heat instantly rise to my cheeks, and I cursed my carelessness in not having been more guarded. Yes, I had often considered what my life must have been had I married Captain Devereaux. But that possibility was long past now and could scarcely be admitted to, especially to my unwitting successor in his affections.

Cassandra came to my rescue once again. "I should think it is a subject talked of in every naval family," said she. "Our own is no exception. And now, more recently, we have all had the information of Mrs. Crowe to feed our imaginations. One cannot help but think about it, but that hardly means we would choose a life at sea, even if we could."

"Exactly," I agreed, shooting Cassandra a grateful look.

The moment passed, and Bernadette none the wiser for it. It had, however, served to shed some light on my friend's line of thinking. Clearly, I was not the only one who had entertained the idea of a life as a navy wife. But there were currently two candidates vying for the office of *her* husband, for Charles continued his efforts to please her as well. For more than one reason, I desired that his gentle attentions to my good friend would carry the day in the end, although I had no very high hopes that they would. A week into our stay at Sidmouth, I took opportunity to test the waters on his behalf.

"It seems you have acquired not one but two devoted suitors," I observed to Bernadette in a neutral tone. "What a lucky girl you are."

We sat together on an accommodating rock high above the town, admiring the impressive view from the cliffs of Peak Hill and resting from our long ascent. I had taken care that the others had wandered out of hearing before initiating this conversation.

"I daresay they are only being kind to me on account of my ankle," said she in return, blushing with a pleasure that belied her self-deprecating words. "Who would have thought that my being clumsy would work so much to my advantage?"

"Dear Bernadette, you are too modest. I think there may be more in their special attentions than mere kindness."

"To own the truth," she said in a conspiratorial whisper. "I would not be displeased if there were, at least on Captain Devereaux's side. He is a gentleman well worth catching, I should think! Oh, and I mean no slight to your brother by saying so. No doubt he is equally worthy, only… only still a little young."

"Perhaps by some estimations, but he is of an age with you – two and twenty."

"Really?" She paused in thought before continuing. "To be sure, twenty-two is a fine age for a *woman* to be married, but your brother seems little more than a boy. I prefer a man who is well established, do not you? One who has lived a little more in the world."

I nodded in comprehension. "One who has had time to collect a little wealth about him. Yes, that would be ideal. My brother cannot compete with Captain Devereaux there, sadly."

Bernadette squeezed my hand with affection. "Much as I would adore being your true sister, Jane, I could not consider marrying Charles if he should ask me."

"Yes, I see that now. You will be kindest, then, in not encouraging him. Allowing him to hope falsely would only lead to grief."

"You are quite right, and so I now resolve it."

"And what of Captain Devereaux? Do you intend to accept him, should he ask? Are you in fact in love with him?"

Bernadette's eyebrows shot up in surprise. "Well, you do not lose any time, do you, Jane?"

"Why should I mince words with you, dear friend? But you need not answer if you think my questions officious. I should take no umbrage, I assure you, even were you to tell me to mind my own business. *I* would certainly make free to do so in your place."

"I could not for the world say any such thing to you, Jane! I love and esteem you like my own sister, or perhaps more. You may ask me anything you like. I only hesitate because I have as yet no definite answer to give you. After all, I have known Captain Devereaux no more than a week. Ask me again when another fortnight is gone."

I said nothing, but it struck me that *I* had not required three weeks to determine if I loved the man... or even one. I had known the answer to that question within minutes.

~~*~~

The descent from Peak Hill was for me every bit as taxing as going up it had been, although in a different style. Bernadette, in keeping with her recently stated intention, declined my brother's escort in favour of Captain Devereaux's arm, and the pair moved off ahead. A dejected Charles then claimed Cassandra as his consolation. The trail being too narrow to admit three walking abreast, they fell in behind me, soon dropping further back and leaving me to fend for myself in the middle, my own thoughts for company.

It seemed that Bernadette had firmly settled on Captain Devereaux now, and I had helped her to do it. That it was for my brother's ultimate good gave me little comfort as I watched them together – she smiling up at the captain beguilingly and he obviously entranced.

No, this would not do, I thought. I must distract myself. I must find my pleasure in the walk – the exercise, the fine summer day, the intricate tangle of undergrowth alongside the path, the tiny creatures that made it their home. If my own powers of observation and reflection on these things were inadequate, I could rely on others. Surely there had been more than enough written in prose and poetry about such things to keep my mind fully occupied! If I could but remember some description of wildflowers, some sonnet or quotation on the glories of nature, I would be safe.

But it was impossible. How could I think when I was every moment overhearing snatches of the conversation going forward between Philippe Devereaux and my friend? I would catch a few words – enough to engage my interest – and then the wind would blow the next sentence away in the opposite direction. She would ask a question, to which I very much wanted to hear the captain respond, but his answer would be carried off to the cliffs or to the valley below.

When we had at last come down about halfway, we entered into a less exposed section of the trail, where the path wound between a rocky outcrop on one side and steeply rising scrub ground on the other. The wind could not find us there, and its disruptive effects died away all at once. Every other sound now stood out in sharp relief against a blank background – the clatter of a pebble dislodged by my foot, the trickle of water in some unseen crevice, the talk of my companions.

Although Bernadette and Captain Devereaux instinctively dropped their voices lower, just as one would upon entering an empty church, the stone wall to one side of us echoed their words clearly enough. I followed at a distance of no less than fifteen feet, and yet I could suddenly hear all. Bernadette's voice was the first I distinguished. She seemed to be in the middle of some eager speech.

"...and so I insisted she go through with it! I could not bear that she should be frightened into turning back from doing what was right, from a thing she herself had chosen and promised, by such nonsensical doubts. *I* would not. When I have made up my mind, I have made it. It does not signify what anybody else may say to me after that."

"Your sister would have turned back then, but for you?"

"She would indeed, I am ashamed to say. She would have left that poor man, now my brother-in-law, standing at the altar. And what a mistake that would have been, for she could never have hoped to find a better, both as to fortune and disposition."

"How lucky for her to have had such a sister at hand to remind her of her own good. I hope she is properly grateful to you."

"Oh, I did not do it for her thanks! And in fact, we never speak of it. I have always supposed it is because Charlotte is too embarrassed by her own behaviour to wish to be reminded."

"Naturally."

Here Captain Devereaux glanced back over his shoulder. I instantly dropped my eyes to avoid meeting his or giving any sign that I was otherwise interested. After a moment, he resumed his discussion with Bernadette in a slightly lower tone.

"I am certain your sister must be an amiable creature, but I cannot help thinking it a pity that she does not possess more of your decision and firmness. One must hope that she will learn these things from her husband, now that she is beyond your influence. For otherwise, what will become of her without fortitude and strength of mind? Stick always to your purpose, Miss Cumphries. Anybody may sway one who is too yielding or indecisive. And, although such a person may seem conveniently compliant at first, even friends will eventually tire of one who cannot be depended on, who proves unreliable in word and deed. No, let those who would be happy be firm. That is what I say."

Were these words meant for me? I could not help but wonder. When he had glanced back before saying them, had Captain Devereaux been hoping that I was not close enough to hear... or being sure that I was? Either way, his indictment of the persuadable character was one more proof of what he must think of me.

Likewise unhappy is the lot of Anne Elliot, whom I now send on a similarly long walk to Winthrop. There she also overhears a telling conversation (one between Captain Wentworth and Louisa Musgrove) to similar effect. Then, afterwards...

> *She had much to recover from before she could move. The listener's proverbial fate was not absolutely hers; she had heard no evil of herself, but she had heard a great deal of very painful import. She saw how her own character was considered by Captain Wentworth; and there had been just that degree of feeling and curiosity about her in his manner, which must give her extreme agitation.*

I go on to describe Anne's weariness – weariness of spirit as well as of body – to reflect how I remember feeling at that point in *my* walk. Unfortunately, I could not write a convenient gig ride home into existence for myself, as I now do for Anne. No, I had little choice but to continue putting one foot in front of the other until at last I tripped and stumbled.

It happened so quickly that I had no chance to prevent it or to stifle the little cry that escaped my lips as I fell to my knees on the rough ground. I was not seriously hurt, only surprised and unable to immediately right myself. As I attempted to stand, I felt strong hands securing my arms and lifting me to my feet. I turned and saw that it was Captain Devereaux. He had done it without a word, and my own sensations made me for a moment perfectly speechless as well. Then the others gathered round and a kind of noisy chaos, full of solicitude for my welfare, arose.

Captain Devereaux carried on, undeterred. He ordered everybody out of the way and carefully ushered me to a nearby style, where he eased me down to sit on the step. Only after accomplishing this did he at last release his hold of me. I was by then just enough recovered to thank him for his kindness before he backed away and allowed Cassandra to take over the primary office of ministering to me.

He had done it. I was returned to safety, and he had been the one to place me there. He could have left it for Charles, who was just as near at hand and in many respects the most proper person for the job. But instead, he had rushed to do it himself. I was very much affected by this view of his disposition towards me.

It seemed that although he could not forgive me, neither could he be unfeeling. Though condemning me for the past, though otherwise indifferent to me, and though actually becoming attached to another, still he could not see me suffer without the desire of giving me relief. My past sins had not completely extinguished all humane feelings in him. And perhaps there was still some slight remainder of former sentiment at work. He had acted on an impulse of pure, though unacknowledged, friendship. Or, at the very least, it was proof of his warm and amiable heart, which I could not contemplate without emotions so compounded of pleasure and pain that I knew not which prevailed.

-16-

Anne found herself by this time growing so much more hardened to being in Captain Wentworth's company than she had at first imagined could ever be, that the sitting down to the same table with him now, and the interchange of the common civilities attending on it – they never got beyond – was become a mere nothing.

Day by day, I continued to strengthen myself against seeing Captain Devereaux and Bernadette together. As one's eyes soon become adjusted to the shock of bright light or one's mind to hearing an unrelenting noise, so my heart built up a kind of callousness of its own. The circumstances had not changed, but I no longer felt the pain as acutely. For that, I was grateful. And my prediction of the sea air doing me good had also come to pass. I felt a healthful bloom as I could not remember experiencing since leaving Steventon. Then I received another welcome restorative in the form of a valuable addition to our group.

After passing a fortnight in Sidmouth, we were all dining together at the York again one day when a note was delivered to Captain Devereaux. He took a moment to read it, his aspect brightening as he did so.

"It is from Captain Bothwell," he announced presently. "He has returned, and now you shall all finally meet him."

We had heard the name before and knew that this was the friend whose presence had drawn Captain Devereaux to Sidmouth in the first place. By extension, he had thereby played a role in bringing the rest of us thither as well. But, having been obliged to travel on business to London, he was away when we first arrived.

"We must call on them tomorrow – Captain Bothwell and his mother," continued Captain Devereaux.

"What? All of us?" exclaimed Mrs. Crowe. "My dear brother, what are you thinking? I cannot suppose that his mother will be wanting or expecting nine strangers to descend on her all at once. At least you have never led me to believe that her health is robust enough or her home grand enough to accommodate such a crowd."

"No, of course you are right, Marguerite. Perhaps I did get carried away in my enthusiasm; I did not think before I spoke. I shall go myself to start, so that we do not overwhelm them."

Mrs. Crowe nodded in approval. "A much better plan. I daresay the rest of us will meet your friend by and by."

Captain Devereaux went on to give us a little history of his acquaintance with Captain Bothwell, Bothwell having been for some time his first lieutenant until earning a ship of his own. "We have had some grand adventures together, I can tell you. And he is a thinking man too – very well read. If I were to be marooned on a deserted island, I could do far worse than to have him as my companion. Between us we would surely find a way to sail home again. And if not, we should never want for intelligent conversation," he finished, with considerable warmth.

"I perceive that you are very fond of this Captain Bothwell," said my father.

"I have never known a finer man, Mr. Austen, and I would gladly sail to the ends of the earth and back again to do him a service if he asked. I warrant he would have done the same for me in the past." Here a frown creased his brow. "Although, unfortunately, his sailing days are over now."

"Oh? How so?" asked Papa.

"Injured in the war," explained Philippe. "Lost an eye for one thing. But he does not let that ruin his spirits. Another reason I respect him so much."

"That is just what I admire about the navy!" said Bernadette. "It is a band of true brothers."

"Yes, but you should not imagine it some kind of utopia, Miss Cumphries," said Charles, "for even brothers do not always like each other. That is true in families as well as the navy. Disagreements and jealousies are sure to arise on occasion, and then, you must stand clear. Some of the fiercest clashes I have ever witnessed have been between so-called brothers."

"Take care, Charles," said Captain Devereux. "You mustn't give away all our secrets. If Miss Cumphries wishes to believe every sailor a saint, who are we to disappoint her?"

Admiral Crowe joined in the discussion. "Miss Cumphries may believe it," he said, "but you will never convince my wife that navy men can do no wrong. She has collected far too much evidence to the contrary over the years, mostly thanks to me. Is that not so, my dear?" he added, turning to his wife.

Mrs. Crowe had our full attention. With a mischievous glint in here eye, she replied, "I shall give you no account of it, I assure you. What secrets I know of navy men, I keep to myself!"

The admiral chuckled, regarding his wife warmly. "Good girl, Marguerite," he said. "Good girl."

Once again I marvelled at the easy way they related to each other, the admiral and his wife. I had always thought that my parents got on well together, and they did. But this was more, a depth of affection and mutual respect as I had rarely observed anywhere. There was nothing at all overt; it was simply understood between them, conveyed in the most seemingly insignificant gestures – the smallest look, word, or touch. And yet the light burned so steadily bright between them that it could not be denied.

Was this merely the natural outgrowth of uncommonly amiable dispositions? Or could it be the hard-won result of having weathered many trials and dangers together over the course of the years? The Crowes never spoke of their troubles, but I wondered if they were very much grieved by their marriage never having been blessed with children. Was this the private sorrow that had bound them together so closely? If so, it seemed to me they had been somewhat compensated in their unspoken affliction.

~~*~~

I admit to being vastly intrigued by the prior information given of Captain Bothwell. I was therefore delighted when a scheme was hit upon that would delay my introduction to him no longer. It was decided that Captain Devereaux would call in the morning at Mrs. Bothwell's house – a modest dwelling close to the sea just off the west road – paying his respects to the widow and then inviting her son to accompany him back to the York to be introduced to his friends.

Accordingly, we were all assembled there at noon to meet him. When it was my turn to be introduced, I saw no sign of especial consciousness in the way he looked at me, no indication that he knew of the history between Captain Devereaux and myself. This was as I could have wished and a relief to have confirmed.

Captain Bothwell was a tall, dark man with a sensible, benevolent countenance and disarming manners – a perfect gentleman. As for his war wounds, there was little in evidence except the black patch covering where his right eye should have been. That was a thing which could not go unnoticed. Some of the others seemed a bit put off by it, as if they could not decide whether to stare or resolutely look away. For me, though, this fearsome specter inspired no dread or even much curiosity. If anything, it aroused my sympathy and a desire to extend kindness. This was no arduous task, for Captain Bothwell was very warm and obliging. I liked him at once.

In the days that followed, I found that Captain Bothwell, now wholly absorbed into our little band, consistently gravitated to my side. And I was glad of it. We had much to talk about, our common interest in all types of literature proving the most fertile source of conversation.

On one such occasion, when the six of us "young people" were again walking along the beach, Captain Bothwell and I launched into a particularly animated discussion. Having already gone through a brief comparison of opinion as to the first-rate poets of the day, we were trying to ascertain whether *Marmion* or *The Lady of the Lake* was to be preferred. Then, instead of settling the initial question, Captain Bothwell added to it by throwing *Giaour* in as well – how did it rank compared to the other two, and how the devil was it to be pronounced?

As this discussion was going forward, I noticed Captain Devereaux (Bernadette on his arm, as usual) drifting ever nearer. He had gone silent himself and seemed to be inclining his ear to hear what we said instead of whatever Bernadette talked of. Once or twice before, since his friend's return to Sidmouth, I thought he might be doing so – artfully attending to our conversation, that is – but this time I was certain. What could he mean by it, I wondered? Was he worried that I might be slandering him or telling secrets? Perhaps it was only a general curiosity, much like I myself had experienced upon accidentally hearing some part of his conversations with Bernadette.

Whatever his motive, I felt I had to let him know that I saw what he was about. So, before I could lose my nerve, I turned to him and said, "Do not you think, Captain Devereaux, that I expressed myself uncommonly well just now, when I was giving my opinion of *Giaour*?"

"What? Oh, I hardly know," he said indifferently.

"Come now, Captain," I prompted. "I am sure you could not help but hear, as close as you happened to be walking." It was bordering on impertinence, but I could not seem to help myself, once I got started.

"Better still," said Captain Bothwell, "perhaps you can shed more light on this question with your own opinion."

"Yes, do assist us, Captain Devereaux," I agreed. "You have already heard our ideas. There must be *something* you could say that would be equally worth listening to."

Philippe glared at me but kept his tone carefully neutral. "When it comes to poetry, I believe there can be no definitive answers, no absolute right and wrong. It is only a matter of what one happens to favour. One person is devoted to Pope, and another can appreciate nothing but Shakespeare. They are both right, since their own taste must dictate."

"There, Miss Jane," said Captain Bothwell, looking at me with earnest approbation. "You were right as always. My clever friend did have an opinion worth hearing, and one not unlike what you were saying to me just the other day – that judging poetry is an entirely subjective thing."

We had paused in our walk, and I risked a glance at Captain Devereaux. I read a certain something in his expression. I saw that he had noticed his friend's admiration of me. A brightness flashed in his eye, which seemed to say, "This man is struck with you, and even I, at this moment, cannot deny your merits."

I did not imagine it, though the look held but an instant before vanishing. Then I said flippantly to him, "All I know is that I could not think of limiting myself to a single author or even to poetry alone. Why should I chuse only one thing when there is so much worth reading? A veritable banquet is spread before me." It was a remark akin to something I recalled saying to him when we first met, those years ago. Did he remember as well, I wondered? There was no telling by his ambiguous response.

"You are quite right, Madam," he said. "We are living in a great age for literature."

Bernadette, who I knew had no taste for poetry or prose, was growing impatient. "Let us have no more of this dull talk," she said presently. "Come with me, Captain Devereaux. Do you see those rocks jutting out into the water? I wish to explore them."

The tide, being lower than usual, had indeed exposed a set of rocks I had never noticed before. As we all moved closer, I could see from the regularity of their shape and configuration that it was no formation of nature; it was a ruin of some man-made effort.

"It looks as if it could be a long-abandoned attempt at creating a sea wall," said Captain Bothwell.

"Indeed," agreed Philippe.

"Let us walk out onto it!" suggested Bernadette. "What a thrill it would be to feel the waves lapping nearly at our feet."

"No, Miss Cumphries," said Captain Devereaux firmly. "It is not safe. The wet rocks will be slippery, perhaps even unstable, and the tide is beginning to return."

Bernadette looked quite put out, but she allowed herself to be held back from approaching any nearer to the perilous rock formation.

I felt as if I had been to the brink and back as well, and my feelings remained in an excited state for some time to come. As fully as I had accustomed myself to Captain Devereaux's continual presence, we still had been carefully avoiding much in the way of direct intercourse between us – rarely speaking, in fact. My boldness in having just now broken that unwritten rule had surprised us both.

Once again, I was grateful for Captain Bothwell's restorative presence. As he drew my attention away from Captain Devereaux and back to himself, I became comfortable again – comfortable and altogether sensible of the gentleman's true value. I had immediately felt his usefulness in distracting me from Philippe and Bernadette, but I genuinely enjoyed his company as well. And the fact that he evidently found *mine* worth keeping did my spirits a world of good.

Perhaps he sensed in me a kindred spirit, someone not unlike himself. It occurred to me that we were both wounded, although in different ways, and we both knew what it was to be slighted – me by my former love and he by those who could not bear to look on his disfigurement. Hence, I was always pleased when Captain Bothwell fell to my lot, and I was well repaid, to be sure, for my efforts to befriend him.

Even in this, however, there was a type of sadness, a necessity for caution, I reminded myself. Had things been different, Captain

Bothwell would have most naturally become part of my permanent social circle. But as it was, the relationship could be nothing more than a temporary delight. His devotion to his old friend would always supercede any regard he held for me, and, except for this brief season in Sidmouth, he could not be friend to us both.

It shall be the same for Anne, I now decide, when I introduce her to the Harvilles and Captain Benwick at Lyme. Although she will be allowed to eagerly esteem these good people, her pleasure in their acquaintance must be likewise tinged with sadness for the knowledge that she will soon be obliged to give them up. They are only on temporary loan to her; they really belong to Captain Wentworth. I write...

> *There was so much attachment to Captain Wentworth in all this, and such a bewitching charm in a degree of hospitality so uncommon that Anne felt her spirits not likely to be benefited by an increasing acquaintance among his brother-officers. "These would have been all my friends," was her thought; and she had to struggle against a great tendency to lowness.*

~~*~~

"Forgive me, Jane, but I must ask," said Cassandra that night when we retired to the bedchamber we shared at our lodging house. "How are you bearing up, dearest?"

I was not surprised by her question. I knew by how solicitously she had been watching over me that she had wanted to ask for days. But I also knew she had been trying equally hard to resist troubling me with questions.

"I saw you talking to Captain Devereaux on the beach," she continued. "What was it about?"

"Oh, nothing much," said I. "I caught him listening in on my conversation with Captain Bothwell, and I could not allow him to get away unmolested. That is all."

Cassandra brightened. "So you made him pay for his indiscretion. Excellent! Were you very severe upon him?"

"No, not very. Not so that anybody else would notice. I believe *he* did, though, at least I hope so. After all, one would hate to be always saying terribly clever things without the sharpness of one's wit sometimes carrying the point home. Do not you agree?"

"Now you sound just like Lizzy Bennet. How delightful!"

"You know that she is my model in all things."

"I thought it was the other way round, Jane – that Lizzy was patterned after yourself. Either way, I am sure Captain Devereaux must have felt the point of your wit!"

"Perhaps I should also flirt a great deal more with his friend. Do you think that would make any impression on him at all?"

"Now I am certain that you are joking. But, Jane," she said, coming to sit beside me, "do be serious for a moment. I cannot believe you are as serene as you seem. No one could think ill of you even if you were full of angry revenge. It must seem as if both the captain and Miss Cumphries have betrayed your affection."

"That is the strange part, Cass. I cannot hate either one of them. Perhaps it would be easier if I could. I have always liked Bernadette, and I still do. It would be unreasonable to blame her, since she has no idea that her attachment to Captain Devereaux in any way harms me."

"Then what of the captain himself? Surely, you cannot absolve him so neatly, can you?"

"No, but I believe I understand him. He is not a cruel man, only injured and resentful. And, although it is a hopeless case, I admit I still love him."

"Oh, Jane!"

"I know," I said with a sigh. "I cannot help it. The world seems to me a finer place because he is alive in it. To see him again, to be with him, even in this limited way – it is more than I ever expected. I must endeavour to be satisfied with that. What other choice do I have?"

"But to watch him courting your friend? How it must pain you!"

"Please, do not encourage me to such feelings! They are all too tempting as it is, believe me. I do sometimes feel like raging against the world in general and Captain Devereaux in particular, but I dare not dwell on such things. No, far better that I should meditate on *your* example, how much you have borne and with such grace. That is where I expect to find my peace in the end, in practicing forbearance and in rising above the circumstances, like you."

"You give me far too much credit, Jane."

"Very well, you may share it with Elinor Dashwood if you prefer; she is every bit as philosophical. What is it she says when she is resigned to Edward's marrying Lucy? Something like, '*after all that is bewitching in the idea of a single and constant attachment, that one's happiness can depend entirely on a particular person, it is not meant to be so. It is not fitting or possible that it should be so.'* Elinor believed that Edward would be happiest in doing his duty to Lucy. And now I must believe the same of Philippe and Bernadette."

"But there is not the same duty to be done in this case; no positive engagement exists. That is, not so far as I am aware, or do you mean to imply that there is?"

"Bernadette has said nothing to me about it. But you must admit that, by his conspicuous attentions towards her, Captain Devereaux has already raised certain expectations. He could not in good conscience walk away from her now if he wanted to, which there is no reason to suppose he would. No, he has committed himself, and we must all accept it. I have, and so must you do, my dear sister. As much as I know you like him, Captain Devereaux will never be your brother-in-law." With an arch look, I added, "Now Captain Bothwell is another matter entirely. One cannot rule him out."

-17-

There was too much wind to make the high part of the new Cobb pleasant for the ladies, and they agreed to get down the steps to the lower, and all were contented to pass quietly and carefully down the steep flight, excepting Louisa; she must be jumped down them by Captain Wentworth... He advised against it, thought the jar too great; but no, he reasoned and talked in vain; she smiled and said, "I am determined I will."

This is how I now begin writing of Louisa Musgrove's accident at Lyme, which will change everything – the course of the story and the outcome for every person involved. At Sidmouth, Bernadette prefigured her in real life.

It happened in this way.

We had all been kept indoors for four days by a continuous and drenching rain. So, when the sun burst out into the open again on the fifth, we were anxious to do the same. All but Cassandra, that is; she was feeling a little poorly and kept to our rooms.

Captains Devereaux and Bothwell appeared at our house early in the day to inquire what the rest of us would prefer. "It will be too dirty to walk into the hills after all this rain," said Charles. "But I think we can safely venture anywhere in town or along the shore."

"Oh, we must go to the shore!" cried Bernadette. "I must see the sea again; I have missed it above all things these many days. In fact, it has made me wonder how I shall exist without it when we must return to Bath."

"To the shore, then," stated Captain Devereaux, "if nobody has an objection. Miss Cumphries's very survival may depend on it."

Nobody did object, of course. The aim was to be together and to stretch our legs with some exercise out of doors. It mattered very little to me – or I suspect to any of the others, save Bernadette – in which direction we walked.

It was a Saturday, and the town bustled with activity. The markets were not our destination, however, and so we skirted round them and headed directly for the seashore. As we neared it, I felt the blustery wind more and more, its insistent breath drying my skin, dragging my skirt fiercely backwards against my legs, and tugging at my bonnet. It was having its effect on the water as well, I noticed when we came within sight, whipping up foam and choppy waves across the surface as far as the eye could see.

"Perhaps we should retreat," suggested Captain Bothwell. "This wind cannot be pleasant for the ladies."

"Oh, no!" cried Bernadette. "We must go on. This is wonderful! It is so refreshing!"

Captain Devereux then looked for my answer.

"No one need be afraid on my account, I assure you. I quite agree with Bernadette." And I meant it. Indeed, the conditions represented an aspect of the sea which I have always found particularly fascinating – its changeableness. If one views it ten days in succession, one will likely see as many faces. It may be smooth as gently rippling azure satin the first, an unrecognisable angry grey mass the next, and something altogether different the third.

So we went forward undeterred, crossing the esplanade and actually out onto the shingle beach. That is when we saw it again, the remains of the forgotten sea wall construction, now sitting high and dry, with gulls perched here and there along its length, their faces set to the wind.

"Look," said Bernadette, pointing and moving in that direction. "The tide is fully out and the rocks are dry. We might walk on them today in perfect security. See, the birds are even sunning themselves."

Captain Devereaux objected as before. "No, Miss Cumphries, you must come back. It still is not safe, believe me."

"Devereux is correct," agreed Charles, calling after her. "Especially with the wind, it had better not be attempted."

But Bernadette continued across the beach ahead of us, increasing her pace and shouting back over her shoulder, "I am determined to do it this time, with or without you."

Seeing that she would not be turned back by mere words, Captain Devereaux belatedly struck off after her. This, however, only made Bernadette run faster, laughing aloud as if it were a game. She reached the rocks without being caught and then began quickly picking her way along the crest of them, out into the sea, with her arms outstretched for balance.

I cupped my hands at my mouth. "Bernadette, please!" I shouted into the wind. "You must come back!"

She either did not hear me or chose to ignore my caution as well. She simply smiled gaily and took another step forward into the gaping maw of the open sea.

By this time, Captain Devereaux had also reached the formation, immediately launching out across it after Bernadette as he continued trying to coax her back. He had nearly caught up to her, and I thought all might yet be well, when I saw an unusually large swell approaching. "Look!" I shouted, though I knew my friends on the rocks could not hear me. Even if they had, there was nowhere for them to take shelter. Charles, Captain Bothwell, and I dashed forward to the water's edge, but there was nothing we could do.

The rogue wave broke and rolled over the rocks, scattering the resting gulls and quickly sweeping towards Bernadette. Finally seeing the danger, she screamed and turned back. It was much too late, however; the wave was upon her in another moment, knocking her off her feet and tumbling her down into the frigid water.

Philippe withstood the wave, but then he plunged into the water on purpose, going after Bernadette.

They both vanished from sight, and I held my breath in suspense. A minute later, I saw the captain's dark head briefly bobbing above the water before disappearing as he dove down once more. It seemed an eternity, but at last he came up again. This time, he had something with him, which he began towing toward shore. Although it looked like nothing more than a lifeless bundle of sodden cloth, I knew it was my friend Bernadette. When he reached a depth where he could stand, Captain Devereaux gathered her body up into his arms and continued forward. His face was stricken with agony; it was more than I could bear.

"Go to him! Go to him!" I cried out. "For heaven's sake, Charles, leave me and go to *him*."

My brother obeyed, letting go of my arm to stride out into the water and meet Philippe. Together they carried Bernadette up onto the beach.

There was no wound, no blood, no visible bruise; but her eyes were closed and she breathed not. Her face was like death.

Oh, the horror of that hour!

After frantically searching my brain as to what needed to be done, I said, "Roll her onto her side with her head lower than her feet. We must allow any water she has taken in to flow out again."

How I knew this, I cannot say. But Captain Devereaux followed my instructions without question. I knelt beside him and began pressing Bernadette's back, hoping that by so doing I could force the drowning saltwater from her lungs. Whether by this method or purely by grace, a small quantity of fluid was expelled. She began to cough and sputter, mildly at first and then with shocking violence as her body struggled for air. Alarming as it was to watch, it was also reassuring proof that, for the moment at least, life persisted.

"Praise God!" exclaimed Charles, and we all echoed his words.

Philippe turned to me again. "What now? There must be more we should be doing for her!"

Just then, Bernadette opened her eyes halfway, and we all froze in mute expectation. But our hopes of an immediate end to the nightmare proved unfounded, for there was no apparent consciousness in our friend's face and her lids soon slipped closed again.

"A surgeon!" said I, in delayed response to the prior question.

"Yes, of course; a surgeon this instant." Philippe caught on the word and began rising as if to fetch help himself.

"No," I corrected. "Send Captain Bothwell. He will know where the surgeon is to be found. And we must get her warm."

"Take her to my house," said Captain Bothwell decisively. "It is the nearest place, and my mother will help you. I will bring the surgeon there." With this, he left us at a run.

"I shall carry her myself," said Captain Devereaux, looking more collected now and obviously eager to be doing something. He gathered Bernadette into his arms again and rose, staggering slightly as he did so.

I had also got to my feet, and I saw this. Laying a gentle hand on his wet sleeve, I looked up at him and said, "Captain, do allow Charles to help you. Please. He wishes to be of use to Miss Cumphries as well."

He nodded, and together the two men carried the corpse-like figure away from the shore and to the Bothwell house.

Under Mrs. Bothwell's direction, Bernadette was conveyed upstairs and given possession of her own bed. Between the two of us, we managed to remove the wet clothes and replace them with dry. Charles was then allowed in to build a fire.

By the time the surgeon arrived, his patient was resting a little more comfortably – still coughing some and out of her senses, but warm and better able to breathe. Yet he would give us no definitive answers as to the ultimate outcome, only saying that he did not regard it as a desperate case. Miss Cumphries had sustained a blow to the head when she fell, which he did not consider life threatening. The more material danger was to the lungs, he explained. Still, the patient had youth and vigour on her side, giving every reason to be hopeful of her survival, if not her full recovery.

This was enough for the moment to give profound relief to those who had been worried he might say that a few hours must end all.

"Thank God!" uttered Captain Devereaux, with a tone and a look which I will never forget, nor the sight of him afterwards as he sat near a table, leaning over it with folded arms and face concealed, as if overpowered by the various feelings of his soul, and trying by prayer and reflection to calm them.

After the surgeon had given his instructions and gone, Captain Devereaux and Charles left for their respective lodgings, shortly returning again in dry clothing, Charles with our mother in tow. Mama was in a pitiable state of agitation, fretting and mumbling something about how she was sure to have the blame for all of this in the end. She went straight up to Bernadette to be assured that the girl still breathed, returning several minutes later a little more composed.

It then seemed fitting for us, all gathered in Mrs. Bothwell's small parlour, to consider what was best to be done as to the general situation. Charles volunteered to immediately ride for Bath to inform Mr. Cumphries of the accident, to which the rest of us agreed. That Bernadette must remain where she was (regardless how distressing it seemed to involve the Bothwells in such trouble) did not admit a doubt either. Her removal was impossible. Mrs. Bothwell soon silenced all scruples; and, as much as she could, all gratitude on this count. It had already been arranged in her mind that her son must give up his room and find a bed elsewhere, so that the patient could have one of her female friends stay to help nurse her.

"It should be Jane, of course," said Captain Devereaux with conviction. "No one could be more proper and capable. You will stay with her, won't you, Jane?" he asked me, speaking with a glow and a gentleness, which seemed almost restoring the past.

I could not immediately answer, so overcome with emotion was I at being addressed by him in this intimate manner, hearing him speak my name again after so many years. I felt my face flush and saw a consciousness on his own before he turned away.

"No, no!" said my mother at this point. "That will not do at all. Miss Cumphries's care is *my* responsibility and I will not shirk it. I feel a duty to her father to look after her personally. Jane had much better go home."

"Might I not stay as well, Mama? Any corner or a mat on the floor of Bernadette's room would suffice for me."

Mama would not hear of it, however. She reminded me that I could walk over every day as it was, and so there was no need to further impose on Mrs. Bothwell with extra people.

I could say nothing to this.

When these arrangements had been decided and Mrs. Bothwell had returned to the sick room, nobody seemed to have anything left to say. It then impressed me as odd that we had been talking very calmly and rationally, making provisions as if we might have been planning an excursion of pleasure or a trip to the market rather than the care of a friend, a bright young woman, whose very life still hung in the balance. My heart was suddenly pierced by grief anew. "What an ill-judged, ill-fated walk on the shore!" I bitterly lamented. "Oh, how I wish we had never thought of it!"

Captain Devereaux's anguish obviously equalled my own. "Don't talk of it, don't talk of it," he cried, bolting to his feet and holding his head with his hands. He turned from us and continued. "Oh God! That I had not given way to her at the fatal moment! Had I done as I ought! But she was so eager, so resolute. Dear, sweet Bernadette!"

I confess my thoughts following this outburst were not wholly charitable in nature. I wondered if – even perversely hoped that – Philippe would now begin to question the justness of his previous opinion as to the universal advantage to be found in firmness of character. Should not today's misadventure prove that, like all other qualities of the mind, resoluteness should have its proper limits? Perhaps when he was more rational again, he might even allow that a more persuadable temper would probably have listened to her friends and avoided tragedy.

I chastised myself at once. Was I now blaming that poor girl upstairs for her own terrible misfortune, cruelly criticising her character when she lay so close to death's door? Abominable! What sort of wretch would do such a thing? And yet I had – proof that I had no right to judge the shortcomings of others so harshly.

My path of penance was clear. I must compose myself and be just. I must show Captain Devereaux that I was not so petty as to resent my sick friend. I would attend on Bernadette with a zeal above the common claims of regard... for his sake as well as for hers. I would also endeavour to wish them both happy when the time came, for it seemed that by this shared experience the two of them were now more irrevocably bound together than before. Beyond her previous attachment, Bernadette owed Captain Devereaux her life, and she would surely devote the rest of it to making her eternal gratitude felt by him.

-18-

If Louisa recovered, it would all be well again. More than former happiness would be restored. There could not be a doubt, to her mind there was none, of what would follow her recovery. A few months hence, and the room now so deserted, occupied but by her silent, pensive self, might be filled again with all that was happy and gay, all that was glowing and bright in prosperous love, all that was most unlike Anne Elliot!

That night, I had the cathartic relief of pouring out the whole story, and all my varied feeling attending it, to Cassandra. I hid nothing from her; I told every action and word I could recall, every wretched thought and my fears for the ultimate outcome.

"How much you must have gone through!" she cried when I finally had done. "And poor Bernadette! What will become of her?"

"God willing, she will recover," I said. "Then I expect she and Captain Devereaux will be married."

"Dearest, how can you speak of it so mildly? I know the idea must still grieve you."

"Of course, but I continue trying to rise above. Do not you think it is very noble of me to desire to nurse my rival back to health? I shall be just like Prior's Emma towards her Henry, who promoted his happiness at the expense of her own. Perhaps, if I can manage to die in the effort, I might even be nominated for sainthood one day."

"Oh, Jane, to make jokes at such a time?"

"One must either laugh or cry, after all, and I much prefer laughing, if I have the choice."

Cassandra considered for a minute. "But alongside the pain, there must be a degree of pleasure to be found in Captain Devereaux's turning to you in his time of need. Surely that means something – a proof of friendship and of deference to your judgment."

"Or perhaps it only signifies that I am valuable to him for what use I can be to Bernadette, the woman he truly admires. Nothing beyond."

But Cassandra was right. Despite my outward cynicism, I could not help but retain within me some portion of the original gratification I felt when Philippe had looked to me – for help in the first desperate moments and then again with his tender words later at the house. He might be in love with Bernadette, but he apparently could not help holding me in some esteem as well. The old regard was not completely extinguished after all.

~~*~~

After services at the local parish church we attended, there to pray very earnestly for Bernadette's full and speedy recovery, I spent the rest of the day at the Bothwells'. Mama had already exhausted herself – more with anxiety than hard work – and felt justified by my presence in lying down for a while. In truth, though, there was little for anybody else to do, thanks to Mrs. Bothwell's efficiency. I insisted on taking my turn watching over Bernadette, but I ended by spending most of my time and energy downstairs, trying to make myself useful in the kitchen.

The surgeon came twice – morning and early evening – to check on the patient's progress. He confirmed what her friends had already observed, that Bernadette was much the same, with no symptoms worse than what they had before appeared. This in itself he counted a victory. A speedy cure must not be hoped, he said, but everything was going on as well as the nature of the case admitted.

In the days that followed, I kept my promise to faithfully attend Bernadette. With me, Mama, Mrs. Bothwell, and sometimes Cassandra, the patient had more nursing than any one unconscious soul could rightly require. God bless Captain Bothwell for what a friend he was to me during that week! With hours of suspense to fill and nothing of consequence to occupy them, I surely would have run mad were it not for him. He was the one who determinedly kept my mind occupied with challenging discussions when I was consigned to wait in his mother's parlour with no other employment. He was the one who convinced me to occasionally break my penance long enough to take some exercise out of doors.

We saw Captain Devereaux frequently but not for any duration. Although he was sure to call at the Bothwell house two and three times each day to enquire after Bernadette's condition, we could never persuade him to stay. If he sat down for more than five minutes together, his foot was sure to begin tapping – slowly at first, and then picking up tempo until it could be sustained no longer. He would then catapult himself from his chair and make some excuse to leave. Most often, however, he did not even attempt staying; he came, received his report, and then he quickly ducked out the door again. I would occasionally espy him out walking as well – alone and at a pace so brisk it was more like a single-minded march. What demons actually drove him on so furiously, I had no way of knowing, but I naturally supposed it was primarily his anxiety over Bernadette's recovery.

When Bernadette opened her eyes on the sixth day following her accident, that recovery was assured. Thankfully, no fever had developed in her lungs, and the surgeon was satisfied that her head would eventually be set to rights as well. Oh, what a happy day that was for all concerned! I was grateful to have witnessed it before going, for we were due to return to Bath.

By this time Mr. Cumphries, whose own indifferent state of health had delayed him, was arrived in Sidmouth to begin overseeing his daughter's slow recuperation. My presence then became even less necessary than before. All my protestations notwithstanding, my parents determined there was no justification for my staying on beyond what had originally been planned, only to give added expense and trouble to others. I was to go home with Papa and Cassandra, and only Mama would remain to continue assisting Mrs. Bothwell with the nursing of my friend. In small consolation, I was at least allowed a brief audience with Bernadette the afternoon before I went.

I sat with her some twenty minutes before she awoke, for although there were longer intervals of sense and consciousness than even the day before, she still slept much of the time. When she did open her eyes, I cleared my throat to announce my presence. Bernadette slowly turned her head, and I smiled broadly at her, truly delighted to see her improvement for myself. "There you are, friend," I said cheerfully, taking her nearest hand. "I cannot tell you how happy I am that you are come back to us. You gave us all quite a scare, you know."

"Did I?" she responded weakly, looking confused.

"Yes, you most assuredly did, although it is probably to be expected that you will not remember at first. You have been quite ill, Bernadette, but never mind that. The important thing is that you will soon be well again. The surgeon himself has said so."

We were both silent a minute, during which time she seemed to be trying to make sense of what I had told her. "Where… Where exactly am I?" she asked presently. "I suppose I should know, but I confess I do not."

"You are at the home of Mrs. Bothwell, dearest. It seemed the best and certainly the nearest place to bring you after the accident."

Then, all at once, a look of horror beset her countenance. "I remember. The wave!" she said, her lip trembling and tears beginning to trail across her face and fall onto the pillow.

I instantly dropped from my chair and knelt beside the bed, hugging her whole arm to me greedily. "Oh, Bernadette, do forgive me!" I pleaded, my own tears stinging at my eyes. "I should not have reminded you of what must be terribly painful."

When she was enough recovered, Bernadette said, "You are not to blame, Jane. I sometimes forget when I sleep, or it seems only a nightmare from which I will awaken. But it was real, wasn't it? I nearly drowned." She shivered involuntarily, as if feeling the deadly embrace of those icy waters once more.

I could not deny the truth, so I nodded my head. "You must try not to dwell on it, though. The danger is long past now. Think only of getting well and getting on with the rest of your life."

"Yes, I will try. Truly, I will." Brightening a little, she added, "Papa is here. Am I correct in thinking I have seen him? My head is so muddled that I cannot be sure."

"Not so muddled as you suppose perhaps. Yes, you have seen your father… and all your other friends as well." I paused and then forced myself to go on. "Captain Devereaux comes frequently to ask after you. He has been very devoted to following your progress these many days. You may not know it, but it is to him that you owe your life, Bernadette. He is the one who rescued you from the sea."

"Oh!" she exclaimed in some alarm. "Then I must thank him at once. Is he here now?"

"No, no," I said, trying to settle her. "Lie still; the doctor says you must not exert yourself. There will be plenty of time for you to thank the captain later… plenty." *A lifetime*, I thought, chagrinned. When Bernadette was calm again, I returned to my chair before continuing. "Now, I came to tell you goodbye, for I must return to

Bath tomorrow. I wish I could stay, but alas, I have no choice in the matter. Mama will be here, though, and I have made her promise to keep me informed of how you are getting on. You will soon be well enough to travel, I trust, so we will not remain apart for long."

I sat with Bernadette a few more minutes, until I could see that she was slipping back into sleep. Then I reluctantly left her, intending to return at once to our lodging house to make preparations for our departure on the morrow. I was intercepted downstairs by Captain Bothwell, however.

He rose and stepped forward when I entered the room. "Miss Austen," he said. "I am sorry indeed that we are to lose the pleasure of your company. I have enjoyed our discussions more than I can say."

"I too," I answered sincerely. "Perhaps we shall meet again, though," I added, knowing how unlikely it should be.

"Yes, yes," he agreed eagerly. "That is just what I have been thinking. It is not impossible, you know, that I should one day come to Bath."

"And should you like to see Bath, Captain?"

"I believe that I should. People say it is a place not to be missed, but you must advise me. Yours is an opinion I have learnt to trust, whereas I would not much credit the common cant."

"You must not ask me; I cannot be impartial as to Bath. My original positive views of the place have since been overpowered by too lengthy an exposure. I suppose it is pleasant enough on a short visit, though. And if you admire man-made monuments and prize the advantages of a large society, then you should by all means visit Bath."

He looked at me very earnestly. "If I come, Miss Austen, it will not be to enlarge my society but to continue the friendships I already value so much. May I hope to call upon you there… you and your excellent family?"

I hesitated, not knowing his true intentions and whether or not to encourage him. Deciding that I should simply be honest, as he had always been with me, I said, "I would be happy to see you in Bath, Captain Bothwell."

He smiled and, to my surprise, took my hand. I believe he was on the point of kissing it when the front door opened and Captain Devereaux came in. After we had all stared at one another for a few seconds, he said stiffly, "Forgive me. I fear I am interrupting."

Captain Bothwell let go of my hand, which I then audaciously offered to Captain Devereaux. "Not at all, sir," I answered evenly, looking him in the eye. "In fact, I am glad you have come, for I was just taking leave. Now I can say goodbye to you as well. Who knows if we shall ever meet again?"

I saw some emotion flash across his countenance as he stepped closer and accepted my hand. All my senses sprang to attention at his touch, at the nearness and force of his supremely masculine presence. For a moment I thought my heart might stop beating on the spot. What was I thinking to deliberately reawaken such dangerous sensations, to invite such exquisite torture? I must have been out of my mind. I suppose I wished to recapture those long-lost feelings, even for a moment, and then make a dramatic exit. In the first, I succeeded. As to the second, however, my object was completely spoilt by what Philippe said next.

"Uh... actually, I do know, Miss Austen. I have just bespoken a supper tonight for your family and mine at the York. So you see we shall meet at least once more after all. I hope that is agreeable to you."

Terribly embarrassed, I reclaimed my hand, which felt as if it were on fire, along with my cheeks. "Of course it is agreeable, Captain," I mumbled. "How kind of you." Then I hastily departed the Bothwell house.

The supper that night was an uncomfortable affair. I had been too bold before, thinking I should never see Captain Devereaux again so that it mattered not. Now, instead of making a theatrical exit with the memory of a private parting to carry with me, I had to endure a veritable crowd followed by an impersonal goodbye.

Captain Bothwell, seated to one side of me, did his best to entertain, but I had not the heart for it, especially when it seemed that every time I turned in his direction, I would see Captain Devereaux frowning at us. No, it would not do; much safer to face the other way, where I had the admiral and his wife to converse with. Mrs. Crowe always met me with a kindness which gave me the delight of fancying myself a favourite with her, and I found the admiral's goodness of heart and simplicity of character irresistible.

Bernadette's sad accident – something we three had not discussed together before – was soon the prevailing topic. Prior to that point, the Crowes had been chiefly obliged to Captain Devereaux for their information of the original incident and of the invalid's current state.

"A very bad business," said Mrs. Crowe. "My brother refuses to censure Miss Cumphries for it, but I cannot help believing the whole misadventure the result of great imprudence. I suppose the thoughtlessness of youth must have the blame. Still, it is frightful to think how long her recovery will require or if there might not always be some lingering effect of the concussion hereafter!"

"Ay, a very bad business indeed," agreed the admiral in a low tone. "A new sort of way this is for a young fellow to be making love, is it not, Miss Austen? He allows his sweetheart to be tossed into the drink so that he can have the credit of saving her life! No doubt effective, but surely there might have been an easier way of securing her affection." He shook with silent mirth at his own attempt at humour.

I smiled, in spite of the subject.

"For shame!" rebuked Mrs. Crowe. "This is no joking matter."

"Now, now, my dear," he cajoled. "Miss Cumphries is out of danger and cannot possibly suffer by what I say. You see that Miss Austen smiles, and she has been a friend of the young lady much longer than either of us. Lest she be brought too low by this crisis, I believe it is our duty to carry on as cheerfully as may be in her support."

"Perhaps you are right," said Mrs. Crowe. "We must not forget that others have suffered besides Miss Cumphries. You, Jane – you and your brother – cannot have come away from the experience untouched."

"I thank you both kindly, but you need have no anxiety on my account. I am no fainting victim, Mrs. Crowe."

"I would hardly accuse you of that, dear, for Philippe has spoken of your cool head in the crisis and your commendable efforts for your friend ever since. I am thinking of the other thing he said – his wish that you would be none the worse for your exertions in the end. Apparently, he has sometimes observed in battle that when a person remains calm in the face of calamity, it is only later that the full force of the event is felt. He was anxious that you should not suffer that fate."

I was nearly overcome by what Mrs. Crowe said, or rather by what Philippe had said to her about me. This was handsome of him indeed, for it had not been necessary for him to speak to his sister of me at all. Yet he had done it, and this – his expression of regard – gave me more pleasure than almost anything else could have. I hazarded a glance in his direction. He was not frowning now as he returned my steady gaze; it was an expression I could not rightly interpret. Sadness? No, perhaps more like regret. I could imagine that my own countenance mirrored his at that moment.

-19-

I remember it rained that next morning as we left Sidmouth – a small, thick rain that almost blotted out the familiar objects discernable through the carriage windows. I had said my adieu to the sea the evening before under a clear sky full of stars, the generous moon illuminating my last view of the shimmering water as well as the way back to our lodging house from the York. Now quickly all the other landmarks, which had become so well known to me during the previous month, slid one by one beyond my reach as well. It was back to cheerless Bath for me, my sister, and my father. Charles was already there, and Mama would come two weeks later, with the Crowes.

Recalling that time and all my attendant sensations, I now write of Anne…

> *She could not quit the mansion-house, or look an adieu to the cottage, or even notice through the misty glasses the last humble tenements of the village, without a saddened heart. Scenes had passed in Uppercross, which made it precious. It stood the record of many sensations of pain, once severe, but now softened; and of some instances of relenting feeling, some breathings of friendship and reconciliation, which could never be looked for again, and which could never cease to be dear. She left it all behind her; all but the recollection that such things had been.*

I occupied myself on my journey with the more gratifying aspects of the memories I carried away from Sidmouth. I had survived seeing Captain Devereaux again – something I had once considered unimaginable – and more than survived; I had come away stronger for it and with more charitable feelings toward him and the events of the past. I was now better acquainted than before with the man who might have been my husband, had the fates smiled upon us. I had seen him mature, successful, honourable, and brave. I had seen him admired and deserving to be. And I had heard myself praised by him once more.

This should have sharpened my loss, and it did, but it somehow made it easier to bear at the same time. I was proud; I think that best identifies the common cord in my collection of disparate emotions. I was proud of myself firstly, that I had behaved with restraint and dignity. Then, I was proud of him – for the man he had become, and also of his recovered regard for me. The naysayers of the past had been proven wrong and I right. I felt exonerated. I had been completely justified in singling him out those years before for my love and esteem, and so I could be proud of my judgment and taste as well.

Captain Devereaux would now do his duty to Bernadette, and I must also be proud of him for that.

I cannot say that I always remained so philosophical in the days and weeks that followed; pride is cold comfort in loneliness, after all. And I was truly lonely that summer when I returned to Bath, bereft of nearly all my friends – having left my mother and important others behind in Sidmouth, as well as those I still missed from Steventon.

The setting itself gave me no comfort, for I had learnt to dislike Bath. Not least among its detractions for me was the familiar din that greeted us immediately upon our arrival – the dash of other carriages, the heavy rumble of carts and drays, the bawling of newsmen, muffin-men, and milk-men. These did not upset my father, I noticed. No, his spirits rose under their influence, and he remarked that, after being so long in retirement at the seashore, there was "nothing like the cheerful sound of a little activity." I suppose everybody has their own tastes in noises, as well as in other matters, and sounds that are quite innoxious to one ear may be most distressing to another. For me, it was a sad thing indeed to exchange the natural music of wind and wave for the mechanical clatter of town.

And now I am not alone in thinking so; Anne Elliot, for one, agrees with me. Having been compelled by my pen to resign all the pleasantness Lyme and Uppercross had comprised, she is come to Bath as well, just as I designed from the beginning she should.

Anne entered it with a sinking heart, anticipating an imprisonment of many months, and anxiously saying to herself, "Oh! When shall I leave you again?"

And yet, she comes to Bath revived and refreshed by the enlivening circumstances of the near past. Her time in the encouraging company of the Musgroves and Crofts, her bittersweet reunion with Captain Wentworth, her bracing experiences in Lyme: these have conspired to, in some measure, restore her bloom. Even Sir Walter notices his daughter's improved looks. He observes to Anne that she is less thin in her person with a complexion greatly improved. Is it the work of the liberal application of Gowland, he wonders? It is not, rather of a more effectual balm – the unguent of human warmth, given in generous measure by the companions just left, but never at home.

To her surprise, Anne finds kindness and friendship in Bath as well. Once again, it is not through her family, who are as cold towards her as ever. It is not in her noble relations, Lady Dalrymple and Miss Carteret, who are soon discovered to be in residence. No, it is through a renewed friendship with her old schoolfellow, now a widowed Mrs. Smith, and in the particular attentions of her cousin Mr. Elliot, recently reformed and pardoned. He will presently propose to flatter and adore her, as she deserves to be.

While he cannot compare with Captain Wentworth for romantic appeal, Mr. Elliot does come replete with impressive virtues, among them the advantages of birth (as heir to Kellynch and to Sir Walter's baronetage), a gentleman's education, a fortune acquired by his first marriage, and flawless manners. He is a well-looking young widower too, which cannot but enhance the force of his other attractions. I now write to that effect…

He was quite as good-looking as he had appeared at Lyme, his countenance improved by speaking, and his manners were so exactly what they ought to be, so polished, so easy, so particularly agreeable, that Anne could compare them in excellence to only one person's manners. They were not the same, but they were perhaps equally good.

Sir Walter and his favored daughter Elizabeth were won over by Mr. Elliot at once. Lady Russell will soon be seduced by the aptness of pairing him with her young protégé, and by the idea of seeing

Anne become the next Lady Elliot in her mother's place. As for Anne herself, her opinion of her cousin is not yet formed. But it must be expected that she will not be so quick as her relations in dismissing the improprieties of the past, that she will not swiftly be swayed by a handsome face, correct opinions, and an elegant manner. She will, I trust, have the good sense to look deeper, below the polished surface, before committing herself. After all, she has been gifted with a certain sharpness of mind the others lack, and, what is more to the purpose, she has experienced the profound love of a worthy man once. For better or for worse, it seems unlikely she will easily accept anything much inferior now.

However it might end, Mr. Elliot is without any question Anne's pleasantest acquaintance in Bath; nobody can equal him.

Unfortunately, there was no entertaining Mr. Elliot waiting for me upon my return to Bath, not even a Mrs. Smith or a Lady Dalrymple to expand my confined society. Although I did thankfully have a sister who was a *far* better companion than Elizabeth Elliot! Through all my disappointments and losses, I kept Cassandra near me, the best and truest friend. My brother Charles stayed on in Bath with us temporarily, and my Aunt and Uncle Leigh-Perrot resided there on a permanent basis. Beyond these familial supports, I turned to my pen to find companionship, not by composing stories – for I never found Bath an inspiring place to create – but by writing letters. I wrote to Henry and Eliza in London, to Catherine and Althea Bigg at Manydown, and finally to Madam Lefroy, whom I knew I had sadly neglected of late.

In this case, there was an awkwardness to overcome in apprising my former mentor of events at Sidmouth. Captain Devereaux's name must be mentioned; that did not admit a doubt. Yet I could not have spoken it looking straight forward into her eye. Consequently, I was glad to have the protection of time and distance in choosing my words. Should I risk provoking her by expounding on the excellence of the man I had lost, in large part by her persuasion? I was tempted. Or should I be kind? Should I pretend there had been no especial significance to me in seeing him again? Impossible! In the end, I praised the captain enough to satisfy my own sense of fairness, but I also endeavoured to allay any fears this information might arouse by speaking of my sanguine expectations of soon hearing his engagement to Miss Cumphries announced.

It was true; I waited in suspense for this or indeed any news from Sidmouth. When I wrote to my friends there, I hazarded no enquiries of Captain Devereaux, yet there was voluntary communication of him sufficient to satisfy me. My mother reported, among many other things, that the captain's spirits had been gradually recovering. As Miss Cumphries improved, he did likewise; he was become much calmer and more composed than the tormented soul he had shown himself to be that first week. Apparently, he had visited Bernadette with faithful regularity since then – frequently, but only for a very few minutes each time. Mama attributed this brevity to a commendable disinclination of doing the patient harm, fearing what ill consequences an extended interview might excite in her delicate condition. And now he had taken himself off altogether, to Plymouth for a week, till her head were stronger. This was Mama's initial report.

Her second carried little of Captain Devereaux in it beyond her casual mentioning of how much he was liked by Mr. Cumphries – for himself and especially for saving his daughter's life. A letter from Mrs. Crowe confirmed all – that the invalid continued to recover apace, and that Mr. Cumphries had handsomely declared to the admiral and herself how much he looked forward to the honour of their two families becoming more nearly connected as soon as might be.

Here was the final nail in the coffin. With the father approving of the match as well, there would be no escaping for Captain Devereaux. Although I had no real reason to suppose he wished to escape Bernadette, I admit I had held out a slight, irrational hope that his previous preference for me might have been rekindled so far as to make him reconsider his plans to marry my friend instead. Even should this have been the case, however, it had come too late to save him. His conspicuously courting Miss Cumphries for weeks had rightly raised expectations. His rescuing her from the sea, their bodies drenched and clinging together as they were, had forever bound the two of them together. With Bernadette having already clearly shown her own wishes to the world, only her father's outright refusal of consent could have honourably freed Captain Devereaux. Now that faint possibility had been snuffed out.

~~*~~

Mama followed us by a fortnight in returning home to Bath, delivered by the Crowes from Sidmouth, as had been previously arranged. The unexpected turn was that Captain Bothwell had ridden north with them, going so far as to accompany them up to greet us when they all arrived in Sydney Place.

"Why, Captain Bothwell!" I exclaimed on the occasion. "This is an unexpected pleasure. I had not thought to meet with you again so soon."

"I daresay you had not, Miss Austen, but here I am nonetheless."

"So I see. Were you no longer needed by your friends at Sidmouth, by your mother?"

"No indeed, I was of very little use to anybody there, I assure you. Miss Cumphries was doing well enough three days ago to be moved into her father's lodgings. So my help is not wanted any more by my mother. Devereaux will not miss me either, not with his interest so much engaged with Miss Cumphries. They are to be married, you know."

"Oh!" I started, and I required a moment to recover myself. So there it was. Not completely unforeseen, but still... "No. No, Captain Bothwell, I did not know it for a certainty."

"I trust you cannot be *too* surprised, Miss Austen; we could all see where the thing was headed. The only wonder was what they could be waiting for."

"Yes, I suppose so. And it is now finally quite settled between them?"

He nodded.

"Well then," I responded, attempting a cheerful expression. "What excellent news, this." I could think of nothing further to add. After all, it was only the period to the end of a sentence already written, the outcome we had all long predicted, as Captain Bothwell said.

"Yes, it is," he agreed more heartily. "I hope they will be very happy. Now, as I was saying, since nobody wanted me in Sidmouth and I had been so keenly anticipating a visit to Bath, I decided there was no time like the present for it. So here I am. What do you say to that, Miss Austen?"

"I will repeat what I said before – that it is a pleasure, sir, to meet with you again so soon. How long do you intend to stay in Bath?"

"I have no fixed plans. I will stay as long as my friends want me, I should think," he said with an earnest look. "If I begin making a nuisance of myself, though, you must be sure to tell me. I would not distress you, or my excellent hosts for the world."

"Certainly," I said lightly, "but I hardly think that probable, Captain. After all, it is just as likely you will tire of us first. I cannot speak for the Crowes, but I have no acquaintance of rank to whom to introduce you, no power to collect good company about you."

"I care nothing for rank, Miss Austen. There is far more to good company than high birth, according to my way of thinking. My idea of good company is a collection of clever, well-informed people such as yourself, who have compassionate hearts and a great deal of conversation. That is what I call good company, and I believe you would agree with me."

"You claim to know me very well, sir."

"Not at all. I only admit to having a great desire for knowing you better than I do at present, and of already suspecting that I could never grow tired of your company." He said this with a warmth that conveyed sincere friendship and perhaps hinted at even more.

So, in many ways, I had the superior to a Mr. Elliot after all. Captain Bothwell was perhaps not so fashionable or charmingly mannered, but far more honorable. And he was likewise determined to pay me every possible attention, to do what he could to ensure my comfort and happiness. I was flattered. I was gratified that such a worthy gentleman saw value in me, especially at a time when I knew myself to be forever divided from the one man I truly loved.

Although I had no expectation of anything serious developing, I thought a little flirtation might serve to lift the spirits without doing either of us any harm. I hoped it might do us both good, in fact. I had long wondered about Captain Bothwell's history and imagined a tragedy was hidden somewhere in his past. His determined joviality seemed to me a guise intended to mask some inner sorrow, much like the patch he wore served to cover the battle scars beneath. I thought perhaps, with my encouragement, he might make progress in overcoming whatever his trouble was.

-20-

When I began Anne Elliot's story (as well as this companion piece of my personal remembrances), I made a vow to provide my heroine with a more felicitous conclusion than providence has seen fit to authorise for me. And so it is at this point that the two stories – hers and my own – must begin to diverge once and for all. It is at this point that I can no longer sustain the pretense of our paths running parallel. Until now, there have been more similarities than differences, which will not be the case henceforth. For, rather than hearing that her captain is finally engaged to another, as I did, Anne hears the reverse. She hears from reliable sources that Louisa Musgrove, instead of being to marry Captain Frederick Wentworth, is to marry James Benwick.

> *In her own room Anne tried to comprehend it. Captain Benwick and Louisa Musgrove! Their minds most dissimilar! Where could have been the attraction? The answer soon presented itself. It had been in situation. They had been thrown together several weeks. Louisa, just recovering from illness, had been in an interesting state, and Captain Benwick was not inconsolable. He had an affectionate heart. He must love somebody.*
>
> *She saw no reason against their being happy. Louisa had fine naval fervour to begin with, and they would soon grow more alike. He would gain cheerfulness, and she would learn to be an enthusiast for Scott and Lord Byron; nay, that was probably learnt already; of course they had fallen in love over poetry. The idea of Louisa Musgrove turned into a person of literary taste, and sentimental reflection, was amusing, but she had no doubt of its being so. The day at*

Lyme, the fall from the Cobb, might influence her health, her nerves, her courage, her character to the end of her life, as thoroughly as it appeared to have influenced her fate.

The conclusion of the whole was, that if the woman who had been sensible of Captain Wentworth's merits could be allowed to prefer another man, there was nothing in the engagement to excite lasting wonder; and if Captain Wentworth lost no friend by it, certainly nothing to be regretted. No, it was not regret which made Anne's heart beat in spite of herself, and brought the colour into her cheeks when she thought of Captain Wentworth unshackled and free. She had some feelings which she was ashamed to investigate. They were too much like joy, senseless joy!

Oh, fortunate, fortunate Anne! Thanks to my contrivance, her way for happiness is now cleared by this strange turn of events. Were such a thing to occur in real life, however, it might be rightly credited a miracle. How else could one account for such an unexpected outcome – that a young woman should be so materially changed by a fall as to subsequently attach herself to a man with whom she had nothing in common before, that the formerly high-spirited Louisa Musgrove should now prefer the dejected, thinking, reading Captain Benwick? And yet so it is, with Anne Elliot the possible beneficiary.

Would that there had been such miracle for me.

But there was no Captain Benwick for Bernadette to fall in love with at the critical moment, only possibly a Captain Bothwell, who had been less interested in cultivating a new literary garden in her fallow mind than in reaping the already well-grown harvest in mine.

This is not a tragedy, I tell myself; it is simply the way matters unfolded, and we can rarely direct events around us to suit our personal wishes. And yet, as I write these things down so many years later, a new doubt enters my mind. In hindsight and in light of Anne's contrasting fate, I cannot help thinking, "If only I had been less quick to form a friendship with Captain Bothwell. If only I had not monopolised his time, but had instead encouraged him to interest Bernadette in some of his ideas…" What might then have occurred? Would anything have changed for us? Might Bernadette's affections, so much in need of an object to fix on in her condition, have transferred to him? Would Captain Devereaux, like Captain Wentworth, then have been freed to reconsider his choice, even to renew his addresses to me?

It gives me no peace to think so, since I cannot go back and change a thing. It is better to believe that events transpired exactly as they should have. It is more beneficial to accept that suffering has a useful purpose, despite the fact that I do not always understand it. Whether my life would have been happier with Captain Devereaux than it has been without him, this is impossible to say. All that can be known for certain is that it has been a *different* life – not empty, not devoid of joy and purpose, simply different. I have not been given the gift of marriage and the gratification of bringing up my own physical children. Instead, I have been gifted with time to nurture a communion of a different sort – one of the mind – and with the raising up of my small clutch of literary offspring, who, I dare to hope, will long outlive me. I could not have done both.

Yet the little drama of my strange love affair with Captain Devereaux does not end here. There is at least one more act in the play left to be revealed.

~~*~~

Captain Bothwell continued his steady attentions to me in Bath, a fact which could hardly go undetected by anyone in our household. And, just as everybody noticed, everybody had an opinion about it. My brother Charles was least forthcoming, only going so far as to comment to me on several occasions that Captain Bothwell was undoubtedly "a very fine fellow." My sister did not dispute this, but she did caution me against risking the captain's heart by raising false hopes. My mother made her sentiments known by how ready she was to spare me from household duties every time Captain Bothwell called, and by the gracious smiles she bestowed on him. It was my father, however, who was apparently charged with relating to me their united opinion on the subject, as well as ascertaining mine.

"We have certainly been seeing a lot of Captain Bothwell these two weeks past," he said, coming to sit down across from me. With Charles gone out, Cassandra still up in our room, and my mother scurrying away as soon as he entered, Papa had me alone and cornered in the drawing room that morning. "A fine young man," he added.

I saw that he was awaiting some response from me. Though my father had affected a casual tone, he was unconvincing, and I was immediately on alert. "True," I answered warily, "I cannot dispute these facts."

"Yes, yes, a very fine young man," he repeated. "Not so dashing as Captain Devereaux, perhaps, but every bit as agreeable in other respects. Would not you concur, Jane?"

I assured him that I did and then returned my attention to my needlework.

Presently, however, Papa continued. "And you are not much put off by his…"

Looking up when no more words followed, I saw my father swirling his fingers in the general vicinity of his eye. "No, Papa," I said. "I am not the least put off by the patch Captain Bothwell wears; I never have been. But may I ask to what these questions tend? I cannot help feeling there is a specific purpose in the course of your conversation."

"Very well, Jane. I shall come straight out with it. Your mother and I are wondering if, or rather hoping that, you would look favourably on an offer from the gentleman, should it be forthcoming, which seems likely. I have observed a certain similarity of mind between you, which would go a long way towards making a successful partnership, and I would feel confident entrusting your future to such a steady man. He has proven himself to be of good character, and I understand his resources are more than adequate. It would not be a brilliant match, admittedly, but perfectly respectable. The thing is, we would like to see you well disposed of in marriage, and this may be your most eligible option."

I set my work aside. "You mean it is the best I can reasonably hope for at my advanced age," I said dryly, "and that you should very much like to see me safely off your hands. Once again, I must agree with you, Papa. One spinster daughter may be accepted as a matter of course, but two is something of an embarrassment, not to mention the decided pecuniary disadvantages of such a case."

"Now, Jane, you mustn't put words in my mouth. You are free to do so with the made-up people in your stories, I suppose, but not with me. Your mother and I simply want what is best for you. We always have, despite what you may think, and despite how… how certain matters have turned out." He paused, and I could see him struggling with emotions too near the surface for comfort, hear a slight quavering of his voice when he spoke. "We have done our best, but if we have not always been right in our advice to you, then I am truly sorry for it."

"Dear Papa," I said at once, "I do not blame you any more than I blame myself for having been guided by you. If you erred back then, it was on the side of prudence and safety. I know that. If I was wrong in yielding, it was to the claims of duty and conscience. Let us not now reproach ourselves for such things."

"You are wise beyond your years, my dear, and your kindness to an old man will surely be rewarded. Only do this one thing more for me; keep an open mind about Captain Bothwell. Will you?"

"I will try. That is all I can promise."

"Fair enough. Your sister has sworn she will never consider a second attachment, but I depend upon your being more reasonable. Remember, you owe Captain Devereaux no loyalty. To put it plainly, Jane, he did not die; he chose another. He was perfectly free to do so, of course, but now you must feel at liberty to do the same. I'm sorry to be so blunt, but it is the truth and needed to be said. I pray you do not plan to sacrifice the rest of your life in honour of some misplaced vow of constancy to him. That is my point."

"No, unlike Cassandra, I have taken no such vow, but neither will I marry where I do not love."

He stood and came over to me. "Love is important, my child," he agreed, stooping to kiss my forehead. Then he lifted my chin to look me in the eye. "But so is a roof over one's head, as your mother is fond of saying. I worry about what will happen to my women when I am gone."

"That time is very far off still!" I declared, fervently believing it was true. Although my father's full head of hair was by then completely white, he appeared to me as handsome and vital as ever. "And anyway, you need not worry. Edward, at least, is extremely well set up; he will be generous to us, surely, if and when the need arises."

I was mistaken in both these assumptions. Dear Papa died only two years later, and Edward, who among my brothers could by far best afford to come to our aid, did little to help us. He allowed his mother and unmarried sisters to drift from one place to another for a long time, near poverty and without a settled home, before belatedly doing his duty. Although I am profoundly grateful for our snug little cottage here at Chawton, and I always will be, I am still a bit ashamed of Edward. Even if, as I very much suspect, his reluctance was at the behest of his wife, that is no excuse.

But of course, I knew nothing of this at the time. What did soon became clear, however, was that I could not marry Captain Bothwell.

True to my word, I tried. I tried to forget Philippe and any comparisons to him. I reminded myself daily of Captain Bothwell's merits even as I continued to enjoy his company at Bath. Pausing in our walk up to Beechan Cliff one day, I studied his kind face and attempted to picture what my future might look like if I were to become his wife. We would set up housekeeping in Sidmouth, I supposed, since his mother was there. Nothing grand – I did not aspire to such and he had not the means – but a comfortable house, with a view to the sea perhaps. I would like that. There would be mutual affection if not passion between us. And probably children. That would give me worthwhile occupation...

"It's no good, is it?" I heard Captain Bothwell say, interrupting me from my private reverie.

Shaking myself, I struggled to catch up, to gather what I had missed while daydreaming. My only clue was the great sadness I saw in his eye. "I'm so sorry, what?" I said, admitting my lapse.

"This thing we have been playing at. It's no good is it? We have both tried, but our hearts are not in it. I can see that now."

I understood then what he meant, and I thought of denying it. Instead I said, "No, you are quite right. Dear Captain Bothwell, I wish it could be otherwise. I truly do."

"As do I, Miss Austen. You are the first woman after... That is to say, it has been a long time since I have met someone with whom I thought there might have been a chance. With you, I had the idea that perhaps... We are such good friends, after all."

"But friendship is not enough somehow, is it? I am so relieved that you feel the same. I would not for the world wish to injure you, Captain. And it is not due to anything wanting in you personally. Please believe me. Any woman would be proud to be addressed by a fine gentleman such as yourself."

He frowned and looked away. "Not so, unfortunately. Some cannot even bear the sight of my ugly face – one in particular." He silenced my objection and then went on. "I do not ask for your pity. I only tell you these things as a friend. You see, Miss Austen, I loved a girl once, a long time ago now. Miss Hammermaster and I were to be married as soon as I returned from the war. Instead, when I came home injured, she took one look at me and burst into tears. She could not go through with it, and under the circumstances it hardly seemed fair to force her. I thought, given enough time, she might come round, or, failing that, that my own attachment would expire so I could love another. When I met you, I felt the first real hope..."

He broke off and we were silent. "What ever became of Miss Hammermaster?" I asked gently a minute later.

"She is Mrs. Evanston now, married these six months to a man who presumably has all his body parts in their proper places."

"Then I am truly sorry – sorry for *her*, that is, for she has missed her chance at the better share and instead has chosen what is undoubtedly inferior."

He half smiled at this. "You are a dear for saying so, Miss Austen."

"It is no more than what I sincerely believe. People do not always choose wisely for themselves when it comes to love. Or if wisely, perhaps not fortunately. One's affection must be returned. I understand something about the matter." I went no further, but neither did I attempt to hide anything of what I was feeling at that moment.

Captain Bothwell studied me narrowly. "Yes," he said at last, nodding his head. "I believe you *can* appreciate my situation, all too well, in fact. I thought I observed... That is to say, I wondered before if there might be something... I only wish I had known. Perhaps then... But we need say no more about it if you like. I think we understand each other."

"Thank you, Captain."

"Only tell me this; is there any service I may render you in this matter? I suppose you realize that Miss Cumphries and Captain Devereaux are likely to be joining us here in Bath very soon. Is there any communication to our mutual friend you would trust me to make on your behalf?" Here he gave me an arch look. "Or any act of espionage against your enemy? I would gladly storm the very walls for you, Miss Austen. It would be an honour. The danger to myself must not even be considered."

"I thank you, gallant sir," said I with a deep curtsey before we both broke into laughter. The moment quickly passed, though, and we became sober again.

"Seriously, Jane, if there is ever anything I can do, you must not hesitate to ask me. Perhaps there is still a chance for you."

"No, my dear friend," I murmured. "Too late. I regret that it is far too late... for *all* of us."

-21-

Although I did not accept Captain Bothwell's offer of heroic intervention on my behalf, I did ask that he would remain my friend throughout the weeks ahead. I had come to rely on the warmth of his companionship so much that I could not countenance being deprived of it again at once, especially if I was to endure witnessing the happiness of the engaged couple – something it seemed I could not expect to avoid. They would all soon be in Bath – Bernadette, her father, and Captain Devereaux – as confirmed by Admiral Crowe the following day.

I set off into town that morning on my own, undeterred by the fact that neither of my usual companions – my sister and Captain Bothwell – was available to accompany me on my errands. I was not alone for long, as it happened. For, walking up Milsom-street, I had the great good fortune to meet with the admiral. He was standing by himself, at a shop window, with his hands behind him, in earnest contemplation of some print. I might have passed him altogether unseen, for I was obliged to touch his arm as well as address him before I could catch his notice. When he did finally perceive me, however, it was done with all his usual frankness and good humour.

"Ha! Miss Austen! This is treating me like a real friend, for I might have stayed looking at this odd thing all the day, were it not for you coming by and getting my attention. I can never pass by this window without another attempt to make sense of it. Do you see this ship here in this picture? It must have been a queer fellow who painted it, to think that any sailor would venture out to sea in such a shapeless old cockleshell as that." He laughed heartily. "Why, I would not trust it to carry me over a horse pond! Now then, where are you bound this fine morning, and can I be of any use to you?"

"None, I thank you, sir, unless you will give me the pleasure of your company the little way our road lies together."

"That I will and gladly. Here, take my arm, for I do not feel quite comfortable without a woman alongside. That's right. Now we shall have a snug walk together, and I can tell you the latest news from our friends in Sidmouth as we go along."

After his taking one last look at the picture of the ship, and giving one last shake of his head, we set off. I was eager to hear what he had to tell me, for the chance of its being a more thorough report (or at least more current information) than what had been relayed to me through Captain Bothwell. I was forced to be patient, however, as we were several times interrupted by the admiral's stopping to say a "How d'ye do" to someone of his acquaintance. There were quite as many retired navy men in Bath as he could have wished for, it seemed. Finally, when we had gained the greater space and quiet of Belmont, my curiosity was gratified.

"Well, now you shall hear something that will surprise you, Miss Austen," he began. "But first, you must tell me the name of the young lady I am going to talk about, that young lady that we have all been so concerned for. She is Miss Cumphries, of course, but I always forget her Christian name."

"You mean Miss Bernadette," I suggested.

"Ay, ay, Miss Bernadette Cumphries. That is her name, but not for long," he said with a wink and a knowing look. "T'will be Devereaux soon enough, for she is to marry our Philippe. The girl's father has given his consent and it is all decided." He smiled and looked sideways at me. "But, Miss Austen, I see I have not surprised you after all."

"Not entirely, I admit, for I heard something in the same style from Captain Bothwell."

"Of course. I should have known."

"And surely no one who had seen the two of them together in Sidmouth could have doubted the outcome."

"And still, doubt it I did for all that. Too much discrepancy of mind to suit, was my way of thinking. But you see now that I have been proven wrong. It is not the first time such a thing has occurred, I assure you." He paused to tip his hat to yet another navy man across the street.

Not willing to let the matter drop, I continued. "And this information of yours, it is certainly true?"

"Oh, yes. We have it from Philippe himself. His sister had a letter from him day before yesterday. Like yourself, she was not surprised by the news. She had said it would be so ever since Philippe fished this Miss Cumphries out of the drink. Something to do with propriety and raised expectations. I daresay you ladies comprehend these matters better than a man who has been too long at sea and in the company of sailors as uncouth as himself." He gave a low chuckle. "I am pleased to be wrong in this case, for it is high time my brother-in-law took a wife. I only hope it will be a happy union."

I made no reply to this, and we walked on in silence for a minute. Then I ventured one step further on the subject of interest. "I suppose they are both quite impatient to get on with it too. Did Captain Devereaux mention a date?"

"No, Miss Austen, he did not. He only said something about Miss Cumphries being fully recovered first, although I cannot help but think that this hesitation comes because of the peace. If it were wartime, they would have settled the thing weeks ago, a knock on the head or no. At least she has been deemed well enough to travel now, this Miss… Oh, what's her name again?"

"Bernadette."

"Yes, of course. I must make a special point of remembering it this time, or soon you will begin wondering if I have not had a knock on the head too! Well, never mind, Miss Austen. This much I do recall; they are all coming within the week – the girl and her father, as well as Philippe. Then we shall see how things stand and what we are to expect."

~~*~~

Three days later, Mr. Cumphries sent a message round to our door to alert us to his return and to say that his daughter would require a day's rest from the journey before receiving any visitors. Accordingly, I waited. I hardly knew what I would find or what I should say when I did go at any rate. I had always intended that my feelings for Captain Devereaux should not affect my friendship with Bernadette. But that was when an alliance between them had been only theoretical. Now that it was a fact, it seemed impossible that I could follow through on that aim.

No, my friendship with Bernadette must decrease as her ties to Captain Devereaux increased. I should be sorry to lose her; I had few enough friends in Bath as it was. So it must be, however. I knew I could not bear to visit her as Mrs. Devereaux.

One piece of luck in the situation was that Cassandra and I had been invited by Edward to Godmersham the following month. Charles was to take us, and we would remain there several weeks. It seemed the perfect way to distance myself – literally as well as figuratively. And perhaps Bernadette would be married and gone before I returned. In the meantime, I had to get on as best I could.

She was a changed creature when I saw her.

I had been directed to the drawing room when I arrived, and there I found Bernadette, reclining on a settee and looking as fragile and nervous as a sparrow. My compassion aroused, I went to her at once. "My dear, how glad I am to see you," I said, stooping to give her a tentative embrace. "Are you well?" I drew a chair up close to her.

"Oh, yes," she answered, her words assuring more than her countenance and tone could support. "I shall be completely well in a few more weeks."

Just then, a loud clatter resounded from another part of the house, and Bernadette started quite severely at the noise. For a moment, I thought she might burst into tears.

I reached out to rest a hand over hers. "I daresay one of the servants has dropped something unimportant," I suggested. "Nothing to be alarmed about."

"Of course," she said. "I was only a little surprised; that is all. It is my nerves, you see, Jane. The doctors say they will be the last to recover from the shock I have had. Loud noises frighten me. The silliest things make me cry. And I cannot even bear to look at a body of water." She closed her eyes for a moment and shook her head slightly. "It will pass."

"Oh, Bernadette. I had no idea."

"How could you? You mustn't feel sorry for me, though. I am getting a little stronger every day, and I have my friends to support me. Papa has been an absolute darling about this whole thing, and then there is Captain Devereaux…"

Although I had known the topic must be discussed, this mention of his name still caught me off my guard and sent a jolt right through me. "Ah yes, Captain Devereaux," I repeated feebly as I searched for a more appropriate response. "I heard the good news. Allow me to wish you joy in your upcoming marriage. How happy this must make you both."

"Thank you. Yes, I am very lucky – not only that the captain wishes to marry me, but that he was there to rescue me in the first place. I owe him my life; I think it was you who first told me that, Jane."

"Yes, I believe so."

"Captain Devereaux has been so kind to me since then too, standing by me even when nobody knew if I would recover completely or not. A lesser man might have used my illness as an excuse to cry off. I would hardly have blamed him if he had. The marriage vows say 'in sickness and in health,' but that is as to what happens afterward. No one ought to be required to take on damaged goods at the outset."

"Oh, Bernadette, you must not talk so slightingly about yourself. As you have told me, you will be completely well again in a few more weeks. Captain Devereaux is a lucky man to get you, I should say. I hear your father is very well pleased with him also. Is it true?"

"It is. Here again, we have been fortunate in finding no opposition. He says he could not have chosen for me a better man, had he searched the world over. In fact, Papa was in favour of the wedding's being to take place as soon as possible."

She did not say this with the enthusiasm I might have expected. So I enquired, "But you are not?"

"Not at all. I would wish to be stronger and entirely back to my usual self before attempting it. Besides, I know that Papa will miss me terribly when I go away; I am all he has now, with my mother gone and my sister married."

"He would not wish you to sacrifice your happiness for his, however. Still, I think you are right to wait."

She brightened. "Do you really?"

"Certainly. There is no reason to rush, as far as I am aware. And marriage, although a blessed occasion, is a substantial undertaking nonetheless. One ought not to attempt it in a weakened condition, as you say."

"Exactly, and so I have told my father!"

"I trust he gave you no trouble about it, once you explained how you felt."

"No trouble, or at least very little. He always lets me have my own way in the end. Anything I want, my father is sure to see that it is done. When I was but a girl, I told him I wanted a pony. So he arranged it, never mind the excessive bother and expense it turned out to be. It is no different now I am all grown up. I wrote to him from Sidmouth, before my accident, to tell him I wished to marry Captain Devereaux, and Papa will make sure it happens... just not immediately."

"Not until you are completely ready."

"Exactly. And you know, I would much rather be married when it is cheerfully warm. It is too late to arrange a wedding for this autumn, and Bath is so cold and damp in the winter months. Spring, or even summer, will be much more commodious. Do not you agree?"

"I agree that it should be done according to your wishes – yours and Captain Devereaux's, of course. If you do not mind my asking, what does he say about a date?"

"Oh, it is just as you would suppose; he is all accommodating and undemanding. Everything is to be done when and how I desire it."

"Then you will find no difficulty there either. That must please you."

"I cannot reasonably fault him for it, except it occurs to me that it might be more flattering to me if he were not so very patient. A man violently in love should not be quite so willing to wait for his bride, should he?"

"Bernadette! You quite shock me," I protested, while at the same time feeling my face grow warm for remembering how impatient Captain Devereaux had been to make me his wife those years ago. "We are not barbarians, after all; we are ladies and gentlemen. I believe forbearance – his, as well as yours – is a very commendable thing, and it will do you good service in the end, I trust. Take time to get better acquainted first, unless you would rather know as little of your marriage partner's defects as possible going in. I have sometimes heard that is the best way, but I cannot think it sound advice myself."

"Nor can I. Dear Jane, you are right, as always. It is much better to be sensible about these things, and not to let oneself be run away with by illogical feelings. After all, I chose Captain Devereaux as much with my head as with my heart. I must not blame him if he has done the same."

This comment gave me pause, and I hesitated before asking, "You do love him, though, do not you, Bernadette? I trust you would not be planning to marry him if you did not feel what you ought."

"When you fall in love someday, my dear friend, you will discover for yourself that it is a difficult thing to measure. I do not think

I am really the romantic sort to begin with – not like the passionate heroines we read about in Mrs. Radcliff's novels, at any rate – and yet I am quite certain I love Captain Devereaux well enough to be happy. There is but one thing in the situation that I could wish to change, and that is his profession. I would wish him out of the navy as soon as may be."

I was stunned. "You cannot be serious," said I.

"Perfectly."

"But I thought you revered the navy. I distinctly remember your saying so when we were all together at Sidmouth."

"That was before I nearly drowned! The picture is entirely altered now. Surely you can understand that, Jane. Now the idea of my husband venturing out to sea fills me with paralysing dread. And I could never go with him on a voyage, as some captain's wives do. Think of Mrs. Crowe! How many places she has travelled to with the admiral. It would be out of the question for me; I cannot bear the thought of ever setting eyes on the sea again, let alone setting sail across it!"

"Perhaps that feeling will pass in time. As you say, your nerves are still not fully recovered."

"No, Jane, my mind is quite made up, and my father agrees with me. With the peace, there is very little demand for sailors anymore, so it is perfectly reasonable that Philippe should expect to make a change."

"He captained a boat even before the war – a commercial vessel it was then. It is in his family, Bernadette. It is in his blood. He would never give it up willingly. He would certainly never consent to being idle." I then perceived that I had stated this with more authority than I had any right to claim. "At least that is my impression of him," I corrected. "You, of course, are in a better position to judge."

"Oh, he would not be idle. My father is prepared to offer him a very fine position in the bank. He will have occupation – a safe, dry occupation – and we would be able to live in London, instead of some crude port town."

I tried to picture Captain Devereaux in a businessman's suit instead of his naval uniform, captaining a desk in a stuffy office rather than breathing salt air from behind a ship's wheel. *Impossible! It must never be!* my soul strained to cry out. I could not bear to think of him so sadly brought down, domesticated beyond all recognition. Instead of saying what I felt, however, I was obliged to restrain myself. I took a deep breath to calm my agitated feelings and then asked, "Does Captain Devereaux know all this? Does he understand what you and your father have planned for him?"

"Not as I have just told you, no. And before you censure me, Jane, hear me out. I have tried to talk to him about it ever since we became engaged; honestly, I have. I wanted to give him a hint to start him thinking. But whenever I suggest we should begin making plans for the future, he says it can wait. He says I should concentrate only on getting well for now, and that there will be time enough later for the rest. So what am I to do, since he will not listen to me?"

"You must *make* him listen, Bernadette. Now, before you are married. He must not find out your feelings and plans only after the wedding, when it is…" I stopped myself saying the rest.

"When it is what?"

When it is too late! But here again, I did not say what I wanted but what courtesy demanded. "Oh, nothing. I only meant that it is important that you should be honest with him from the beginning. It would not do to start off your marriage on the wrong foot. Do not you agree?"

Bernadette did agree, or perhaps she only said the words to appease me. For, despite my cautions, she seemed remarkably unconcerned, as if she still presumed Captain Devereaux would happily acquiesce to her wishes when the time came.

I could not be so sanguine and considered that it might have been better had she never told me so much, given that I was powerless to do anything about it. Rather, I was then sentenced to anguish over the business in her stead. It alarmed me that my friends – for so I considered them both – could be blindly walking into a most unfortunate future. The thought of Captain Devereaux being made to give up his seafaring ways at his wife's behest did not bode well, in my opinion. Nor did the idea that he might refuse to do so. What satisfaction was to be found for either of them then? One would surely end by resenting the other. The only question was which?

-22-

Anne would see if it rained. She was sent back, however, in a moment by the entrance of Captain Wentworth himself, among a party of gentlemen and ladies, evidently his acquaintance, and whom he must have joined a little below Milsom-street. He was more obviously struck and confused by the sight of her than she had ever observed before; he looked quite red. For the first time, since their renewed acquaintance, she felt that she was betraying the least sensibility of the two. She had the advantage of him in the preparation of the last few moments. All the overpowering, blinding, bewildering, first effects of strong surprise were over with her. Still, however, she had enough to feel! It was agitation, pain, pleasure, and something between delight and misery.

He spoke to her, and then turned away. The character of his manner was embarrassment. She could not have called it either cold or friendly, or any thing so certainly as embarrassed.

After a short interval, however, he came towards her and spoke again…

These things I now set down in Anne and Captain Wentworth's book. They are meeting again, in Bath, for the first time since their parting after Louisa's accident, and more importantly, for the first time since his being made a free man again. And what a meeting it is, embodying a myriad of hopes and fears, agitations and ecstasies, not only for the mere fact of seeing one another again, of thrilling in each other's presence, but also for what may follow. Anne had quite enough to feel indeed! Added to the sentiments already mentioned, she is now at liberty to feel one more: hope, glorious hope. Although the ultimate outcome is not yet secured, the insurmountable obstacle has inexplicably been surmounted, and all things are possible again.

How very different by necessity were my sentiments when I saw Captain Devereaux again in Bath.

It was at Molland's; it did rain; and he was embarrassed. This much is true. But in every other particular, it was more like I have since imagined and written of the meeting between another pair, a pair by the names of Edward Ferrars and Elinor Dashwood, when they knew themselves to be divided forever, also through an engagement kept more by honour than affection.

Cassandra and I were waiting for the weather to improve before continuing on our way, when I chanced to catch a glimpse of Captain Devereaux out in the street. A minute later, he was opening the door and walking through it. We were suddenly face to face again.

I had known he was coming to Bath and that we must in all likelihood meet. It had been only a question of exactly when and where the event would occur. I knew also that when we did meet again I must congratulate him on his engagement. And still I was unprepared for the flood of sensibility which overtook me when I saw him that day. I supposed I had rather hoped he would look somehow different and less attractive, now that he was officially unavailable. Instead, he was just the same, as handsome and appealing as ever. My brain turned to jelly and would not function. Words failed me. My spirits nearly did as well. He was equally discomposed – uneasy and not knowing what to say. So we, neither of us, said a word. We just stood gaping at each other, three feet apart.

It was Cassandra who broke the awkward silence. "Captain Devereaux, how pleasant to see you again. I hope you are well."

The captain shook off his reverie and turned to my sister. "Miss Austen, how kind. Yes, I am very well. I trust you and all your family are in health also."

"We are, thank you. And we have heard that you are to be congratulated."

This was my prompting to likewise meet my obligation. "Yes, do allow us to wish you joy, Captain," I said more blithely than I intended.

After he accepted our compliments with evident discomfort, Cassandra excused herself on the pretense of wishing to make a purchase of Papa's favourite marzipan.

And then we were alone. In spite of the various noises of the room, the slamming of the door and the ceaseless buzz of the persons walking through, I could attend to no one but Captain Devereaux and he to me. I was struck, gratified, and confused at this. My breath came quickly, and I felt an hundred things at once. All I knew was that I did not wish the moment to end, and that I must say something, anything, to sustain it.

"You were... You were a good while at Sidmouth, I think," I finally observed. "It must have been a dreadful time of suspense for you."

He gathered himself before answering, "Yes, it was, but I did my best to keep occupied. I walked and rode a great deal. The country round about is very fine. The more I saw, the more I found to admire."

"I should very much like to see Sidmouth again."

"Indeed? I should not have supposed that you could have found any thing there to inspire such a feeling. The horror and distress you were involved in – the stretch of mind, the wear of spirits."

"The last part was certainly very painful, yes. But one does not love a place the less for having suffered in it, not unless it has been nothing but suffering, which was by no means the case at Sidmouth. Previously, there had been a great deal of enjoyment – so much novelty and beauty. Altogether my impressions of the place are very agreeable."

There was a pause while he seemed to be deciding whether to say more or keep his next thought to himself. Then he moved a little closer to me and dropped his voice. "Miss Austen, I can only imagine what you must be thinking of this news, this engagement between Miss Cumphries and myself. What I mean is..." He broke off and a look of consciousness passed between us.

"I am thinking nothing at all," I lied, "other than my wish for you both to be very happy. You have done the honourable thing, Captain. You have stood by my friend through her illness, and now I hope your steadfastness will be rewarded."

He shook his head. "You are very good to say so. It has been all my own doing, though, this unfortunate business."

Since I could not acknowledge what I believed to be his true meaning, I deliberately misunderstood him. "You must not be so severe upon yourself, sir, taking the blame for Bernadette's accident. You warned her against the danger, and then saved her when she fell. Certainly this must exonerate you in everybody's eyes."

"Not in my own, I assure you. I had been carelessly playing at something I had no business doing. And now the ramifications, the persons affected..." He looked away, and I could see him struggling for composure before he was able to continue. "Miss Austen... Jane, I believe I have wronged you more than anybody."

I inhaled sharply at this and then took a moment to relish the sincerity of his admission and the warmth of his gaze before responding. "You are mistaken, Captain," I said. "You owe me no apologies. As your friend, naturally I am proud that you have done your duty. Beyond that, however, I do not see where I enter into the matter. It is Miss Cumphries you must now look to please. My feelings can no longer be any of your concern."

"It is as you say, regrettably so. I suppose I must take my comfort in the fact that you still call me your friend. You will never know how much that means to me, Jane."

It was more than I could bear – hearing him utter my name, the anguish in his voice and expression, the tender way he looked at me. I knew I must extricate myself before all self-command was lost. "Will you excuse me, Captain?" I said hastily. "I see the rain has let up, so my sister and I must be on our way."

"Of course," he said, stepping back to unbar my way. "I have no right to detain you any longer."

I found Cassandra at the counter, laced my arm through hers, interrupting her purchase, and all but dragged her from the shop.

I would have been particularly obliged to my sister if she had walked by my side all the way to Sydney Place without saying a word. I had never found it more difficult to listen to her. Though nothing could exceed her solicitude and care, just then I could think only of Captain Devereaux. I believed I understood his present feelings, and the flutter of spirits that information excited in me was not to be recovered from immediately. No doubt I would be wise and reasonable again in time, but not at once.

~~*~~

I made brief visits to Bernadette in the days that followed, never staying long for fear of encountering Captain Devereaux there or of revealing too much of my hidden sentiments to my friend. Continuing to improve in strength and spirits, Bernadette was soon ready to make her first foray back out into society. An evening concert had been decided on, with all her friends alongside.

My family was the earliest of all our party at the rooms; and as Mr. Cumphries and his daughter must be waited for, we took our station by one of the empty hearths in the octagon room. We were hardly settled there when the door opened again and Captain Bothwell walked in alone. I was the nearest to him and, making yet a little advance, I greeted him instantly. He joined us in waiting as we filled our time with talk of the weather and of the concert we were to hear. Admiral and Mrs. Crowe were the next to arrive, followed lastly by Bernadette, supported on the arms of both her father and Captain Devereaux. With the whole party now collected, we marshaled ourselves and proceeded into the concert room.

Many eyes turned our way when we entered, not to see me or most of the others. They doubtless strained for a look at the young lady who was by then known in all Bath as one who had come through a most harrowing experience in Sidmouth, dually celebrated for having been drowned and also for having survived it. Captain Devereaux must be looked at as well, of course, earning his share of admiration for the twin heroics of saving Miss Cumphries and then proposing marriage to her.

Our party was divided and disposed of on two contiguous benches. I had maneuvered so well as to place Cassandra on my one side and Captain Bothwell on the other in the foremost bench, my motive being to escape the unhappy prospect of observing Bernadette and her escort any more than absolutely necessary.

My mind was in a most favourable state for the entertainment of the evening, as it was just occupation enough to distract me from my troubles. In fact, I had never liked a concert better, at least during the first act. Toward the close of it, in the interval succeeding an Italian song, I endeavoured to decipher some of the words from the performance for Captain Bothwell, with whom I shared a concert bill.

"I am a very poor Italian scholar," I said by way of an apology when I had given up the attempt. "It is a love song, and so perhaps does not bear too close a translation; it would hardly be proper to discuss such things."

"I thank you for trying nonetheless," said he. "A little Italian is still something I cannot help but admiring. And it is but one of your many accomplishments. The fact that you are modest of your own claims is simply another of your charms."

"For shame, Captain!" I protested, even as I laughed. "This is too much flattery. You cannot be sincere."

"On the contrary, my dear Miss Jane. It is no more than half as much praise as you deserve. The world must be made aware, and I am happy to do it." Dropping his voice and leaning a little closer, he added, "After all, I did volunteer myself as your champion. Miss Cumphries must not have all the attention tonight."

This induced me to glance over my shoulder at the lady mentioned. Instead, my gaze fell on the gentleman beside her: Captain Devereaux. He had been looking my way too, at least it had that appearance. He immediately masked his expression, however, and withdrew his eyes.

During the tea break, when we were all moving about, except Bernadette and her father, Captain Devereaux continued to avoid me. I noticed he did not speak to Captain Bothwell either, not for the entire length of the interval. It was unaccountable.

I now write Anne into a similar scene and sensations:

The anxious interval wore away unproductively. The others returned, the room filled again, benches were reclaimed and repossessed, and another hour of pleasure or of penance was to be set out, another hour of music was to give delight or the gapes, as real or affected taste for it prevailed. To Anne, it chiefly wore the prospect of an hour of agitation. She could not quit that room in peace without seeing Captain Wentworth once more, without the interchange of one friendly look.

I was just as anxious for a friendly look from my captain. I say 'my captain,' when of course he really belonged to Bernadette. But that is why a friendly look was all I hoped for. After our conversation at Molland's, I did not think it more than what should be reasonable, more than my due. Yet here was a return to the grave and disapproving Captain Devereaux.

Between songs, I heard him speaking behind me of the concert, owning himself disappointed. "…In short, I must confess that I shall be just as happy when it is over."

I could not keep silent while he was so obviously and inexplicably discontented. In hopes of encouraging him, I turned and said, "Perhaps it does not measure up to what one would expect in London or Paris, Captain, but it is certainly finer music than anything I have been accustomed to in the country. I will say that much for the claims of Bath. I am certain you will think better of this next song.

Although I am unfamiliar with it myself, Captain Bothwell has just been recommending it to me most enthusiastically."

Philippe's mouth hardened at this. "No," he declared, glaring at Captain Bothwell. "I doubt a mere song could be worth my staying for, despite what anybody may say. I shall remain only to be of service to Miss Cumphries."

Bernadette smiled at him and squeezed his arm, which seemed to give him some discomfort. The picture of them so closely connected pained me as well, that is until I was suddenly struck by a new idea, one which I could not dismiss. Could it be that he was jealous, I wondered, jealous of Captain Bothwell's marked attentions to me? It would be unreasonable, but that did not signify in the least. Reason plays very little share in affairs of the heart.

The more I thought about it, the more certain I became that jealousy for my affection was the true and only explanation for his behaviour. Thinking back, I could now see there had been signs of it even in Sidmouth – his over-listening of my conversations with Captain Bothwell, dark looks in our direction when we were together – but I could not have believed it before. Perhaps it had been that same jealously that had rekindled (or at least made him aware of) the esteem he still felt for me.

For a moment, the gratification I felt at this was quite exquisite. But alas! It could be nothing more than a private satisfaction. The consciousness had come too late to be acted on. It could lead to nothing, for he was bound to another.

-23-

I saw Captain Devereaux several times more in Bath over the course of the next two weeks, always in company with some one or other of our mutual friends. On a few of these occasions, he was pleasant to me; at others he confirmed by his churlishness that it vexed him greatly to see Captain Bothwell attentively by my side. If Captain Bothwell noticed the change in his friend's demeanour, he did not say so to me. I suspected he not only knew of Philippe's jealousy, but courted it on my account. Regardless, I hoped the friendship between the two men survived this charade, which would be over soon enough.

None of these incidental meetings with Captain Devereaux provided opportunity for another intimate conversation such as we had shared that day at Molland's, which was no doubt just as well. For what was there to be gained by our further exploring into forbidden territory, by a more frank acknowledgement of the persisting bond between us? What could be hoped for beyond the opening of new wounds?

Finally, the day of my departure for Godmersham was upon me. Since it would put an end to any further encounters with Captain Devereaux, I welcomed it with a kind of bittersweet relief. The thought of never seeing him again wrenched me with anguish, and yet there was one thing still worse: standing by to watch him marry another woman. I hoped to be spared that rare form of torture by spending as little time as possible in Bath. After a month or more with my brother Edward and his wife Elizabeth at Godmersham, Cassandra and I were invited to the Biggs at Manydown Park. Perhaps a visit to my brother James at Steventon might be arranged too. In the meantime, however, there would be one more perilous gathering to face at Bath.

My parents had organised an afternoon party at Sydney Place in consideration of our going away – Cassandra's and mine, with Charles as our escort – to which all our friends were invited. The guest list, of course, included Captain Devereaux.

Alternatively, it is an *evening* party to which my pen now dictates Captain Wentworth should be invited – most particularly invited. Anne cannot help being a little ashamed of her father and sister when they condescend to present the card to him, as if the insolence of the past is nothing that their current overtures will not easily erase, as if he must consider it an honour to be asked to attend the baronet and his family.

The truth is, though, that the Elliots have been long enough in Bath to understand the importance of a man of such an air and appearance as his. Captain Wentworth will move about well in their drawing-room. That it is all that signifies. But Anne sees the hint of distain in the captain's eye, and she cannot be at all sanguine of his accepting the engagement. I write…

> *She closed the fatigues of the present, by a toilsome walk to Camden-place, there to spend the evening chiefly in listening to the busy arrangements of Elizabeth and Mrs. Clay for the morrow's party, the frequent enumeration of the persons invited, and the continually improving detail of all the embellishments which were to make it the most completely elegant of its kind in Bath, while harassing herself in secret with the never-ending question, of whether Captain Wentworth would come or not? They were reckoning him as certain but, with her, it was a gnawing solicitude never appeased for five minutes together. She generally thought he would come, because she generally thought he ought; but it was a case which she could not so shape into any positive act of duty or discretion, as inevitably to defy the suggestions of very opposite feelings.*

Poor Anne.

No, lucky Anne! She will be kept in dreadful suspense no longer. Surprising events are about to unfold, revolutionary events, events of a morning such as she will surely never forget. Once again, these things I now create as counterpoints to what occurred in my own life, although to a different end. They owe their crucial essence to my own history. They are a true reflection of all that was best and brightest between Jane and Philippe, now refashioned for Anne and Frederick.

I do not begrudge them their good fortune. On the contrary, I rejoice for them as I continue their story:

> When she reached the White Heart, and made her way to the proper apartment, she found herself neither arriving quite in time, nor the first to arrive. The party before her were Mrs. Musgrove, talking to Mrs. Croft, and Captain Harville to Captain Wentworth, and she immediately heard that Mary and Henrietta, too impatient to wait, had gone out the moment it had cleared, but would be back again soon, and that the strictest injunctions had been left with Mrs. Musgrove to keep her there till they returned. She had only to submit, sit down, be outwardly composed, and feel herself plunged at once in all the agitations which she had merely laid her account of tasting a little before the morning closed. There was no delay, no waste of time. She was deep in the happiness of such misery, or the misery of such happiness, instantly.

Instantly in Captain Wentworth's presence again. Looks are exchanged, a telling conversation overheard, a letter of vital importance written by the gentleman and read by the lady after he is gone:

> I can listen no longer in silence. I must speak to you by such means as are within my reach. You pierce my soul. I am half agony, half hope. Tell me not that I am too late, that such precious feelings are gone for ever. I offer myself to you again with a heart even more your own, than when you almost broke it eight years and a half ago. Dare not say that man forgets sooner than woman, that his love has an earlier death. I have loved none but you. Unjust I may have been, weak and resentful I have been, but never inconstant. You alone have brought me to Bath. For you alone I think and plan. Have you not seen this? Can you fail to have understood my wishes? I had not waited even these ten days, could I have read your feelings, as I think you must have penetrated mine. I can hardly write. I am every instant hearing something which overpowers me. You sink your voice, but I can distinguish the tones of that voice, when they would be lost on others. Too good, too excellent creature!

You do us justice indeed. You do believe that there is true attachment and constancy among men. Believe it to be most fervent, most undeviating in – F.W.

What woman could read such a letter and not be moved? Anne Elliot cannot. For her, it is fresh agitation and all-consuming happiness at once. And yet no tranquillity will be possible until she speaks to him, until she hears the avowal of his love repeated by his own lips; her ears must confirm the impossible things her eyes have seen written on the page before she will believe it.

They meet again on Union-street.

There they exchanged again those feelings and those promises which had once before seemed to secure every thing, but which had been followed by so many, many years of division and estrangement. There they returned again into the past, more exquisitely happy, perhaps, in their reunion than when it had been first projected; more tender, more tried, more fixed in a knowledge of each other's character, truth, and attachment; more equal to act, more justified in acting. And there, as they slowly paced the gradual ascent, heedless of every group around them, seeing neither sauntering politicians, bustling housekeepers, flirting girls, nor nursery maids and children, they could indulge in those retrospections and acknowledgments, and especially in those explanations of what had directly preceded the present moment, which were so poignant and so ceaseless in interest.

Of what he had written just then in the letter, nothing is to be retracted or qualified. He has loved none but her. He had meant to forget her; he had imagined himself indifferent, when he had only been angry; and he had been unjust to her merits, because he had been a sufferer from them. At Uppercross he had learnt to do her character justice again, but only at Lyme had he begun to understand himself. By then, however, it was too late. In his resentment, he had attempted to attach himself to Louisa Musgrove. Instead, he had only succeeded in entangling himself. He had remained, lamenting the blindness of his own pride and the blunders of his own calculations, till suddenly released by the astonishing intelligence of Louisa's engagement with Benwick. Then at last he could do something. He would go to Bath at once and try Anne again.

"Was it unpardonable to think it worth my while to come, and to arrive with some degree of hope? You were single. It was possible that you might retain the feelings of the past, as I did; and one encouragement happened to be mine. I could never doubt that you would be loved and sought by others, but I knew to a certainty that you had refused one man at least, of better pretensions than myself. And I could not help often saying, 'Was this for me?'"

All other questions and misunderstandings are soon done away with, all former objections soon consigned to their proper places, till Anne has nothing left to either wish or fear. It is expeditiously settled between them that they are to be as happy together as humanly possible, with only enough regret from the past remaining to remind them never to take their current felicity for granted. Captain Wentworth, especially, feels the truth of it.

"This is a recollection which ought to make me forgive every one sooner than myself. Six years of separation and suffering might have been spared. It is a sort of pain, too, which is new to me. I have been used to the gratification of believing myself to earn every blessing that I enjoyed. I have valued myself on honourable toils and just rewards. Like other great men under reverses," he added with a smile, *"I must endeavour to subdue my mind to my fortune. I must learn to brook being happier than I deserve."*

Who can doubt what will follow? A Captain Wentworth and an Anne Elliot, with the advantage of maturity of mind, consciousness of right, and one independent fortune between them, cannot fail of bearing down all remaining resistance, all the want of graciousness among her friends. These will be as a minor annoyance, not worthy of their notice – the hum of a passing insect, the possibility of a shower. For the insect's days on this earth are few, and the shower will soon be driven off by the power of the irrepressible sun.

So shall their love be, the captain and his lady: bright, never ending, a life-giving force. It will warm all those who gather round them, bless all those who wish them well, and scorch with unquenchable fire any person who dares attempt to come between them. Anne and Captain Wentworth are incandescent; they are untouchable, living on forever in a state of bliss beyond the reach of most mere mortals. This is my gift to them.

No, that is not entirely true. I cannot claim credit, for I am become merely the scribe. I may have first set them loose on the page, but the lovers have long since taken possession of their own story. They have determined their own course. They have dictated to me what will be their outcome. In truth, I am the one who has been the recipient of a gift, for they have allowed me to look on. They have shared with me their thoughts and feelings. They have given me joy in their own finding of happiness.

This is true of all the others as well: Catherine and Mr. Tilney, Emma and Mr. Knightley, Elinor and Edward, Marianne and Colonel Brandon, Jane and Mr. Bingley, Elizabeth and Mr. Darcy. Who am I forgetting? Oh, yes, Fanny Price and Edmund Bertram. They have all given me joy. They have filled my life with meaning. They have been my true friends and most comforting consolation over the course of these many years.

These are treasures I will carry with me always, to the end of my days. I hope that I may in some form also take them with me when my time on this earth is done. I believe it cannot be long. For months now, even as I continued at my work, I have had the sensation of my life slipping away, sifting inevitably through my fingers like so much sand. I begin to think that this persistent illness of mine will not be satisfied until it has claimed me completely.

If God ordains it, then who am I to complain? Though I should be sorry to leave the pleasures of this world, I will not be sorry to leave behind its pain and heartaches. I will go when He calls me, confident that the best is yet to come, that the blessings of heaven will far outshine what I leave behind.

But first, I am determined to finish my own story, that of my ill-fated romance with Captain Devereaux. Though our conclusion cannot compare to the lofty heights Anne and Captain Wentworth have now achieved, our final chapters must have their proper share. They not only contributed vastly to that other couple's happiness by inspiring what I have written in their book. But our finale, for its own sake, I think, very much deserves to be told.

-24-

As I related before, my parents had organised an afternoon party at Sydney Place in consideration of our going away, which was to be the last time I would see Captain Devereaux. That is, if he would come at all. I was by no means confident of his appearing at my father's door that afternoon or even certain I should desire he would. I wondered if either of us could bear seeing one another again, knowing that the end of that brief interval would part us, probably forever. The previous meeting between us – a chance encounter on the street, as it happened to be – had been far less laden with significance. Perhaps that would be as Philippe would prefer to leave it. Yes, let that impersonal, inconsequential five minutes of nothingness be our epilogue. It would be fitting that the thing should die, not with a terrible wail but with an inaudible whimper.

He did not come.

Bernadette arrived with her father at the appointed time. So did my aunt and uncle, the Crowes, and a handful of other guests. But a half hour passed and then a whole, with no sign of Captain Devereaux. Although I had convinced myself it would be for the best if he did not come, I was crushed by disappointment nonetheless. I could not help feeling it, and no doubt I looked it as well, for Captain Bothwell soon came to my aid. This also was to be for the last time, since he was going away in a few days himself, away from Bath and returning to his mother in Sidmouth.

Captain Bothwell – once again acting with the easy kindness that usually marks an older acquaintance than he really was – began with a little light-hearted banter, telling me an amusing anecdote about something which had occurred that morning, how he had seen two women arguing over a fish at the market, only to have the thing run away with by a stray dog instead – no very satisfactory outcome for either fishmonger or patrons.

A few minutes later, however, the captain drew me aside from the others, to an open window where there was at least a little breeze to counteract the stifling air of that hot September day. I could see by his manner that he had something very particular he wished to discuss. He wasted no time broaching the intended subject either. His countenance taking on a serious, thoughtful expression, he produced a small parcel from his pocket and began unwrapping it.

"Look here," he said, displaying an oval miniature painting of a young lady – a rare beauty according to the rendering. "Do you know who this is?"

I shook my head, not wishing to hazard an awkward guess.

"It is Miss Hammermaster, of whom I told you. Mrs. Evanston, I suppose I should say now, but she was Miss Hammermaster right enough then. She had this portrait drawn for me – a present before I went off to the war – that I should carry it in testament to her promise of marrying me when I returned."

I dutifully admired the picture as he so obviously wished me to do. "She is a lovely woman," I said sincerely, "and it was laudable, the sentiment with which she gave this to you. Although things did not turn out as you had hoped, perhaps carrying the picture brought you at least a little luck, for you did survive to come home."

"Aye, that is something." He glanced back down at the painting in his hand. "I still take this out from time to time, just to look at her face. I suppose it is wrong of me, now she is another man's wife. I might do better to have the thing made over to her husband, rather than keeping it to remind me of…" He stopped and shook his head. "How little I thought then that… Well, no matter; it is all in the past." He tucked the miniature back into his pocket with a sigh.

Searching for a word of consolation, I finally said, "She loved you once, though. That knowledge must be some comfort to you."

"I don't know about that, Miss Austen. Has such knowledge been any comfort to you?" He closed his eyes a moment and rubbed his forehead. "Forgive me. That was unfair. No, I take no comfort in such fickle affection as Miss Hammermaster felt for me. I cannot even call it love, for her actions fly in the face of the ideas I have long held on that subject. But perhaps it was not her fault. Perhaps it is not in a woman's nature to be constant when confronted with adversity."

In this I saw an opportunity to return to more comfortable ground. It was an opening for debate, which would do us more good than melancholy recollections of the past. "I can by no means allow such a statement to pass by unchallenged, Captain Bothwell!" I said. "Any woman who truly loves must be capable of constancy, even more so than a man. We do not forget you, so soon as you forget us."

"Indeed? This is an extraordinary claim you make for your sex, Miss Austen. On what do you base it?"

I could see that I had at least succeeded in distracting him from his troubles. His eyes brightened as he entered into the spirit of the discussion.

"It is perhaps our fate rather than our merit," I continued. "We cannot help ourselves. We live at home, quiet, confined, and our feelings prey upon us. You are forced to move on by some exertion. You have always a profession, pursuits, business of some sort or other to take you back into the world. Continual occupation and change must further assist a nature already more inclined to inconstancy."

"No, no, I will not allow it to be more man's nature than woman's to be inconstant and forget those they do love, or have loved! I believe the reverse is true. Just as our bodily frames are stronger, more capable of bearing rough usage, so it is with our feelings. They are also stronger and will weather the heaviest storms."

"Even if I were to grant you your assertion (which, however, I am not prepared to do), your own analogy will not support you. Man may be the more robust, but he is not the longer-lived, which exactly explains my view of the nature of their attachments – violent, perhaps, but burning out too quickly."

"We may never agree, Miss Austen, but let me just observe that all histories are against you, all stories, prose and verse. They all speak of a woman's fickleness."

"And they were all written by men. No, spare me any references to books. Men have had every advantage of us in telling their own stories. Education has been theirs in so much higher a degree; the pen has been in their hands. I will not agree to books proving anything."

"Then how is the question to be decided between us?"

"I am persuaded that it never shall be, Captain Bothwell. As you said yourself, we may never agree. We each began with a little bias towards our own sex, and then we have built every circumstance that has occurred within our own circles to support it. We cannot bring forward as evidence our friends' experiences, not without betraying a confidence. And as to our own…"

"Yes, we each know something of the matter. But it is not a thing that admits to being weighed and measured, is it? I cannot prove – nor do I wish to – that my suffering has exceeded your own."

"That is just what I think. And I hope I do justice to men such as yourself, Captain Bothwell, men who have hearts. I believe you capable of everything great and good. I believe you equal to every important exertion and every domestic forbearance, so long as – if I may be allowed the expression – so long as the woman you love lives and lives for you. All the privilege I claim for my own sex is that of loving longest when all hope is gone."

I could not immediately have uttered another word; my heart was too full, my breath too much oppressed. Whereas I had intended to divert the conversation into safer territory, instead we had come full circle, arriving back round at the crux of the matter again.

"You are a good soul," cried Captain Bothwell affectionately. "There is no quarrelling with you, is there? And I shall miss our spirited debates. How sad that we must now be parted."

I was just about to say something of my wish that we might meet again, when a small noise called my attention outside. Captain Bothwell and I both had our backs partially turned to the open window until that point. Now we pivoted in unison to locate the cause of the sound we had heard. I looked down at the street and there, at a distance of only a few feet away, was Captain Devereux, looking back up at us.

I started violently at seeing him, and I felt my face grow hot in an instant. How long had he been standing there, I wondered? What had he heard me say? Had his quick mind penetrated my meaning, understood that he had been at the very core of all that I had spoken? There was no time for further conjecture, however.

Philippe had his finger to his lips to silence any exclamations on our side. He said nothing himself, only signaling with his other hand that one of us should come down to him, although it was not immediately apparent which one. Captain Bothwell, naturally supposing it should be him, raised his eyebrows in question and pointed to himself. No. Captain Devereaux shook his head and turned his beseeching gaze more distinctly towards me. I was the one Captain Devereaux wished to see.

I hesitated. Would it be proper, I asked myself. Would it be wise to speak to him alone? What could he, an engaged man, have to say to me that did not bear being heard by Captain Bothwell, Bernadette, or any other?

Almost inaudibly, Philippe whispered the word. "Please."

His look was so urgent, so pleading, that I could not deny him. In truth, I did not wish to deny him. I hesitated no longer. I shrugged one shoulder at Captain Bothwell and began a casual stroll across the room towards the exit. A smile at one guest here, a word to another there – nothing out of the ordinary, nothing to draw any undue attention. Then, when no one appeared to be looking my way, I slipped quickly and quietly down the stairs and out the door.

It is silly, I know, but in doing so I felt like an inmate escaping, a prisoner fleeing my captors, certain that at any moment I would be discovered and dragged back inside where I belonged. My heart beat wildly as if I were risking great danger. In truth, nothing much would have happened, even had I been found out. But no one came after me. No one, I believe, even knew I was missing from the party for those fifteen or twenty minutes except Captain Bothwell.

As soon as I emerged from the door, Captain Devereaux was at my side, taking my elbow and steering me down and across the street into Sydney Park. Only after we were well away from the house did either of us speak.

"Thank you for seeing me," he said presently.

"Are you not coming in, Captain?"

"No, I had been pacing the sidewalk, trying to make up my mind to do it when I saw – and heard – you and Bothwell in earnest conversation at the window."

I shot him a sharp, sidelong look.

"Yes, I know. Over-listening conversations is a bad habit, one for which you have reprimanded me before. Believe me, my conscience smote me at once, but then I was hearing things which overpowered me and I could not turn away." He stopped, faced me, and took both my gloved hands in his. "Jane," he said with feeling, "you pierced my soul by your words, and I am in agony. Dare not say that man forgets sooner than woman, that his love has an earlier death."

He broke off and released my hands. I saw he was struggling, and yet I knew not how to help him. "You disagree?" I finally asked softly.

"I not only disagree, I know this to be false! And yet…" Here, he stopped again, closed his eyes, and dropped his chin to his chest. He drew a deep, shuddering breath, in and out. When he had regained mastery of himself, he continued. "I know it to be false, Jane, and yet honour prevents me saying more. You comprehend me, though. You grasp my impossible situation. The only thing I am at liberty to hope now is that we two may be finally and completely reconciled… as friends… before you go away. Even this may be asking too much.

"I had been angry with you for so long, Jane. It was probably unfair of me from the beginning; I *know* it was wrong of me to continue indulging such feelings as I did. For this I will forever pay the price. I shut my mind and would not understand you or do your motives justice. But I swear I am a wiser man now – wisdom painfully acquired – and my resentments are all done away with. Your slate is wiped clean. If I could only be assured of your absolution as well, I believe I could face the future with some measure of peace."

"You apologised to me once before, at Molland's. Remember?"

"I tried, but you would not listen then."

"I am listening now, Philippe."

He smiled a little at this, at hearing me use his Christian name again, I suppose. "Good," he said. "Do not pretend that I have nothing for which to ask your pardon, because I know better. I have spoilt our last chance at happiness, haven't I?"

I started to protest, but he went on.

"No use in denying it; it is true. But we had best not speak of it. I will only ask you this. Will you accept my apology and say that I am forgiven? Can you do that, Jane? Will you at least consider it?"

"There is no need to consider. I forgive you, Philippe, freely and with all my heart."

He looked me in the eye very directly, judging the sincerity of my answer. Apparently satisfied, the tension in his countenance eased, the taut muscles of his jaw relaxed. I saw relief in his expression, relief, gratitude, and perhaps a measure of inner joy. "Thank you," he said after a moment. "This shall have to be enough for me."

We had taken our conversation, our advance toward the acknowledgement of our true feelings, as far as we dared go. It would not have been right to go further, nor was there any need. I knew without a single doubt that Captain Devereux and I understood each other. We had communicated our meaning in every look exchanged and by the pungent undertones of our words. Although our love could not be declared openly, it was nonetheless blazing through from just beyond the veil.

All too soon it was time to put such otherworldly thoughts behind us. We both felt it. After one last thoughtful pause, we turned back toward my door and toward harsh reality.

"And now, we must both take courage and move forward along our separate paths," said the captain.

"Yes, we must," I agreed.

"My course is clear. My fate is already marked out for me. But you, Jane, what will you do? Shall you marry my friend Bothwell? He is an excellent fellow, you know. He would take good care of you." He said this as if he had made up his mind to do it, though it pained him deeply.

"I agree; he is the very best of men, but I shall *not* marry Captain Bothwell. He is more like a brother to me, and that would never do. No, I shall be content enough to remain single. I will always have my sister for companionship, and I shall never want for occupation."

"You will pursue your writing ambitions then? Excellent! This is a worthy goal for you, and one day I hope to hear you are a great success, a celebrated author."

"Indeed, sir, I hope you hear of no such thing! For it should mortify me exceedingly to have my name bandied about like some person of notoriety. No, my books must be the popular ones. People may look at and talk about them as much as they like. I will remain in the shadows, or perhaps more like a fly on the wall, listening to what they say."

"Anonymous?"

"Exactly. After all, it is not thought respectable for a lady to have a profession, and novels are still not considered quite the thing."

"The person – lady or gentleman – who takes no pleasure in a good novel must be extraordinarily stupid. But, perhaps you will be the one who converts them, Jane, the one who converts the whole world to reading novels. It is a pity, though, that the world will never know to whom they are indebted for their enlightenment."

In the years since that day, I have revisited this, our last conversation, many times. In a small way, I have perhaps fulfilled Captain Devereaux's prophecy. Four novels from my own pen have now circulated out into the world, all published anonymously. I have hope that there may eventually be more. *Susan*, now become *Catherine*, has been kept waiting far too long, and Anne Elliot's story deserves to be read as well. I am happy for my books' modest success. And I am equally happy for my quiet spot beyond the scrutiny of the public eye.

It has been a good life – different from the one I once so dearly desired, but no less valuable for all that. If I could but know with certainty that my dear Captain Devereaux is also well, I should be entirely content. But I do not know it, and I suppose I never shall.

-25-

I never saw Captain Devereaux after that last day at Bath. He returned me to my father's door; he kissed my hand; we each took one last look; and then he resolutely strode away.

I desperately wished to call him back. Despite the pact we had just made to be strong, I felt like giving in to every weakness, like indulging my selfish side, like snatching that remarkable man away from my poor friend and keeping him for myself. Would he have deserted Bernadette for me had I asked him to that day? Perhaps, but it would have been his undoing. He would have lost all respect for himself, as well as for me for having tempted him to act against his principles.

I could not do it. I let him go, and I decamped for Godmersham the next morning, where I remained until the end of October.

When I returned briefly that November to Bath, I found a note Bernadette had left for me at Sydney Place.

My dearest Jane,
Papa has been recalled to London – some pressing matter at the bank – so I, of course, go with him. You must write to me there from now on, for I do not know when if ever we shall come back to Bath. Things are now in a fair train for a June wedding. I continue to regain my health and strength apace, so I expect to be fully recovered by then. I know you will be wondering whether or not I have discussed the future with Captain Devereaux, as you so sternly advised me to do. Let me have the pleasure of setting your mind at ease on that score. We have now ventured onto the subject, and he means to make no difficulties about it. It is settled

that we are to be the happiest couple in the world. I hope you will be present to wish us joy on our wedding day. Write to me often, Jane. I shall send more details of the date, etc., as soon as our plans are in place.

*Yours ever,
Bernadette*

I did answer her letter, congratulating her on the continued improvement in her health as well as the improvement in her understanding with Captain Devereaux. After that, however, I thought it most prudent to allow our friendship to die the quiet death of abject neglect, and our correspondence soon came to an end. I could not be continually hearing of Bernadette's plans and her happiness with Captain Devereaux, not if I wished to retain my sanity and get on.

That was my one simple goal: to somehow get on with my life, whatever sort of life it could be without Captain Devereaux. As I had told him, I expected to remain single – both because I believed I could never love anyone but him, and because I was not likely at seven-and-twenty to have another choice. I was a little mistaken in this last part, however.

Cassandra and I went on to Manydown Park at the end of the month, where, I am sorry to say, I behaved very badly. Perhaps it was the knowledge that Captain Devereaux meant to compromise his future by Bernadette's wish that made me think I could consider compromise as well. At any rate, when Harris, the younger brother of our good friends Catherine and Alethea Bigg, awkwardly proposed marriage to me there, I disgraced myself by accepting him. Then I further disgraced myself by taking back my promise the next morning. Although to preserve the engagement would only have compounded my error, correcting it was nearly as dreadful, and it is to this day an embarrassment which I would prefer to forget.

After that humiliation, I consoled myself with work. I had made very little progress on my writing in the time since we had come to Bath, but now I threw myself into the endeavour as if my life depended on it. I have often thought since that the occupation did indeed save me by giving me light and purpose at a very dark time. I believe writing was my true calling all along, my destiny with which nothing was allowed to interfere – no husband, no children, no domestic distractions. It comforts me to think so, that I was only deprived of one set of pleasures for the fulfillment of another, equally as good or perhaps better.

So I set about a comprehensive revision on the manuscript of *Susan* that winter, infusing it with new life and poignancy – things drawn from my recently expanded experience in the field of romance. I added a phrase here and there, a bit of dialogue or a description of feeling as it had not been in my power before to envision. The same is true of the other novels. All of them were either written or revised to convey the more mature understanding I afterward possessed because of knowing Captain Devereaux. His influence is everywhere apparent... to me, at least. His fingerprints and mine mingle on each page. The books are become our true offspring – his and mine together – for I could not have produced them without his help.

I soon stopped trying to put Captain Devereaux out of my head (something which had already proven impossible) and started accustoming myself to his peaceful and permanent residence there. No matter what occurred, no one could take him from me completely, not as long as I remembered him. And even now, more than a decade after these events, not a day passes without my thinking of his dear face, without recalling some noble act or a tender word he once imparted. He is ever before my mind's eye, ever established in my heart as deserving love and esteem. He is my muse, my mentor, and my inspiration.

When I was finally satisfied with *Susan*, I entrusted the manuscript to Henry, who was able to sell it for me to Crosby & Company that following spring. It seemed that I would soon have my first novel published, and I was delighted. Here, I thought, was something I could build a future on. Here was evidence that I had something of value to offer, the product of my mind and of being at liberty to dedicate myself to my work. I had been right to reject the security and comfort Harris Bigg-Wither had offered me. I hoped this first taste of literary success would begin to convince my less-optimistic family members of the same.

Nothing comes easily, however, and several years more would elapse before my words at last found their way into print. Yet the promise had been made, and it carried me through the lean times. I believed in my ultimate right to success, even when nobody else did. I could not give up the dream of publication, of sharing my stories with the world, for it was all that I had left to me, that and the slim hope that I might someday see Captain Devereaux again.

~~*~~

That May (1803) brought surprising news to Bath, as to the rest of the world. Napoleon had broken the peace and the war against the French was back on again. This meant Charles and Frank were needed by the navy at once, and I could not help wondering if Captain Devereaux would be going away as well. Or perhaps he had already given up his commission in preparation for his upcoming marriage. Having severed my ties to Bernadette, I had no way of knowing. I was, therefore, completely unprepared for the letter that arrived for me shortly thereafter. I at once discerned the hand that had written the direction. It was from the man himself – Captain Devereaux. With every part of my being quaking, I spirited the precious missive away to read it alone in my room. This is a faithful transcription:

My Dear Miss Austen,

Please excuse the extreme liberty I take in writing to you directly, but I must speak by such means as are within my reach. I would come to you in person this instant if I could, but my ship sails with the tide, and who knows when my next chance might be?

You will by now perhaps have heard that Miss Cumphries has called off our engagement. We had reached a critical impasse, you see. The details are not something she would wish me to repeat. It will be sufficient to say that Miss Cumphries could not bear to think of the sea and I could not bear to give it up. As there was never any true depth of affection (on either side, I am now convinced), it is for the best. I suppose I should properly pretend to be sorry for the break, but I will not be false with you, Jane, never again. Too much time has been wasted as it is.

I feel compelled to say it once more, now that I am at liberty to speak openly. The fault has been mine, wholly mine. Had I done as I ought when I first met you in Sidmouth (or even sought you out before that, as soon as I had established my fortune – dear God, how I wish I had done so!), none of this would have happened. They say pride makes fools of us all. I know it surely made one of me, driving me to act against my own interests, to punish you for a perceived wrong, long past, by feigning a preference for Miss Cumphries. Before I could come to my senses, I was too deeply entangled to free myself. I had thrown away our second chance. I had lost the only woman I ever cared for by recklessly becoming bound to another.

Being caught in the trap of my own making was probably no more than what I deserved. But that I involved you, and that other innocent victim, this is unconscionable. And yet, by some miracle, purely by the grace of God, I have been given leave to hope that things may still be put right. Tell me not that I am too late, that such precious feelings as we once expressed and later revived, are now gone forever. I offer myself to you again with a heart even more your own than when you almost broke it four years and a half ago. I have loved none but you, Jane. Unjust I may have been. Weak and resentful I know that I have been, but never inconstant.

You said last September that you had forgiven me with all your heart. Too good, too excellent creature! Is it possible that your heart could do still more? Could you persuade it to love me again?

For you alone I now think and plan. For you alone I shall fight and return. The dream that you may then, at long last, be my wife – this must sustain me. I go now, uncertain of my fate. Do us justice, my darling. Consider that there is indeed true attachment and constancy among men. Believe it to be most fervent, most undeviating in... -P.D.

What I felt upon reading this letter may be imagined. Over and above my absolute astonishment, there was something more near to pure joy than I have ever experienced before or since. My heart was given wings that day. Philippe was free, honourably free! He would not be shackled to a woman he did not love or a profession which would surely have made him miserable. Everything was explained. What I had supposed and he had implied before our final parting was all now confirmed. Most importantly, he loved me, he wished to marry me, and this time we would not be put off by anybody's objections.

I longed to shout, to laugh and cry aloud! At the same time, I was afraid – afraid to break the spell, afraid to risk awakening from the dream by making any sound or sudden movement. But such news could not be kept bottled up for long. I had to share it, and my dear sister must be the first to know. I had calmed myself sufficiently to go in search of her when she came to me instead.

I heard a soft knock. "May I come in?" she said, opening the door a crack.

"Yes, yes, come in! It is your room too."

"I do not wish to intrude, but I saw you had received something in the post. I could not help wondering what it meant."

I went and embraced her at once, still holding onto my letter. "Oh, Cass, it is merely the best news in the world! I can scarce believe it. Here. It is from Captain Devereaux. You must read it for yourself, for I will not quite trust that it is real until you have confirmed it for me."

Giving me a quizzical look, Cassandra took the letter and sat upon the bed to study it. I was too overcome by nervous excitement to be still, however; I paced the confines of the small room, all the while watching my sister's reaction to the writing before her. At every moment, she was reading something that surprised her. This I verified from her incredulous looks and little exclamations. She did not speak, though, until she had finished.

"You should not have allowed me to read something so personal, perhaps," she then said with downcast eyes.

I saw her heightened colour. "It is a very good letter, though, is it not?" I said teasingly. "I thought the captain expressed himself well, with intelligence and sincerity of feeling, especially at the last."

She looked at me and smiled, a twinkle in her eye. "Indeed. It is a most excellent letter, to be sure." Then her tone changed as she handed it back to me. "But can this be true? Not about his loving you, for I do not doubt that for one minute, but that he should have been released from his definite engagement to Miss Cumphries? And what is this business about the sea?"

"Yes, it must be true for he would not lie or even joke about such a thing. As to the sea, this is what I know. Although I did not think it my place to mention it to you before, Bernadette confided to me, months ago, that she has an absolute horror of the water since nearly drowning at Sidmouth. She could not bear the thought of setting eyes on the sea ever again."

"And yet she expected to marry a sailor?"

"It was her plan that Captain Devereaux should give up the profession to work at her father's bank in London. From something she wrote in a letter, I thought he had agreed to do so."

"Apparently not."

"As you say. He was honour-bound to marry her, but not to give up his career for her. Thus the impasse he mentions."

"So he is really and truly free, free to marry you when he returns from the war. Oh, Jane, how wonderful! Could you have believed that things would end in this happy way?"

My heart was too full to speak, and my eyes had already begun spilling over with tears of joy. Seeing this, Cassandra took me in her arms and let me cry until my quaking sobs turned to peals of giddy laughter, in which she immediately joined me. There was nothing else for it; the pent up suspense and surprise must come out at last. And, once the dam had been breached, there was no stopping the flood from pouring forth in full measure unto exhaustion.

Mama heard the uproar and came to investigate. She found us both on the floor, where we had collapsed when we were too helpless to support ourselves any longer. "What's this?" she demanded. "Have you both been infected with some sort of violent lunacy?"

Cassandra and I just looked at her and then at each other before bursting afresh into nonsensical mirth.

-26-

In due course, I shared my good news with the rest of my family. Although the salient fact was exactly the same as it had been several years before – that Captain Devereaux wished to marry me – the reception of my announcement was entirely different this time. Once the confusion over Bernadette's prior claim was cleared away, there was general celebration at the idea rather than disapproval, relief rather than reproach. Mama declared that she had always liked the young man. Papa philosophised about how patience and prudence will pay in the end, and was I not now glad that we had waited?

Although I said nothing in rebuttal, I still could not understand why I should rejoice in having been kept waiting an extra five years for my happiness to be established. I only hoped it would not be much longer than that.

Everything depended on the war. How would it end? When would England's sailors be coming home? How many would be lost before it was all over? Speculation abounded, but I do not recall a single person venturing an opinion for what really occurred – that the conflict would wage on another dozen years. Such a calamity could hardly have been imagined, let alone predicted. For better or for worse, my suspense over when Captain Devereaux might return to me did not comprise nearly so long a term.

They say that trouble comes in threes, and so it did for me. It stalked me relentlessly, humbling and punishing me until I could no longer see the use of going on. One does, of course. One has no choice. But I have never known a blacker time.

First, my old friend Madam Lefroy was killed in a fall from a horse. It happened in December of 1804, on my birthday in actual fact. Though we had been less close recently, divided by distance as we were, I felt the loss of her exceedingly.

I had no time to recover before the second, even harsher, blow fell a month later, when my dear father followed my friend to glory. His death was nearly as sudden and nearly as unexpected, the nature and brevity of his illness having little prepared us for the melancholy outcome. Had I a husband and a family of my own by then, I might not have suffered so much as I did. But my father had always been my mainstay, my tower of strength. I had unconsciously assumed he would continue to be so, at least until I married. Now he was gone, which would have been devastating enough, but his income expired with him, multiplying our misery. We three Austen females were forced by our suddenly reduced circumstances to move to cheaper lodgings in Gay Street, and so on from there.

I thought that things surely could get no worse, and then they did.

In April, the final disaster was visited upon me. Henry came early that month from London to pay us an unexpected call. Ordinarily, his arrival would have lifted my spirits more than almost anything else. It was clear from the beginning, however, that this time would be different.

He had come in quietly with no fanfare to announce him. I first espied him just inside the front door, his head bent close to my mother's and speaking in low tones.

"Henry!" I called out in surprise, quickly starting down the stairs to meet him.

Both he and Mama turned toward me wearing expressions of decided grimness. My steps instinctively slowed. I was no longer in such a rush to discover what had been so important as to bring my brother to us from town. His countenance told me it was nothing good. His focused gaze gave me to believe it was no general misfortune, but something to do most particularly with me.

"What is it?" I asked warily, though I was already certain I would be happier not knowing.

"Jane," said Henry with obvious pity in his look and tone. "Do come and sit down." He took my arm and gently guided me to our small parlour.

I followed him as one in a trance, my senses immediately numbing themselves against the shock of whatever disaster he meant to relate. "Is it Eliza?" I asked, not really believing it could be the case.

"No, it is not Eliza," he answered. Having settled me on the sofa, he drew a chair up so that he could sit directly across from me and close enough to hold my hands. "I do I have some bad news for you, Jane, but it is about Captain Devereaux."

A violent wave of nausea instantly swept over me. My breath first caught in my throat. Then it emerged a second later in some cross between a sob and a cough. "Is…? Is he…?" I could not complete the question; I could not bear to say the words. I fought to contain the panic and the tears that threatened to overwhelm me, and at the same time I longed to give in to them.

"No, he is not dead," Henry quickly informed me, "at least we do not know that he is. Missing: I suppose that would be the most accurate way to think of him."

"What do you mean by that, Henry? Explain yourself this instant. I must know the truth, whatever it is."

"The truth is that no one seems to be entirely certain what happened. We comprehend this much, however. Captain Devereaux and his ship were serving under Nelson as part of the blockade at Toulon, when a French contingent broke through the line just at that point." Henry paused to allow me to digest this much.

Steeling myself, I finally said, "His ship was lost in the battle, then, and he was not picked up among the survivors."

"No, I'm afraid it is worse than that, Jane."

"Worse! How could it possibly be worse?" I demanded frantically, the tears beginning to flow in earnest now.

"It was reported that his ship allowed the French fleet to pass without a shot fired and then joined them on their break-out run. They are known to have made it past Gibraltar, possibly sailing for the new world. No one can say for sure what their destination was, only that nothing has been heard of them since."

Although I tried to comprehend what he was telling me, it made no sense. "But… But why on earth would he assist the French?"

"I wish I knew." Henry dropped his gaze to the floor for a minute before looking up again. "He is being called a traitor, Jane. Some are even saying he has been one all along, that he came to this country expressly for such a purpose, to put himself into a position where he could betray the English to the forces of his native land at a critical moment."

I was stunned. "Impossible! It must be a lie! You know it as well as I, Henry."

"I do not believe the charges either, and yet I am at a loss for how else to account for what has happened. Why should the navy lie about such a thing? Why should they invent such a damning slander? And if they did not invent the story, how is it possible to interpret matters in such a way as to render Captain Devereaux guiltless in the case?"

"I have no answers, but that does not change the fact that there must be another explanation."

"He is charged with treason, Jane," Henry said grimly. "He will face court-martial if and when he ever returns."

This was devastating news, although the thought of him returned to England alive had to be better than the alternative. "Well, at least then he would have a chance to tell what really occurred, to defend himself and clear his name."

"I wish that were the case but, contrary to what you might suppose, courts-martial are not instituted for the purpose of discovering the truth. They are chiefly convened to demonstrate very publicly the perils of running afoul of the crown. This is accomplished by exacting heavy punishment on those already found guilty in the minds of the powers that be. No, we must not wish for that. We would do better by our friend to pray he never sets foot on English soil again, for if he does, he will surely hang."

Thus died all my hopes of domestic happiness, all my dreams of Captain Devereaux's returning from the war to marry me. Not only was he likely never coming back, I had now to pray that he would not attempt it. Those who were lost later that year in the Trafalgar action were celebrated as heroes. But I could not even take that small comfort. I had to hear Captain Devereaux called a traitor wherever I went, to hear his name abused and his infamous treachery reviled at every turn.

Henry was right. The case against Philippe had already been decided. There would be no justice for him in court. People's minds might move on to other things; fresher scandals would soon take precedence there. But the navy had a long memory. Traitors must be made an example of, regardless how old their crimes.

We later heard the news that the Toulon fleet, to which Captain Devereaux's ship had supposedly become attached, was intercepted in July at Cape Finesterre. His ship was not among them.

Did this mean the earlier reports had been wrong? Not necessarily. Ships were lost at sea all the time, and not always as a result of combat. Did the new information tend to support the idea that Captain Devereaux was alive or that he was dead? I could imagine a reasonable case for either one.

For weeks, I tortured myself with such unanswerable questions and impossible conjectures. I went to sleep thinking of what might have happened to him, dreamt about one horrible fate or another nearly every night. Sometimes, upon first awakening, I thought it had been just that: only a dream. Then cold reality set in once more and those icy fingers of fear clutched at my heart again.

I was afraid, not for myself but for him. Despite my worry and loneliness, I was snug and warm at home in England. Meanwhile, he might be shackled in some dank French prison or, worse yet, dead with his body mouldering at the bottom of the sea.

I prayed and I waited, waited and prayed. As months passed and then years with no further word, it became clear that I must somehow reconcile myself to never knowing what had happened. Just the same as for countless others, war had swallowed up the man I loved, and only God knew what had become of him.

I had no choice but to get on with my life, and so I did.

Cassandra, Mama, and I, joined by our dear friend Martha Lloyd, moved from place to place until finally coming to rest here at Chawton in 1809. Here is where I was at last able to make good on my pledge to Captain Devereaux of earnestly pursuing my literary ambitions. Here is where the darling children of my pen finally took life and grew. From here they have gone out into the world – *Sense and Sensibility* first, followed by *Pride and Prejudice, Mansfield Park*, and *Emma*.

I love them all dearly, and yet it never ceases to amaze me that other people – total strangers from modest to highest birth – also find them worthwhile knowing. They are not epic tales of grand adventure or important personages. They are only the stories of rather ordinary families with ordinary problems, living in country villages and manor houses, such as one might meet with every day. These seemed to me to be the very things about which to write. And I am gratified that so many others have taken my literary offspring into their hearts and homes as well.

In all this, Captain Devereaux has had his part, as I have said before. His words, character, and mannerisms have found their way into every book. More significantly, the feelings excited by him in me have informed my writing of the heroine in love, in all of her elations and agonies.

Some might argue that, considering the ultimate outcome, I would have been better off had I never received Captain Devereaux's letter, that it would have been kinder not to have raised my hopes for a bliss which never came to pass. With such an assertion, I would most strenuously disagree. In fact, I would not be convinced to part with that treasured letter for any price. It is to this day my most cherished possession. Because of it, I know I was once well and truly loved by a man of superior worth. That can never be taken from me.

To Captain Devereaux and to our unconsummated love I hereby dedicate the work of the last year, both this autobiographical account and the novel its events inspired. I am grateful to have been given enough time to complete them.

These two now lie alongside one another before me. Their pages are written in the same hand. Their stories merge as almost to form one body. Indeed, they are so fiercely intertwined as to be impossible to cleanly divide. When one is wounded, does not the other bleed? And yet they must now go their separate ways, for the happy twin is destined to venture out into the world... as soon as I and the other have made our escape from it.

What people may hereafter say about my life, I cannot control. My biographers, if any, must do the best they can with the sources available to them. It is necessary that this, my own account – of love lost, found, and lost again – shall remain for some time to come concealed from their eyes. For now, the story belongs to me alone... to me and to that one other.

Part Two

-27-

March 1817

Although my sixth novel was well and truly finished months ago, it seems this volume, its companion, was not. I find that I have, after all, some things more to tell.

I put down my pen that day last August with the gesture of solemn finality appropriate to the occasion. Then I sat a moment, gathering myself for the effort of raising my feeble frame to a standing position, so that I might wind a string round the manuscript I had so lovingly wrought. *The Elliots, by A Lady*: the title plus my usual epithet written in my own hand on the foremost page.

During the time it took to write it, my strength had gradually ebbed away to the point where I sometimes wondered if I could go on. Yet there was no turning back. The story consumed me. It dominated my thoughts, waking and sleeping. It demanded to be told. So I had obediently forged ahead. That other world, Anne and Captain Wentworth's, was always with me, its characters and events becoming as real to me as those persons and proceedings belonging to my own household.

Like a spider, I had carefully spun the tale's intricate pattern. And then I neatly knit up all my loose ends, seeing to it that, unlike in real life, everybody not greatly at fault had been returned to tolerable comfort at the last. It set my mind at ease to know the good-natured Miss Musgroves would be suitably married. And I had even taken the trouble of putting the ailing Mrs. Smith in the way of a secure future. More importantly, however, Anne and her captain were reconciled, and their happiness would not be again threatened by objections at home or by want of money. No separations of war or debilitating illness either. As author of their lives, if not of my own, I had been able to do that much for them.

In our case – mine and Captain Devereaux's – the ravages of time have consumed far more than the eight years lost by Anne and Captain Wentworth. Our second chance passed us by long ago, and there can be no third…

As I wrote these things down, the door creaked and I looked up to see my mother bustling into the room. "Are you still at it, Jane?" she asked. "What have I told you about overtaxing yourself? All this exertion cannot be good for you in your weakened condition."

I drew a weary breath. "These are only a few notes, just for myself. I have given up the idea of writing any more novels."

"Well, thank heaven for that! These tales of yours may have produced a little money, which is always welcome, humbly circumstanced as we are, but I daresay what they have cost you is a vast deal more than can ever be measured. I am convinced within myself that, were it not for this unhealthy fascination with made-up stories, you should have been married and settled long ago instead of languishing here at home. You should have recovered from your disappointment and learnt to like somebody else. Heaven knows you had your chances, before you lost your bloom…"

"Mama," I interrupted, putting a hand to my fevered brow, "I refuse to have this conversation with you yet again. Not now; I am far too tired." I slowly rose from my table and turned to go. Although climbing the stairs might take my last ounce of strength, I cared not. I simply had to get off by myself and rest a while.

"It is no wonder that you are ill, Jane," Mama called after me, "the way you have dissipated your energy."

Again, my mother was entirely wrong. Whatever was amiss with my health – and even the various medical men seemed to have no very good idea about that – it was nothing whatever to do with my work. Writing had not been killing me; it was the only thing that had kept me alive, all that made it worthwhile to drag myself from bed each morning. Now, however… Well, that did not bear thinking of.

The flight of steps before me looked truly insurmountable. There were fourteen of them in all, and I had come to count the conquering of each one a small accomplishment to be duly noted and rewarded by a minute's rest. And so I began the epic climb once more.

Despite what I told my mother, I had in fact started another novel – one about an odd collection of people who are overly worried about their health and seeking relief at a seaside resort town, which I have named Sanditon. I had in mind my own fruitless pilgrimage to Cheltenham last May, where the mineral springs failed to do me any good. This new story, which I began in January (when I was feeling a great deal better than before or since), was my way of poking fun at myself, of trying to joke myself out of the idea that I was truly ill. It has always been my way to laugh at a thing that would otherwise require one to cry. Sickness must be considered a dangerous indulgence at my time in life, and so I have resisted it as long as I could.

Though it was but four in the afternoon when I achieved the refuge of the room I shared with my sister, the early hour seemed no deterrent. If there is anything advantageous about having sunk to the level of a hopeless invalid, it is that no one thinks it odd that I should have a lie down in the middle of the day. For a long time I fought the distinction – that of being an invalid – but no more. Denying one's own frailty is a form of pride, one that I can no longer afford to maintain.

I should have the room to myself, I knew, since Cassandra was away. She had gone to Berkshire to comfort my Aunt Leigh-Perrot upon the death of my uncle, although one could argue that my sister might just as well have stayed to comfort my mother instead. It is not that Mama was overly close to her brother. The truth is, she had been for years anticipating a substantial legacy from him when the time came, and imagining how nicely such a windfall would relieve our relative poverty. But her hopes were all for nothing; not a single farthing did he leave her. The disappointment had thrown her into a foul temper indeed.

My eyelids were already heavy when I collapsed onto my bed. This retreat was a temporary measure, but I knew a more permanent release from life's struggles could not be far off. Every moment took me a heartbeat nearer the end, every breath brought me closer to my last.

This awareness of my own approaching mortality did not grieve me overly. I was resigned, and, particularly when the pain in my back grew excessive, I welcomed the coming of death. In fact, I sometimes thought I could hear the beckoning call of dear friends from the other side of the great divide. They were waiting there to welcome me. My newly arrived uncle had joined my father, Madam Lefroy, and my cousin Eliza (Henry's wife), who left us nearly four years past after an agonizing illness. Perhaps I would then at long last also be reunited with my dear Captain Devereaux, if he had indeed traversed that path before me.

In the meantime, sleep provided a gentle respite from the day's trials. I hoped that I might dream of him again, not tangled in the horrors of some unknown fate as I did at first, but enjoying a better existence supplied by my imagination. I could by no means control where my mind chose to wander while I slept. But, in recent years, it had more often conjured up images of Philippe in happier circumstances – reviving and even improving upon one of the more felicitous scenes from the past or depicting an agreeable alternate present. If I found myself with him there, so much the better. And if I died rather than awakening, I might never have to leave him again.

~~*~~

I did in fact dream of Captain Devereaux, although not in the way I had hoped.

The dream began harmlessly enough, even pleasantly. I saw my captain on the far side of an expanse of open water, standing on a distant shore, his earnest gaze cast in my direction and his hand outstretched, as if to help me across to join him. He looked just the same as he ever was: young, strong, vital, and wearing his impeccably groomed naval uniform.

On some level I knew it made no sense he should be completely unchanged after so long, or that I could observe all this so clearly, for I was also aware that he was in fact very far removed from me. But such is the nature of dreams.

My heart went to him at once, and I likewise reached out my arm. But it was no use. Although it had seemed perfectly reasonable to try, now it became clear that we could never touch; we were too far apart. The captain then cupped his hands about his mouth and called out to me. What he was saying, I could by no means tell. No matter how hard I strained, I could make out not a single word.

"Philippe! Philippe, I am here!" I called back. It came out barely more than a whisper, however, and I could see that he had not heard me either.

There was a beautiful young woman at Captain Devereaux's side, a person whom I did not know. She seemed to be afraid of some concealed danger, for she was forever glancing over her shoulder, into the bank of heavy fog behind them, and pulling urgently at the captain's arm.

"Stay with me!" I cried out. And yet I could feel him slipping away as the fog inexorably advanced, soon to swallow him up completely.

Just before he disappeared from my sight, I saw him toss what appeared to be a piece of paper into the waves at his feet. The offering floated gently in the gulf between us, drifting steadily towards me but remaining maddeningly out of reach. Was it an important message of some sort? All I knew was that it came from Captain Devereaux, and was, therefore, of infinite value.

I simply had to lay claim to that paper. I willed it to come to me, and just when I thought I might succeed in retrieving the prize, a fish surfaced to gulp it down. Lost forever! Worse still, the fish then transformed itself into a sea serpent, growing to terrifying proportions. It fixed its cold, ugly eye on me and began slithering in my direction. I wanted to run but my feet seem rooted to the ground. I could not move, and the monster was coming straight for me. There was no escape; another second and the thing would overtake me. It opened its fearsome mouth to devour me. I opened mine to scream…

I clawed my way back to consciousness with my heart thundering loudly in my ears. When my head cleared, I soon apprehended the truth. No monsters here; no serpent's jaws. I was safe on my own bed.

Long afterward, however, the images of the dream still clung to me, their tendrils twining into my mind and constricting my heart. I considered that perhaps this was only a new symptom of my advancing illness. Fever could play tricks on one's brain, after all. But I was more disposed to believe the nightmare came to me as a harbinger of some sort, that it was laden with a significance which I was at a loss to interpret. If that were true, the dream seemed to reinforce the idea that Captain Devereaux was alive and that he still cared for me – things I had nearly lost the hope of. Or was it the reverse? Was he waiting on the other side of a different divide, waiting to bring me across death into the afterlife? I could take little comfort in either explanation. There was such a dark menace about the way the scene had played out, such a threat of imminent danger, that it stirred fresh fears within me, both for the captain and for myself.

-28-

I could hardly decide what the disturbing dream might mean, if anything, and a full day passed without entirely ridding myself of the feeling that it held special significance. It was all dismissed, however, that next morning when the post arrived.

Even before that, my spirits were elevated, having happily awoken with far more vigour than usual. This was the nature of my strange illness, the unpredictable pattern. I might seemingly be at death's door one week and substantially revived the next. One time I might be nearly too weak to hold a pen and another I felt equal to almost anything. I could never tell if I was coming or going, so I gave up trying. I learnt to simply be thankful for good days like this, when I possessed enough strength to dress, come downstairs, and help with the breakfast things. This also allowed me to get the first look through the letters, where, to my great delight, I found one from Mrs. Bothwell.

I have never forgotten Captain Bothwell's kindness to me at Sidmouth and Bath, now so long ago, and we have, through his wife, maintained a loose sort of correspondence between ourselves ever since. He still lives in Sidmouth, married these seven years to a very pretty, goodhearted young woman named Kate, whom I have had the pleasure of meeting twice. They send me word each time another child is born to them – four at last count – and I have returned the favour at least often enough to keep them apprised of my whereabouts and activities.

These indirect communications with Captain Bothwell, as well as an occasional letter from Mrs. Crowe, have been my only tangible connections back to a time when Captain Devereaux was still among us. We have all missed him in our own ways – his friend, his sister, and myself – and, with the passing of each additional year, it has become more and more difficult to pretend to one another that he will ever return.

After recognising the feminine hand that had addressed it, the next thing I noticed about the newly arrived letter was its thinness. This was not the corpulent packet I usually received from the Bothwell household, several pages containing all the little domestic details and descriptions that I had come to expect and enjoy so much. No, this one was far less weighty. When I broke the seal and unfolded the paper, I saw it was just a single sheet beginning in Mrs. Bothwell's tight scrollwork and then changing to another, which I took to be her husband's.

My Dear Miss Austen,
  I hope this finds you in better health than when we heard from you last, and that it was only a touch of the rheumatism after all, although I cannot be quite comfortable that this is the case. It would be so very like you, Jane, to make light of something altogether more consequential than you are willing to admit. Regardless, I trust that the thing we have now to tell you will work a beneficial effect. At the very least, it will certainly surprise you. But it is not really my news to share, so I will now consign this letter over to my husband, who is better able to do the job:

  Miss Austen, this is your old friend Bothwell here. And now you must prepare yourself for a shock. No, it is not another Bothwell child. It is that, at long last, I have heard from our mutual friend. You know who I mean, but I dare not even write his name lest someone of an uncharitable nature should get wind of it. In case this letter should somehow fall into the wrong hands, the less said here the better. I trust we will both receive a fuller explanation in due course. Suffice to say that he is alive, he is currently abroad, and he is very desirous of returning to this country.
  In addition, he has enquired about you most particularly, Jane, asking – no, demanding – to know where you can be found. It seems he had attempted to reach you in Bath, where he last knew you to be, and naturally received no answer. In accordance with his wishes, then, I have sent him your current direction. But at the same time, I advised him against coming. Knowing the danger as you do, I felt

certain you would agree with me. He seems determined, however, and so I expect you will hear from him soon.

Even now, there are those who are on the lookout and who would gladly profit at our friend's great expense. The threat, of course, is not limited to the gentleman himself. Any person who knowingly gives aid or shelter to such a man also puts himself at peril of the law. So I reminded him, as I now do you. This may prove a more effective deterrent, since he will be less willing to risk your safety than his own.

I do not have a solution to this dilemma, my dear. I only mean to put you on your guard, lest the thing should blow up in our faces. What a tragedy it would be for him to be taken now, after having miraculously survived so long under hostile conditions. Our prayers are with you both.

Yours,
Bothwell

I was by this time sitting down, having begun to shake uncontrollably as soon as I discovered the subject of Captain Bothwell's discourse. Captain Devereaux was alive! I rejoiced that I was alone, for I would not have been capable of hiding my profound discomposure, not even to save my life. Instead, I was joyously free to feel and show all the attendant agitations without fear of detection. It was too much to comprehend, too much to bear! Could it be true, I wondered, that after all these years apart, he would finally come back to me? I was filled with the thrill of hope to think so… but also with great alarm at the risk involved.

Oh, how I wished Captain Bothwell had been present bodily, not merely on paper, for I desperately needed to talk to someone, someone I could absolutely trust. My next thought was for Cassandra, but here again I was thwarted by her absence. I would send and beg for her to return home at once; I must have her with me. But in the meantime, there was Henry. Yes, Henry would do very well.

Suddenly excited and wanting to be doing something, I threw my cloak about my shoulders and went outside. "I am going to walk over and see Henry for a bit," I called to my mother, who was in the vegetable garden again.

Mama looked up in surprise, wiping her dirty hands on her green apron. "Are you certain that you should, Jane?" she called back.

"Oh, yes. It is a fine afternoon, and I am feeling much stronger today. The fresh air and exercise will do me good."

"Very well. I suppose you know best what you can endure."

She turned back to the seedbed she had been tending. I hurried on my way, spurred on by the prospect of sharing my exciting news with my favourite brother. Although I was truly sorry for Henry's misfortunes – Eliza's death and, more recently, the collapse of his bank – I could not be sorry that these events had ultimately brought him to Chawton. He had finally taken orders and now served as curate of the village.

I found him in the church, standing at the elevated pulpit and in the midst of a recital of his sermon for Sunday.

Glancing up at the noise of my entering, he exclaimed, "Why, Jane! What brings you here? Are you well enough for such an exertion as this?"

"I am well, Henry, I assure you!"

Having descended from the pulpit by this time, he added, "Nevertheless, you should sit down and rest." He gestured to a spot in the foremost pew.

"Oh, no," I said. "It is far too gloomy and cold to sit in here. Are these great blocks that make up the walls of your church stone or ice? Sometimes I wonder."

"To the garden, then. Here, take my arm."

"A much better idea," I agreed. "Oh, Henry! I have so much to tell you."

"Have you? Yes, I can see that you are nearly bursting with it." We settled ourselves on a sunny bench and he went on. "Now, what is this all about?"

"It is a great secret, but I know I can entirely rely on you, dear brother."

"Of course, you can."

"Here," I said, handing him the Bothwells' letter, which I had brought with me. "Prepare yourself for a shock and read this."

He did so without question or delay, although the minute it took seemed an age as I waited impatiently for him to finish. I stood up. I laughed at his initial surprise. I sat down again. And I mirrored the growing concern I read on his countenance as he continued.

Finally, he refolded the letter and returned it to me. Covering my hand with one of his own, he said, "Well, Jane, this is news indeed. What do you intend to do about it?"

"I hardly know. I only received the letter an hour ago and decided to come straight here."

"Good. You should tell no one else, not Martha nor even our mother. I do not imagine that either of them would deliberately betray our friend, but the fewer people who know about this the better."

"I *must* tell Cassandra; I can never hide anything from her. You know it is true."

He nodded ruefully. "Very well, but it can go no further. Are we agreed?"

"Yes, yes, but what am I to do, Henry? If Captain Devereaux really intends to come, what shall I tell him?"

"Do you wish to see him? Do you still have feelings for the man after all these years?"

"One does not stop loving a person simply because that person has been absent through no fault of his own." As a widower still mourning for his Eliza, I knew Henry could understand this explanation.

He nodded solemnly. "Well, then. We must think of how it can be best managed. We must be careful, but I should think that a single clandestine visit might be arranged without too much difficulty."

"No, Henry, that will never do! If Captain Devereaux feels the same as before, we must marry this time and be together always. Nothing must be allowed to hinder us." Then I suddenly remembered myself and my face fell.

"What is it, my dear?" asked Henry.

"What a fool I am to have allowed my emotions to run away with me in this manner! They have carried me off to a dream world and made me forget my own mortality. I have no business speaking of 'always,' when for me that may be a very brief period indeed. Perhaps I should count myself lucky were I to hang on long enough to enjoy the one clandestine visit with Captain Devereaux you propose."

"You have been very ill before, and you have always improved again."

"Yes, but these upturns never last. Today I feel as if I might live to be ninety; tomorrow I may find myself on death's doorstep once again."

We both fell silent, and I could see that Henry had descended into a deep contemplation, from which I had no wish to rouse him prematurely. I had asked for his help, and somehow, hope against hope, I expected him to come up with a terribly clever solution to an impossible situation. After a few minutes, however, he shook himself and sighed.

"What is your opinion?" I asked.

He gave me a weak smile and patted my hand again. "You must give me more time to consider, Jane. I do have an idea or two, but nothing that bears discussing at this time. Just know this, I pledge myself to do whatever I can to assist you, my darling sister, and Cassandra will feel the same. Write and ask her to come home. Tell her you are not well and you need her. That is near enough the truth. When she returns, we three will put our heads together and arrive at some sort of plan. Perhaps you will have heard from the captain by then and we will know more of his intentions."

The idea of a letter arriving from Philippe sent my heart soaring once again, in spite of myself and my sensible cautions.

I watched the incoming post with a very sharp eye from that day forward, every morning hoping for his letter and every morning experiencing a crushing disappointment when it did not come. Meanwhile, I did as Henry advised. I told no one of Captain Bothwell's information to me, and I wrote to summon Cassandra home on the pretense of my health taking a turn for the worse.

The following Sunday, after services, Henry pulled me aside for a brief tête-à-tête. "I had unexpected visitors yesterday," he told me in low voice, glancing about to be sure he could not be overheard.

From his grim expression, I knew this was not good news. Instantly on alert, I waited for him to continue.

"It was two men from the admiralty sniffing round and asking questions about Captain Devereaux. Did I still consider him a friend? Had I heard from him? Did I know his whereabouts? That sort of thing."

"Good heavens, Henry! What did you tell them?"

"I told them the truth – that we had been friends at one time, but that I had neither seen nor heard from him in over a decade. I did not feel obliged to go beyond that. But it proves that Captain Bothwell has not exaggerated the danger. I'm sure by now he has reccived a similar visit, he and the Crowes as well, although they will have had to be more evasive in their answers than I was."

"Very true," I said, trying to absorb this new information. "Will these men be questioning me too, do you suppose?"

"I should imagine not, or they would have done so the same day they came to me. Our whole family is known to have been acquainted with him, but these strangers would have no reason to suspect the captain had any special connection to you, unlike your friend from Bath. What was her name?"

"Miss Cumphries, now become Mrs. Fuller, I believe."

"Ah, yes. Well, we must be careful all the same. These inquiries, coming just now as they do, are evidence the navy is somehow aware that Captain Devereaux may be about to resurface and that they are still very much interested in apprehending him."

"We cannot allow him to come, then! We must somehow impress upon him that the danger is too great. No matter how desperately I wish to see him, nothing is worth the risk."

"You can try to dissuade him but, as Captain Bothwell said, he may be too determined to listen to anybody's cautions."

After this upsetting news from Henry, I watched the post more diligently than ever. I felt it was now imperative that I should intercept Captain Devereaux's letter without anyone else seeing it. And then I must save him by warning him away. It was my responsibility to do so. If he should come to England for my sake and be taken, I could never live with the guilt. And yet, living with guilt or any other kind of regret was not likely to be my problem, since there was a very good chance I would be dead before long.

Seeing Philippe once more would have been my last wish too, were I honest. If he felt the same, was it my place to deny him? I was by no means convinced that I could persuade him against his own inclination in any case. And yet, it surely was my duty to try, to protect him and also my family. There would be ramifications if any of us were discovered to have aided a notorious fugitive. There could be criminal charges, as Captain Bothwell indicated in his letter. I imagined that even a suspicion of collusion could damage the careers of my navy brothers, Charles and Frank. I had no right to risk that. Then what was I to do? Everywhere I looked, I could see disaster, and yet I could not imagine turning Captain Devereaux away.

Day by day, I grew more anxious. I could not eat, nor could I sleep properly with these things worrying my brain. When I soon began feeling more unwell, I suspected it was in no small part because of this very strain. My excuse for summoning Cassandra home had been a self-fulfilling prophecy, coming true almost immediately.

As fate would have it, my sister and the long-expected letter – both of which were delayed to the point of my distraction – would turn up almost simultaneously.

-29-

How much of this latest sudden decline was due to my illness itself and how much to my mounting anxiety over Captain Devereaux, I cannot say. But when Caroline and Anna happened to call at Chawton Cottage during that distressing period, they found me quite the invalid, not so much as bothering to properly dress myself and unwilling to leave my room. Indeed, I had worked myself into such a state that I was barely able to hold a coherent conversation. What a sad impression they must have had of their Aunt Jane that day. I am sorry for it too, as it will likely turn out to have been our parting view of each other.

My nieces were not the only ones worried by my deterioration; my mother had become quite alarmed as well. She had seen me recover from bad spells before, but this was different. There was a new sort of fevered distraction about me. And since I was unwilling to tell her the whole truth, to reveal the other contributing factor, the blame for my decline was all laid to the account of my illness. Soon, having had no satisfactory results from the local men who had been attending me, she decided to send for a surgeon of greater renown, a Mr. Giles Lyford, who came all the way from Winchester to see me.

After a thorough examination, which I did not enjoy in the least, he industriously set about curing me, applying various treatments and physics, which I enjoyed even less. He was a decent man, however, and despite the insults to my modesty and comfort, his measures seemed gradually to remove the evil. I did feel a great deal better for his ministrations, at least temporarily.

Mama saw me improved and felt she had got her money's worth. In fact, she complimented herself on her good judgment for having sent for the surgeon when she did. Mr. Lyford was less sanguine. Before he went away, he said he could not rule out another relapse, and he therefore recommended my removing to Winchester, where he could more easily supervise my long-term care. This invitation would prove not only necessary but convenient for me as well, although I did not know it at the time.

The day after Mr. Lyford had gone, my letter finally arrived.

There was no notation of the sender's identity on the outside, but I knew immediately it was from Captain Devereaux. The sight of his handwriting brought back a rush of feelings from the past, an uninvited wave of reminiscences, and it set my entire frame to trembling. It was as much as I could do to maintain a morsel of composure until I had squirreled the missive away with me to my room.

Even then I did not rip it open at once; it was far too dear for such brutal treatment as that. Instead, I sat and stared at it, transfixed, turning it several times in my hands, running my fingertips over the rough paper, and then bringing the thing to my nostrils to inhale deeply of it, in the unlikely event that some faint scent of the sender might still be detectable there.

Only when I felt I was calm enough to read it rationally did I finally break the seal and smooth the paper flat across my lap. As I began to read, the words nearly came alive on the page. It was as if the clock had been turned back and I could once again hear his rich, mellow voice with that slight shade of a French accent.

> *My Dearest,*
>
> *Do I presume too much by addressing you thus after so long? What you must think of me, I can only imagine. What you have been told of my supposed treachery, I know all too well. If you ever cared for me, do not judge until you hear the truth from my own lips, I beg you.*
>
> *What is important now is that you should know for me nothing has changed. In my mind, you are still the darling girl who captivated me so completely all those years ago. My enemies may have had custody of my body while we have been apart, but they could never imprison my heart, for it still belongs to you and always will. No one can ever usurp your position there, and I cherish the memories of our two brief seasons together to this day. I want nothing so much in this world as to live out the rest of my years with you by my side.*
>
> *But I fear that one thing has changed; I hear that you are become very ill. Is it so, my darling? I pray it is not. I*

pray that even by the time this letter reaches you, you may have fully recovered your health and strength. That it should be otherwise would be too cruel to bear contemplation.

Now that I am finally at liberty to do so, I am determined to come to you at once, despite the danger. No matter what it may cost me, I must see your dear face again, hear your voice speaking my name. Am I being unreasonable? Or dare I hope that you will be pleased to see me, that at least a remnant remains of the regard you once felt for me? Bothwell tells me that you have never married either, just as you said you would not, and this gives me some reason for optimism. My love for you is undiminished, and I am your most devoted servant always.

P.D.

I will have arrived in Dover by the time you receive this. If you are able, send word to me there (addressed to Peter Danvers, general delivery), as to where and when we may most safely meet. I am afraid we must be terribly circumspect about this, my dear. The danger is quite real, as I am certain you will appreciate.

So there it was in black and white. He still loved me and was determined to see me again, come what may! He was already in England too, a fact that both thrilled and terrified me – to know he was so close and yet in danger every day he remained.

The most important questions were answered. I would have to be satisfied without knowing the rest until, as he said, I could hear the truth from his own lips. The recollection of that phrase set my mind off on another reverie, a commemorative tour of the handsomely rugged geography of Philippe's entire person, not only his full lips. His image rose up quickly before me; it was never far away. But was the picture still accurate, I wondered. It had been so very long since I had seen him, and he had apparently experienced great hardships in the interim. I had to prepare myself for finding him much altered... as he surely would find me.

It occurred to me then that Captain Devereaux had quite literally entrusted his life to me, gambling that I still cared enough to receive him, believing that I would not betray him to the authorities. It would never have entered my head to do so, of course, but he could not know that. It was proof, even more so than his words, of his sincere devotion to me and his desire to cast his lot in with mine.

I read the letter once more, wishing to delight in the best parts on this second, more leisurely perusal. As I did so, I discovered that, excepting the final chilling lines, every word was worthy of being enjoyed again. He had called me "dearest." He had begged to be given the chance to explain himself. He had declared that his heart still belonged to me and that he was willing to risk all for the chance that we could be reunited.

I was so caught up in these gratifying sentiments that I did not at first hear the commotion from below. Cass! Cassandra must finally be home, I realised when I came to myself. I tucked my letter into my pocket and hurried downstairs.

~~*~~

How I got through the rest of the day, I hardly know. I am a selfish creature and, in my extreme perturbation of spirits, I wanted my dear sister to myself, to unburden my heart of all that had taken place since she had gone away. And yet I was forced to put up with sharing her with my mother and Martha, who quite naturally were glad to see Cassandra as well.

She had greeted me at once when I came downstairs. "Oh, Jane, you should never have let me go away if you were feeling poorly," she said, tightly embracing me. "I am so sorry I could not contrive a way to get home any sooner. But Mama says you are better again, thanks to the man from Winchester." She then held me at arm's length to examine me. "Though I must say you look a little flushed to me."

I felt my cheeks warm still more under her scrutiny. How could I possibly explain at that moment that my present state had far more to do with a different gentleman entirely? I simply nodded and embraced her again, taking the opportunity to whisper in her ear, "Oh, Cass, I have so much to tell you! Not now, though, for it is a very great secret."

She gave me a chastising glare, for which I could not blame her, since I had thus sentenced her to long hours of suspense. When at last we were alone, retired to our own apartment for the night, my sister wasted no time. With the door barely closed behind us, she demanded, "Now, Jane, do explain yourself. What can account for this agitation? Is it your health?"

"Have no fear. It is not my health, which is truly improved again, thanks to Mr. Lyford's efforts. It is something else altogether – a most unexpected development, information which cannot leave this room. Oh, Cass, you will hardly believe me when I tell you, but I have had news of Captain Devereaux at last! Can you guess? He is alive, he still cares for me, and he is coming."

She clapped her hand over her mouth to muffle her exclamation of surprise. "Captain Devereaux?" she repeated when she had regained her self-command.

"Yes, it is true. Quickly, come and sit down," I said, indicating the chair she favoured in the small alcove attached to our bedchamber. "I have two letters for you to read. Here. This one is from the Bothwells. Its arrival is what really made me summon you home from Berkshire."

She took it eagerly and read it straight through. When she seemed to have sufficiently digested its revelations, I handed her the second. "From Captain Devereaux," I explained. "It came just this morning. I had not yet recovered from its effects when you arrived."

She hesitated. "Are you certain I should read it, Jane? Communication between lovers is a private affair, not intended for anybody else to hear."

"He would not mind. And after all, you read his other years ago."

"I would not have, had I known what it contained."

"This one will be far less shocking, I promise you. Besides, you must know all if you are to properly advise me, and I desperately need your advice, Cass. I am in a quandary."

"Very well, then." She looked dubious, but she complied, bending her head over the second missive. "Another excellent letter," she said wistfully when she had finished. "Nearly as good as his first, if I remember correctly."

I sighed. "Yes, I quite agree."

"Who else knows of this business?" she asked.

"Only Henry, and so it must remain because of the danger of discovery. Henry has had men from the admiralty come round asking about Philippe."

"Oh, no!"

"It is true. So you see that, although I cannot manage this on my own, neither can I risk involving anybody beyond what is absolutely necessary – both for their sakes and for Philippe's. You will help me, though, will not you? I know it is a great imposition and a risk…"

"Of course I will help you in whatever way I can! You should never doubt that. You are as much a part of me as my arm or my leg. To serve you is to make myself happy, Jane."

I was quite overcome by this handsome sentiment, and I felt exactly the same. I would have gladly risked anything to bring Cassandra's Mr. Fowle back to her, sacrificed whatever it might require to see her reunited with the only man she had ever loved. I nodded, and I knew we understood each other completely. "Then we must meet with Henry as soon as possible, just we three, to discuss what is best to be done. Perhaps between ourselves we may hit upon some inspired idea for how I might manage to safely see Captain Devereaux again."

-30-

We seized an opportunity the very next day, one created by my sister's expressing a natural wish to see her brother after having been away. Mama made no difficulty when Cassandra further declared that she intended to take me with her as she went to find Henry, so we set off directly after breakfast.

Henry adopted a serious expression when he saw the two of us entering the church, and he immediately ushered us into the vestry, where we could speak undisturbed.

"I have heard from our friend," I began once we were settled behind the closed door. I could barely keep my voice steady for my excitement. "He is at Dover, awaiting my instructions for when and where he might see me."

"He is determined to come, then?" asked Henry gravely.

"Yes, quite determined, no matter the risk, he said. Cassandra has read his letter and she will confirm it."

Cassandra nodded. "This is all a very new idea to me, and I can by no means see any good solution, though we talked and talked half the night through. Jane expects she must be satisfied with one visit, but I cannot be satisfied for her with so little. She should have more time to be happy – as much time as God sees fit to give her on this earth. After already having been kept apart so long by misfortune, I cannot bear to think of two people, so attached to one another, meeting and then having to part yet again. Impossible! You understand these things better than I do, Henry. Is there no chance of proving the captain's innocence and removing the indictment that hangs over him?"

Henry, who had remained standing, rubbed his chin in thought. "I cannot say it is impossible, but I believe it highly improbable. His voluntarily surrendering to court-martial should not be considered;

the risk is far too great. No, I have thought and thought, and it comes down to this. He may hope to evade the law for a short time but not with impunity. If he must come – something I still think inadvisable – I'm afraid he must have his visit and then quickly leave the country again, this time forever."

Cassandra and I both gasped at the awful finality of my brother's pronouncement, the seeming harshness of his words made all the more devastating for the truth they embodied. I hardly knew what I had expected him to say, but not this. I had never allowed myself to think in such bleak terms. I suppose I had been holding out hope for some miracle to save us. But Henry was right; I saw that now. Philippe simply could not stay in England. Too many people knew him and knew of his reputed treason. They also knew of the offered reward. All it would take was one person, one greedy or overly patriotic person, to spot him. No, that would never do.

I burst out with, "Then when he leaves the country, I will go with him." The words, which were out of my mouth before I knew what I was saying, sent an immediate thrill through me. At once my imagination set to work, depicting the scene before my mind's eye – my beloved and I standing arm-in-arm aboard some picturesque sailing vessel, our faces set into the wind as we made for the continent, or perhaps America, and the idyllic future that awaited us there.

I was alone in these pleasant musings, however; my siblings instead looked shocked, even horrified. They stared at me as if I had suddenly grown a second head or at the very least that I had pronounced I intended to fly to the moon. I was therefore obliged to defend what I had actually said. "Why should you be so surprised? It is the only logical conclusion. Cass, you say Philippe and I must be together always, and Henry says the captain must leave the country as soon as possible. Since you are both correct, what other option is there?"

Cassandra was the first to respond, although not completely coherently. "But... but your health! Your home... your place in the world? To leave everything behind? No, I... And being known to have run away with a man who is not your husband!"

"He *would* be my husband, as soon as it could be managed."

"I know that is what you both want," she continued, "but the marriage could not take place openly, probably not even legally in this country, since no one must know his right name. To our neighbours, it will appear as if you have eloped with some stranger at best..."

"…and with a traitor at worst," Henry added, "if anybody should have recognised him. Need I remind you, Jane, that it is not only your reputation that would be compromised in such an event? Your mother – your whole family – could be implicated in the crime of harbouring a fugitive, once it is known that he has been here and has been received. Is that what you want?"

"No, of course not! I would never wish to harm any of my dear family."

"Henry!" pleaded Cassandra. "Do have a heart."

"Forgive me," he said, his tone softening. "I do not mean to be cruel, my dear Jane. I vowed to help you and I will. But I trust that part of keeping that vow is pointing out pitfalls before you stumble into them. Those officers from the admiralty could be back at any time, so one thing is sure. It would be safest for all concerned that the gentleman of whom we speak should not come to Chawton at all."

We were silent for a time, my temporary elation at the idea of flying off with Philippe vanished, replaced by renewed discouragement. When further discussion accomplished nothing, we three were forced to close our conference with no viable plan in view.

"I am so sorry, Jane," said Cassandra as we walked slowly home.

I attempted a smile. "It is not your fault; not Henry's either. I know you both only desire what is best for me. It was wrong for me to expect so much, to think that a simple solution could serve for such a complex problem. Just for a moment, though… Well, never mind. Perhaps things will look clearer tomorrow."

I truly hoped so, for I would soon have to write to Philippe, and at that moment I had no clue what to tell him.

~~*~~

Another sleepless night followed, during which I made little progress, though I grappled with the problem from dusk until dawn. A glance in my looking glass the next morning confirmed that the night's wrestlings had had their telling effects, leaving my face drawn with dark circles beneath my eyes. My appetite was off again as well.

At the breakfast table, Mama gave me a chastening glare. "You had better eat something, Jane," she warned, "to keep up your strength. Remember what Mr. Lyford said. If you show any signs of relapse, I am to pack you off to Winchester straight away. I will not hesitate to do so either, although I needn't tell you we can ill afford the expense. Never let it be said that Mrs. Austen refused to do what was right by one of her children."

I could have kissed my mother on the spot, for from her mouth, of all unlikely places, had come the elusive answer to my dilemma. It was instantly clear to me. She had accidentally provided the wise and perfect solution, which none of the rest of us had been able to conjure up by long hours of serious contemplation.

"Winchester!" I told Henry the next day, Cassandra and I having gone to see him again upon this latest inspiration. "I simply must go to Winchester! Do not you see?"

"No, I most certainly do not. Do you mean to remove to Winchester on account of your health?"

"Yes, but not *only* that. It will be my way of exiting Chawton without importunate questions being asked. It will also be my way to meet Philippe with less risk to him and to my family. Nobody, except Mr. Lyford, knows me there. Oh, and young nephew Charles at the college, but I wouldn't expect to see much of him. More importantly, I should think it far less likely that anybody will notice Philippe there either, for he will hardly be expected to turn up in that location." I paused to allow Henry to assimilate this new information.

"There is a deal of sense in what you say, I suppose, about going to Winchester I mean. But what then?" he asked. "Will you give the gentleman up and return home in the end?"

I took a deep breath before answering. "No, Henry. I have been turning the question over in my mind since the idea first occurred to me yesterday. And I am now convinced that there are only two possible conclusions to this business, neither of which will allow me to return to Chawton. I must therefore be resigned to giving up my home and family, to giving up the life I have known in the hopes of a new one." Although I heard my sister's muffled sob beside me, I did my best to ignore it, as well as the choking lump in my own throat. "I do not say 'a better life' for I have been happy as I am, for the most part. But I must believe it is the life I was meant to have. And after all, what more could any of us ask for than that?"

"I could dashed well ask you to explain yourself plainly," said Henry with indignation. "Your sister is crying and I still have not the slightest idea what you are on about, Jane."

"Of course not. I must begin by telling you what I have already told Cassandra. Much as I might like to believe otherwise, I know that I have still not entirely overcome whatever illness has been plaguing me these many months. By going to Winchester, I intend to give Mr.

Lyford every chance of curing me, once and for all. But it may be that, despite his best efforts, I will succumb to it at last. That is one very probable outcome, and I would only be deceiving myself to think otherwise."

Henry said nothing to this, but I could see him struggling to keep his countenance, and there was a glistening of tears in his eyes.

"Oh! My dearest brother," I exclaimed. "You mustn't be downcast by what I say. Instead, help me keep my courage up. I do not wish to die, I assure you, but neither am I particularly afraid. If it is to be, however, I pray the end will not come before I have seen Captain Devereaux once more and know him to be safely away again. If, however, as I would much prefer, Mr. Lyford is able to do me good, to at least improve my condition enough to travel, I intend to sail with Philippe in whichever direction he wishes to take me. All that matters is that it be some place where we can live out our days together, safe from further persecution."

"And never to return again?" asked Henry.

I shook my head. "A person cannot return from the grave, and that is what people must think – that Captain Devereaux was never in this country and that I am dead and buried. It is the only way to avoid scandal. It is the only way Philippe and I will be left in peace."

"You mean to counterfeit your own death? Why, I never heard of anything so preposterous!" Looking completely exasperated, Henry called on Cassandra for help. "Cannot you make your sister see sense?"

"I have tried, believe me, but in the end I find I cannot fault her reasoning. Much as the idea of losing her grieves me, I am disposed to think that in her place I should do the same." Cassandra hesitated before continuing. "And, if you will forgive me saying so, Henry, I suspect that you would be capable of trying something equally wild to have your dear Eliza back. Now, admit it. You would give the rest of us up without a thought for that chance."

Henry took a minute to silently debate the point with himself before answering dryly, "I might at that." He then heaved a great sigh. "Very well, Jane. If this is truly what you want, I will throw my weight behind your outlandish scheme one hundred percent. It has been a good long while since I had a proper adventure. This will undoubtedly be one worth remembering. We shall all enjoy telling the tale one day, I daresay."

"Perhaps one day, Henry," said I. "Perhaps one day a long time from now. But while any danger remains, it must stay a dark secret. Agreed? Let us make a pact of it, the three of us."

And so we did, clasping hands and swearing to carry the daring plan through to the end, regardless of the consequences. Then we huddled together to discuss the particulars, like conspirators plotting an infamous crime.

"I will feign an exaggeration of my symptoms if necessary," said I, "so that Mama will agree to send me off."

"Naturally, I will go with you to Winchester," said Cassandra. "It is what I want and what everybody would expect, that I should stay by your side as your companion and nurse."

I nodded and squeezed my sister's hand before moving on to the next topic. "Transportation could be a problem, though, and an added expense. I do feel a bit guilty for inconveniencing my dear family... and especially for deceiving them."

"Not at all," said Henry. "You deserve the best chance possible of a full recovery. And it is for their own protection that we keep the truth from the others, at least until you are... uh... until you are..."

I provided the word. "Gone. Let us just say gone, Henry. That will serve for either case."

"Very well, then. As I was saying, it is for their own protection. This way, if questions ever arise, they can honestly say they knew nothing about the business. As for transportation, I believe we can count on James and Mary for the loan of their carriage on the occasion."

"Yes," I agreed. "Mary is not a liberal-minded woman, but that is just the sort of thing she would do handsomely." I paused a moment. "There is one more thing, Henry – a favour."

"I am at your service."

"Thank you. After I am gone, will you watch over my darling children? My novels? I do not wish them forgotten, though I must leave them behind. I would like to think they will carry on in my absence, to outlive my death, real or supposed. I will therefore entrust them all to your care, if I may."

"Of course," he replied. "It will be my honour."

That night, after Cassandra was fast asleep, I took out pen and paper to write two important communications by the light of my candle. The first was my letter to Captain Devereaux, confirming my love and relaying my plan to meet him in Winchester. The second was my will.

-31-

I had intended to begin waging my campaign the very next morning, conjuring up new as well as old symptoms aplenty to impress upon my mother the absolute necessity of my going to Winchester. But again, the thought alone seems to have been sufficient to bring on the real thing. I woke feeling far more tired than when I had gone to sleep, and I was so weak that I could not get out of bed. Within days, the dark blotches, which I could never have feigned, obligingly re-appeared on my skin. The only conscious effort I had to make to advance my objective was to no longer hide what I was feeling. Now, when my back ached, I groaned aloud instead of stifling myself. Now, I did not bother to deny that I was very ill indeed.

My family was genuinely concerned at this most frightening turn, as indeed was I. And, when the limited talents of the local medical man yielded no appreciable result, Mama's mind was made up for Winchester without my even having to suggest it.

Although the course of action required was decided quickly enough, it could not be enacted without considerable exertion. Letters had to be written – one to Mr. Lyford to warn him of my coming, and another to James to secure the loan of his carriage to take me thither. Winchester lodgings had also to be found. Then there was the packing together of all that Cassandra and I might need for a stay from home of undetermined duration, and the funds necessary to support us through it.

All these arrangements I observed and yet was powerless to assist in. Mama, Martha, Cassandra, and Henry: they all buzzed and fussed about me, fulfilling my every need and providing every tender comfort within their reach. And the others rallied round as well, visiting and contributing what they could.

It is a humbling thing to find oneself utterly helpless, and yet it can be a gift as well. One who is too proud to admit a weakness will never experience the compassionate care of others. It is only when that person is brought low, dropped to the bottom of a deep pit, that he or she will look up for relief and find it.

Such a one was I, although I did not know it before then. I had privately taken satisfaction in my own abilities and often thought myself a cut above my company – not perhaps by society's standards, but by my own. Now where were my grounds for boasting? What benefit to me was my intellect in this situation? Could I think myself well again? When I was unable to even raise my head from the pillow, could I by my own efforts expect to add one minute to the length of my life?

Only God could do that. He would ultimately decide the length and course of my days. In the meantime, He had already sent his ministering angels round me, I perceived, in the form of my friends. I had never known such tenderness and love as they showed me through my illness. Or perhaps it had been there all along, and I had failed to properly appreciate it. In any case, I understood as never before that I was blessed. And there were moments when I felt as if I might wish for nothing better than to die there, peacefully, at home, and cradled in the bosom of such a family.

But we are not made that way. We are made to cling to life so long as there is hope. And I still had the hope of getting well and the hope of seeing Captain Devereaux again. These things compelled me to continue forward, to not give in just yet.

So, I said goodbye to my mother, knowing it would be, in all likelihood, the last time I would see her on this side of heaven, and I allowed myself to be carried off to Winchester. Cassandra travelled with me in my brother James's carriage, with Henry and my nephew William riding escort alongside.

"They will surely be soaked clean through," I said as I watched the rain running down the windows, heard it pattering on the roof of the coach. I was reclined on the makeshift bed that had been arranged for me, bridging across from one set of seats to the opposite. Poor Cassandra was crushed into the little space leftover. "If I were not such a wretched invalid, we could all have ridden inside where is it dry. What a bother I am."

"Don't be silly, Jane," she replied, straight faced. "If you were not an invalid, we would hardly be going to Winchester in the first place."

She meant it in jest, I knew, and I laughed at her joke – one more proof that she really is the witty one. "Of course, you are right," I agreed. "It would seem that even my mind is failing me now. More evidence of what I was saying, Cass. I am become a dreadful burden, especially to you."

"Let us have no more of this kind of talk. It is for me to decide if I am overburdened, not you. And I can always call on Mary to help with the nursing if it becomes more than I can manage."

I sighed. "I think we can hardly stop her coming. She sounded so determined in her letter," said I, referring to the note that had arrived from Steventon parsonage along with the carriage, wherein my sister-in-law had volunteered her services.

"Now, Jane, although Mary is not a favourite with you, you ought to be grateful for her kind offer."

"I know you are right, and I *am* grateful, but I fear she will become a complication we can ill afford. If she comes, how are we to prevent her from meeting with Philippe and from documenting every detail in that ever-present diary of hers?"

"Yes, I see what you mean," said Cassandra. "Honestly, why a person who lives such a retired life should keep a diary at all, I have never understood."

"Nor I."

We jostled along several minutes in relative silence, with only hoof beats, the jingle of harness, and the creaking of the carriage timbers to fill our ears. The rocking motion had nearly put me to sleep when my sister spoke again.

"We could work them to our advantage, I suppose."

"Work what to our advantage?"

"Mary and her diary. If we are careful, it might be possible."

"I still have not the pleasure of understanding you."

"Forgive me. I was only thinking aloud. Jane, I truly believe you will recover from this illness. And when you do, you intend to create the false impression that you have died instead. Correct?"

"Yes, what of it?"

"Well, it occurs to me we might want some independent documentation to that effect, for the record. You said yourself that, for you and Philippe to get away and be left in peace, everybody must believe you are dead and buried. Otherwise, there will always be people who will pursue you, importunate questions for your family to answer."

"Precisely. That is what this whole scheme is meant to forestall."

"Henry and I will support the false report, of course, but it would do no harm to have a third person to confirm it – an eyewitness above suspicion."

"Our sister-in-law would be that, it is true. She is nothing if not painfully honest and forthright. Do you think we could really deceive her, though? Would it be right to do so? And what about Mr. Lyford? How are we to convince him to go along with this charade? Oh, Cassandra, I had not considered!"

Cassandra reached for my hand. "All in good time, Jane. Let us see to getting you well first. I trust the rest will sort itself out in the end."

There was sense in what she said. No point in worrying too much about questions that might never come into play. If I did not recover, I would be saved the need for contriving solutions to these difficulties. If I did recover, it would be well worth the trouble of doing so. In any case, there was no turning back.

~~*~~

I felt excitement building in my chest as we neared our destination. I began thinking less of difficulties and of what I had left behind, and more for what lay ahead. It would be an adventure either way. I had always liked Winchester for its own sake – the beautiful cathedral especially. Now it was where my fate would be decided. In Winchester, God willing, I would see Captain Devereaux again. Perhaps he was in town already. That thought set my heart to fluttering despite my weariness.

We stopped at Mr. Lyford's house in Parchment Street only long enough for Henry to go to the door and announce our arrival.

"Lyford said he would come to you tomorrow morning," Henry reported upon his return to the carriage.

We drove on to College Street, where we had arranged to rent rooms, but attaining those rooms was no easy task. In my dependent state, I had to nearly be carried up the narrow flight of stairs. I was especially glad for young William's presence then, for it was an awkward business and I doubt as to Henry's being able to have managed it on his own. Once more I apologised for my helplessness, and once more I was assured that my friends considered it a privilege to be of service to me.

The best feature of our apartment was the neat little drawing room, which boasted a bow window with a view to the street, the old city wall, and Dr. Gabell's garden. It was a pleasant room, but as I looked about myself I could not help wondering if I would ever leave that place again. Were those four walls, with the faded paisley paper peeling at the seams, the last sight my eyes would behold before closing forever? If so, the glories of heaven were sure to be the more impressive for the dramatic contrast.

I had no complaints, however. My surroundings did not signify. My only point of agitation was in worrying over Captain Devereaux's safety and pondering when I would see him. Otherwise, I was content in knowing that I would have a secure place to rest my head and the care of my friends.

"William must be off in the morning, but I will stay on for a few days," Henry told me when I was settled, reclined onto the sofa. "Until Mr. Lyford has been to give his opinion and..." Here he checked to see that our nephew had left the room, as had Cassandra. "And until the other gentleman has arrived as well. I would like to see him again and to judge for myself if I can entrust my sister's future to him. After that, I'm afraid I must return to Chawton and to my duties there. But I will come at a run if you send for me. You must not hesitate to do so. Understood?"

"Oh, Henry, you are too good! I shall miss you terribly, and never to be given a chance to repay your kindness either!"

"Let us have none of that, Jane. I have already been well and fully paid, I promise you," he said self-consciously. "Now, while we have a moment to ourselves, tell me more of what you would have me do about your books."

I lay back and closed my eyes for a minute. I could see them all in my mind, lined up side by side on the shelf: *Sense and Sensibility,* my first born, as it were, and therefore always special; *Pride and Prejudice*, my most popular and promising child; *Mansfield Park*, the one I feared would never be rightly appreciated; and *Emma*, who had the dubious honour to be dedicated to that contemptible fellow, His Royal Highness, the Prince Regent.

I looked earnestly at my brother. "As I said before, I would like to think they will carry on in my absence, the ones already published, that is. And it would please me very much if the other two could find their way into print as well – Catherine's story and Anne Elliot's too. You will discover the manuscripts in my trunk at home, along with a lot of my other scribblings – mostly childish nonsense I wrote long ago and did not have the courage to throw into the fire as I ought to have done. Do whatever you please with all of that. It is only the novels that concern me. And perhaps no one will want them either, in which case you mustn't feel as if you have failed me. All I ask is that they be given a fair opportunity, as the others were."

"I will do my best."

"I know you will, Henry. What do you think of their chances?"

"Excellent, I imagine. In fact, I expect a queue to form for the rights to publish two more works, just become available, by the author of *Pride and Prejudice.*"

"You are partial to me, though. We must not suppose everybody else will be so enthusiastic."

"I will find a publisher; that is my promise to you, Jane. Might I ask one favour in return?"

"What is it? Although it hardly matters; I could deny you nothing you really wanted."

"It is only this. After you have sailed from England with your captain, might I have the privilege of telling the world who gave these 'darling children' of yours birth? I know how you have always despised the thought of living with notoriety, but..."

"But since I will be as good as dead, one way or the other, what harm could it do? Is that what you are thinking?"

"Not exactly, no. It is more that I am proud of you, Jane – of you and of what you have been able to accomplish. I think it is high time others became aware of it too. I would handle the business with the utmost decorum, I promise. Nothing showy or crass. Still, I will abide by your decision. So, what do you think? May I have your permission to announce that the authoress people so admire is none other than my youngest sister?"

I had heard the catch in his voice.

We all spoke of my impending death in theoretical terms; we all pretended I would survive instead, that I would live to make my escape into oblivion with Philippe. But Henry knew the truth. He knew it was likely my death would be more than theoretical, that his sister would be gone from this world, not just gone from his sight. Perhaps it would give him comfort in that melancholy hour to see me receive some acclaim, even posthumously. I could do that much for him.

I gave Henry the authorisation he sought, since it obviously meant so very much to him. I told him he was free to reveal my identity upon the publication of the final two books. It did seem only right and fitting that, with the collection of my works then complete, they should all be brought together under the correct name. That elusive creature known as 'a lady' must not have the credit for them in perpetuity.

-32-

I spent a miserable night, the unfamiliar bed as well as the bumps and bruises of the road contributing an extra share on top of the discomforts of my illness to which I had become accustomed. It left me more disheartened than ever and struggling to find any cause for hope. The second night in a new place was sure to be better, I reasoned. More significantly, I would see Mr. Lyford soon and begin taking positive steps toward at least the chance of recovery. He had helped me before, so I felt confident he would do everything within his power to assist me again. However, I also knew it might take more than human wisdom to bring about my cure. Here again, I had some basis for optimism in that I was assured that many people were praying for God's intervention on my behalf.

I lay in bed, only half awake, when, at around ten o'clock, I heard a knock sound at the outer door – Mr. Lyford, I presumed. Cassandra had been up for hours, having first tended to my needs and then leaving me alone again to rest. From my situation, I could not see who came in, but I knew it was a man from the voices I heard in low conversation following. A minute later, there was a tap on my door and Mr. Lyford came in.

"What have we here?" the familiar, portly gentleman asked with a smile as he came towards me. "I had not thought to see you again so soon, Miss Austen. I suppose you could not resist the invitation to visit my fair city after all."

"No, sir," I answered. "I was so determined to come, and I made such a nuisance of myself at Chawton, that my mother finally relented, just to be rid of me."

He laughed gently. "It is good to see that your wit and good humour have not deserted you."

"I trust they will be the last to go, Mr. Lyford. But as for the rest…"

"Yes, yes, your sister has told me. The same bad business as before, it seems. Well, I shall just have to cure you again, only this time I must make it stick. Well then, may I begin?"

I consented, offering up my humble person for his inspection.

He stooped over me and set about his work with the professionalism and efficiency which had given me confidence in him the first time we met. He looked and listened, pressed and prodded, spending a good ten minutes in his examination, and saying nothing until he had finished.

"It is bad this time," I said, observing his serious expression.

He eased himself down to sit on the other bed only a few feet away. "I will spare you any useless platitudes. Instead, I shall pay you the compliment of dealing honestly with you, Miss Austen. Shall I?"

"By all means."

"Very well. As you say, then, it is bad. Your malady has returned with a vengeance, more vicious than before, it seems."

I suddenly remembered my strange dream of a few weeks back. Was this dreaded illness the monster I had foreseen then, the beast which would rise up to devour me, to keep me from Philippe? I shuddered and said, "The thing seems determined to swallow me up entirely this time."

He nodded thoughtfully. "It is true that I consider your condition quite grave, my dear. And yet it is also true that I have seen some who were far worse off than you live to recover. You must not lose heart. You must fight this thing with all your strength, physical as well as strength of mind. Then I think there may yet be a chance."

His words did not much encourage me. At that moment, I felt as if, were my remaining strength – body, mind, and spirit – poured together to be measured, the quantity would have fit nicely into a thimble with room to spare.

"May I come in?" Cassandra asked from the doorway.

Mr. Lyford rose at once. "Why, certainly, Miss Austen. Your sister and I were just having a bit of a chat."

"Have you formed an opinion, then, Mr. Lyford? What are we to do?"

He directed his reply to us both, turning first to one and then the other as he talked. "I still believe we were on the right course before, so I will pursue that line of action again. In addition, though, I intend to consult with a few colleagues for their opinions. Perhaps one of them will have heard of some new remedy for this sort of thing which we might try. The science of medicine is advancing at such a pace in this modern age that it is difficult for any one man to keep up. I am not too proud to ask for help. I will exhaust every available resource on your behalf. You may depend on it. It will, however, take time, so I hope you have come prepared to stay for some weeks."

Cassandra answered the surgeon's question, looking to me to ensure my concurrence. "We are prepared to stay as long as it takes, Mr. Lyford, to do whatever is required to make my sister well, once and for all."

"As am I, Miss Austen," he added. He then faced me again. "We shall begin your treatments tomorrow. I will see to the body, but I am pleased to know there is another gentleman here in town to minister to your soul."

I gave him a puzzled look, for indeed I had no idea to whom he might refer.

"The Reverend Mr. Danvers stopped at my door the other day to enquire if you had arrived yet. May I give him your direction when next he calls?"

"Reverend Danvers?" I asked, still mystified.

"Yes. Old family friend from Sidmouth, he said. Tall gentleman, a bit shy of fifty, I should think. Do you not know him?"

Philippe! I then perceived that Mr. Lyford must be speaking of Philippe. So he had come indeed! He was still safe and in Winchester at that very moment. My heart swelled to hear it; it was too full for words. Cassandra had to rescue me once again.

"Oh, yes, Mr. Lyford," she hastened to say. "We know him very well. An old friend of the family, as he told you. It is only that we are surprised to discover him here. I suppose our mother must have sent for him. How kind. By all means, you must give him our direction at your earliest opportunity. He will be a great comfort to us all at this difficult time, to Jane especially."

As Cassandra talked, she had skillfully distracted Mr. Lyford's attention from me and then escorted him to the door. Although I liked the man, it was a relief to have him gone, for I could not have begun to hide my discomposure. Captain Devereaux had come, and perhaps there was yet time. No matter what transpired afterward, I felt I could bear it if I could but see him once more before I died.

Send him to me soon, I prayed. *Dear God in heaven, he must come soon.*

That was my sole focus and goal – to hang on to life long enough to see Captain Devereaux again. With his impending visit in mind, I submitted to my sister's efforts over my hygiene. She washed me, tidied my hair, and insisted I clean my teeth – things I would not have had the energy to attempt on my own. She said no sister of hers would, in an unpresentable condition, receive a guest, at least not while she could help it.

The looked-for guest did not call that day, however, and it was only Mr. Lyford who came again the next, bringing his prepared draughts and his instructions for how I should take them at regular intervals. He charged my poor sister with this and everything else encompassed in my care.

Henry was with us for much of the day as well. But unlike Cassandra, there was little for him to do. Except for his conversations with me, he was consigned mostly to hovering, fretting, and pacing.

My job was simply to rest – very nearly the only thing of which I was capable anyway. I must have fallen asleep again after the few bites of supper I had been able to take, for the next thing I knew, Cassandra was shaking my shoulder and speaking to me in a low but insistent tone. "Jane," she said. "Jane, you must rouse yourself."

I reluctantly opened my eyes. "What time is it?" I asked. "Am I due for another dose of the physic?"

"Half past seven, and no, it is not time for your medicine. It is something else altogether. Oh, Jane, he is come at last. Captain Devereaux is here to see you, so you must rouse yourself at once."

I was fully awake then, or at least I hoped I was, and that this was not just another especially vivid dream of an event so long wished for. But I could hear male voices in the adjoining room – Henry's and another – and there was no mistaking to whom the other belonged, though many years had passed since I had last heard it.

That awareness startled me into action. "Help me sit up a bit, Cass," I insisted, "and do let me have a look in the glass." My sister obediently did as I bid her. She eased me to a sitting position and piled pillows behind my back to keep me there. Then she gave me the hand mirror. I could not approve of what I saw in it, however, not of the thin face or the blotchy, pallid complexion. "Is he much changed too," I dared to ask.

"Some, yes," she answered as she fussed over my hair. "The years have not been entirely kind to him either, from what he told us before I came in to you. Doubtless you will hear the whole story in good time, but for now you must simply be glad he is come. Be gratified in knowing he has travelled far and risked much to be with you again. Only the most ardent admiration could have motivated such exertions. Therefore, you cannot suppose he will care if you fail of your very best looks at the moment. He knows you have been ill."

Nevertheless, I tried pinching some colour into my cheeks before giving Cassandra permission to send him in.

"Do you wish me to stay with you while you speak to him?" she asked.

I considered. Would my sister's presence ease or magnify the awkwardness of the reunion? I could not be certain, but I felt as if Captain Devereaux had earned the right of a private audience. "Thank you, no," I said. "We will deal as best we can on our own, but you may leave the door open if you think it more proper."

Cassandra squeezed my hand, kissed me on the cheek, and said, "Take courage, dearest. This is what you have wished and prayed for. I trust, now that the moment is arrived, it will not by any means disappoint you."

-33-

Although it was evening, it was also the end of May, when the days are long, the result being that there was still sufficient light coming through the window to illumine the form of the tall man who paused in the doorway.

My breath caught in my throat. It was he indeed! Strange to see him wearing a cleric's collar instead of his naval uniform. But there was no mistaking the familiar architecture of that face, though now disguised with a neatly trimmed beard and somewhat remodeled by the effects of time. A bit too thin, I thought, and with a few lines added to further attest to the harshness of life. But his warmth of expression overshadowed all else, and his lopsided smile gave me to know he was still my own dear Captain Devereaux.

"Hello, Jane," he said.

"Philippe," I murmured. It was all I could manage.

I reached for him then, and he came to me at a rush. In a moment he was at my side, kneeling, kissing my hand, and then ardently pressing it to his chest as he gazed at me, devouring me hungrily with his eyes as if he were a starved man who could not get his fill. I felt just the same.

"Jane, my dearest Jane!" he cried. "To be here at last... Oh, how I have longed for this day!"

I was silently thanking God he had arrived in time.

"You are not well, though. I am so sorry. I should have come sooner. The war and then all that followed... but I ought to have found a way."

"Never mind," I whispered. "Never mind. I am sure it could not have been helped, any of it. And you are here now. That is all that signifies."

I tentatively stroked his intriguing new beard. He brushed away a tear that spilt across my cheek and then allowed his hand to linger there. We were both weeping by this time, though I could hardly have said whether primarily for joy or for sorrow. In those initial minutes, we bore the whole weight of years of deprivation as well as the shock of their sudden relief, the intense feelings made more bittersweet for the uncertainty of what the future held for us. I could not dwell on such things at the time, however. I could only tell myself what I told him. All that mattered was that he was finally back where he belonged – with me.

A lengthy interval expired with nothing very intelligible – or at least repeatable – passing between us. It was all sensibility, tears, embracing, the hurried exchange of private pledges, the confirmation by word and gesture of our mutual passion and enduring devotion. It was a necessary exercise in sweeping away the intervening decade, the cruelly coarse sands of time that had come between us. All this was right and essential before we could calm ourselves enough to speak of other things. And all this was sealed with one very long, very fervent kiss to remove every doubt, after which I was spent. With a contented sigh, I leant back against my pillows.

At that moment, Cassandra poked her head through the doorway. "Are you well, Jane?" she asked. "You mustn't tire yourself overly. Your visitor can come again tomorrow, you know."

I murmured words of reassurance, and she withdrew again.

"Perhaps your sister is right," said Captain Devereaux. "You must be tired." He reluctantly started to rise, but I clung to his hand like a lifeline.

"No, pray, do not leave me," I pleaded. "Not yet."

I suppose it should have been enough for one day, and I should have rightly been content to drift off to sleep for the night, to allow the pleasing reality of his presence to migrate directly into my dreams. But I could not let go. *We* could not let go. There was a sense between us that this might be our only chance, that we must wring every bit of goodness out of the meeting in case it would be our last as well as our first. I knew my condition was grave; he did as well, having already spoken to my doctor. And his own life was at risk every minute he remained in England.

"Very well," he said drawing up a chair to sit close by my side. "I certainly have no wish to go. I have so much I want to say to you, so much I must tell you. I will not be easy until you know the truth about what happened in the war. I am no traitor, Jane! You must believe this."

"Oh, I do," I assured him. "I never for one minute thought that you had really behaved treacherously, as the reports we heard claimed. I knew there had to be some error."

One side of his mouth tugged upward a fraction at this. "Excellent creature, you do me justice after all. Yes, some error indeed. No one could have been more surprised at those reports than I was myself when I heard them not long ago."

"Tell me how it was."

"Are you sure? I would not wish to tax your strength just so that I might have the relief of unburdening myself."

"Nothing would contribute more comfort, I assure you, than hearing your story. It would be lifting a burden for me as well, sorting out a mystery that has long plagued me."

"Of course. This is how it happened. I had not purposely allowed the French force to escape Toulon unchallenged," he said in disdain. "While it is true I fired no shot when they broke through our blockade, it was only because they were clearly out of range. That was part of the admiral's plan, that the loose arrangement of our ships would entice the French from port, which it did. The gaps in our line, however, not only enticed them out, it allowed Villeneuve's fleet to evade us entirely. So, I did the only thing I could. I fell into pursuit, mistakenly expecting my compatriots to join in the effort."

"But the others did not go with you?"

"No, not one of them. Perhaps they hesitated too long, and then found the winds against them. I cannot say. The only thing I am sure of is that I was alone when, after we had passed Gibraltar, the French fleet, joined by their Spanish allies, turned to engage my ship in battle – if one can call such an uneven match a 'battle.'"

I gasped at the picture this description formed in my mind. "You had no chance, then, horribly outnumbered as you were."

"No," he said solemnly. "No chance at all. My crew fought bravely and died heroes, although it seems they will never be given their due now. That offends me more than anything else. Only a handful of us lived through the conflict, and I alone, so far as I know, survived the long imprisonment at Cadiz following. There is no one left to tell the tale excepting myself, and *I* will not be believed."

"So you have been in Spain all this time? Not in a French prison as I have often thought of you."

"One prison is much like another, I suppose, but yes. As an officer, I might have been treated a little better than my men, which may have made the difference. In any case, I would never recommend it. Nothing but dankness, disease, boredom, and discouragement. No wonder the spirit eventually succumbs."

"Oh, good God! This is worse than I had imagined. How did you endure it so long?"

"One has no choice. One must endure or go mad. It becomes a challenge of the mind as much or more than the body at some point. I was near to death on several occasions and would almost have welcomed it. Instead, to keep my sanity, I set little tasks for myself – puzzling problems of mathematics in my head, attempting to learn the Spanish language I heard spoken round about me, committing to memory passages from the Bible or any other book I was lucky enough to lay hold of. Having a goal to accomplish, no matter how small or seemingly inconsequential, gave me a motive to cling to life a little longer."

"Yes!" I cried. "I have felt the same at times during my illness. Having a story to finish writing or even simply the goal of saving my sister and mother the grief of my dying – these things gave me a reason to go on."

"I see you understand. The most powerful incentive for me, however, was my determination to keep my commitments to those I loved – to you and to my younger sister. I had promised I would return to marry you and, long before that, I had vowed to find out what became of Simone during the revolution and to help her if I could."

"I remember. You told me so the first time we met. Were able to keep that vow at last? Did you find your sister?"

"I did, thank God. Had I known you were ill, I would have come directly. As it was, though, I decided to post a letter to Bath for you, which I now know you never received, and then I went to France in search of Simone. It took weeks and weeks, but my painstaking enquiries finally bore fruit, leading me to a little village in the south. There I discovered her – in sad circumstances, but alive and safe. Luckily, friends had been able to spirit her away to that place when the trouble erupted. She has been living there ever since, using an assumed name."

"I can only imagine how delighted she must have been to see you again."

"Very much so, yes, as I was to see her, although it grieved me to find her in such mean estate, especially when I think of the care with which she was brought up, the better conditions she had been raised to expect."

"Where is she now? Still in France?"

"No, I have resettled her in Italy, along with the portion of the family wealth I was able to recover – some portable property my father had hidden away in case of emergency. She will be comfortable there… she and her child." He stopped, closed his eyes, and shuddered slightly.

"Is… is there something amiss with the child?" I asked.

He continued with some difficulty. "Not exactly. The little girl, my niece, is a sweet thing. It is only her origins that I find upsetting. Her father was… That is to say, she is the result of my sister's being required to put up with a brute of a landlord, who would have otherwise turned her out of his house and over to the authorities. This was at a time when it would have gone very badly for her if he had. Simone assures me the filthy beast is dead now or I would have felt compelled to avenge such barbarous treatment – my clear duty, since I failed to protect her in the first place as I ought to have done. If I had only stayed in France all those years ago…"

"What could you have accomplished more than your father and brother did? Your life would have been sacrificed along with theirs and your sister no better off for it. You made the only choice possible under the circumstances… and you brought others away to safety with you. Think of that instead."

"Dear Jane, what a capable defence you mount for me against my own conscience," he said wistfully, stroking my cheek again. "At least I can do something for Simone now. My idea is that we will join her in Italy… once you are well enough to travel, of course."

Here he dropped his eyes from mine. He knew as well as I did that it might never be, but neither of us could bear to acknowledge that fact aloud.

"Italy sounds divine," I said instead. "I should be pleased to be warmed by the Mediterranean sun, and to meet your sister too."

"Very good. We will talk much more about it tomorrow." He searched my face, and a shadow clouded his own countenance. "But you *are* tired now, I see. And here is your sister again, come to tell me it is high time I was gone."

I protested as I had successfully before, this time to no avail.

"I must go, for your sake," he said. "But I will return in the morning, I promise." He pressed his lips to my hand once more and then released it.

"Do be careful, Philippe," I urged him.

"I will, and the name is Peter Danvers, Madam," he said with a wink and his best British accent. "Reverend Danvers to you." He pulled a pair of spectacles from his pocket and perched then atop his nose, completing the disguise. At the doorway, he looked back, gave me a parting salute, and then he was gone.

I felt as if all the air had been forcibly drawn out of the room – and out of my lungs – by his leaving. A suffocating atmosphere of foreboding, too thick to breathe, rushed in to take its place.

"You are unwell, Jane," said Cassandra, hurrying to my side. "More so than usual, that is. What is it? Truly, you look very ill. Did Captain Devereaux say something to upset you?"

I ignored her question and focused my entire being on the supreme effort of drawing my next breath. This finally accomplished, I said, "Oh, Cass, I shall never see him again."

~~*~~

So strong was my fear, so overpowering my impression that I would see Captain Devereaux no more, that all my sister's sensible counsel and lengthy reassurances could not dislodge it.

"You saw how well disguised he is," she said in part, "what care he has taken over his appearance. Why, I would hardly have known him myself, had I met him on the street. He is a clever man too, and he will take no unnecessary chances. You may be sure of that. This meeting has simply overexcited you, and overtired. A good night's sleep will set you right. You shall see."

All the same, after she had fulfilled her other duties to me, I insisted she bring me paper and pen so that I could write these things down before I slept, lest I were to die in the night without having completed the final chapter.

I took no comfort when I did not die but awoke with the dawn instead, for it only proved I had been mistaken about how the ultimate separation would occur. Perhaps it had been *his* demise instead of my own I had foreseen. Perhaps, notwithstanding Cassandra's confidence in him, he had been discovered and taken away as soon as he parted from me. My stomach lurched at the thought of Philippe behind bars, Philippe standing trial, Philippe being led away to the gallows. No! If anyone must die, I much preferred it should be me, for to be left behind again – to have him travel on without me, more irretrievably than before – was unthinkable.

Whether it was a true miracle, I do not know, but it happened that a ray of the rising sun at that moment passed through the window, reflected off the glass of a small watercolour picture hanging on the wall opposite, and shone squarely on my face, nearly blinding me. Closing my eyes against the brightness, I thought of Saul, who became Paul, and how he had been struck down by a dazzling light from heaven while on the road to Damascus. Was this God's way of getting my attention as well?

I was instantly ashamed of the weakness of character my unbecoming state of near panic indicated. I remembered that I had previously vowed to trust Providence for the future, asking only that I be allowed to see Philippe once more. God had kindly granted my request, but I had failed to do my part. To where had my feeble faith flown? It was inconstant as the wind, apparently, blowing first in one direction and then another.

And yet faith was not built in times of ease, but in times of testing, I reminded myself. I had often heard my father say so, across the dinner table as well as from the pulpit. Neither was faith something I was required to muster on the basis of my own strength. Fortunately, it was built on a much more concrete foundation – on God himself, not me or any other undependable mortal. His ways were infinitely higher. He was unchanging and true. He viewed everything from an eternal perspective, of which I was incapable, and yet he had taken the trouble to send me this personal sign. He would surely work all things together for good in the end, as He had promised.

Deep in my heart, I believed this. And I knew, despite the current crisis, that I could trust Him absolutely. Live or die, Captain Devereaux and I were safe in His care. A profound peace filled me to overflowing then, one that never again quite deserted me in the difficult days to come.

-34-

I was awake long before my sister that morning, meditating on these things. Lying there quietly in my bed, I observed Cassandra when she finally arose from hers. For the first time I noticed how slowly she moved – slowly, stiffly, and in considerable pain it seemed to me, like an old woman, though she was barely beyond her prime. It was hard work, not age, which had wrought the change in her – the work of caring for me. This understanding cut me to the quick, and I immediately determined to do something about it. I could not prevent my own decline but I would not drag my beloved sister down with me.

"You must send for Mary at once," I said.

"Oh, good morning, Jane. I did not know you were awake. What did you say?"

"You need help here, Cass, and you must send for sister Mary at once."

"Nonsense, Jane. I can manage well enough on my own. I have Henry, after all, and Mr. Lyford. Moreover, you said yourself that Mary would be a complication we can ill afford, not to mention the fact that you can barely abide her presence."

"I know what I said, but we also agreed such considerations must be secondary to my getting well. Even if I begin improving at once, it may be weeks before I regain my strength. So I will continue to need help for some time to come – too long for you to carry on alone. And you know as well as I do that Henry will be of no use. Nursing is not a man's province. Besides, he is leaving soon. I must put aside my dislike of Mary, and we must indeed accept her kind offer of help. It is the only sensible thing to do."

Cassandra did not concede at once. By the time she had gone through the morning's chores, however – seeing to it that the helpless invalid was fed, washed, dressed, and every other necessary function attended to – I believe she was beginning to appreciate the wisdom of my advice. She wrote to Mary later that day.

Although I was calmer about the possible peril of the situation in general, thanks to my early morning epiphany, it was still a great relief when I heard Captain Devereaux arrive. Mr. Lyford had just left me, and I could hear the four of them – the surgeon, Philippe, Henry, and Cassandra – conversing in the outer room while I tried to compose myself. I was grateful Cassandra had taken the time to fuss over my appearance a little and to arrange me in a semi-seated position again, just in case he came.

He tapped on the door and enquired, "May I enter?"

"Yes, by all means," I answered eagerly, rallying my paltry reserves of strength for this important visit.

He came and stood before me, taking up my hand and studying me for a minute, frowning slightly as he did so.

I was gratified to see love and compassion burning in his eyes, but there was also an unbearable measure of pity. "You mustn't scrutinise me so narrowly, Captain," I said with forced brightness. "Mr. Danvers, I mean. I fear you do not like what you see. Although last night I may have had you fooled, the daylight has surely undeceived you. My plans are ruined and all my secrets revealed. Well, at least you have found out in time, unlike many a man who has committed himself in haste only to be disappointed when the veil is removed. Think of poor Jacob, discovering after it was too late that he had married the wrong woman entirely!"

He attempted a smile at this. "If memory serves, Jacob only waited seven years for his Rachel; I have waited more than twice that for you, Jane. Now I only wish I could do something to relieve your suffering."

"Oh, but you can. You are! The sight of you has done me more good than all Mr. Lyford's potions, believe me. If I recover…" I saw him wince. "That is to say, when I recover, he shall have to share the credit of my cure with you, which I daresay will vex him greatly." I had to pause a moment to catch my breath before continuing. "Now, let us have no more talk of sickness. I am in too cheerful a frame of mind for that. You must instead keep your promise to tell me about Italy. Bring your chair up close as before and talk of the future. Tell me all about the place we are to live when we go away."

I was satisfied that the worried furrows on Captain Devereaux's brow had eased a bit. Still, the effort of this pretty speech had cost me, and I was therefore only too happy to relinquish responsibility for the conversation entirely to my handsome companion. Keeping hold of his hand, I leant back against my pillows to gaze upon and listen to him.

"You will adore Italy, Jane," he began with obvious excitement. "The people are very hospitable and the climate ideal. I cannot wait to introduce my sister and to show you the palazzo. I leased it with you in mind, so I hope you will approve."

"A palazzo? That sounds very grand."

"Oh, no, I would not wish to excite any expectations of opulence. It is exceedingly comfortable, true, but I would hardly call it grand, except for the canal itself, of course. When one lives in Venice, one must have a house on the main canal. There is a certain quality to the light there that is utterly fantastic and unlike any other place in the world. It defies description, but you will experience it for yourself soon enough."

"Heavenly," I murmured. "Tell me more – all the little details."

He humoured me in this, continuing on with only an occasional word of encouragement. I soon closed my eyes to better imagine the scenes he described – the distinctive architecture, the Italian cuisine, the golden, rolling countryside. As Philippe talked, I began mentally constructing the timeless stone façades of an Italian villa to replace the dingy apartment walls surrounding me; substituting the lapping of waves against gondolas for the clatter of a vendor's carts on the street outside; trading the damp English fog for dry, Mediterranean heat.

I was soon transported to a picturesque, iron-railed balcony overlooking the Grand Canal. Philippe was beside me, of course, stroking my arm reassuringly. Yet when I opened my eyes, I discovered to my dismay that Philippe was no longer himself; he had become someone else. It was Mr. Lyford who now sat with me, Mr. Lyford's hand that had rubbed my arm to rouse me. I was no longer in Italy either.

"Mr. Lyford?" I said in some confusion.

"Good afternoon," he returned. "So sorry to wake you from your gentle slumber, my dear."

I shook myself to clear the cobwebs. "Not at all, sir. I am always pleased to see you."

"It seems to me your colour is a little better today. How do you feel?"

"Oh, my! Still weak as a kitten, I'm afraid, but in less pain. I feel a good deal calmer about my situation too. There must be some value in that."

"I suppose we have the spiritual counsel of your Mr. Danvers to credit."

I nodded. It was true in the main.

"Good man, that Mr. Danvers. And yes, calm is far better for the health than excessive agitation. Only mind that you do not become so complacent as to no longer care whether you live or die. We are in a war of sorts, and you must be prepared to fight, as I told you before."

"I will fight to live, Mr. Lyford. Have no fear on that head. Thanks to Mr. Danvers's coming, I have more reason than ever for getting well."

Mr. Lyford proceeded with the business he had come for. He examined me and bled me, and he instructed my sister in the administration of the various soups and elixirs he prescribed. After he had gone, I believe I slept again. And then Henry was my next visitor.

"What became of the captain?" I asked when my brother entered my room.

"He sat with you for an hour or more before he went away," said Henry.

"I dozed off right before his eyes, I suppose. Oh, dear, how tiresome he must have found me."

"Never mind that. I daresay you will both get over it. I hear from him that you are to go to Italy when you are well, and to live there in some kind of style from the way Captain Devereaux describes it."

I smiled weakly. "Yes, so he tells me. And he is Mr. Danvers now, Henry. We had best practice calling him by that name, even amongst ourselves, lest we forget and give him away in front of others one day."

"Right you are, Jane. Now you are thinking."

"Not an easy thing, is it, this art of concealment, especially when one has been raised to be completely forthright? Father would lose all respect for me, I suppose. And I can see Mr. Darcy scowling at me too. '*Disguise of every sort is my abhorrence,*' he is saying."

"Mr. Darcy kept a few secrets of his own, as I recall. And the idea of invention is not entirely foreign to you either, when you think of it. You have spent the better part of your life constructing fictional tales of one sort or another – volumes full."

"Imagining a fictional life for somebody else and living one yourself are two very different things."

"Well, you had best get used to it. When you leave this place, Miss Jane Austen will cease to exist, according to the plan. But who will you be then? By what name will you be known in your new life?"

The question took me by surprise and set my mind into a sudden flurry of activity. "I cannot say. I have never before given it any thought, but what an intriguing prospect! I always take great delight in choosing names for the people in my stories. How much more so to choose one for myself! But perhaps I will travel as Mrs. Danvers, at least until we are out of the country."

Henry glowered. "Humph, I cannot say that I much like the sound of that. Run away with the man first and marry him later if it suits you? I hate to point this out, Jane, but it sounds a deal like something one of your less respectable characters would do."

"Are you thinking of Lydia Bennet? Or perhaps Maria Bertram?"

"Quite."

"Well, then it is possible I have more in common with those ladies than you or I had supposed."

"Do not tease me, Jane. A brother feels a heavy responsibility to defend his sister's honour, especially in the absence of her father."

I could not help laughing, weak as I was. "Oh, Henry, you are a darling, but need I remind you that I am no girl? I am a woman of one-and-forty. I believe your duty to my honour expired years ago."

"There is no expiration on defending virtue, at least there ought not be. I would be much happier knowing things had been done properly, that is all."

"I declare you are become a Puritan in your old age, Henry! Would you have the banns read out in Winchester Cathedral, then? You know it is impossible. Or perhaps you have money to spare and mean to purchase us a special license. In that case, remember to have a little something extra on hand to buy the silence of the man who performs the ceremony. No, my dear brother, it will not do. Under the circumstances, I simply cannot be married to the gentleman anywhere on this side of the channel. Your scruples notwithstanding, Mr. Danvers and I shall have to wait to be properly married until we reach the continent. I promise to send you word when the deed is finally accomplished, though. Perhaps that will ease your conscience. In the meantime, you must trust us to behave as we should."

-35-

Henry departed the next morning after extracting a promise from both Cassandra and myself that we would send for him again the moment he was needed. Such assurance I readily gave. Indeed, it was the only way I could have been convinced to part with him – the idea that I could and would see him again.

We expected Mary from Steventon any day, and for her to then take up Henry's recently vacated cot in one of the side rooms. Although I had been the one to insist on summoning her, for Cassandra's sake, I had agonised about it ever since. There were two principal problems, as I saw it: to keep her, along with everybody else, in the dark about Captain Devereaux's true identity; and to prevent her from deliberately or accidentally disrupting our carefully concocted plan for escape.

After hours of rumination on the subject (I had very little else to do, in truth), I decided the second problem was easily solved. We could simply dismiss Mary to return home to Steventon, her help no longer needed, as soon as my health sufficiently improved, if indeed it did so. With her well clear of the business, I would supposedly take a sudden turn for the worse and promptly expire. Immediately after Philippe and I were safely away, she, along with the rest of my near relations, would be informed of the truth before any rumour of my theoretical death ever reached their ears. At least that was the strategy. The idea that anyone I loved might suffer unnecessary grief on my account, even momentarily, made me most uneasy, especially when I considered the disaster which resulted when another lady feigned her own death. Juliet's plan had been sound, I considered. She had simply entrusted her message for Romeo into the wrong hands, to be delivered too late. I would take no chances; I would send my letter – the one I had already begun composing in my mind – by express.

I did not like keeping Mary in the dark any more than I did the rest of my family, but it had to be done, for their own protection as well as Captain Devereaux's. I trusted that, once everything was thoroughly explained, they would all forgive me.

As to the idea of Mary's remembering the captain, that was more uncertain and so more difficult to account for. The two had met only once – twenty years ago at the party at Steventon celebrating Henry and Eliza's marriage. Since then, the captain had changed substantially, thanks to the inevitable working of time and to his deliberate alterations. Even the last vestiges of his French accent had nearly vanished, I had noticed. These things were highly in our favour. Although Mary's mind was keener than most, it still seemed unlikely that her penetration would go so far as to discover a former slight acquaintance in the face of a person taking pains not to be noticed, and whose name would have had no reason to be mentioned again in her presence in two decades' time. We would need to be more circumspect with her in the house, but I had every reason to hope Mary would accept Mr. Danvers (as Mr. Lyford had) for the person he presented to be: a clergyman of my acquaintance, come to give me counsel and encouragement in my hour of need.

The testing of this theory, however, was to be put off for some time, as I soon learnt when Captain Devereaux came that afternoon.

I had been sleeping again, this time on the sofa in the drawing-room, for I could not seem to keep my eyes open for much more than an hour or two at a stretch. Now it actually *was* the captain who sat beside me when I awoke.

"Philippe," I said when I saw him there. We were alone, but with the door ajar as usual. I could hear Cassandra humming and moving crockery about in the tiny kitchen.

"Peter," he corrected with a smile.

"Yes, well, you will, neither one of you, find it very amusing that I should always be asleep in your presence, as if I did not care a straw that you had bothered to come. I am sorry for yesterday, really."

"No need for apologies. I only worried that my talk had been so tedious as to bore you into unconsciousness," he said sardonically.

"Do you often have that effect on ladies, Mr. Danvers?"

"Ladies? No, I have had no recent experience with the fairer sex, I assure you; it is on men that I have practiced the art. Something I was working on in prison, actually, a tactic for escape. Bore all the guards to death, or at least out of their senses, and I would walk out a free man."

"And were you successful? Is that how you made your escape at the last?"

"After a fashion. I believe they were so weary of me by the end of the war that they were glad for an excuse of letting me go, for here I am, you see."

"Yes, I do see," I said, savouring the sight of him and wishing I could go on doing so forever. "And I shall be very happy to have you practice all your arts on *me* from now on. I cannot promise to become bored with you, however, no matter how diligently you try."

"Not even after twenty or thirty years?"

Twenty or thirty years – what a heavenly thought. "No, not even then," said I.

"Very well, I suppose with you I must find my satisfaction in other ways." He gave me a significant look, which nearly took my breath away.

"I sincerely hope you will, Mr. Danvers." After thoroughly enjoying the moment, I went on. "Oh, but you shall not always be Mr. Danvers, I daresay. Who will you be when we arrive in Italy? Who will I be, for that matter?"

"You will be my wife, of course. As for your name, how should you like being addressed as a countess?"

I could not help laughing; the idea was so absurd. "I, a countess?"

"Why not? You are as noble as any lady I have ever known. And there is some justification for it too. An old family title. It would have been my brother's, of course; now I suppose it belongs to me, should I choose to use it. But we needn't decide now."

Indeed, I could not. Henry was correct when he had said I must become accustomed to living a fictional life, but it would require some serious adjustment in my thinking to adapt to the idea of living it as a countess – a challenging masquerade indeed for an ordinary clergyman's daughter. How unfortunate that my cousin Eliza was not available to advise me. She had managed the feat with some style in her day.

While I had been occupied with these musings, Philippe had risen and gone to one side of the bow window. He pushed the half-drawn curtain away a few inches and peered out one corner. I saw his expression darken.

"What is it?" I asked.

"Oh, probably nothing," he said dismissively. "Just a curious man down the street. I have seen him several times now, and he seems to have nothing better to do than to follow my every move. But possibly it is only my imagination playing tricks."

"You think him a spy for the admiralty, then?"

"The thought has occurred to me. More likely he is simply a mercenary out for the reward."

"Then you must get away from here at once! You must indeed, Philippe."

"There is wisdom in what you say. Perhaps it would be best to make myself scarce for a while. Shall you mind if I leave you?"

"Terribly! But do anything rather than being arrested now, after all you have come through."

"I do have some business to attend to elsewhere in any case. I must see my sister Marguerite... and Bothwell too. He is holding some money for me – funds essential for our future. If that fellow out there is really following me, I could lead him a merry chase in the process."

"You mustn't speak as if it were a game; the stakes are far too high."

"My darling, I promise to take no unnecessary chances – not with my own safety or with the welfare of my friends either. I will lead my shadow much astray and then double back to my true destination without him. I shall be very clever, I assure you. All things considered, however, I believe it will be wiser for me to keep on the move rather than to stay in one place too long."

He had come back from the window to his chair by me, but now he was on his feet again and pacing. This, as much as his words, revealed his anxiety to be gone. I truly did not desire he should stay at his peril. I only wished I could get away as well. Oh, to escape the sickbed and go adventuring with him – to see the Crowes and the Bothwells again!

He seemed to read my thoughts. "Would that it were possible for you to come with me," he said.

"I should like nothing better, but in this case you must carry my love to our friends for me."

"That I shall, and I depend on finding you vastly improved by the time I return. When I saw Mr. Lyford the other day, he said he would be consulting with some very learned London men on your behalf, and that he expected to return with something beneficial. His optimism has taught me to believe as well, else I would hardly consider leaving your side for one day."

I could not let on that I was less sanguine about a recovery. I knew he must go, and with a clear conscience. "Shall you be off immediately?"

"Yes, the sooner, the better. Those who can arrest me may have been sent for and already on their way here. If this man has indeed identified me, he will be eager to collect his reward."

Philippe had taken care to keep his tone relatively light, despite the serious tendency of our discussion. And yet I heard the genuine concern he strove to hide, which heightened my own. "Go tonight then," I told him, "as soon as it is dark."

"I think I will at that." He passed an unconscious hand through his dark hair, now interwoven with grey at the temples. "Jane, it is possible that officials will come to question you – you and every other person in this house – once they discover I have given them the slip."

"We will be ready for them. We shall not give you away, depend on it."

We were both silent, studying each other as if trying to determine whether or not we each believed the words we had spoken so decidedly, if we truly felt the confidence we had expressed. In reality, all I could think of was that he was leaving that very night, and only God knew if I would ever see him again. I should have had a thousand more things to say to him before he went. However, I could think of only one. "Will... Will you hold me before you go?" I ventured. "I know it might not be entirely proper but..."

His expression, previously drawn taut with the strain of anxiety, now melted into a warm, off-centered smile. "I will do better than that," he said. Drawing the draperies closed first, he came to my side once more. "Will you dance with me, Jane?"

The idea both delighted and mystified me. "We have no music," I pointed out, "and you know I am barely able to stand, much less dance!"

"We shall not be held back by such trifles." Bending over me with arms outstretched, he said, "If you will permit me?"

Comprehending then what he intended, I nodded.

"Put your arms about my neck," he instructed, and when I had done so, he lifted me from the sofa in one easy motion. "There," he said softly, holding me against himself. "This will do very nicely."

Oh, the rapture of that hour! – caught up in Captain Devereaux's strong embrace, held close to his heart and near enough to be aware of his breath in my hair and his scent in my nostrils. He began to hum then – a low and indistinct melody next to my ear – moving his feet in time until we were slowly turning about the drawing-room. I rested my head on his shoulder and allowed myself to be entirely swept along in the dream. It was not a proper dance; it was a vast deal better – doubtless inappropriate for the barely acquainted, but ideal for the couple who is married (or very soon to be so). With our bodies moving together as one and my face separated from his by less than a hand's breadth, it was the easiest, most natural thing in the world that our lips should be united as well. And so they very often were.

I cannot say how much time we passed in that exquisite attitude. It was both an eternity and yet not nearly long enough. Eventually, he did go, however, and I was once more alone. I bless Cassandra for her discretion – and especially her absence – throughout the whole of that extraordinary tryst. I shall never forget it, even should I live to be a very old lady. It served to rejoice and fortify me for yet another separation from Philippe. Of what duration this one would be, I had no idea.

-36-

Mary came on Friday, June sixth – she *and* her diary. Cassandra told me Mary began scribbling in it almost as soon as she arrived, though never within my sight. What she found worthwhile recording for posterity, I do not know. There could be nothing more remarkable available to her than the ebb and flow of my illness and the comings and goings of our household. Scant fare indeed, for, with Captain Devereaux gone out of town, few came visiting except Mr. Lyford. He was not so very interesting a subject, truth be told, and neither was I. Nevertheless, Mary continued documenting, undaunted.

I loathed the thought of being so closely observed, especially with my proposed plans for deception on my mind. I was glad for two things, however – first, that Captain Devereaux had got away without my sister-in-law's seeing him, and second, that her presence made it possible to divide the load, shifting a considerable share of the nursing her way. Mary was a very willing worker; I must say that much for her. If anything, she was a little too keen, inclined to take charge more than strictly necessary or wanted.

"Now I am come," I heard her tell Cassandra, "you shall have a rest. You must go and do as you please. I can manage things here very well on my own."

Cassandra did not abandon me entirely to Mary's mercy, but she did, with my encouragement, leave the house much more frequently – to attend church, go to the market, or simply take the air on a walk. I was hopeful that the change would soon restore her.

From the way Mary looked at me with pitying eyes and a sorrowful bearing, and the way she spoke to me with excessively sweet and scrupulously careful words, I immediately perceived that she considered my chances very grim indeed. This did not trouble me overly. I intended to live or die quite independent of her opinion in the case. No, it was not for myself I worried. My concern was that she would distress others of my family with her dire reports, for she wrote letters as eagerly as she did entries in her diary.

Perhaps she meant it as a kindness, by way of preparing my loved ones for the inevitable conclusion. I freely admit that I should have had the charity to grant her this reasonable benefit of doubt. It is a terrible failing of mine that I have often seen unkind motives where they may not have existed, especially in people I dislike. Mary Lloyd Austen had been a lifelong family friend, and yet, unlike her sister Martha, I could never warm to her. In that, she was Jane Fairfax to my Emma. Yet I am reminded that Emma was wrong about Miss Fairfax, and it is possible I had been wrong about Mary too.

Besides, it did seem as if Mary's prediction of my demise would come true. For weeks, my life had perched perilously close to the precipice, and so it continued after her arrival. Then one day Mr. Lyford came in quite a tremble.

"I've got it!" he announced as he entered the house, his eyes bright with excitement. "After all this time, I have finally found the answer, Miss Austen. At least I think I have."

I was reclining on the sofa, as usual; Cassandra was out; but Mary, who had admitted him, followed the medical man to my side. "What?" she asked. "What are you saying, sir? Please do make yourself clear."

"It is just this. I believe I finally have at least a rudimentary understanding of this illness we have been dealing with." He then returned his attention to me, drawing up his usual chair. "I began reciting your troubles to a few colleagues of mine in London, from whence I have just this moment returned. The one fellow identified the syndrome immediately as something he had come across several times before. In fact, he described your odd collection of symptoms and the vacillating course of the disease so accurately, that I would have sworn he had been looking over my shoulder these two months past. As it turns out, he has become something of an expert in it. I count it as something of a miracle, my coming across him just now. For, had I searched throughout all England, I could not have met with a person more capable of helping us."

I was at once caught up by his excitement. "Does it have a name, this illness of mine?" I asked.

"No, not yet. Perhaps my colleague will name it after himself, as so often happens, although I cannot think Higgenbottom's Disease very distinguished sounding. More important to us than a name, however, is a treatment. Would not you agree? And your illness, Miss Austen, *does* have one of those, I am happy to say!" He brought out a large, brown apothecary's jar from a parcel he carried with him, handling it as reverently as if it contained an ancient, parchment scroll written on by the hand of God Himself. "Do you see this, Miss Austen?" he asked, holding the translucent bottle to the light so that a vague outline of its contents could be seen. "This may be your salvation. I had these tablets compounded for you in town, according to Higgenbottom's exact specifications. If all goes as I hope, you will be well, once and for all, by the time this jar is empty! So let us waste no time in beginning."

He extracted the cork stopper and tipped from the bottle into his hand one coarse, rather brownish lump, roughly the size and shape of an almond.

I stared at the thing, incredulous. Could this unpretentious-looking substance truly be the extravagant miracle we had so long prayed for? Was it possible that a cure was at last come within my reach? It seemed too fantastical to be imagined that in the end it might be as simple as swallowing a series of tablets. The illness had been so very tenacious that I should have thought it would require great exertion or the enduring of some terrible ordeal to finally loosen the demon's grip and be rid of it. But it seemed I was not to be subjected to a harrowing surgery after all, or to any other unique form of torture. I was not even told I must dip myself three times in the Jordan River.

"Bring us a glass of water, will you, Mrs. Austen?" I heard Mr. Lyford saying to Mary. Then he turned to me and asked, "Do you think you can manage a tablet of this size? If not, it can be steeped into a tea, but the effect will be weakened and the taste bitter."

"Then I had rather swallow it whole," said I.

"Down it quickly, then. Do not allow it to linger on the tongue."

As soon as Mary returned, I took the tablet from Mr. Lyford's hand, dropped it into my mouth, and immediately chased it down my throat with the full glass of water.

"Good girl," said Mr. Lyford. "The same twice a day until these are gone. There may be a little upset here at first," he said, patting his ample belly. "But nothing worse than what you have already come through."

Somewhat belatedly I thought to ask, "What is in this medicine of yours, Mr. Lyford? What is it that I am taking?"

He winked at me. "Eye of newt, hair of rabid dog, boar's milk…"

Mary gasped behind him – no doubt the reaction Mr. Lyford had hoped for.

He laughed. "You must forgive my teasing you, Mrs. Austen," he told her. "My spirits will not be repressed tonight. The mixture is really quite complex, though – plant extracts, minerals, and so forth. But think of it as the crushed petals of a few fresh flowers if that seems more acceptable."

Mary sniffed. "This hardly seems a joking matter to me, sir."

"I should not care if these tablets *were* comprised of newt and boar," I rejoined, "so long as they have the desired effect."

"A very sensible attitude," said Mr. Lyford as he rose and bowed first to Mary and then to me. "If you will excuse me now, Mrs. Austen, Miss Austen, I must be getting home and changed out of these travelling clothes."

"Sir, I cannot thank you enough," said I.

"Get well, my dear," he said, patting my hand. "That is all the thanks I require… that and paying my bill, of course. Ha!"

The new medicine did make me feel worse for a day or two, just as Mr. Lyford had predicted, but after a week I was decidedly better. The improvement held and continued the next week and then the next to where I was soon up, walking about the room at length, and able to tend to my own needs. I received a visit from my nephew Charles, who attended Winchester College. I read letters and wrote them. I even made an expedition out into the town in a sedan chair. In short, I seemed well on my way to a full recovery.

Although I had rallied before, this was decidedly different. I began feeling like my old self again – the person I had been prior to the illness beginning. I had nearly forgotten that lady, so long had she been missing. I had forgotten what it was to move with energy, to live without pain. Now I began to resurrect that person from the past, slowly at first, then by leaps and bounds.

In the beginning, I could not trust the positive trend; I had been disappointed by false recoveries in the past. But with each day's improvement, my optimism grew until I finally allowed myself to believe that I would indeed be fully well again, something Mr. Lyford now claimed as a certainty. Cassandra concurred, or so she said. Only Mary held out for a gloomier prospect, a circumstance that inspired me all the more to survive, that I might thoroughly disappoint her.

Had Captain Devereaux been beside me to share in this triumph, my joy would have been complete. But he had not returned, and neither had any letter from him arrived. No one came from the admiralty to question us either, however, which I at first counted as a great blessing, until I apprehended the fact that they would likely not bother with us if they were already fast on their real quarry's trail. I told myself that not one of these facts necessarily portended something ominous. There was no definite proof that Philippe had even been identified. It could simply be that he had determined the risk of any attempted correspondence being intercepted was too great. And he likely travelled a longer, more circuitous route to throw off any person who might be following.

If my beloved's protracted absence meant he was taking every possible precaution against apprehension, I should be well satisfied. It had also preserved him from even a single exposure to my sister-in-law, which must be deemed another advantage. Cassandra and I had at last succeeded in convincing Mary that her help was no longer needed, and she had returned to Steventon none the wiser.

Except for Mr. Lyford's short, congratulatory visits, I had those next few days alone with Cassandra, for which I will be eternally grateful. We spent hours and hours in conversation, laughing and reminiscing over the past. Now that I was nearly assured of having a future – something which had long been in doubt – equal enthusiasm was given to conjecturing about that period. What would my life be like with Philippe? Would the warmer climate of Italy agree with me? Would I ever accustom myself to the idea of being a countess?

Cassandra continued as my watchful guardian while I increased my activity to build my strength. I even persuaded her one particularly fine day to venture out on foot with me. I believe it was nearly more than her maternal solicitude could bear, however. "Are you certain you are warm enough?" she asked more than once. "We must turn back the moment you feel the least bit tired."

Walking out of doors for the first time in over a month felt simply wonderful, yet I could not justify a repeat of the exercise at the expense of my sister. She had done enough for me, much more than I could ever repay. And now she was prepared to make one final sacrifice; she was prepared to give me up.

Papa had predicted the day I was born that I would be a plaything and companion to Cassy, and so I had been for all of my life. In a house full of boys – my father's pupils added to my own brothers – it was to be expected, I suppose, that we two girls would band together. And yet I believe we were even closer as children than most sisters in the same circumstances would be. We were virtually inseparable. When I was only seven, for an example, I insisted on leaving home and going away to school with my ten-year-old sister rather than be parted from her. My mother is known to have said on the occasion that if Cassandra's head had been going to be cut off, then I would surely have had mine cut off as well. This story has been retold so often as to become the stuff of family legend.

Had either one of us been the least bit lucky in love, Cassandra and I would have been quite naturally and amicably parted long ago, when the first of us married. Instead, we had carried on together, united as adults by the common isolation of our spinsterhood in much the same way we had been bound together as children by the common distinction of our femaleness. It had come to seem as if nothing short of death would ultimately part us.

Now, however, the painful separation was finally to occur by a more auspicious means. Cassandra and the rest of my family would recover. I had no fear on that head. They would still have each other, and they would take comfort in the knowledge that I was alive and happy. *My* loss was to be more than amply compensated by Captain Devereaux and by the adventure of a new life, if all went well.

With Mary out of the way and my health recovered enough that I could travel, things were in a state of readiness. We could proceed with the last step in the plan as soon as Captain Devereaux appeared. But still he tarried, and I could not help feeling a little more uneasy with the passing of each day that brought no news of him. Clinging to my faith that all would be well, I tried not to listen to the dissenting voices in my head, which were disagreeably persistent. They told me something must have gone terribly, terribly wrong.

~~*~~

It is perhaps unkind of me to say it, but the first portent of disaster presented itself in the person of my sister-in-law. Mary's uninvited return to Winchester within just days of her removing from it took us so much by surprise that Cassandra and I had no opportunity to prepare ourselves. Neither had we any chance to consider the implications and defend against them.

"I simply could not be comfortable at Steventon," she told us upon her unexpected arrival. "I could not help feeling I neglected my clear duty by being there when I had the powerful impression I was needed here. What if Jane should have another relapse, I asked myself, and no one available to assist Cassandra? It would not do. I made James call for the carriage at once, and here I am."

"But really, Mary," I protested, "there is no need. As you can see, I am very well, even more so than when you went away. Although I am grateful for your concern, I am afraid you have wasted your time in coming."

Cassandra supported me with similar words.

"No, my kind sisters," Mary rejoined. "I shall not be persuaded by such dissembling, how ever well intentioned. In times of need, more help is always preferable to less, and never let it be said that I shrunk from my responsibilities to my husband's family. While you remain in Winchester, I shall remain likewise, completely at your disposal. There is no more to be said about it."

We could hardly turn her from the house, especially after such a speech. But her arrival could not have been more ill timed. Only an hour later came another knock at our door. For the second time that night, I pictured Captain Devereaux standing outside it, and for the second time I was mistaken. Cassandra opened to reveal my brother Henry instead. I fairly flew into his arms.

"Jane!" he cried, receiving me with a laugh and twirling me about once before setting me down again. "Mary wrote that you were somewhat improved, but this is more than I had hoped for, to see you looking so nearly recovered! Oh... Mary," he added, "I had not thought to find you here as well."

"Mary has just arrived," explained Cassandra. "Her conscience would not allow her to stay away when she might be of use to us still. Was not that kind of her, Henry?"

"Indeed," said he.

"And what brings *you* here at this time," I asked my brother. "I am delighted to see you, of course, but had not yet summoned you. I had not expected... that is, I was not planning..." I stopped awkwardly, being unable to say more with Mary present.

Henry seemed equally unsure of himself. "Yes... well... it is a matter of some urgency that brings me, Jane." He glanced from me to Mary to Cassandra and back again. "A piece of news about our... our mutual friend, actually. I am afraid it must be addressed at once; it cannot be put off to a more... convenient time."

By this I took him to mean that it would not wait until Mary could reasonably be got rid of. He felt the need to proceed despite her presence, and I was impatient to hear what he had to say. "I understand, Henry," I assured him. "You must by all means say what you have come to say. Afterward, we will deal with the consequences as best we can."

"Jane may understand," said Mary, "but I most certainly do not. What is all this cryptic business about consequences, urgent messages, and a mysterious mutual friend?"

"You shall know in good time," answered Cassandra. "Let us all sit down first."

Quickly pulling the two chairs from the small table over to near the sofa, we did so. Then Henry began at once. "I am come by the request of Mr. Danvers," he said.

Mary immediately interrupted. "And who, pray tell, is this Mr. Danvers? I do not know anybody by that name."

Henry looked at me once more as if to see whether I wished to stop him saying what would follow, but I did not do so. "Well, if you must know, Mary," he continued, "among other things, Mr. Danvers is the gentleman your sister Jane is going to run away with this very night."

-37-

At Henry's shocking pronouncement, Mary exclaimed in alarm and looked very near to fainting.
    I felt much the same. "This very night?" I repeated in amazement. "Indeed, Henry, what can you be talking of?"
    "Apparently it must be now or never, Jane, although I still have no idea how it is to be accomplished. Here. You two had better read this while I try to catch Mary up." Before returning his attention to his sister-in-law, he handed me a letter.
    I knew at once it was from Captain Devereaux. My hands shook as I opened it. Then I leant toward Cassandra, and together, we silently read the brief missive.

> *Henry, my good man, I very much require your assistance.*
>   *You should know that I pray for your sister daily. I have never wavered in my devotion to her, whether in war, peace, sickness, or health. My fervent hope is that she is not only still willing to throw her lot in with mine, but also now well enough to travel. If so, I mean to collect her at once and be off immediately thereafter. If she is not, I must say my farewells and look forward to her soon joining me abroad. Either way, I cannot delay. Either way, I will want your blessing and the exercise of your services on our behalf before I go.*
>   *I have finally completed my other business and must not stay in this country any longer. I am now fully convinced that I have at least one man on my tail who means me harm. So far, I have, through stealth and cunning, managed to stay a step or two ahead, but I dare not slacken my pace or weaken my vigilance. Consequently, I intend to come and go*

from your sister's place of residence before these mercenaries know anything about it, if possible, thereby sparing myself being captured and sparing your family the inconvenience of awkward questions.

Toward that end, I must beg you to meet me at your sister's house on the seventeenth. Bring the tools of your trade and keep your wits about you. We shall need the best ideas at hand to overcome the formidable obstacles before us. I am your humble servant and, I shall presume to add, your brother – P.D.

"He desires that Henry should marry the two of you before you go," said Cassandra in some awe when she had finished reading. "He has deliberately worded this and everything else with cautious ambiguity, but his meaning is plain enough."

"Is that true, Henry," I asked, interrupting him from Mary. "That you are to marry us? If so, you must have somehow put him up to it."

"Not I. It was all his own idea, I assure you, and an especially honourable one it is too. You understand that he remains in ignorance of your current condition, Jane, and yet he intends to formally bind himself to you either way. Notice his reference to wanting the services of my trade, his illusion to sickness or health, and how he calls me brother at the end. Nothing could be clearer. The deed will be done here after all, before you travel, and I am to have the privilege of performing the ceremony. Although the marriage cannot be recorded in this country, I make no doubt it will be acknowledged in the sight of God. That is what signifies most." Henry then resumed his explanations to Mary, who sat in rapt attention.

I could not believe it. That morning I had no more thought of being a wedded woman before I slept again than I would have expected it to snow that warm day in July. And yet the evidence was before me in Captain Devereaux's letter, which I then examined a second time, tears filling my eyes as I did so. He was alive and safe! This was the most important fact. He was also coming to-day, and we were to be married and depart at once. Emotions of every kind assailed me – joy and excitement as I thought of finally being united with Philippe, nervousness at the continued threat of danger, and also a crippling grief as I glanced at my brother and my sister, whom I might never see again after that night. One look at Cassandra's face told me she was feeling the same. Without a word we flung ourselves into a desperate embrace and for some minutes allowed our tears to flow unhindered.

"...and that is why the rest of the family has been kept in the dark about this. It is for their own protection," said Henry as he finished his informative dissertation to his sister-in-law.

"Now you know, Mary," Cassandra added in a warning tone as we broke from our embrace. "So now you too are bound to keep Jane's secret and ensure her escape, same as Henry and myself. You are not to give her away – not now, not ever – neither you nor your diary. Do you understand?"

"Of course I understand, Cassandra," she said indignantly. "I am not a child that one must take by the hand and speak to slowly. And I should like to know why you suppose I cannot keep a secret. I daresay I am as able to do so as the next person. It seems an unholy sort of business to me, I must say. Still, I know my duty; I will do as my husband would wish me to. If his sister desires to run off with some mad man, it is clearly none of my affair. The reputation of the family must be preserved. That is above all. Now, when am I to see this Captain Devereaux?"

Immediately, there came another knock at the door. For a moment no one moved, and then Henry took charge. "That must be he. Jane, you answer it. The rest of us will wait in the other room so that you can have a bit of privacy." After throwing closed the curtains, he followed Cassandra and Mary out while I went to the door.

I took a deep breath, smoothed my hair and my skirt, and opened the portal wide. There he stood, Captain Devereaux, looking just the same as when he had gone away a few weeks before – just as striking and desirable as ever. *I* was the one who had changed dramatically, and for the better. His eyes lit up at the sight of me.

The captain quickly stepped in and closed the door. "Jane, Jane," he repeated as he gathered me tightly into his arms, lifting me off my feet. "It is a miracle," he said in a voice thick with emotion. We exchanged a deep and lingering kiss before he finally released me and began peppering me with excited questions. "Are you as well as you seem to be? Is your brother here? And has he told you of my plans?"

I laughed. "Yes, Philippe, I am very well indeed. Henry is here, just on the other side of the door – and also Cassandra and Mary, who now knows all. But can it be so? Are we really to be off tonight?"

"If you will marry me first." He became instantly serious. "Will you, Jane?"

"Of course I will, as soon as my head stops spinning! This is all happening so fast." Captain Devereaux kissed me again, which only made my head spin more. Then we called the others out from their hiding places to join us.

The next half hour was comprised of reunions, introductions, explanations of what had transpired over the last month, canvassing the difficulties of the current situation, and deciding how best to go forward.

"The last thing I meant to do was to lead danger directly to this door," said Captain Devereaux, shaking his head. "I had been so painstakingly careful to be sure I was not followed. However, despite all my efforts, it seems I have failed. I saw a familiar looking horseman behind me when I came into town, and he may this moment be crouching in the shrubbery across the way, waiting for his opportunity to strike."

We took in this information soberly and continued to scheme amongst ourselves. Travelling by night was suggested as a precaution against discovery, and not boarding a public coach until well away from the vicinity. Mary, who no doubt perceived her marginal role in the proceedings, sat quietly by through most of this discourse. When she saw we were getting nowhere in overcoming our difficulties, however, she abruptly interrupted.

"Oh, for heaven's sake! You must take my carriage," she declared in exasperation.

Surprised by this sudden outburst, we all turned to look at her.

"You must take my carriage for your escape," she said again, directing her reproachful speech primarily at Captain Devereaux. "There is clearly nothing else to be done! You have a long way to go, and you cannot possibly expect my sister Jane, just recovering from illness as she is, to travel on horseback. Besides, anybody who may be chasing you will be expecting a man travelling fast and alone. He will not be looking for a sedate married couple in a carriage."

After a minute's rumination, Philippe answered. "I thank you for your generous offer, Mrs. Austen, and there is some truth in what you say. Still, I hardly think that I could stroll out the front door, a lady on my arm or no, without being detected. Even if we should manage to drive away, a carriage can be easily overtaken by men on horseback. We should not get two miles."

"Must I think of everything?" she demanded of no one in particular. Then she turned once more to Captain Devereaux. "Consider, sir. They will not follow the carriage if they believe it is someone else who has driven off in it, if they believe you are still in this house. It will be our job to be sure they do."

Mary had our full attention now, and we simply waited in astonished silence for her to reveal the rest of her plan.

"We shall fool their eyes, these spies of yours, by giving them what they expect to see instead of what is actually before them. Henry and Jane must go out by the back way and return in the carriage, being sure to draw attention to themselves before reentering this house. When the same couple later emerges to drive away again, perhaps just after dusk, no one will pay them much heed. Only this time it will have been you, Captain Devereaux, in Henry's place. You two are of the same general height and age. If you were to dispense with your beard and dress in Henry's distinctive clothing, including the hat and an upturned collar, I daresay you could pass for my brother in low light."

Since no one could fault Mary's logic or suggest a better plan, it was decided. Mary sent word to have her carriage made ready for our use, and then Henry and I slipped away. We returned to College Street an hour later, having used the contrived outing to good purpose. I had been able to procure a few items needed for the journey. We also took the opportunity to say our private goodbyes.

"What a mess I am leaving you and Cassandra!" I moaned.

"None of that now. We are glad to do it, and you must have no regrets."

"But how will you manage to carry it off? There is a sham funeral to plan, and perhaps questions from the admiralty to be answered."

"We will manage, Jane. Have no fear. There is nothing that can be proven against any of us by the authorities, should they bother to inquire, which I doubt very much they will. And I intend to persuade Mr. Lyford to be of use in your final arrangements. Medical men have a longstanding tradition of stealing bodies and burying empty coffins, I believe. They must know how it can be done."

"Henry, this is all quite shocking. What makes you think Mr. Lyford would be a party to such a thing?"

"If necessary, I shall simply inform him of the true facts in the case and make him consider the implications. He is no fool. Although he will doubtless resent being unfairly seen as having failed to cure you, I would wager he will be even more reluctant to be known to have aided a notorious traitor, allowing him to evade justice. The point is, we will manage it somehow, Jane. You are not to worry."

I had no choice but to accept this. We had come too far to turn back now.

In order to be sure we were noticed by everybody round about, Henry and I staged a noisy argument as we exited the carriage and leisurely made our way to the door of the house. Although we could not be sure of an audience, so far Mary's plan seemed to be working to perfection.

Back upstairs, we found Mary and Cassandra rearranging the furniture – "for the wedding," my sister explained. "Mary sounds gruff," Cassandra continued to me in a whisper, "but I think she is profoundly affected by the romance of the thing."

The sofa, so long my abiding place, now faced the empty hearth, before which Captain Devereaux and I were apparently meant to take our vows. I also discovered that my intended was now beardless and more handsome than ever. I could not resist reaching up to stroke my hand across that newly shaven cheek, and I came away with fingers nearly singed by his heat. Or was that only my imagination?

"Can we begin?" Philippe said, still looking at me. "The wedding, I mean."

"Ah," said Henry, "I see we are a little impatient."

Impatient? What irony! I reflected that rarely had two people ever been forced to be *more* patient. We had waited for this moment for nineteen years and a half. Now at last, barring any immediate and violent incursion by bounty hunters, we would finally be married. I could wait no longer. "Yes, let us begin at once," I agreed.

Henry nodded. "Very well; have it your own way," he said. Retrieving his book of common prayer, he opened to the marked page and looked at the groom. "I suppose we had best make this an abbreviated version of the ceremony?"

"If you please, sir. It is nearly dusk, and we should be off as soon as possible."

Cassandra and Mary took their seats. Philippe and I stood in front, facing Henry.

"Now, then," my brother began. "I publish the banns… No, that's not the part we want. It's 'dearly beloved.' Yes." He cleared his throat and tried again. "Dearly beloved, we are gathered together here in the sight of God, and in the face of this congregation…" Looking at our congregation of two, Henry shrugged and went on. "…to join this man and woman in holy matrimony, which is an honourable estate, instituted of God in the time of man's innocency, signifying unto us the mystical union that is betwixt Christ and his Church…"

I could have recited nearly all of it, word for word – the miracle at Cana, the charge to never enterprise marriage lightly or wantonly, the causes for which matrimony was ordained – so many times had I heard the service growing up, read out by my father at St. Nicholas's, the Steventon parish church. I could never hear the words since without thinking of him and remembering that I had always supposed he would one day perform the same kind office for me. His absence from that role and the others missing from our tiny congregation sounded a note of sadness within the otherwise joyous hymn.

"...I require and charge you both that if either of you know any impediment, why ye may not be lawfully joined together in matrimony, ye do now confess it."

Silence. All impediments had at last been removed. No more objections to spoil our contentment. No more raging tyrants of war to keep us apart. No more want of money to deprive us of the essentials of married life. We were finally free of these hindrances.

"Philippe Devereaux, wilt thou have this woman to thy wedded wife, to live together after God's ordinance in the holy estate of matrimony? Wilt thou love her, comfort her, honour, and keep her in sickness and in health; and, forsaking all others, keep thee only unto her, so long as ye both shall live?"

Looking tenderly at me, Philippe said, "I will." Then it was my turn to answer the same question, which I did with alacrity. We joined hands for the formal plighting of the troth and the giving of the ring. Philippe slipped a simple gold band on my finger with the words I had so longed to hear from his lips.

"With this ring I thee wed, with my body I thee worship, and with all my worldly goods I thee endow."

There was a prayer, and then Henry concluded with, "Forasmuch as Philippe and Jane have consented together in holy wedlock, and have witnessed the same before God and this company, and thereto have given and pledged their troth either to other, and have declared the same by giving and receiving of a ring, and by joining of hands; I pronounce that they be man and wife together, in the name of the Father, and of the Son, and of the Holy Ghost. Amen."

So it was accomplished; we were married, in the sight of God if not in the sight of any lesser governing body. I wondered if my face was shining as brightly as my new husband's was. He grinned so wide that my cheeks ached for him. In truth, my whole body ached for him, but there was no time to think of that then. We were still in potential danger and would be as long we remained on English soil.

When no one at first stirred, Henry offered, "I could go on. The curate is invited to give a sermon. And there are instructions, prayers and psalms aplenty, including one beseeching the Almighty to make you fruitful in the procreation of children. Would you like to hear it?"

"No, thank you, Henry," said Philippe. "I think Jane and I will be happy with or without that particular blessing." He kissed me to seal the bargain and then addressed Henry again. "However, my dear brother, I will trouble you for the loan of your clothes instead, if I may."

Henry laughed and slapped Philippe on the back. They retreated to the bedchamber to accomplish the task. That was the signal for we ladies to spring into action as well. We did what women do best in such situations; we promptly broke into tears.

"It was a beautiful ceremony," Mary sobbed out, liberally blotting her puffy face with her handkerchief.

"I am glad you were here for it after all," I told her, finding that I meant it. "I will never forget your kindness, Mary, or your generosity in the loan of your carriage." I embraced her and then turned to Cassandra. She was trying to be brave, but her self-control was crumbling. I found I could not speak. My choking emotions would not permit it, and besides, I had no words. A final irony, I thought – a writer without words.

As usual Cassandra read my thoughts. "Do not say anything," she advised. "There is no need."

It was true. She knew exactly what I was thinking and feeling without my speaking, just as surely as I did of her. Instead we clung together until the last minute, unwilling to be parted from each other one second sooner than absolutely necessary.

Shortly, I heard the men returning and knew what it meant; it was time to go. I kissed my sister and my brother one last time, and then I took my husband's arm.

"Are you ready?" he asked.

I looked up into his intelligent face – the face I had loved for a lifetime, now my husband's. Smiling at him, I blinked away my tears and said, "Yes. I am ready."

-38-

No one paid any attention to the ordinary-looking couple who returned to their waiting carriage and drove quietly away from College Street that evening. And when a day or two later the admiralty's man, upon making discreet inquires at Number 8 about a fugitive sighting, learnt that the family above was in mourning, he decided to pursue such an unpromising lead no further.

Philippe and I travelled to the coast without incident and sailed safely away from England within a week's time. By then my family had long since received my farewell letter, copies dispatched to every household by express. I knew I could rely on Henry, Mary, and Cassandra to explain the rest.

> *Be not alarmed, my dear ones, if you should hear reports that I have succumbed to my long illness at last. Although these reports will circulate and they must be believed by all the rest of the world, I wish those closest to me to know the truth. I am not dead; I am simply gone abroad to begin a new life. And, at the risk of sounding like Lydia Bennet, if you cannot guess with whom, I shall think you (those who have cause to know) great simpletons indeed. For there is but one man in this world whom I love – whom I have ever loved.*
>
> *Although the existence and gravity of my illness were entirely genuine, by the grace of God I am completely well again. Rejoice with me! It is only in this fortuitous outcome which you may possibly have been deceived, and this for your own good. It was a necessary ruse, for reasons with which you will become acquainted shortly. For the same reasons, I must beg your cooperation in this enterprise. As I*

said before, it is imperative that everybody else believes I have passed from this world forever. So you must keep this good news in private and make a respectable show of grieving in public, lest your neighbours think you cold-hearted. Consider it a chance to revive the spirit of our celebrated Austen family theatricals. I have every confidence you will mourn me creditably. I am only sorry I will not be there to see it.

Forgive me my flippancy. I do not take this necessary separation lightly. Indeed, deciding on this course was not an easy choice, but I believe it is the right one. I can go forward only by telling myself that we will all meet again – if not in this life, then in the next. For now, I hope you will wish me and my new husband well and happy. I will daily be praying the same for each of you. All my love,

Jane

The bells tolled and my coffin was buried in Winchester Cathedral – empty, but for a sack of dirt of approximate weight. So I am advised by a missive from Henry, which was the first to find its way to me here in Italy. He, Edward, Francis, and my dear nephew James Edward dutifully attended the casket to its final resting place, accompanied by Mr. Lyford.

As it turns out, my doctor's assistance was not the least bit difficult to procure. Although Henry had been prepared with coercive threats of various kinds, he admits that none of his heavy-handed schemes were necessary in the end. It seems Mr. Lyford's generous nature and a certain fondness he felt for me were enough to secure his cooperation. He has earned my eternal gratitude by all the good he has done me. And it gives me pleasure to think I might have done him a good turn as well. I trust that, partly because of what he learnt in treating me, he will go on to greater things by way of his profession.

All my dear family rallied to my cause, as I knew they would. It may have been begrudgingly at first, as in Mary's case. But once decided, they carried it off with admirable spirit and enterprise. I am particularly impressed with the creative sentiments – ones I so clearly do not deserve – by which they memorialised me. Henry, according to Cassandra's information, wrote the inscription for my gravestone, extolling the benevolence of my heart, the sweetness of my temper and the extraordinary endowments of my mind! I blushed to read such misguided but well-intentioned nonsense. And James apparently wrote a poem of equally flattering and equally undeserved praise. I may have fancied myself gifted with words, but perhaps the facility for fiction is more widely spread throughout my family than I had before considered.

Cassandra's beautiful sentiment on the occasion touches my heart most particularly. It is more believable as well, in that I feel much the same at being divided, possibly forever, from her.

"I have lost a treasure – such a sister, such a friend as never can have been surpassed. She was the sun of my life, the gilder of every pleasure, the soother of every sorrow. I had not a thought concealed from her, and it is as if I had lost a part of myself."

Alas, I can never return to her, but I live in the hope that Cassandra may one day come to me. If not, our letters must suffice, as they have done so ably during many briefer separations past. Meanwhile, should an excess of familial affection in my heart demand an object closer at hand, I do have a dear new sister-in-law and niece here in Italy, under the same roof, upon whom I can now lavish it.

I cannot deny the deep and still-bleeding wound being torn from home and family has inflicted upon me. But otherwise I do not regret for one minute my decision to go. I am thriving here in this my second life, my health and happiness burgeoning to new heights day by day. Is it the convivial Italian climate? Or is it the indisputable benefits of married life that so agree with me?

The climate here *is* wonderful. The month is now December, and yet I am perfectly comfortable sitting in the open air late into the afternoon while I write these things down. Life and commerce pass by twenty feet below, transported afloat on the Grand Canal. Philippe was right about Venice. It is indeed a magical place unlike any other, at least in my limited experience. For all its antiquity, it remains as fresh to me as the day I first arrived a few months ago, following our flight from England.

What form this "second life" will take, I cannot foresee. I will have leisure for writing more novels if I so choose (under a different name, of course), and yet at this moment I feel no urgency to do so. It is as if that hunger has at last been satisfied, as if that occupation belonged to the woman I left behind. Perhaps my creative bent will find a different instrument of expression in these new environs. I have always harboured a secret desire to paint, but without the practical means of exercising it. Now is my opportunity. At least I plan to give myself license to try. I will never lack for inspiration, surrounded as I am by beauty and by museums full of master works.

Or perhaps domestic concerns will fully occupy my time. I am a married woman now, after all, and there is still at least a chance of children…

"There you are, my darling," says my new husband, pushing aside the heavy drapery to join me on the iron-railed balcony. A now-familiar thrill races through me as he bends to brush my lips with a tempting kiss. Then, our faces only inches apart, we exchange a knowing look, a flicker of a smile passing between us.

"What have you got there?" I finally ask, hearing the crackle of paper in his hand."

"Ah, yes. I was momentarily distracted, but I came to show you this item in the news. When I saw it, I recognised at once that it would be of singular interest to you. Just there," he says, pointing to a small paragraph near the bottom of the page.

I address my attention to the article he indicates in the English language paper:

<u>Author of Popular Novels Identified Posthumously</u>
It is now known that the well-received novels **Sense and Sensibility**, **Pride and Prejudice**, **Mansfield Park**, and **Emma** (as well as two more titles only now coming to light) were written by the daughter of an obscure English clergyman. Unfortunately, she will write no more, having succumbed to an undetermined illness at the age of one-and-forty. She reportedly died five months ago on the 18th of July, and was subsequently buried at Winchester Cathedral. Thanks to the efforts of her brother, Mr. Henry Austen, **Northanger Abbey** and **Persuasion** have recently been published in a four-volume set prefaced by his biographical notice identifying the authoress as his deceased sister, Miss Jane Austen.

"Your favourite authoress and mine, dead," says Captain Devereaux, now restyled Le Comte de la Fontaine. "Sad news indeed."

I frown and slowly shake my head. "If it were true, but surely there has been some error."

"What? Do you think the newspapers invent these things?"

"I daresay they do not. More likely, they are simply misinformed. No, this report does not upset me, I assure you. Although I am glad to be told that there are now two more of her books out in the world, thanks to this fellow. Uh… what was his name? Oh, yes, Mr. Henry Austen. I am quite certain that this business about Miss Austen herself is a gross falsehood. I feel it in my bones. In fact, I would wager anything you like that she is every bit as much alive as I am. Will you take my bet?"

"O-oh, no!" he says, laughing. "Be so foolish as to make a wager against *you*? Not likely – not when I see that particular gleam in your eye. I perceive, Madame la Comtessa, that you know much more about this business than you are telling."

"You think me clairvoyant, then? What if I told you that I have already dismissed this report about Miss Austen as of next to no importance, and that the gleam you see in my eye is entirely for you, husband."

"If that be the happy case, my dear, then I will call you a mind-reader instead, for you seem to know my thoughts as well as I do myself." He takes up my hand and brings it to his lips. "So then, come with me, my darling exile," he says.

"But I am not yet finished writing in my journal," I protest.

"Later. Your journal will wait; I am not so patient."

Without another word, I lay aside my work and allow Philippe to lead me inside through cinnamon-coloured velvet curtains.

The End

Author's Postscript

I am a novelist, not a historian, and I feel most comfortable in the world of fiction. So, when the idea for this book came to me, I viewed crossing over into the lives of real people with some trepidation. My intention was to write a plausible alternative for Jane Austen, my favourite author, without contradicting any of the known facts. But I quickly discovered that wasn't going to be easy.

First, for me to learn everything that is supposedly "know-able" about Jane Austen would take years. At the same time, however, hard facts and specifics about her are in limited supply. She didn't leave a diary behind, and she didn't achieve enough fame in her own lifetime for biographers to begin taking notes. We do not even have an accurate image of what she looked like.

Much of the pieced-together information about Austen's life comes to us via family remembrances and through the surviving letters she wrote herself. These sources are incomplete, open to interpretation, and potentially biased. I used this to my advantage. It occurred to me that if Jane Austen wished certain truths expunged from the record or carefully constructed falsehoods added, she would likely have found ready co-conspirators in her own family, as I have suggested in the story line. And "blanks" in documentation left me free to invent what might have happened.

That being said, allow me to share a few fact-versus-fiction specifics.

The general timeline presented in this book is accurate, to the best of my knowledge. Jane Austen lived at Steventon, Hampshire, where her father was rector, for the first twenty-five years of her life. When Reverend George Austen retired, he moved his family to Bath. After his death in 1805, the Austen females found themselves in reduced circumstances and were without a settled home again until

1809, when they were given the use of the cottage at Chawton by Jane's wealthy brother, Edward Austen Knight.

Anna Lefroy (whom Jane called "Madam Lefroy") was Jane's close friend and mentor for many years. Tom Lefroy was also a real person in Jane's life, with whom she had a brief but flagrant flirtation. Harris Bigg-Wither, an unappealing family friend six years Jane's junior, did propose marriage. Jane, at age 27, accepted him at first but then reversed herself the next morning.

Other than her aunt and uncle (briefly mentioned), the people Jane meets and interacts with in Bath and Sidmouth are invented, as, alas, is Captain Devereaux. He is a product of my own fevered imagination. But, since authors constantly draw upon their own life experience, it didn't seem so improbable to me that Austen might have based her character Captain Wentworth on someone she had actually encountered.

In addition, during the years they spent in Bath, the Austens did take summer holidays at seaside locations, including Sidmouth, with Charles Austen joining them for the summer of 1802. According to something Cassandra told a family member years later, Jane had had a romance with an unnamed man, who was supposedly a clergyman, on one of these visits to Sidmouth. Cassandra reportedly considered this mysterious gentleman to have been the one true love of her sister's life. He was expected to propose, but then came the devastating report that he had died.

Here, as with the question of which of Jane's letters were preserved for posterity and which ones were destroyed, Cassandra has been the filter through which we have received our information. What we are told about her sister is only what Cassandra wanted us to know or believe.

Jane Austen's death is, of course, the most difficult obstacle to overcome. She began feeling unwell around February of 1816 and, by the time she finished writing *Persuasion* (originally called *The Elliots*) in early August, her health was failing from a still undiagnosed illness. Symptoms improved for a time, and then worsened alarmingly in April of 1817. In May, she was sent to Winchester for medical care, accompanied by her sister. Mary Lloyd Austen joined them in June to assist with the nursing. Despite the efforts of her physician Mr. Lyford, Jane died there on July 18th.

Or did she? I prefer to believe she cheated death. I prefer to think of her living out her days abroad, a permanent but sublimely content exile, alongside the man she loved for a lifetime.

I will leave you with this excerpt from the last chapter of *Atonement* by Ian McEwan, which ably sums up my reasoning:

Who would want to believe that they never met again, never fulfilled their love? Who would want to believe that, except in the service of the bleakest realism? I could not do it to them... No one will care what events and which individuals were misrepresented to make a novel. I know there is a certain kind of reader who will be compelled to ask, "But what really happened?" The answer is simple: the lovers survive and flourish... I like to think that it isn't weakness or evasion, but a final act of kindness, a stand against oblivion and despair, to let my lovers live and to unite them at the end.

Respectfully,
Shannon Winslow

About the Author

Shannon Winslow specializes in fiction for fans of Jane Austen. Her popular debut novel, *The Darcys of Pemberley* (2011), immediately established her place in the genre, being particularly praised for the author's authentic Austenesque style and faithfulness to the original characters. *For Myself Alone* (a stand-alone Austen-inspired story) followed the next year. Then in 2013, *Return to Longbourn* wrapped up Winslow's *Pride and Prejudice* saga, forming a trilogy when added to the original novel and her previous sequel. Now she has given us a "what if" story starring Jane Austen herself. In *The Persuasion of Miss Jane Austen*, that famous author tells her own tale of lost love, second chances, and finding her happy ending.

Her two sons now grown, Ms. Winslow lives with her husband in the log home they built in the countryside south of Seattle, where she writes and paints in her studio facing Mt. Rainier.

Learn more at Shannon's website/blog: www.shannonwinslow.com. Follow her on Twitter (as JaneAustenSays…) and also on Facebook.

Printed in Great Britain
by Amazon